Christine Holt

HOUSE OF ASYLUM

Christine
x

A CIP catalogue record for this title is available from the British library.

ISBN 978-1-7391961-1-0 (Paperback)

ISBN 978-1-7391961-0-3 (Kindle)

First published 2022

To Ethan and Orlissa – I dedicate this book to you as sometimes we drive each other crazy but the smiles, laughter, hugs and seeing you happy makes it all worthwhile.

An ancient secret protected through centuries of time unearthed by those deemed to be lunatics. Life, death and the aftermath…

Chapter One

The lunatic asylum was disturbing at the best of times, but the evening's events were exceptional. The night sky was churning with a menacing energy and the wind was howling, carrying the voices of tormented souls. Creaking from the strain, bare trees waved their bony limbs, vying for attention. Rain lashed down, the tears of demented spirits.

The storm outside mirrored the brewing energy within. In the fading light from the fire, Catherine Fawcett discreetly observed the other female patients from the safety of her hospital bed. There were the screamers like Nelly, only in her early fifties but the paranoia seemed to have prematurely aged her. With thin, greying hair, bony frame and withered skin, Nelly would have been burned at the stake in ancient times.

Then there were the moaners like Ethel, who were terribly sad and cried all the time. Day after day, Ethel sat in her favourite armchair by the bay window, mumbling and sobbing to herself. Her clothes swamped her tiny frame, having lost so much weight over the last few months. Catherine had heard the doctors on the ward-round describe Ethel's personality as, 'Dull and depressed as her appetite'. No wonder the poor old lady was melancholy on hearing their remarks.

The last group were the wanderers and the rockers, always moving, unable to relax or stay still, their eyes sunken, surrounded by dark circles of exhaustion.

Catherine concluded that every woman on the ward was either searching for something or hiding from something; a perverse game of hide and seek. If only she had fulfilled her dreams of becoming a doctor, she could maybe have cured these haunted souls.

Lightning appeared in the unstable sky, briefly illuminating the dark ward. Seconds later a deadly rumble of thunder roused the inmates. Catherine felt spooked at the depth and power of the noise and pulled the covers up to her chin for protection.

Nelly's eyes screamed silently on hearing the thunder. "Heaven has fallen into the hands of the devil," she cried with a voice so deep she sounded possessed by demons. Slumping onto the wooden floorboards, she crawled backwards to hide under her bed, pulling the covers over her, hoping Beelzebub's minions would not find her there. "He's sent her here to kill us, in our beds!"

Goosebumps trickled down Catherine's arms, a tickling chill that made her shiver. Did Nelly know her secret? Was Nelly referring to what had transpired nearly twenty years ago? The paranoia was disabling, too many questions and too many possible answers. There was no other explanation though, somehow Nelly knew her past, that she was a murderer. A secret no one else knew. The secret that had tormented her for eighteen years, leading to this awful confinement. Her nerves were shattered, the daily unpredictable grind was soul destroying. She could not contemplate this asylum being her forever home, it was more like a tomb, as if she was being buried alive, suffocating under the weight of sorrow. Somehow, she had to distance herself from Nelly's remark. Close the door on the past. Lock away those dreadful memories. Tomorrow was an important day, she needed to be focused, to be sharp, but the raging storm was preventing her from sleeping. She tried to concentrate on her answers for her next psychiatry session.

At the previous appointment, Doctor Wainwright said he had seen a vast improvement in her sense of reality. If only she knew what he was going to ask her and what he wanted to hear. One of the things she had to admit was Sam Thompson was dead. He had been found guilty of murder and was publicly executed for his crimes. Last time, Doctor Wainwright had kindly answered her question as to why she could not find Sam's grave. He was buried within the gaol walls in a communal plot. Mourners were forbidden from visiting these mass graves as a deterrent and punishment for a heinous crime having been committed. Being denied a Christian burial and no headstone on a grave prevented the possible ascension to heaven and immortalisation of criminals. Catherine had made a mental note of those answers. If she sounded convincing tomorrow, that she believed this was the truth, then maybe she could finally be free.

As Nelly continued to whimper under her covers, reciting prayers and occasionally banishing demons from her presence, which was now upsetting other residents, two nurses tried to persuade her into bed. They spoke gently, reassuring Nelly that it was just a storm outside and that she was safe in here. The younger nurse sat on the floor and held Nelly's withered hand.

"Their voices whispering, annoying me, in me head, scaring me. Telling me things I don't want to hear." Nelly started tapping her head with her index finger.

Catherine scrunched up her eyes and covered her ears with her trembling hands in a feeble attempt to block out the world.

"They are rattling the windows, angry they are. The demons, I feel their breath. Cold draughts, chilling me bones, making me shiver."

"Come on love, into bed, where it's warm and where you'll feel protected," said the older nurse, her pristine white uniform seeming to glow in the dark, making her appear like an ethereal goddess. "You'll not feel the cold draughts from the windows if you're tucked up in bed and those whispers are just the wind, it's blustery outside." The presence of the nurses sufficiently reassured Nelly for her to slowly make her way from under the bed when a sudden gust of wind forcibly splattered rain against the windows. Everyone jumped at the awful sound, as if stones were being pelted at the glass panes.

"Oh my goodness, that gave me a fright!" said Catherine, her blood pounding through her veins. Nelly retreated to the safety of her underground bunker.

Leaving her younger colleague sitting on the floor to deal with Nelly, Nurse Jones turned to face Catherine and whispered, "You prepared for tomorrow?"

"My mind resembles those storm clouds," said Catherine. Her eyes flitted over to the uncurtained height of the paned windows. "I have so much information swirling around inside my head. What a mess."

"Picture a magical rainbow when the sun finally emerges."

Catherine smiled. "Comforting words, thank you."

"Now try and get some sleep if you can, although in this madhouse, I doubt it." Nurse Jones winked, "And good luck for tomorrow, for you certainly don't belong here anymore."

"I really hope that's true, although in a strange way I will miss everyone."

"Really? Even Maggie over there? Bless her, no wonder she's skin and bone, she never sits still, wandering these corridors day in, day out, mumbling incessantly. I'm exhausted just watching her."

Catherine propped herself up on her elbow and rested her head in her hand. "Still searching for her baby; two years and she cannot move on. Such a sad story."

"Now I can see your eyes are glistening with tears." Nurse Jones was heartbroken at the insight Catherine had to everyone else's predicament bar her own, having lost eighteen years of her life to her delusions.

"True, but I feel useless at how much sorrow and suffering there is in the world. Life seems so cruel and unfair."

Nurse Jones tutted but kept her voice low, "No wonder you ended up in here, so stop worrying about everyone and everything. I don't mean this in a nasty or selfish way but, for once, think of yourself, think happy thoughts about you and your dreams."

Sobbing was heard from the far end of the ward. Catherine and the nurse stopped their conversation to see who was upset. Ethel was in her seventies yet here she was crying, asking for her mother who had sadly died years ago. Her aged hands were held aloft as if waiting for her mother to pick her up from her crib. Ethel was searching for a comforting love, being cuddled in her mother's arms, needing her soothing heartbeat.

Before Nurse Jones left to tend to Ethel, she whispered, "I mean it, look after yourself and enjoy life. Be the one carrying the light in the darkness, not the one worrying if you're gonna burn the house down, yeah?"

Lightning once again lit up the dark room. "I'll try," said Catherine half-heartedly. Menacing thunder rumbled once more, reverberating through her bones.

Chapter Two

The office of Doctor Wainwright had a grand but homely atmosphere. The crackling fire was welcoming and the autumnal tones in the room were warm, if maybe a little dark for the depressed souls residing in the asylum. The furniture was familiar, as if you had happened upon your grandmother's parlour. Catherine's closed medical file lay on the red leather topped desk. Also on the desk was a framed photograph and Catherine deduced this was of Doctor Wainwright, his wife, his three sons and two daughters.

A quill and ink were neatly placed to what would be his right-hand side. On the other side of his desk stood an ornament of a black eagle. Behind the desk, was a floor to ceiling bookcase, housing medical textbooks and novelties such as a skull, a wooden ship, a small telescope, and a globe. Above the dark wooden panelling, pictures adorned the other three red walls. There was an eclectic mix of landscapes, religious scenes and exotic animals. Over the door, a boar's head watched over the room. Immortalised on a wooden plinth, the adornment was creepy. The staring eyes forever watching, the turned ears as if listening, the elevated snout smelling fear of nearby prey, the teeth eternally ready to devour and tear, she detested taxidermy.

Catherine wondered if today's situation was a test. Never had she been left alone in his office. Doctor Wainwright had only just commenced their session when he excused himself from the room for an urgent matter. She pondered the situation. Maybe she was meant to read her medical file, it would show initiative, an inquisitive nature, the ability to take control and make informed decisions. The alternative option was to sit there, refuse temptation, demonstrate the ability to be morally correct and make decent choices. Trying to be sane increased her insanity.

As a distraction, she continued to scan the room to prevent herself from over-thinking. To the far side of the room there was a mahogany coat stand holding a top hat, an expensive looking overcoat, an umbrella and a cane. Four red leather armchairs were placed at an angle to ...

The door opened and in walked Doctor Wainwright. "My most sincere apologies, Catherine, things to sort." His brown tailored suit perfectly matched the room's decor.

"I can imagine you are a very busy person."

"Unfortunately, yes. Now, where were we?"

Catherine wondered if he analysed every single word. "We were discussing last night's storm."

"Yes, frightfully unnerving for delicate minds." He opened the file, placed his glasses onto his nose and read through her notes.

With a receding hairline, his forehead started from the crown of his head. As if to compensate, his eyebrows were long and unruly, creeping upwards like poison ivy. Catherine wondered if he had ever tried combing them.

His right hand reached for his quill. "So, for today I have a list of questions, some I have asked you previously, but I wish to review your answers. I want you to answer truthfully."

"Yes, of course."

"Name?"

Too easy, she immediately thought there must be a hidden meaning to his question, "Catherine Fawcett."

"Today's date?"

Oh, that was a tricky one. Having been in the asylum for the last few months, Catherine had lost her sense of time. "I believe we are still in October and that it is Thursday. But to be honest I would be guessing at the date." Her heart sank, such a simple question yet she felt disorientated. She prayed that this would not influence any decision on her sanity.

"Close enough, it is Thursday 29th of October."

"Thank you for clarifying."

After writing in her file, he lifted his head up to ask, "Where are you?"

Catherine was unsure how precise she needed to be. "I am in your office at the Cumberland and Westmorland Lunatic Asylum on the outskirts of Carlisle."

"Excellent. You appear to be sufficiently orientated to time, place and person."

A sense of relief trickled through her body at the positive sounding words.

"Why were you admitted here?"

Her heart started pounding, "I ... lost someone very dear to me ... I felt lost ... I ... started wandering, physically and mentally, looking for him ... my parents ... they ..."

"What did they do, Catherine?" He stopped writing and paused, looking over the top of his glasses to observe her.

A sudden hot flush travelled from her palpitating heart to her brain, she felt on fire. "They saw my increasing confusion and they locked me in my room." Her cheeks burned with ferocity.

"How long were you there for?" asked Doctor Wainwright.

"Many years."

"What year is this?"

"1863."

"Hmm."

Catherine was convinced 1863 was the correct year.

"Why did they lock you in your room?"

"They were concerned for me. They saw my distress. I was wandering, searching for Sam, I was distraught."

Doctor Wainwright continued making notes as they conversed. "Why were you distressed?"

"I could not accept his passing. I was lost without him."

"And are you still lost?"

Catherine preferred direct questions. "I believe I have found a way."

There was a lull in the questioning. Doctor Wainwright continued to scribe, "We should be grateful when we find the correct path in life."

Another pause, Catherine was unsure whether to respond or not. There had been no question, only a statement. Her heart was racing, her mind was over-thinking. She decided silence was better than confirming any delusions.

Doctor Wainwright opened the top left drawer to the desk and retrieved an envelope which he placed next to the photograph of his family.

"Where is the path leading you, Catherine?" His fingertips met, forming a pyramid. Repeatedly, he spread his fingers, returning to the closed triangular shape.

"I would like my own place, the freedom to do what I want to do, to read, to walk, to explore."

"And how will you fund this newfound freedom?"

Now it was Catherine's turn to say, "Hmm."

"The asylum is a pauper institution, funded by the local counties who refer into these facilities. Your parents no longer have wealth, they are not poor by any means, but they would be unable to fund an independent lifestyle and you are unmarried, a spinster of this parish."

Catherine wanted to roll her eyes but thought better of it.

He leaned forward onto the desk, "In a previous session, you stated you dreamed of being a doctor. What sort of employment would you consider undertaking now?"

This was not going according to plan. How could she be so foolish as to not consider how she would survive on her own. For many a year she had been wealthy beyond most people's wildest dreams, money had never been an issue, had never been important, until the day it was gone.

Doctor Wainwright pushed the envelope on his desk towards his patient. "Please, open it."

Trying to suppress the subtle tremor in her hands, she leaned forward from her chair and retrieved the package from the desk. She sat back in the chair. Something heavy was in the envelope.

"Go on then," prompted the doctor.

Catherine sighed to calm her nerves. The envelope was already open, she slowly lifted the rear fold and looked inside.

"What is it, Catherine?"

The pause was too long, she had not expected this, she had to say something, remain focused, state the truth, without fear, without anger, without emotion. With a faltering crack to her voice she said, "It is a key."

Doctor Wainwright smiled, his right eye almost closing to a playful wink, "Very perceptive, but you know I need more." He raised a bushy eyebrow.

Her body suddenly felt weary, heavy by absorption of life's cruel memories.

"It is ... the key to ... Sam's house."

"Could this be your home, a way for you to live the independent life you crave?"

"I'm not sure I could ... the house ... it holds too many memories." Catherine quickly stuffed the key back into the envelope and placed it on her lap, protected by her crossed hands.

"Then another suggestion is you sell the house. With the proceeds you could live quite comfortably for many a year, giving you time to seek employment. How do you feel about that?"

The house held too many secrets. Selling the property was not a viable option. If the new occupants were to find ... Catherine shuddered and quickly discounted the notion. "I am being totally honest with you as you requested. I cannot sell the house for personal reasons."

Doctor Wainwright nodded, "Thank you for your honesty, I appreciate that. I did have one more surprise for you today, but it will now have to wait for next time. Prior to your next session, I request you visit Sam's house, face your past, exorcise those ... hmm ... I'm sure you understand what I'm implying. I will arrange for one of the nurses to accompany you. Depending on the outcome of your visit, we can possibly discuss you leaving here and starting your new life elsewhere. I'm sure you will be delighted, if not a little intrigued, by the final surprise I have in store for you." He stood from his chair and bowed his head out of courtesy. "Good day, Miss Fawcett."

Catherine stood from her chair. She also bowed her head as a sign of respect, mirroring the doctor's manners. Her feet were heavy, refusing to move. Another week here, this place was intensifying her fears. The pretence of being a lady. The difficulty in remaining lucid, orientated, positive, when everyone else was insane. Sam's home, Fernleigh, the murder house, the rotting skeleton, she doubted her ability to face her past and it not affect her future. The maggots were already gnawing away at her brain.

Chapter Three

Children with feeble minds were encouraged to attend specialist schools. However, the challenging behaviours of some children resulted in them being admitted to adult mental institutions. Nurse Story was petite and appeared so sweet that everyone believed her to be a child, until she opened her mouth. Physically, she gave the impression of being young and naïve, but she was no fool. She had an ability to sense things whilst appearing to be preoccupied with other tasks.

A few days ago, Nurse Story had been encouraging Jeannie to get dressed after suffering a particularly severe bout of melancholia. Nurse Story was standing at the side of the bed, chatting with Jeannie about the awful weather, whilst passing layers of clothing to her patient. Without the acuity of looking, for all this happened behind her, she could sense Delilah wandering the ward and had accurately predicted that she had sauntered over to Annabelle's bed. Whether she had heard the atomised particles spraying into the air or had detected the faint smell of lavender, Nurse Story questioned Delilah if she had sought permission to use Annabelle's perfume and if not, to apologise for using her personal items without consent. At the time, Catherine had been impressed by the nurse's astute assessment, perfectly using her senses to reach an accurate conclusion.

When it was announced Nurse Story would accompany her on the trip to Fernleigh, chills shivered through her body, creating miniscule yet multiple hills of doubt to climb.

With a military stance, the nurse commanded, "Wrap up warm for it's cold outside and our carriage awaits."

Catherine put on her coat, gloves and bonnet. "I predict rain too for the sky is menacingly dark."

Although only small, Nurse Story marched along the long gloomy corridors of the asylum. Catherine was almost trotting at times to keep pace with her guardian. The nurse opened the door. Fresh air wafted inside, and Catherine paused to take in the feeling.

The ladies made their way outside and were greeted by the raucous cawing of crows nesting in the trees. A few birds swirled low, the dark clouds too heavy and laden for the crows to reach higher realms. Catherine prayed this was not a warning sign of impending doom.

As they approached the carriage, a tall thin man with rosy cheeks and bushy sideburns opened the nearside door and tipped his cap as a courtesy to his passengers.

"Thank you," said Catherine, as she climbed into the carriage.

Nurse Story smiled and nodded to the gentleman, "Fernleigh, Scotby village, please."

Other than the horses' hooves creating a soothing, rhythmical noise and the creaking of the wooden joints of the carriage, the journey commenced in silence. Catherine was thankful, for it gave her the opportunity to see places she had not laid eyes upon in almost twenty years. The storm had obviously been ferocious, for trees had been felled, limbs torn from trunks, and leaves were scattered everywhere.

Catherine briefly looked sideways at her travelling companion. The nurse's feet were dangling, her limbs not long enough for them to touch the carriage floor.

Nurse Story must have sensed the glance for she broke the silence and asked, "How are you feeling?"

Catherine questioned why everything seemed to be a test or maybe it was paranoia, part of her psychosis. From everything she had recently learned, honesty seemed to be the way forward. Lies, diversions, excuses, they created false paths, convoluted trails and bumpy rides, she did not want to trip herself up. "I am feeling quite nauseous if the truth be told." She held a pristine, white handkerchief to her nose.

"Why does visiting a house make you feel this way?"

Oh no, another question, these people never stop searching for answers. "I lost my very dear friend. Despite him being completely innocent of the crimes in which he was found guilty, he was hanged in public like a common criminal. I now accept he has gone, but I will never stop loving him. Coming back to his home, after all these years, I'm not sure how I feel, but if this is part of my journey, to put me on the path to being well, then it is a road I must endure."

"You still insist he is innocent after all these years. What makes you so sure?" Nurse Story appeared so sweet with her large blue eyes, rounded face and delicate pink lips but her voice was level, with no signs of accusations or disbelief. She was matter of fact, showing little emotion.

17

"For I know who killed those people. The police knew, the jurors were told, the judge heard Sam's pleas, yet they still convicted him on circumstantial evidence."

"So, who killed them?" asked the nurse.

Catherine remained silent. Years of screaming, wailing, tearing at her clothes, smashing her room, insisting everyone needed to know the truth resulted in her incarceration and being deemed insane. She would not repeat the same mistakes. Silence can be louder than shouting. People did not always want to hear the truth.

As predicted, rain started to fall, misting up the carriage windows. Catherine used the back of her gloved hand to wipe away the condensation which was distorting her view. Almost twenty years had passed since she had visited Scotby village, and the changes were considerable. There were certainly more houses as well as a small grocery store and the streets were more landscaped as the residents had tended to their gardens over the years. Although the village had changed, the road to Fernleigh was still recognisable. The house came into view.

Her beating heart became unstable, making her feel anxious. Her stomach churned with pent up emotions: fear of the known, fear of the unknown, fear of change, fear of stagnation, fear of failure, fear of success and the guilt of seeking happiness.

The carriage stopped as did her respiration. Rain was now pouring and through the wet, misty windows, Fernleigh stood there like a brooding shadow, blocking the light. The garden, with its overgrown hedges, trees and shrubbery looked unloved and neglected. She felt sad that Sam's dreams of a haven were now just a wilderness.

A silhouette of a man appeared at the carriage window, making Catherine twitch and suck in air with fright. She immediately turned to her companion. Nurse Story had obviously seen and heard her fear, for her eyebrows were raised as if in question. The thin man opened the carriage door and helped the women to alight. The rain pelted down but Catherine did not flinch, seemingly in a trance, staring at the house.

"Shall we?" asked the nurse.

The rain was stinging, and the nurse used the hood of her cloak to shelter her from the downpour. Catherine continued to stare at the house. September 30th, 1845, it had rained that day too. She recalled being soaked through; her hair had been plastered to her face. Her clothes had stuck to her skin, the weight of her dress had been heavy, the layers of material soaking up the rivers running through the streets. The chills, the shivers.

"Catherine, we need to make a move!" said Nurse Story with a now exasperated tone to her voice.

They made their way to the closed garden gate. The metalwork had seized, and it took Catherine a few attempts to release the mechanism. The gate creaked on its rusty hinges. The path was barely visible, the weeds had reclaimed it for nature, but Catherine did not notice as she focused on the front door. There was one step up to the property. A pile of crispy, brown leaves had collected in the corner of the once decorative porch. The paint on the woodwork was cracked and peeling, the property looked shabby.

Now sheltered from the direct rain, Catherine paused in the small porch area to search for the key in her pocket.

Becoming more impatient the nurse said, "Hurry up! I'm getting drenched here!"

Hearing the commanding voice made Catherine turn around and look behind her. She had momentarily forgotten Nurse Story was there. The nurse's black cloak was soaked through, with water dripping from her hood onto her nose then onto her shoes, like a trickling waterfall.

"Sorry," said Catherine and she suddenly focused on the task set by Doctor Wainwright, to revisit Fernleigh and face her demons. She placed the key in the lock and turned it to the left and heard a click. The key was realigned, pulled out of the lock and placed back in her pocket for safe keeping. Catherine opened the door to the past, present and her potential future.

Chapter Four

"So, when you walked through the door, how did you feel?" asked Doctor Wainwright.

Without thinking, Catherine immediately answered, "Sad."

"Can you expand on that?"

Catherine did not want to expand on her answer. She questioned why sadness was an insufficient answer. He obviously wanted drama. Maybe she should cry, scream with desperation, collapse in a heap on the floor, cling onto his leg and plead for his assistance.

"Everything was sad. Rusty metalwork, rotting wood, peeling paint, decay, debris, devastation. On the outside Sam's dream was dying. Yet inside the house, I could sense a glimmer of hope. As if the house was waiting for someone to love and to be loved and cared for by someone special."

"Could you be that special person?" Doctor Wainwright tapped his fingers whilst waiting for her reply. When met with silence he continued, "Could you keep Sam's dream alive?"

Finally, Catherine answered. "Oh, I so wish I could, but honestly, I cannot. Too many sad memories. As I walked around the house, I kept wondering how different life may have been with Sam by my side."

"Tell me again about your relationship with Sam, please."

They had discussed this before in a previous session. She could remember her exact answer, "He was my soulmate. I'm sad that it took me so long to realise this."

"Are you perhaps grieving the loss of your dreams as well as Sam's dreams?" Doctor Wainwright raised his eyebrow.

Mourning the loss of a fantasy, grieving for the loss of something she never possessed in the first place, she pondered on whether Doctor Wainwright thought her foolish. "I'm grieving the loss of Sam, his innocence, the injustice, fate has been cruel to us both."

"Ah, so rather than grieving you are angry?"

"Yes, I suppose I am." A brief delay. "Was," she quickly added. Her eyebrows furrowed.

Doctor Wainwright was making notes in the file. He paused to dip his quill in the ink bottle. "So, as you walked around the house did different rooms evoke different reactions?"

Now it was Catherine's turn to pause. She did not want to answer this question. "No, I don't believe so. There was sadness everywhere." She feared the sound of her palpitations would reveal her true feelings.

"In her report, Nurse Story said you had a noticeable reaction in the first room on the right. She witnessed tears in your eyes, a tremor in your hands and a pallor when you approached the fireplace." He paused to see a reaction.

"It was the first room we entered, that is all," offered Catherine. Her body tried to remain perfectly still, but her eyes were restless.

He continued, "On entering the main bedroom, you opened the top drawer of the right bedside table, glanced at a newspaper clipping, then started shaking once more. You appeared distraught." His eyes once again observed her reaction.

She cleared her painfully dry throat before speaking, "The newspaper detailed Sam's hanging and the alleged but false crimes he had committed. Once again, it evoked sad memories."

Doctor Wainwright continued, "But Nurse Story reported that the weirdest reaction was in the kitchen. You stared out of the window at the garden for an extraordinarily long time. You appeared to be in some sort of hypnotic trance, transported to a different world. Nurse Story had tried communicating with you, but you were oblivious to her presence." The doctor put the report down and removed his glasses.

Catherine became aware her fingers were fiddling nervously, as if they were subconsciously admitting their guilt. She quickly clasped her hands in her lap to stem their movement. She recalled standing in the kitchen, looking out over the overgrown garden, thankful that nature was hiding her secret. She had been in a trance, transported back in time, imagining what the body would look like now. Was it just a collection of bones, or preserved and identifiable? Her immediate thoughts had been too much time had passed and the body would be so decayed that recognition would be impossible. Then she remembered they had buried personal items too. Doctor Wainwright coughed, and she realised she was once again in a different world.

Catherine quickly offered, "The grounds were all overgrown, it was pouring with rain, it was a quagmire. Sam wanted a magical garden. It was to be his sanctuary. I was overcome with heartache by the sorry state of the place." She was hit by a revelation, "The house and grounds reflected me, how I feel inside. Neglected, in a sad state of repair, mourning the loss of the person who loved me, wanted me, the future we planned together. Time has taken its toll, crumbling, weathered, older but the potential is there. There is so much love to give, if only someone would right those wrongs and create something magical out of heartbreak. I have only just discovered that person is me."

Doctor Wainwright smiled with contentment and sat back in his chair, looking at her with a physical as well as mental perspective. "In our last session we discussed you being discharged from this establishment. Is this house a place where you could reside? Would this residence provide shelter, warmth, comfort, a sanctuary for your mind, your soul?"

On hearing this, Catherine suddenly realised her mistake, she had not been forced to visit this house to exorcise demons from her past. She wanted to smile, almost laugh at how foolish she had been. She had worried unnecessarily, believing she would be asked about *the skeletons in the closet* as well as the literal ones. The doctor was not aware of the turmoil she suppressed each day. He was oblivious to her secret. He only wanted to find her somewhere to live.

"Sadly, I admit I do not have the strength of character to reside in his home. As hauntingly beautiful as it was to feel so close to Sam, as I've already said, the house provoked too many sad memories."

"I admire your honesty. We know your parents are no longer able to provide you with an income and you stated in a previous session that you could not imagine moving back in with your parents, to stay in the room in which you were incarcerated for many a year. And as this house in Scotby is unsuitable this leaves us with a predicament." He scratched his head, "As far as I understand, Sam left you the house in his will. I am aware that I have also asked you this before, but would you be willing to sell Fernleigh?" He formed the familiar triangular shape with his hands and fingers.

"No!" She would explode if he asked her to expand on this. It was Sam's home and with what went on there, she could not live with the consequences of selling a haunted house and risk the new owners revealing her secret. Doctor Wainwright stared at her from across his desk, his fingertips tapping his lips. Her dreams of being free were fading, her options were depleting, she could sense it by the uncomfortably long silence.

"Do not look so dejected, Catherine. Letting go of the past, in this instance Sam's house, must truly be a testing time for you. It is clear to me, you still love him even after all these years and having his home, well, it is the last link, as painful as it may seem, the uncoupling of that link is a step too far. Maybe in time you can finally let go and find peace."

Although not entirely true, Catherine accepted his analysis for she did not want to expand on the finer details and the truth to unfurl. Keeping the house

22

was self-preservation. Selling the house would be self-sacrifice. The truth on this occasion was to be avoided.

Doctor Wainwright continued, "There is one option we have not discussed. I briefly mentioned at our last session that I have a surprise for you." He put his reading glasses back onto the end of his nose. "The asylum is funded by local taxes for paupers unable to pay for their care. However, we also receive funding from private benefactors, those socialist entrepreneurs wanting to share their wealth for the greater good. They are also interested in medicine, and psychiatry, and furthering our knowledge about the links between mental and physical health. This particular benefactor wishes to remain anonymous, but your case has caught their eye. They are willing to fund a simple lifestyle, to give you time to trial living on your own once more. They ask for nothing in return, other than to see you well and once again able to contribute to society." He looked over the rim of his glasses. "What are your thoughts so far?"

There were so many questions to ask, she did not know where to start. "Do you have any specific details as to where I will reside, the accommodation, the street? Are there any terms to accepting this generous offer? Is there a way of saying thank you for this charitable gift?"

Doctor Wainwright laughed at Catherine's sudden animation. "I have never seen you so energised. Your vibrancy is a delight to see. Indeed, I have more information. I shall read the offer to you in its entirety."

Catherine could not believe the words she was hearing. Rose Cottage could soon be her home. There was a small triangular shaped backyard, enough to house a washing line and a mangle. To the side of the house was a vegetable plot. To the front of the house was a pretty garden with rose bushes and shrubs which she had to keep tidy as part of the offer.

Immediately, she was picturing the scene in the summer, with sweet smelling fragrances wafting through her window. The house was seemingly small but cosy and situated in the village of Edenvale, along the banks of the River Eden. The setting sounded peaceful, perfect for convalescing, with access to beautiful walks and surrounded by stunning, natural landscaping. She would receive a monetary contribution, sufficient to live on for basic rations combined with the vegetable plot if tended to with purpose. The arrangement would be reviewed on a monthly basis by way of weekly letters and if in agreement, Catherine's progress would be shared amongst a select group of benefactors and superintendent staff in order to discuss and hopefully progress mental wellness and rehabilitation back into society. If within three months, Catherine had proven she was capable of living independently, could manage her finances and integrate with her immediate neighbours in a supportive and collaborative way, then she would be free to go her own way.

With animated glee she asked, "Where do I sign?"

Chapter Five

The asylum's Recreation Hall was impressive. The vaulted ceiling was supported by decorative truss beams and was almost cathedral like in its grandeur. With three tiers of windows, the hall was bright and cheerful. At the far end of the hall was a stage draped with palatial red curtains.

Even though Catherine was being discharged today, the inmates were given their daily tasks to complete, which supposedly helped with having a sense of purpose, encouraged exercise and promoted respectful interaction. Her job for the day was to set up the hall for this evening's entertainment. There was to be a quartet with a penchant for Gregorian chants and a ventriloquist with a variety of puppets. *A strange combination of acts.*

As per the instructions, Catherine laid out the tables and chairs precisely. She had been assigned the task with another patient, Margery, who had been diagnosed with dementia. The lady was a little hunched at the shoulders but strong and always on the go. Pleasantly confused, she smiled all the time despite her memory issues. They sat on two spare chairs around the fringe of the room.

"What do we do now?" asked Margery.

"That's us done. I think we deserve a treat." Catherine admired their hard work.

"I'd like a whiskey," said Margery.

"I'm not sure that will be on the menu at this time of day, but you never know." Catherine winked at her friend.

"So, what do we do now?" asked Margery.

"We'll go and get a drink."

"I'll have a whiskey please."

Catherine decided it wasn't worth arguing over. "I'll try my best." She got up from the dining chair and adjusted her skirt and bodice.

"What am I supposed to be doing?" asked Margery.

Catherine held out her hand, "Come with me, we'll get a drink together." They walked out of the hall hand in hand with Catherine leading the way.

"Where are we going?" asked Margery.

Working with Margery was always hard work, Catherine tried to say something different each time to avoid repetition. Then she reasoned that repetition was maybe what Margery needed.

"We are going to get ourselves a drink, for all our hard work."

As they walked along the long corridor with its large windows on one side and numerous closed doors on the other, they followed the curve of the tiled wall around to the first door on the right which was the entrance to their ward. They knocked loudly to gain access.

The door opened and everyone shouted, "Surprise!" The staff and residents had gathered to say goodbye to Catherine. Colourful bunting decorated the walls and they had kindly prepared a small buffet of food.

Nurse Jones came up to her and gave her a lovely hug. "We are so happy for you. Take care and keep in touch, yeah?"

Catherine was overwhelmed by the gesture, "I don't know what to say, I'm honoured to have such lovely friends."

Some of the crowd cheered. Nelly, the screamer with the long, grey hair walked up to Catherine with her arms open, then unexpectedly slapped her across the face.

Nearly everyone gasped with shock.

"Nelly, no! You know that is wrong! You'll be restrained again if you hurt people!" Nurse Beattie was tall for a woman and towered over Nelly. Her voice did not rise, it was low and said in a calm but stern manner.

The nurse attempted to pull Nelly away from the crowd, but the grey-haired woman turned to face Catherine once more, "The devil will not let you go, he will not be defeated. You'll be back here soon, in Satan's house, he likes you being here, mark my words." As the nurse dragged her down the ward, Nelly's head rotated as far as it could. Seeing Catherine out of the corner of her vision she said, "He's watching you, mark my words, you're his favourite, all prim and proper like but I know what you did. He confided in me." The nurse hauled Nelly into the quiet room.

Everyone stood there in awkward silence until Nurse Jones asked, "Are you all right, Catherine?"

Tears welled in her eyes and her hands were shaking. "I'm fine, thank you for asking. This has reassured me why I should not be sad at leaving but rejoicing in having some freedom." With the back of her shaking hand, she gently touched her cheek. There was no transfer of blood, but Nelly's words stung more than the slap.

Nurse Jones had seen the concern, "Here, let me take a look at your face." She tenderly supported Catherine's jaw and moved her head slowly side to side. "It's red but there are no scratches, no blood thankfully."

"Thank you," said Catherine with slight failure to her voice.

"Come on then let's have some food," suggested one of the other nurses.

The group dispersed and staff and residents soon began to enjoy the small party. Those assigned to the kitchen had prepared some pastries, breads and some little vegetable sticks on which to nibble and dip into some relishes. Catherine tried to make her way around everyone, thanking them for their kind well wishes. A little while later, a man announced her carriage was ready.

"It's time for me to go, thank you everyone, thank you so much. Be kind to each other, take care." Catherine waved, picked up her case and turned to walk away.

"Good luck, we'll miss you."

She did not look back to see who had said those final words.

In her possession was one large piece of luggage which had started out as a reasonable load to bear but the asylum corridors were vast, and by the time she got to the waiting carriage the leather trunk had become a burden. With a groan of effort, she lifted the heavy weight onto the carriage floor then climbed onto the forward-facing bench seat. The dappled white horse moved off on command.

The asylum was quickly out of sight and with complete surprise she burst into tears with sheer relief, possibly even joy. She wiped the salty water from her cheek and was reminded of the slap she had received from Nelly. The words still haunted her, "The devil ... he's watching you ... he confided in me ... you'll be back here soon." Catherine shivered at the thought.

By the position of the weak sun setting in the west, the carriage was obviously heading east which she hoped was towards the village of Edenvale. She had never heard of this place before, but the cottage and its location sounded idyllic, no wonder the residents wanted to keep their village a secret to the outside world. There were few houses to be seen so far, only a couple of farmhouses and some fields housing sheep and cows.

In the middle of nowhere, the carriage slowed to an eventual stop. Looking out of each side window, all she could see were hedgerows, shrubby bushes and autumnal trees. She heard a thud, and the carriage shook side to side, the man had jumped down from his bench seat. He appeared at the window. "This is as far as I can go. You'll have to walk the last mile or so."

Catherine got out of the carriage and realised their predicament. Two workmen had cordoned off the area with rope. They were on their hands and knees further down the road, painstakingly laying small stones to form a new road. "Thank you, sir. Do I owe you anything?"

"No, miss, courtesy of the asylum." He tipped his cap and climbed onto his seat.

After a few minutes of walking, her leather trunk became so large and heavy, that she was beginning to waddle like a duck. As she approached the workmen, they stopped, tipped their caps and asked her where she was going. They confirmed she was heading in the right direction for the village of Edenvale but no offer of help with the case was forthcoming. This did not bother Catherine; she was enjoying the freedom of finally being allowed out on her own. The feeling was wonderful.

By the time she reached the outskirts of the village her boots were covered in mud, and she smiled because she did not care. She had never been out walking on her own for years. Yes, she had participated in the upkeep of the kitchen garden and had strolled around in circles in the asylum grounds but to walk somewhere new felt amazing.

Exhausted, she plonked the trunk on the ground and rested her hands on her hips, taking in the first view of the village from the top of the hill. From her pocket, she unfolded the piece of paper given to her by Doctor Wainwright containing the address of Rose Cottage and a simple map of the village. The Wheatsheaf Inn was on her right as per the map. Once more, she picked up the case and waddled down the hill towards the village green. The houses were so pretty, more beautiful than she had imagined. At the right-hand side of the green, just before the grass sloped steeply away, was a grey monument, a monolith of speckled stone which was also drawn on the map. Behind the monument was an imposing residence built of red sandstone which Doctor Wainwright had also drawn on the map. Her heart started pounding, this meant Rose Cottage should be to the left, just around the corner. As the stone-built cottage came into view, it was as perfect as she had hoped for in her dreams.

Tied to the metal gate was a wooden sign, *Rose Cottage.* She released the latch and followed the pathway to the front door. She plonked the heavy trunk on the ground. Above the door was a stained-glass window, colourfully stating, *St Martin's Cottage.* Strange for the cottage to have two names.

The key was in her right hand, she was shaking with a mix of emotions, she wanted to cry but instead tried to smile. She turned the key in the lock and the door creaked open.

Surprisingly, even on this overcast day, inside was light and not the typical dark and overpowering fashion of heavy drapes and fussy wall coverings she was expecting. Parts of the stone walls were exposed, whilst other areas were plastered and painted white. It was simple. It was home.

"Oh, I love it!" she said to herself.

With her muddy boots removed, she walked around the room in her stockinged feet taking everything in. It was the one room, long and relatively thin but it was perfect. There was a small, open fireplace, stone hearth and a red brick surround topped by a rustic oak beam as a mantelpiece. A simple, wooden clock in the centre of the mantlepiece stated twenty minutes past two. There was a blue and white checked armchair and a brown, two-seater leather sofa. To either side of the chimney breast were wooden shelves housing well over a hundred books. Dotted around the walls were paintings of pretty houses, set in stunning landscapes, with sea, countryside or mountain views.

By the front window was a round table with a white tablecloth. A candlestick was the centrepiece. Two simple, dining chairs were neatly tucked away under the table.

The oak staircase was open to the downstairs room but beneath the angle of the stairs was a built-in cupboard. Catherine peeked inside to find a few boring but necessary items such as a broom.

Through a rustic wooden archway, the kitchen area was square with a clean stove. Some kindling was already neatly stacked ready for use. She looked out of the window over a tiny backyard. The promised washing line and mangle were there.

Catherine started to unbutton her overcoat, a once beautiful, blue design with a high collar that had seen better days. She removed the coat and flung it over the armchair. Her parents would have had a fit by her untidiness. Taking in the excitement of every step, she climbed the wooden staircase. Upstairs was one room, housing a large bed, an armchair, a double wardrobe, a chest of four drawers and a washstand. The room was spacious and private, she felt truly blessed. A sigh escaped her upturned lips, maybe she had finally been forgiven of her sins.

With nobody watching, she jumped on the bed in a totally childish way which felt wonderful. As she lay spreadeagled on the bedspread, she did not have a care in the world.

"Oh, I love it! I love it! I love it!" she exclaimed and then squealed with delight. Closing her eyes, she sighed deeply and for the first time in years she felt sheer contentment and freedom. The layers of sheets and blankets felt so soft and warm, allowing her body to sink into their inviting depths. They must have been freshly laundered as the faint smell of sweet peas lingered on the fabric. She could not help but smile. Slowly, her happiness faded away as she thought about the hard bed she had recently endured in the asylum. The frame had groaned each time she moved. Her bony shoulders and hips had felt bruised when trying to sleep on her side. She spiralled to further depths on thinking about the blood-stained mattress on the floor when she was— a noise from the white-washed walls interrupted her thoughts. She lifted her head off the pillow and looked around the room. Nothing to see. Grateful for the interruption, she forcibly stopped herself being depressive and she once again closed her eyes and prayed thanks for the comfortable bed. The smile returned.

Perfection was maybe an impossible dream for the groaning noise from next door returned, like how a method actor would play a tortured ghoul. She got up from the bed and placed her ear to the wall. Silence. She crept along the floorboards, trying to listen for sounds from next door when she came across a mirror hanging on the wall. Her breathing became laboured, and she could feel a flush to her cheeks. She had not seen her own reflection in years. Reluctantly, she slowly side stepped until she could see her countenance in the framed mirror.

An older, wiser lady gazed back at her, wondering where the young, innocent girl was hiding. The once glossy, auburn hair was dull, the once twinkling blue eyes were a cloudy grey, and the fullness of youth had been swept away in the storm. The groans were now internal.

Chapter Six

The setting sun drew Catherine's attention to the time, so she put on her leather boots and blue overcoat and studied the simply drawn map given to her by Doctor Wainwright to find the location of the store. With a small amount of money in her purse, she went in search of provisions.

As she walked along the street, she discreetly looked at her neighbour's house. The sign on the gate read, *Bluebell Cottage.* The front garden was rather scruffy and there was little to see inside the property as the windows were draped with net curtains.

The next house along the street took her breath away for all the wrong reasons. Set back from the road on an incline, the gothic style abode seemed out of place for a quaint village. With its asymmetric design, ornate wood, intricate brick work, square tower, cone-shaped roof and metal spire, the house oozed spooky eccentricities. Catherine scurried past the abode and focused on locating the shop.

A bell rang above her head as she opened the store's door. To her right was a large floor to ceiling cabinet displaying a colourful assortment of bottles, jars and packets. There were baskets on the floor containing various goods such as kindling. To her left was a wooden counter and more cabinets and shelving, displaying everything one could possibly need. A plump, middle-aged woman with a ruddy complexion appeared through a small door. "How can I help you, me love?"

"I need a few things as I have just moved in today."

"I'm guessing Rose Cottage?"

"Correct." She smiled. "Catherine Fawcett."

"Lovely to make your acquaintance dear. I'm Sally Dawson and I live on the farm just over there." She pointed in the direction of the cordoned off road.

"Ah yes, I spotted that on the way in."

"We stock the usual stuff such as bread, milk, cheese, meats, flour, and we try an' produce as much stuff as we can ourselves. Everything is lovely and fresh or baked by my own hands."

Catherine rattled off the list in her head. Sally Dawson packaged each item as they chatted.

"The house over there with the gothic architecture, who lives there may I ask?"

"The one up the hill with the mill stones as part of the wall?" Catherine nodded. "That's Eden Hill House. Creepy, isn't it? It's an orphanage for children who are strange. Occasionally, you see them going for walks. They have a band and sometimes they'll do a performance on the village green but otherwise you rarely see them. Weird little mites they are."

"And the imposing, red sandstone house on the opposite side of the green?"

"They come and go at all times of the day and night. Not sure to be honest what goes on in there, but they are quiet, they'll not bother you. A few of them go to church on Sundays, apparently."

Catherine searched her purse for the correct change, "And the house next to mine, Bluebell Cottage, does anyone live there?" She handed over the coins to pay for her items.

"Now I'm not too sure. It was a young woman and a boy, well I say boy, but he must be in his teens by now, not sure if it's her son or brother. They have lived there for a while, but I heard she wanted to move back to her hometown, to be closer to her family. I'm not sure if she's gone already. I haven't seen them in a while."

Not wanting to appear too nosy, Catherine changed the subject, "And water, is there a pump or well nearby?"

"Around the corner, over the railway bridge and to the right, there's a wooden sign to show you the way."

"Thank you, Sally, you have been most kind and welcoming."

"Not at all deary, feel free to pop in anytime and ask."

Catherine carried her shopping back home, only briefly glancing at the gothic abode. She was convinced that someone was watching her from the tower window.

Back at Rose Cottage, she tidied away her shopping and was just about to put the kettle on when there was a knock on the front door. Confused, as she was not expecting any visitors, she wondered who could be calling. With some uncertainty, she opened the door and saw an elderly gent. He took off his checked flat cap, revealing a wart and liver-spotted bald head with hair only around the sides. Appearing anxious, he stood there twisting his cap, as if wringing out a dishcloth.

"Me house, I'm lost," he stated.

"Erm, well …" It seemed silly to ask him where he lived if he was lost. "What does your house look like?"

"It has a green door."

"And what is the view from your house? What can you see?" asked Catherine.

"A stone, I see the grey stone." He continued to wring out his cap.

"And do you live with anyone? Do you have a wife?"

"No, she died … well I think she did." Like standing on hot ash from the fire, he transferred his weight from side to side.

"Is that your house over there, directly facing the stone?" offered Catherine but then she noticed the blue door.

His anxiety continued, the shuffling steps, the hat wringing, there did not appear to be any recognition of his home amongst the houses surrounding the green. Having not yet taken off her overcoat, she headed outside with the confused gentleman. Arm in arm, they walked around the edges of the green in search of a green door.

As they walked towards a sandy coloured brick house which faced the stone monument, an elderly woman opened the blue front door and bellowed, "Vincent, you were supposed to be going to the shop for milk."

"Is this your wife and home?" asked Catherine.

"Yeah, I think so."

The chubby woman stood there relying on the support of two canes, "He'd lose his head if it wasn't stuck on." She tutted. "Vincent, you were only going there." She nodded in the direction of the shop.

"I think he got lost," suggested Catherine.

"Bless him, he's easily confused these days, he's lost his mind and I've lost the use of me legs but together we cope, don't we love?" Vincent walked down the path and into the house.

"Would you like me to get the milk for you?"

With a smile, she politely said, "Oh that would be so kind. Thank you." She then turned, the smile gone and shouted, "Vincent, give me the money and the bottle!"

A few seconds later he appeared at the door with the requested items.

"Just come in when you've got it, me legs couldn't cope with opening the door again."

Catherine once again walked to the shop, refusing to look at any of the windows of the gothic residence.

The bell above the shop door announced her presence and Sally Dawson appeared from the back room, "You again! What you forgot?"

"Vincent from over there wanted some milk but he got lost on the way so I'm helping out."

"Ah yes, the Kavanaghs, bless them, Vincent and Vera, yeah, he's starting to get a bit dippy in his old age. They are lovely though, hearts of gold." Sally filled the bottle full of milk. "Sad story, but I'll leave that for another day."

Catherine was intrigued but respected the statement.

She walked back to the Kavanagh's yellow brick house and tapped on the knocker which was a lion holding a ring in its mouth. As instructed earlier, she opened the door and shouted, "Here's your milk!" Silence. The hallway was gloomy with dark furniture and wallpaper. "Mrs Kavanagh? Vincent? Here's your milk!" Rather than walk into their house, she left the bottle on the console table in the hallway with the remaining pennies and closed the door, thankful to be going home.

Chapter Seven

After unpacking and finding places around the house for her personal belongings, Catherine noticed a chill setting in the air and thought about lighting the fire. As an inpatient in the asylum, one of her daily jobs was to fetch coal from the cellar and light the fire in the day room. Being one of the younger and fitter patients, she was expected to retrieve coal whenever supplies were running short. Catherine had detested the cellar, the smell of dampness, the oppressive darkness and the dirt. The spiders and rats had also bothered her but the memory of what she had found there one evening would forever torment her thoughts. Evelyn was lying over the coals having slashed her own throat with a knife she had hidden up her sleeve. Desperately poor since her husband's fatal accident, her only option had been to place her three dear children in the workhouse and for her to seek refuge in the adult workhouse down the road. Hoping this solution would be a temporary measure, she had found herself unable to cope with the backbreaking work and the guilt of abandoning her children. The melancholy had been overpowering and taking her own life had seemed to be the only way to ease her pain. Having been admitted to the asylum, she had seemed to improve, occasionally laughing, at times singing, but obviously this was a mask she was hiding behind. Catherine shivered and tried to forget the image of Evelyn sprawled over the coals and instead tried to think of the times they had chatted, and Evelyn had mustered a genuine smile. Catherine made the sign of the cross and whispered, "Rest in peace dear Evelyn."

The living room fire provided a warm glow as well as heat allowing Catherine to peruse the books which were scattered in a visually pleasing display on the shelves either side of the chimney breast. There were works of historical fiction and romance from the Tudors through to the Regency period.

There were factual historical books such as *The Rise and Fall of the Roman Empire, William the Conqueror* and another entitled *The Hammer of the Scots*. There was also a bible.

Amongst fact and fiction were practical books on a variety of subjects such as embroidery, knitting, cooking, gardening, carpentry and painting. There was also a book titled *Self-Help* by S. W. Smiles which looked quite interesting, but one book stood out amongst the many on the shelves. From the binding, it looked professionally crafted, with gold lettering along the burgundy spine, *The Story*. Catherine carefully removed the horizontal book from between its upright neighbours. The pages were expertly folded and intertwined with red thread. She flicked through the first few pages. The book appeared to be a diary with neat handwriting and a few simple pictures. She placed the book under her arm, lodging it between her elbow and waist, whilst she studied the remaining books on the shelves. This was the only one she was remotely interested in reading.

The fire was now roaring, yet she lit a couple more candles for extra light. Sitting comfortably in the blue and white checked armchair, she loosened her hair, allowing the auburn curls to fall freely over her shoulders, and opened the book.

November 1958

Joyce sauntered over to the living room window, pretending to admire the beautiful countryside view from their detached, stone cottage. The autumnal hues were breath-taking. The leaves had turned, and some were falling as she eavesdropped on her husband's telephone conversation. From her new vantage point, she could see him standing in the hallway. John was so animated that Joyce could not help but wonder about the seemingly good news. His eyes were smiling, and his voice was a few notes higher than usual. His excitement was contagious. Joyce felt her heart starting to race with curiosity.

John's body language was morphing as his right hand held the heavy receiver to his ear and mouth. His cheeks inflated, then he blew out a discreet sigh. From the mouthpiece, the coil swirled down like a helter-skelter to the telephone base. John kept winding and releasing the cord around his index finger, now appearing nervous. Joyce was convinced there was an element of bad news. His fingers were now combing through his silky brown hair, finishing with a pose of clinging on to the back of his neck for dear life as he huffed and puffed to what the other person was saying. His fingers left a trail of red marks.

Joyce tiptoed closer to the door. John was no longer in view, but she could hear muffled sounds from the mystery caller. The voice had a feminine tone, but it was hard to say with certainty. Joyce went from a state of intrigue to inquisition, with so many questions needing answered. Her heart now racing for different reasons.

Finally, she heard John say his goodbyes and the receiver was placed on the base. She quickly pretended to be busy by fluffing up the pink cushions on the blue couch. The cottage had been built in 1780 but they had recently refurbished the downstairs rooms to a modern interior which Joyce had fallen in love with, having seen an article in a glossy magazine. The decor didn't really fit with the house's exterior, but she thought surprises were good. John walked through to the living room.

"What was that all about?" asked Joyce.

"I need a beer first." He wandered through to the kitchen and got himself a drink from the fridge. He took a couple of gulps. His hands a little shaky.

"Come on then, hurry up, don't keep me in suspense." Joyce sat on the edge of the sofa, her legs daintily together and to the side. She adjusted the sea blue scarf around her neck. Her husband started to laugh. "What's so funny about that?"

"Sorry, I wasn't laughing at you. I've been offered a job."

"You never told me you'd applied for a job," said Joyce with a quizzical look on her face.

"That's because I haven't."

"What's the job? Where's the job? For whom? Doing what?"

John laughed again, seemingly in a daze, "That's another strange thing." He sighed deeply and took another big swig of his beer. "I'm not at liberty to say."

"Stop with all this nonsense and mystery. Just tell me what you can say then."

He took another mouthful of beer. "Dear Lord, where do I begin?"

On Monday, John had received a phone call at work, from a woman calling herself Mrs Briggs. She seemed to know a lot about him, declaring she was impressed when researching his career, detailing the various positions he had held and had asked if he was interested in a prestigious position along similar lines, but doubling his already excellent salary. John had been reluctant to engage over the phone, doubting her sincerity as she was vague on the employment details and the offer seemed too good to be true. He had thanked her for her interest and suggested if she could be so kind as to put something down in writing, he would consider her offer but he never did, thinking it all a joke, probably a wind up from one of his mates. Two days later, by official recorded post, an envelope had arrived at home marked, *Strictly Private and Confidential.* Inside was a detailed offer of employment, a formal contract, confirming his employer, place of work, professional role and responsibilities. The telephone call today was confirming the acceptance of the offer and a few other details.

"Where's the letter then?" asked Joyce.

"I can't show you."

"Why are you being so … so …evasive about all of this?"

"Because that is part of my new contract as I have sworn on and signed the Official Secrets Act." John finished the dregs of his beer.

Rarely was Joyce quiet but she took a few moments to analyse what she had heard. By then, John had been to the fridge and back for another beer.

"Is there anything you *can* tell me about this new job?"

John took three gulps of beer and tried to be discreet about an emerging burp before replying, "We will have to sell the house and move from here."

On hearing those words, Joyce was conflicted, feeling sad about moving from such an idyllic location. They had a lovely cottage with stunning views over countryside, but the house and garden were quite small. With only two bedrooms, she would have liked something bigger for she dreamed of starting a family. By moving away, she would miss her family and friends who were all relatively close by. Then she smiled, thinking about the possibilities, imagining the dwelling they could buy if John was going to be on double his current salary. A luxury, modern penthouse overlooking a harbour or maybe a grand town house in London or an impressive Georgian abode with an acre of land in the country. Realising she was dreaming, she looked over at John and there were now two empty bottles of beer on the table. His brow was furrowed.

Even though he wasn't working today, he still wore a blue silk tie which contrasted nicely against his white shirt. Eight years older than Joyce, he had aged well, the few little speckles of grey adding to his distinguished good looks.

Joyce plucked up the courage to ask, "Can you at least tell me where we will be moving to?"

John slapped the top of his thighs then sprung to his feet. "To the middle of nowhere by the sounds of it." He made his way into the kitchen for another beer.

Chapter Eight

Catherine had not slept well. This was no surprise or cause for concern, for she was in an unfamiliar place, in an unknown village, after spending months in a lunatic asylum with all its strange noises. The silence of the night had been disturbing.

Prior to bed, she had been reading *The Story,* which had added to her state of uneasiness.

After washing, dressing, breakfasting and tidying up, Catherine decided to go for a walk and explore the village and surrounding area. She walked past the Kavanagh's yellow brick house, noticing the bedroom curtains were still closed but a fire was on, evidenced by smoke swirling from the left-hand chimney.

As the path continued steeply downhill, a beautiful old church with an octagonal tower came into view on the left-hand side. A sign stated, *Welcome to St Constantine's Church.* On her right was a long building with a sign stating, *The Ferryman's Cottage.* The downhill path ended abruptly at the water's edge. The impacted dirt road changed to sandy grass and continued right along the river. On each bank was a small jetty, but no boat or ferry could be seen.

Further along the sandy footpath was an exquisite stone bench, sculpted into powerful angel wings. Layer upon layer of realistic feathers were carved into the sandstone. Anyone sitting on the bench would feel like they had the protective wings of a guardian angel wrapped around them, keeping them safe from harm whilst they admired the stunning view.

In a commanding position, high on the other side of the river was a large residence with terraced gardens forged from the sandstone. Water cascaded down an ornate man-made fall, decorated with gargoyles, dragons and images of war. The water flowed down stone steps, surrounded by an archway, into the gently flowing river. Catherine was mesmerised by the intriguing sights and pleasing sounds.

The footpath ascended through ancient woodland. With barely any analytical thoughts, Catherine felt happy and at peace with the simplicity of nature. The earthy smells, birds chirping, the wind lightly rustling remaining leaves, the sound of the river flowing below, she was healing from within. Life continued despite adversity; nature had to carry on surviving.

The woodland path suddenly forked. She stopped, unable to make a conscious decision without some effort. The left path continued downhill heading towards the river. The right path continued to wind uphill. On first impressions, the left path appeared more interesting with a layered rock formation peeking through the trees.

As she slowed her pace to carefully descend the stone steps, she could see the left path was soon to end. A stone wall circumvented the natural rock abutment, and a spiked metal gate barred the way. To her right was the towering layers of natural stone she had seen jutting out from the woodland hill. To her left was a sheer drop of approximately forty or fifty feet to the river.

Out of curiosity, she tried the handle of the metal gate, but was disappointed to find it locked. To see what the metal gate was protecting or hiding, she stood on the decorative metalwork with the tips of her toes and leaned to her left, in order to gain further perspective. There appeared to be three separate openings to a network of caves.

With her way blocked and little else to see or do, she retreated her steps and decided to head back to the village. She would take the right uphill path another day.

On walking past the yellow brick house once more, Vera was standing by the front door. "Sorry lass, I can't remember ya name or even if you told me, but Vincent's gone missing again. Have you seen him on ya travels?"

"I'm so sorry but I saw no one on my walk down by the river and through the woods. My name is Catherine, Catherine Fawcett."

"Call me Vera, and well, you've met Vincent. And thanks for getting the milk yesterday." Her face suddenly contorted in pain, and she struggled to transfer her weight from one side to the other. "I'll have to go inside. Me hips are killing me slowly but surely. Come in lass."

Catherine had a quick look around the edges of the green, but Vincent was not to be seen. She walked down the path to the blue front door and stepped inside.

The hallway was dark with a few homely items to brighten the dreary interior. There was the console table on which she had placed the milk and money. A potted plant added a little interest. At the bottom of the stairs was a coat stand holding two brightly coloured shawls and an overcoat. On the floor was a wicker basket filled with wood and a metal container filled with coal. There were numerous paintings on the walls. She heard Vera calling

41

from the room on the left, so she made her way inside. There were patterns everywhere. The wallpaper above the dark panelling bore green foliage, the red rug an exotic Persian masterpiece, the curtains were green with gold stripes and the burgundy suite was partially covered by a floral throw.

"So, what has happened to Vincent?" asked Catherine.

"Well, we have separate rooms as he's a terrible snorer and yet I can still hear him from my room, and I'm not too sure if he went to bed last night or if he left this morning. What time is it now?" She answered her own question by looking at the grandfather clock in the far corner. "Just after ten, well he could have been missing for hours."

"I have been down to the river. I saw the beautiful waterfall and the stone caves with the metal gate. He was not there." Catherine wanted to ask about the caves but knew this was not the time to interrogate the woman.

"Where is the silly old sod?" Vera was obviously upset. She did not know what to do with herself.

"If you feel it would be helpful, I'll ask around the village for him if you'd like?"

"Would you do that? That would be really helpful. Sorry but I've forgot ya name again."

"Catherine."

"I'm Vera, Vera Kavanagh." She struggled out of her chair and looked out of the front window in search of Vincent.

"Does Vincent have any family or friends here? Does he have a particular place he likes to frequent?"

"No, I don't think so, other than the pub but that won't be open yet. He's a lazy git at heart so this wandering is so unlike him." Vera was trying to make light of the situation, but Catherine could see her pain. "He'd always moan if I sent him on errands, but he'd do it. He'd do anything for me. Bless him." She dabbed her handkerchief to each eye. "Otherwise no, no family or friends round here. We did have four children but sadly they died when only bairns. We gave up trying after little Molly."

Catherine was reminded of her work at the funeral parlour. Grief was an awful emotion to deal with for there was no right or wrong approach. Everyone was different, the only thing to do was be there for that person through their sorrow.

Vera waddled back over to her armchair and plonked herself down. Catherine approached the old lady and offered her hand which Vera kindly took and simultaneously they gently squeezed. This appeared to be the time to leave, there was sadness and a cloak of darkness in the room, Catherine did not want any melancholic thoughts to invade her mind. "I will do my very best to find Vincent."

As the sitting room was stifling, Catherine was thankful for the cooler fresh air as she walked out of the door. First, she would walk around the village green and see if she could find any clues to Vincent's hiding place. She walked past the large red residence, which was now on her right, wondering if he could be in there. The building reminded her of a gentleman's residence, an exclusive place where women were forbidden to attend. Men together, whisky flowing, card games, smoking, clouds of intoxicating fumes swirling around the room, solving problems, putting the world to right. It was a plausible idea that Vincent could be there, but Catherine was doubtful with it being early in the morning.

On her travels, she walked past many beautiful houses, some were quaint, others were grand, but she particularly liked a blue and white house, it looked so pretty, like an iced cake.

She stood outside the store and peeked in the windows. Vincent was not there. There was a choice of a road leading downhill with more beautiful houses or the road which bends to the right with white cottages. She had walked that way yesterday afternoon to fetch water from the well. Undecided which way to go, she called into the store.

Sally Dawson ducked her head to come through the small doorway. "You again!" she stated with a smile. "You are definitely my best customer at the moment."

"I'm on an important errand." She explained about Vincent Kavanagh's disappearance.

"Well, he's not been in here this morning. I'll take him back home if he does."

"The road there, where does it lead?" asked Catherine, pointing down the hill.

"It takes you to the railway station, but it's only used for deliveries at the moment, not for passengers." A sudden look of horror appeared on Sally's face. As she continued, her voice conveyed a slight tremor, "There's a bridge to cross the train tracks and another bridge over the ..." She hesitated enough to heighten Catherine's concern, "The area's known locally as Suicide Point."

Catherine was horrified by the answer. "I think I need to go there." She had to forcibly swallow to dislodge a lump that was growing in the back of her throat. "And the road that way, where does that go once past the well?"

"It's currently impassable. They are digging up the road and laying down water pipes. We can't wait to have proper running water in the village, but it's taking a long time. There's only ever two men working on it. I don't think there will be any problems that way, Vincent wouldn't get past the waterworks."

"The walk down by the river, the metal gate, I think there may be caves. Is there any possibility he could be in there?" asked Catherine.

"Haven't been there for years. As far as I know, no-one ever ventures there. I've no idea who may hold the key, or if there's even a key to be had. Sorry."

Catherine was none the wiser. She thanked Sally for her help and left the shop. The village was like a ghost town, so quiet and still. Although Edenvale was classed as a village, she was surprised by how large the area felt when searching for a missing person. There were too many houses to knock on each door at this stage. With the thought of Suicide Point on her mind, she headed to the train station.

Chapter Nine

Continuing her search for Vincent Kavanagh, Catherine headed downhill towards the railway station and Suicide Point. Grand residences, all built to different but elegant styles, lined the sides of the road. Further down the hill was a house of Georgian appearance. A sign above the front door squeaked in the breeze, *Lawson's Lodging House*. There appeared to be stables to the rear for horses and space for carriages.

Rounding a corner, a waist height wooden fence came into view and the railway tracks soon became evident. The station master's house was on the far side of the rails. A metal bridge painted red, cream, black and gold traversed the double tracks. Catherine ascended the steps and stood on top of the bridge, taking in the views along the train lines. No sign of a body, alive or dead. With an air of grace, she continued down the far side and loitered on the platform, as if waiting for a train.

The station master's house was typical in design, with fancy fascia woodwork in pristine white. A woman was busy in the garden. She wore simple, brown clothing and a flimsy bonnet. Catherine tried to catch the woman's attention by waving but to no avail.

"Hello there! Sorry to bother you. I'm looking for Vincent Kavanagh, the man from ..." she did not know the name of the house. "He lives in the yellow house overlooking the village green."

The petite woman walked towards Catherine, "Sorry dear, I've not seen anyone around here in the last hour or so. Then again, I have been busy." Looking exhausted, she carefully placed the hoe onto the perfectly manicured lawn and put her hands on her hips, seemingly thankful for the respite from tidying the flower beds in preparation for winter.

There was no polite way of saying it, "I'm also looking for Suicide Point."

The woman raised her eyebrows in question, "You are not thinking of doing anything stupid, are you?" Whilst waiting for a reply, she used her forearm to wipe the dewy perspiration from her brow.

Catherine rested her gloved left hand on her chest, "Oh goodness me, no, it's to put Mrs Kavanagh's mind at rest about her husband."

"My sincere apologies for asking, but my mind has been troubled by the gruesome sights I have witnessed over the years." The woman removed her gardening gloves and discarded them next to the hoe. She opened the pristine white gate and approached Catherine. "Come with me, I'll show you the site." The two women walked along the platform which narrowed to a single pathway along the side of the house. "As you can see, there are two sets of train tracks running along this viaduct with limited visibility ahead due to the trees and the bend. Yet people take the chance of running the line to get to the other side of the river. This less than a minute walk over the train tracks saves folk an hour trip to get to Great Corby over there." She stopped talking to give Catherine time to take in the surroundings. "Nowadays, whether they walk the line to deliberately kill themselves or whether unfortunate accidents, no one knows but there have been a few … incidents." The woman grimaced at the thought.

"This is Suicide Point? They are hit by a train?"

The woman nodded her head. "However, there is another option if they are so desperate that they cannot wait for a train." Catherine followed her along a narrow-slatted path a few feet below the elevated train line, their heads now level with the parallel tracks. From being on the firm station platform, the ground suddenly disappeared as the precarious position of the viaduct was realised.

The consistent gaps between each wooden slat revealed the churning River Eden below. Catherine's stomach felt like a trapeze artist doing dangerously high somersaults with no safety net. "We must be a hundred feet in the air!"

"When this was built in the mid-1830s it was supposedly the tallest viaduct in the world."

"Wow!" managed Catherine, her legs suddenly feeling wobbly as they traversed the wooden planks.

"Suicide Point is here." The petite woman could barely see over the tall, cast-iron railings. "As you can see, further to our left is the steep embankment covered with trees. Further to our right is the river. If they jump here, at this precise point, they land on the hard path with nothing to cushion their fall, ensuring they meet their maker." She peered through the painted white railings to gain a better view of the riverside path one hundred feet below. "Nobody there, no blood stains, I think we can safely say Mr Kavanagh hasn't been here."

46

"Thank goodness for that." Catherine looked around. Wooden slats were stacked in a neat pile in the corner. "Why have they cordoned off the path from there? Why not close the pathway before Suicide Point?"

"They haven't closed it. They are continuing the walkway all the way to the other side."

"But will this not encourage more people to …"

The woman understood the pause and continued, "No, I personally believe the train track deaths are mainly accidental. I reckon they study the timetables of the trains, make an educated guess that the track will be safe, but trains run late, there are freight trains which are not timetabled, there are trains for the railway maintenance workmen and there are now rumours of a Royal Train being commissioned. Anyway, if people want to kill themselves, they'll find a way, pathway or not."

As silence now ensued following a rather macabre conversation amongst strangers, the women turned around and headed to firm ground where air did not swirl beneath their feet and the sight of flowing water did not create queasiness.

"Thank you, you have been most helpful."

"No trouble, I hope you find Vincent."

Heading uphill towards the village store, Catherine suddenly realised that out of all the houses in the village, Vincent had knocked on her door, so she went back to the cottage to check if he was there. After a quick freshen up and a cup of tea, she went back outside to continue her search. She looked over at the Kavanagh's house. Vera was standing in the bay window. On seeing Catherine, she shrugged her shoulders and shook her head. Vincent was obviously not home.

Catherine decided to knock on a few doors and the house next to hers was first on the list. The gate was partially off its hinges and needed a little shove to open the angled metalwork. She navigated the uneven path and knocked on the door. Convinced she heard noises from within, she knocked once more on the rapper, a small orb and claw shaped design. The laced curtains seemed to briefly flutter but no one answered the door.

Avoiding the spooky, gothic orphanage, she justified the decision that it was unlikely Vincent would make the long walk through the grounds to climb the numerous steps to the front door. Instead, she crossed over the road. Of all the houses around the green, Sycamore Lodge was the filthiest, but she decided to knock on the door anyway. The pathway to the house was uneven and covered in slippery, green sludge from the surrounding trees. The garden was unkempt and dreary. The place felt dark, damp and unloved. Leaves piled in a corner. The windows were grimy, and the curtains were drawn. No one answered to the sound of the three loud knocks on the cobwebbed door. Catherine quickly made her escape.

47

Next door was a very tall house, grand and imposing but again there was no answer from this door. She assumed they must be working.

Catherine then visited the pretty, blue and white house. Surprisingly, a young man appearing to be in his early twenties answered the door of Hazel Dell. Although his clothes were a little worn, they were clean with a delicate, soapy smell catching the breeze. She had imagined an old, frail lady living there, for the house was so pretty and feminine. The young man mumbled as they chatted, seemingly quite shy, as he kept his head low, hiding behind his long fringe.

Catherine introduced herself and the young man offered his name as Mark. He confirmed he was acquainted with Mr Kavanagh but had not seen him wandering today. On Catherine's suggestion, she wondered if anyone else in the household had seen Mr Kavanagh, so Mark shouted for his mother and grandmother, and Catherine could hear their replies.

Mark had a gentleness about him, "Sorry we can't help, but I'll keep a lookout for him and let Mrs Kavanagh know."

"Please do and thank you."

The gentleman's residence was next on this side of the green. The gravel pathway crunched under her feet so there was little chance of making a stealthy entrance. By the time she reached the property and climbed the stone steps, a butler answered the door.

"How may I help you?" he offered with a slight bow of his head.

"Please forgive me for the interruption but I am trying to locate the whereabouts of Vincent Kavanagh. The gentleman who resides there." She pointed to the yellow house. "He appears to be missing."

"I personally have not seen Mr Kavanagh for some time, but I will ask the others on your behalf."

"The others?" asked Catherine.

"Staff and guests. Who shall I inform with any information?" The butler cocked his head to the side.

"You may advise Mrs Kavanagh or myself, Catherine Fawcett. I am residing at Rose Cottage." She pointed to her house on the opposite side of the green.

They made their formal acquaintance and said their goodbyes. As she walked away from the residence, she had an uneasy feeling about Mr Schubert yet could not quite pinpoint why. His eyes had wrinkled as he smiled, his coarse red hair was neatly combed over to the side, he was smartly dressed, well-spoken and his manner was welcoming but something felt peculiar. There was something familiar about him. She pondered that he may know the anonymous benefactor who was funding her expenses or that Schubert may know the owner of Rose Cottage and was made aware of her presence. Horrified, she realised he may know of her predicament and the reasons to her seeking asylum in the village. Recalling his overall demeanour, she wondered if it was smugness, possibly. Insight, more than likely. An air of superiority, definitely.

As she was so close to the Kavanagh's house, she called in to check Vincent had not suddenly appeared. Vera invited her into the warmth of the living room.

"No, he's still not here. Me mind is churning with worry. Has he fallen in the river? Has he walked along the train tracks and been splattered to pieces? Has he jumped off Suicide Point and made a bloody mess for someone to clean up?" Vera was visibly distraught, her hands constantly fidgeting.

"Let's not worry ourselves unnecessarily." Catherine walked over to the armchair and was almost overcome by the heat from the fire. She placed her arm around Vera's shoulders. The lady was trembling and obviously not from feeling chilled.

In detail, Catherine told Vera where she had been and with whom she had spoken about Vincent's possible whereabouts. Vera had started trembling again at the mention of the train tracks and Suicide Point, but Catherine quickly reassured her that she had thoroughly checked those areas and there was no sign of Vincent. The mention of Mr Schubert at the red sandstone residence had also rattled Vera's nerves and she was adamant that Vincent would be highly unlikely to step foot in that place.

Chapter Ten

Catherine felt guilty at leaving Vera in such a sorry state, but she needed to go home. The heat from the fire, walking miles in search of Vincent, exploring the caves and the woods, her feet felt raw and blistered, as if they were about to explode out of her laced-up boots. It was the furthest she had walked in many a year.

As soon as she stepped over the threshold to Rose Cottage, she kicked off her boots, leaving them where they landed and she sat in her armchair, thankful to have the weight taken off her swollen feet. She closed her eyes and sighed with relief.

The Story, the diary she had been reading came into her thoughts. The book was upstairs on the bedside table. She wanted to collect it but her motivation was missing, just like Vincent. She looked at the stairs, too many steps to contemplate at this precise moment. Her eyes closed once more but all she could think of was the handwritten pages and the strange content of the book. Reluctantly, she forced her feet to the floor, stopped at the kitchen to light the fire and put the kettle on to boil. Tentatively, she made her way upstairs to retrieve the book. Her feet were throbbing with the effort. She gingerly hobbled back down the stairs, waited for the kettle to boil and made a pot of tea. Placing the book and tea tray on the small round table within easy reach of her armchair, she pulled up the footstool and started to relax.

She assumed *The Story* was written by a previous resident of the cottage. As of yet, there was no name or date, and she resisted the urge to flick through to the end of the book to see if the author had signed her name. It felt like the author was female. The handwriting was decorative, and the occasional pictures of flowers were delicate. *The Story* was a bound leather notebook with blank pages, allowing the owner to write a story, keep a diary or draw a picture. This book seemed to be an account of the goings on around the village green.

Catherine wondered if the author was also from the asylum. This house was possibly a refuge, a stop gap for those considered well enough to be allowed back into society. She shuddered, wondering if everyone in the vicinity knew she was a former lunatic. How embarrassed she felt at the stigma, that everyone in the village probably knew her secret. The variety of books on the shelves was probably a way to keep a lunatic busy and distracted. There were practical books, on topics such as cookery and sewing, and she wondered if this was a way of encouraging someone to live independently and be self-sufficient.

Trying to stop the worrying thoughts she opened the book.

1st May

Three minutes past eleven

The Kavanaghs are late in commencing their daily walk. Mrs Kavanagh is certainly not as spritely as she was. She waddles like a duck and her hips are so rotated that her feet are forever at ten minutes to three. I'm convinced she will one day trip herself up with her canes. Mr Kavanagh appears as shifty as ever, always on the lookout as he props up his wife. With his bowed legs, he looks like he has been riding a horse for hours on end.

Twenty-three minutes past eleven

The young man from the sweet confectionary house walks over to the monument. I am guessing he is the grandson of Mrs Humphries. He sits on the stepped surround, leaning back against the grey eyesore on the green. His hair is an unruly mess and as always, he flicks his head frequently to move his fringe from his eyes. I love those wavy, brown locks.

Twenty to twelve

Finally, she is here, skipping over to the boy. She is wearing a loose-fitting ensemble today, mainly white, but with snippets of pink. She appears gay. The boy's face lights up on seeing her approach. They are oblivious to their surroundings, seemingly much in love. The animation in their countenance, so wonderful to see. They head downhill towards the river, probably to escape prying eyes.

The Kavanaghs have made it home safely.

Two o'clock

What a sight to behold! The children from Eden Hill House are spilling onto the green. Having had time to study them on a few occasions, it appears to me that each child seems to have some sort of simple mind or physical deformity. The little girl, having four or five years, always catches my eye. Today, she is wearing a blue dress, overlaid with a pristine white pinafore. The layers of her garments fail to hide her metal calliper with the brown leather strapped onto her right leg. Her hair is golden in the sun, such perfect ringlets cascading over her shoulders. Each child bears an instrument today. The ringleted girl holds a triangle. They are standing in the middle of the green, grouped according to their instrument choice such as wind or percussion. I feel embarrassed by my ignorance for I fail to identify any of the tunes played but they are all hauntingly beautiful and melodic. The finale created tingles down my arms. They live barely a few feet from this cottage, yet I have never heard them play or rehearse and with a band of this size, this is most peculiar. However, I am most grateful for the performance. This has lifted my spirits.

Just before six

That will be Mr Kavanagh off to the Inn. I wonder if I will see him stagger home. This is most unlikely, for I will be fast asleep by then.

Fifteen minutes past six

Mrs Dawson locks up the shop.

A quarter to nine

Two unknown gentlemen arrive at Oak Bank Hall. Heaven only knows what takes place in that residence.

Catherine closed the book for this was the last entry for that day. The author seemed obsessed with the goings on in the village. She was reminded of one of the ladies at the asylum, oh now what was her name, Williamina, yes, Mina for short. Her hair was always neatly tied in a bun. She was obsessed with trivial annoyances yet could not cope with the more important functions of life. Asymmetry, something slightly rotated, she would go around the ward picking up an individual crumb or speck of lint, walk to the fire, throw the offending item on the coals and go in search of other irritations to destroy or align.

Was the writer of this diary so fascinated with precise timings to be considered a lunatic? Diary was the wrong description, they were observations, the obsessive recording of events to the exact minute. Catherine wanted to know who this person was but would read *The Story* to its natural conclusion, rather than deliberately try and unearth information on the previous occupant of the house.

Chapter Eleven

Rain lashed against the bedroom window and the roof felt liable to being whisked away into the swirling winds. Catherine could not sleep. She got out of her cosy bed and put her feet to the cold floorboards. Her heels were tender, and she had to hobble over to the window. Trying to peek from behind the curtains, she could barely see outside for the windows were misted with condensation.

Her plans for the day were to check on Vera's wellbeing and to see if Vincent had returned home. If not, she would visit the Wheatsheaf Inn and then on to the outskirts of the village where the workmen were laying the new road. Someone must have seen something. However, with this weather, all she wanted to do was to go back to bed which she did.

An hour later and still in bed, Catherine wondered what to buy from the store as cooking and baking had never been her strong point. Since arriving at Rose Cottage, she had lived on ready to eat foods such as bread and cheese. When they were wealthy and she resided at Petteril Bank House, set in extensive grounds leading down to the River Petteril, her parents had employed a maid who had cooked most of their meals. When in the asylum, the other residents had complained whenever Catherine had been involved in the meal preparation, so she was soon relegated to tending the garden and preparing the vegetables for the meals. Secretly, she had been pleased to be outside in the garden for she loved the fresh air and exercise.

Today, she would try and concoct something from scratch. If her budget stretched to the luxury of meat, she would also buy an onion, a carrot and a turnip and make a stew. She could throw it all in a pot and give the mixture a stir every now and then.

She pulled on her dressing gown and went downstairs. Her feet were beginning to loosen a little with each tender step. She boiled herself an egg then sat by the window at the small dining table, nibbling at her meagre breakfast.

Despite the atrocious weather, a man emerged from the road between the Kavanagh's house and the gentleman's residence. He was trying to run, battling into the wind, the tails of his long black coat flapping behind him. Occasionally, he looked over his shoulder, the wind almost blowing him over at times. In the inclement conditions, his crimson cravat added a splash of colour as it poked out from his turned-up collar. Holding onto his top hat, he scurried past the various houses on the opposite side of the village green and headed down towards the railway line. He was now out of sight.

Catherine considered that maybe he was staying at the Lawson's Lodging House and was desperate to get out of the rain. She looked at the clock on the mantelpiece, eight thirty-two. She thought about writing it in *The Story,* then grimaced, not wanting to become obsessed, like the mysterious author, by detailing all the goings on in the village. Two men then hurried past wearing long, shapeless overcoats and flat caps, running the same route as the gentleman. They too disappeared round the corner towards the train station. Maybe they were due to catch a train.

Feeling a little chilled, she took a jug of warm water upstairs, washed herself down, got dressed and pinned her hair up as tightly as possible, intending to venture outside at some point if the weather settled down.

She had few items of clothing with her. She had written to her parents to inform them of her new address, and she was hoping they would visit and bring her some different attire. Everything in her wardrobe was so old fashioned. Everything seemed bigger, flouncier and wider nowadays. With her incarceration nearing twenty years she had barely been outside, and clothing had been the last thing on her mind. The clothes she owned were still beautiful, but they were now fading, bobbly and worn.

Taking the weather into consideration, she chose a high-necked blouse made from thick cotton with plenty of ruffles which added extra layers and therefore protection from the wind. The skirt she chose was a simple, brown affair. She had taken up the hemline, for she detested her skirt becoming sodden when dragging through mud and rain. Her mind briefly returned to the day of Sam's hanging, how she had walked back to his home, Fernleigh, in the torrential rain, her skirt soaking up the water. How chilled to the core she was that day, the start of her confusion. Deliberately, she stopped herself from reliving the past. If people thought her immodest at showing her ankles, well she was now of an age where she did not care. She smiled to herself, thankful for how far she had come in not worrying about what other people thought.

The rain poured for three solid hours and Catherine could not believe the clouds could hold so much water. Finally, at twenty-nine minutes past eleven the rain started to abate. That stupid book, she was becoming obsessed with the time, like the author of *The Story*. For a moment, she wondered if she was the author of the book. *Of course I'm not*, she thought. She then scolded herself for being silly.

Catherine pinned on her most protective bonnet, put on her outdoor attire and made a quick dash over to the yellow house. She knocked on the door and did not wait for a reply, Vera had said on a couple of occasions to just shout and come in, but the door was locked. At first, Catherine thought that Vera was maybe sleeping late, but it was nearing time for lunch. Her stomach flipped at her next thought, which was something dreadful had happened to Vera. Maybe she had fallen and was lying on the floor in agony or God forbid, the woman had collapsed and was lying unconscious or worse.

The single, central windowpane in the door was frosted so she could not see into the hallway. Carefully, she stepped over the low stone border which pretended to be roped edging and carefully made her way over the small front garden which was saturated due to the downpour. Peering through the front window, she could see the room was furnished as before with the curtains, rug, drapes, tables and plants but all the Kavanagh's personal items had gone. All the paperwork Vera had stuffed in the open writing bureau had been taken and the portraits had disappeared, leaving ghosts of their presence on the wallpaper. The fire was cold.

On making her way back to the front door, she closed her right eye so she could look through the keyhole. The cluttered hallway still had the dark furniture and the basket of kindling and the bucket of coal but like the living room, all the personal possessions had disappeared. The coat stand was now bare. It was as if the memory of the couple had been erased.

Unsure on what to do, Catherine decided to go to the shop and buy the few items she needed for her stew. Hopefully, Sally Dawson may know what was going on. The bell announced her entry and the chubby shopkeeper soon appeared from the back. Her face looked grey.

"Are you well, Mrs Dawson?" asked Catherine.

"Have you not heard the news?"

Catherine shook her head. Her stomach tensed at the thought of what was coming next.

"Someone has jumped from the railway bridge." Mrs Dawson sat down on a wooden stool which was behind the counter. She suddenly seemed so small and vulnerable despite her voluptuous size.

"Do we know ... who it was that jumped?" Catherine felt faint at the possible answer.

Mrs Dawson shook her head, "Nobody that I know from around here."

Partially relieved, this meant it could not possibly be the Kavanaghs. "Have you heard anything regarding Vincent or Vera? Their house appears to have been abandoned overnight."

"No, I've not heard anything about them. All this morning's talk has been about the suicide."

"And is it definitely a suicide?"

The shopkeeper gave her a quizzical stare. "I'm not quite sure what you are implying."

Feeling uncomfortable, Catherine tried to justify her question, "I was an undertaker, working in a funeral parlour. I worked with the police during an investigation for numerous murd ... I ... anyway..." She stopped talking. Instead of feeling dreadful at possibly offending someone and having to explain her thoughts and actions, she quickly changed her perspective. The store was the only place to obtain supplies and she did not want to alienate this woman but neither did she feel obliged to justify herself.

Catherine rattled off the required items and promptly paid. She thanked Mrs Dawson for her assistance but decided not to ask this woman any further questions. On leaving the shop and walking towards home, she realised that she was the stranger in *their* village and the locals may consider her to be an outsider, worthy of suspicion until better acquainted. Again, Catherine considered the notion that Rose Cottage was known for being a house of asylum. This village gave the appearance of being idyllic, but all was not as it seemed.

Chapter Twelve

After preparing the rabbit stew, Catherine could not decide whether to venture down to Suicide Point to find out for herself who had made the jump or whether to venture up the road to the Wheatsheaf Inn. Her trip would have to be short for she would worry about leaving the fire and stew unattended. She was reminded of the insightful words from Nurse Jones, 'Be the light in the darkness, not the one worrying if the house was going to burn down'.

On giving the pot a stir, she then made her way down the hill towards the railway station. Despite the rain, people were still congregating on the east-bound platform. The colourful bridge over the railway tracks was permissible but the walkway to Suicide Point was cordoned off. Unable to glean anything from the railway station and the gossiping crowds, she wondered how to get to the road underneath the viaduct. Through the trees, she noticed a sign stating, *99 steps*. On closer inspection there were wooden steps winding down the steep embankment which took her to the bottom of the viaduct. The perspective was impressive for she could see the five spans of the bridge across the river, the railway lines a hundred feet above her head. To her left was another crowd of people, including two policemen.

Rivers of blood trickled from the prone body, the flow enhanced by the wind and rain. She remained calm despite the horrific sight. Being an undertaker had strengthened her resolve for dealing with the dead. People were milling around, discussing in disbelief the fate of the unknown gentleman. Officials behind the cordon were undertaking various tasks. Catherine glimpsed details between the moving crowds. The deceased was a man wearing a long, black coat with tails. His top hat had travelled quite a distance from his body. He was lying at such a twisted angle that his neck must be broken. After a while, a very tall and thin policeman turned the body supine and aligned the head. Her breathing paused at a peek of crimson silk. It was the gentleman she had witnessed this morning, battling into the wind with his collar turned up high. His crushed face was bloodied but he appeared to be tanned compared to the other pale faces standing over him. She walked away from the scene with a melancholy weight on her shoulders, wondering why this man had to die. There had to be a reason behind his story.

Leaving the noise and chaos behind, Catherine wandered along the pathway by the river which brought her to the Ferryman's Cottage and St Constantine's Church, the vicinity from where she saw him emerge this morning. He seemed well dressed for such an early start and his skin tone was exotic. She tried to put the incident to the back of her mind for she did not want to become ill again, taking on the guilt, stress and woes of others.

Walking past the yellow house, she wondered who had moved the Kavanagh's personal belongings so quickly and for what reason. Vera was certainly incapable of such a task and whoever it was, completed the move with stealth overnight. As she headed towards Rose Cottage, she was convinced she saw movement of the net curtains from Bluebell Cottage next door.

On entering her house, the first thing she did was stir the stew in the pot on the stove. The contents were rather watery at this stage, it did not look appetising, almost like dirty dishwater but the aroma was promising. She placed more kindling to maintain the fire. Then she went into the living area and with her ear against the wall, listened for noise from her next-door neighbours. A male and a female voice, conversing in whispered tones, the volume too low to hear specific words. Groans and growls were occasionally heard.

As she was still wearing her outdoor clothing and because the rain had eased to only a drizzle, she decided to walk up to the Wheatsheaf Inn and enquire about Mr Kavanagh, especially since *The Story* had mentioned he frequented there. She gave the pot another stir before leaving the house once more. Better to be busy than wallow in the past on her own.

Walking up the road towards the Inn, she discreetly took in the many lovely houses along the way. Some houses were directly on the road whilst others were set back with a long approach. Edenvale was a very pretty village indeed, every house unique.

She had never visited a public house and for that reason her heart started complaining when she saw the Inn on the corner of the sharp bend. Unsure on what to expect, she took a deep breath and ventured inside.

The interior was gloomy but atmospheric. Red walls, dark furniture and low beams were made cosy by fires either end of the room which were glowing and crackling. The smell from the burning wood was aromatic. Four older men were in the far corner, huddled near the fire. They stopped talking to stare at Catherine.

She approached the bar and waited, her discomfort increasing. The gentlemen in the corner resumed talking, she was hoping not to be the topic of their conversation. They suddenly started laughing gregariously and Catherine tried not to take it personally. Thankfully, a handsome man came through the archway, and he could not hide his surprise on seeing Catherine waiting patiently at the bar. He ran his fingers sideways through his golden hair.

"Good afternoon. What can I do for you?" he offered, followed by a cheeky smile.

"Are you acquainted with Vincent Kavanagh? I was wondering if you have seen him recently." Catherine wondered why she was bothering, especially in light of Vera having disappeared too.

"Vincent ... hmm ... I've not seen him in here for a while. A couple of weeks maybe." He looked over at the men, "Have you lot seen Vincent recently?" They all shook their heads.

"It seems I have reached a dead end. Sorry to bother you." She made to walk out.

"Last night though, when I was walking home after locking up here, there was a horse and cart outside of their house. Two men had crates on the back of it. No signs of Vincent or Vera though. Are you a relative of theirs?"

"No, a concerned acquaintance I suppose."

The man possessed an infectious smile, he leaned over the pumps to come closer to her, "As you can see, it isn't exactly riveting in here." He nodded subtly over to the men, "I'd be glad of your company any time of the day or night. I'm here most days, except Sundays, so please don't be afraid of coming in here. We don't bite ... much." He winked.

"Thank you, I will consider your kind offer." Catherine politely smiled, turned, then headed towards the door.

"Please don't think about it too much!" said the barman, sad at her departure.

The rain had finally ceased, and she continued with her plan to walk the mile to the road works. She was aware of her heels starting to ache. By the time she reached the workers, she was limping. Two men were working on the road.

"Good afternoon, I was wondering if you could help me."

The men used the conversation to stand up and stretch their legs. "Of course. Fire away," said the older man. His hands were filthy with the laborious task he had been undertaking.

"Have you seen an older gentleman, appearing to be in his late sixties, and please excuse me for making a personal comment but he has bowed legs. He has started wandering and we fear he may be lost. Have you seen him in the last couple of days by any chance?"

"Sorry, miss, can't say I have. What about you, Davey?"

"Nah, can't say I have," said the younger man. He wiped his nose on his sleeve.

"Also, I am enquiring about a gentleman who was wearing a top hat, tails and a crimson cravat." Catherine made alternate eye contact between the two men.

The workers made eye contact between themselves and there seemed to be a pause.

"Someone fitting that description arrived here yesterday morning. Looked a bit foreign to me, dark skin and all that. As you can see, the road is still blocked. He got out of a carriage and went down there." The older man pointed with his filthy finger.

"Do you know where the track leads?" asked Catherine. Again, she observed every little sign.

"Erm ... the track leads to a farm down there on the right. If you go straight on it leads you to the woods and the path round to the left takes you back to the village."

"You mentioned the woods, is that where the metal gate blocks the entrance to the caves?"

The men looked at each other again. It was the older man who replied, he put on what appeared to be a pretend smile. "Yeah. It's a lovely walk down there."

Catherine also feigned a smile, "I quite agree. Do you happen to know the contents of the caves?"

The younger lad spoke, "Nah not me. I'd rather be in the Wheatsheaf having a beer." He laughed at his attempt at a joke.

The older man interjected, "Best get cracking, this road will never lay itself. Good day to you, miss." They got on their knees and concentrated on their work.

Undeterred, Catherine briskly walked down the track in the direction of the woods. Her heels were aching, but she wanted to get out of their sight before slowing. She questioned why she was bothered about them watching her walk or indeed why she was bothering about Vincent Kavanagh and the dead, foreign gentleman. She guessed she needed some focus, some distraction from her own problems and this was a way to integrate with the villagers, as Doctor Wainwright had asked her to do.

As the track veered to the left, an imposing sight was to behold, the ruins of what looked like a medieval monastery. The gatehouse was in better shape, perhaps two or three stories high with the roof still intact. The entrance to the grounds was through a stone archway and she meandered between the crumbling foundations. Memories of the library at her previous family home at Petteril Bank House came flooding back. The leather-bound books, the smell of the aged leaves, the sounds of the pages being perused. She recalled reading something about the monasteries and Henry VIII, resolution, revolution, dissolution, something along those terms. How sad, for the monks or nuns who lived there, their home and their livelihood cruelly taken from them by the king.

There was a door to her left, which she did not dare open but on the right was another door already ajar. With some trepidation she peeked inside. The room was small, she could see everything by standing in the doorway. On a shelf to the left were four cabbages, three carrots, and two turnips. Straight in front of her was a large red sandstone slab which reminded her of an ancient altar. To the right was a wooden depiction of the crucifixion of Christ and below the cross was a wooden sign. Other than those few items, the room was bare.

With a fluttering heart, she bravely walked into the room in order to read the engraved sign.

On ringing the Priory bell, sanctuary will be provided for those in need. Under no circumstances will asylum be provided if a crime has been committed within Edenvale.

The Priory and its bell had seemingly long since gone, leaving only this room for sanctuary. She looked around again, contemplating staying in such a small and depressing room with nothing other than a cold slab of stone to sit or lie upon. A shiver ran through her body, the cold and dampness of the room was oppressing. However, a warmth of emotion brought a smile to her face that someone was kind enough to leave a few items of food for those in dire need.

Compared to the dankness of the stone room, the air outside felt fresh, especially having been cleansed by the rain. Continuing along the track, she was surprised by how quickly she was back in the village. The track brought her to the corner of the Kavanagh's yellow house. Since she was passing, she knocked on the door once more. Whilst waiting, she noticed something lying on the floor under a bush. The wooden sign stated, *Buttercup House.* There seemed to be a theme with nature for the houses in the village. She glanced over to the red sandstone gentleman's residence, wondering if it too had a name. *I'm not as daft as they think I am,* thought Catherine to herself as she spotted the sign, *Oak Bank Hall,* hidden within climbing ivy. Oak Bank Hall sounded familiar, then she realised *The Story* had mentioned the name and that the author was oblivious as to what went on there. The author was obviously referring to this place.

She skirted around the green admiring the beautiful houses then sauntered down the paved path to her front door. She noticed a strange mist had formed over the windows. Suddenly, a realisation hit her, and she panicked. As she fumbled for her key, she admonished herself for being so distracted for she had forgotten about the rabbit stew.

Rushing inside, the fire had nearly burned itself out and when she looked inside the pot, it did not smell or appear burnt. She got a spoon and stirred the contents. The items had started to congeal at the bottom of the pot but thankfully the stew was salvageable.

Condensation was dripping down the walls, so she opened the windows and doors to let in some air.

Ravenous, she did not care about the presentation of the food, she just ladled the stew into a bowl and sat at the table. There were too many thoughts running through her head. The strange caves, the priory gatehouse, the depressing sanctuary, the creepy orphanage and the secretive gentlemen's residence, two missing people and a possible suicide or murder. She had to find the link to these seemingly unrelated places and events. Perhaps *The Story* would reveal more clues.

Chapter Thirteen

Catherine sat in the comfortable armchair and was thankful for the respite, her feet finding some relief as they warmed nicely by the open fire. Her heels were painful from walking so many miles. She made a vow not to leave the house tomorrow for any reason at all, other than the house being on fire. With a stretch, she reached for the burgundy bound pages of *The Story* which lay on top of the oak mantlepiece.

2nd May

Twenty minutes past eight

Mrs Dawson opens the shop, twenty minutes late today. She is stomping about like a petty child. Good grief, she appears to be shouting at old Mrs Humphries, who has been patiently waiting outside the store for the last ten minutes. Poor Mrs Humphries has stormed off and is heading back home. Somebody did not sleep tight.

Five minutes to ten

A guest from Oak Bank Hall is walking out of the grounds. His dress sense is impeccable, with his blue cravat and matching handkerchief. He walks with such grace, so upright and proud. He takes his time, nose in the air, he does not appear to be snobby, he truly appears to be smelling the air. He smiles then sighs heavily with a look of contentment. My goodness, I do believe the shop is his intended destination. I pray that Mrs Dawson has shaken off her foul mood.

Seven minutes past ten

Thankfully, he has survived the wrath of Dawson. I can see no obvious purchased items. Oh, surprisingly he is walking past the gentleman's residence and heading down the hill. I am pondering on where he is headed. Church? Cells? Gatehouse?

Eleven precisely

The Kavanaghs make their daily appearance. Mein Gott, I pray for forgiveness for my harsh critique, but Mrs Kavanagh appears to have an exploded canary on top of her head. The milliner must have been out hunting the day that monstrosity was created.

Twelve precisely

If this illness does not kill me, I am convinced tedium will. I dream of being outside and continuing my investigation. Such a beautiful day. The gentle breeze from the window is warm. I can hear birds singing. Perhaps they are calling for their sweet canary friend now nesting in a hat.

Twenty-seven minutes past twelve

The distinguished gentleman returns to the residence with another gentleman. He too is dressed immaculately, oozing wealth. What on earth do they do there? I am convinced they must be part of the secret.

Two o'clock

The children from the orphanage walk in line down the hill. I assume they head to the sandy banks of the river to enjoy the waterfall.

Two minutes to four

Mr Kavanagh is heading up the hill, I am assuming the Wheatsheaf is calling.

Thirty-eight minutes past four

How extraordinary, Mrs Kavanagh is heading over to Oak Bank Hall. From where does she purchase her monstrous hats? A taxidermist? The deceased canary has been buried and she now sports a murmuration of starlings on top of her head which are fluttering in the gentle breeze. Heaven above, the doorman has let her in. Is she part of this too?

Thirteen minutes to seven

Mrs Kavanagh hobbles home, she looks ashen.

Nine o'clock

Various well-dressed gentlemen have been coming and going from Oak Bank Hall all evening. Nothing to report as such but they are up to something.

3rd May

Thirty-six minutes past nine

So tired, I cannot believe I stayed up until midnight and slept in. I hope I have not missed anything of importance.

Eleven twenty-eight

Where are the Kavanaghs for their daily walk?

Twelve o'clock precisely

Something is going on at Oak Bank. Twelve of them outside. They are heading down the hill. Nine men and three women. Young and old, fat and thin, shabby and chic, they are a mixed bunch. Where are they going? A walk along the river? To the cells? The sanctuary? Church?

Seven minutes past one

Mr Kavanagh is most likely off to the Wheatsheaf, that cap must be humming for he wears it constantly.

Nearly two thirty

Still no sign of them returning. Mrs Kavanagh has been up and down at the bay window like a jack-in-the-box.

Twelve minutes to three

A man in a hideous suit is looking at the grey monument. Is the stone the hiding place? Surely not! It is far too small at only four feet high.

Fourteen minutes past eight

Mr Kavanagh staggers home in a dreadful state. Oh my goodness, I'm trying not to laugh but he reminds me of a newborn foal. With each precarious step closer to home, he needs five more to maintain his balance. My sides are aching with laughter, I can barely see the words I write for tears are streaming down my cheeks. He is currently in the bushes at Larch House. I cannot recall having laughed so much in ages. Oh my, he is now upside down in the bushes, his feet in mid-air. I truly hope he has not come to any harm. Oh dear, he may be stuck! Thank goodness no, he has completely flipped over. He is currently out of sight. Here he is, little steps, holding onto the bushes. Gesundheit, he has sneezed once, twice, thrice. Please forgive me for finding amusement in another's misfortune. A sigh of relief, he has made it home. Dear Lord, now he has tripped over the front doorstep and is lying like a starfish and flapping about like one too.

Being the last entry for the day, Catherine closed the book, needing time to take in the information. Her head rested back onto the armchair, and she closed her eyes, trying to fathom what on earth was going on. Oak Bank Hall, she had the impression it was some sort of religious sect. But the cells, what on earth were the cells? Who was imprisoned there and how come the author, she assumed a previous resident of this house, knew about the cells? Mrs Kavanagh, what was her role in all of this? Was she part of this cult? And the monument, was it the hiding place? What did the author mean by that statement and what investigation were they undertaking? What was the illness keeping the author imprisoned in the cottage? Catherine wanted to solve the mystery. She would have to continue reading *The Story*.

Chapter Fourteen

On placing her feet to the cold bedroom floor, she could barely take any weight through her heels. As she walked around the room on tiptoe, the pain gradually eased, allowing her to put her worn silk slippers on her tender feet.

Breakfast was a simple affair of a wedge of stale bread with some fruit preserve. At some point she would have to find the courage to re-visit the shop. She would engage in pleasantries with Mrs Dawson but nothing personal or controversial that may lead to accusations or arguments.

Last night, she had made herself a promise not to venture out of the house today unless the house was on fire but the thought of being cooped up inside on such a pleasant day was unthinkable. Her painful feet would not tolerate a full-on exploration of the village, so she prepared for a visit to St Constantine's Church.

Catherine spruced up her appearance, knowing she would be walking well-trodden pathways and she wanted to be dressed appropriately in a house of God. She washed in warm water from the porcelain bowl then soaked her aching feet for a few minutes before gently massaging them dry with the towel.

With barely a limp, she walked over to the wardrobe and chose a sky-blue dress with a pleated skirt, long puffy sleeves and a high neckline with a lace collar, to which she fastened a brooch.

Before going to bed, she had tied her hair so now she had curls which she loosely pinned up. A dainty hat completed her ensemble.

The sun shining through her windows had promised warmth but as she stood at the front door placing the key in the lock, the day was cooler than she had anticipated. Thankfully, the stillness of the day was a blessing. As she made her way towards the church, her eyes flitted between the Kavanagh's house, the grey stone monument and Oak Bank Hall. The green was too muddy for walking on with the shoes she wore, so she skirted around the edges.

The downhill road was steep as it veered round to the left. The River Eden and church came into view. The lychgate was closed but opened easily and she walked along the path, respectfully inspecting the church grounds. There were few headstones in the graveyard, which was surprising, considering the size of the village and the age of the church. There was a squared off area, with a round stone base and what looked like the butt of a column. Whatever had once stood there had long since gone.

For some unknown reason, she felt anxious at the thought of entering the church. She had never felt this way before about a holy place. She had not been to church for years until she was admitted to the asylum. The doctors and nurses had encouraged a balance between physical, emotional and spiritual wellbeing, so attending church was part of the daily routine. The vicar at the asylum had been an inspiration to Catherine. There had been a particular sermon which had changed her way of thinking. People mostly prayed to God because they wanted something such as money, food, employment, a roof over their head or to be free from pain. People saw God as a masterly figure who could give or take as he desired. Reverend Smythe had proposed a different philosophy, that good and bad things happened to each and every one of us. This was part of life. God was not there to reward or punish, he was there to share your joy and half your sorrow. Reverend Smythe suggested that when we prayed to God, we should be thanking him for being there and for all the small mercies, not to ask for miracles. God knew what people wanted but more importantly God knew what people needed. Things happened in life that might seem strange, or cause suffering but God could see the past, present and future. Everyone was where they needed to be. This perspective on life had really helped Catherine come to terms with her admission to a lunatic asylum. Her prayers were now mainly to say thank you to God for every little joy in her life, and focusing in on all the wonderful things, rather than ruminating on the woes. This generally put Catherine in a positive frame of mind, put the responsibility on her to improve her life and she took nothing for granted. Occasionally, she did request miniscule favours to which she now lengthened her top lip over her teeth and looked towards heaven in shame.

Standing by the door of the church, she surmised that maybe this was where she needed to be on this day. Bravely, she opened the door.

After her initial reservations, the interior of the church was peaceful and comforting with cream and brown tones. Tapestried pew cushions added colour and warmth. Taking her time, she walked along the right-hand side, reading the plaques and dedications to those who had passed over the centuries.

Each arched window depicted a heavenly figure. The main east window was more elaborate and depicted biblical scenes, the bright sunlight creating stunning colours on the floor.

The most striking feature within the church was a life-sized, marble sculpture situated in the northeast transept. There was a woman lying supine holding a child, with another woman standing over her pointing upwards. The artwork was exquisite and the attention to detail was astonishing. Catherine delicately ran her fingers over the cold, silky marble.

Her body jumped when she heard a voice, she thought she was being reprimanded for touching the sculpture. She turned around and saw the vicar.

"Please accept my apologies but I felt inclined—"

The vicar interrupted, "By all means, feel free to touch. Beautiful, aren't they?"

The vicar was small but chubby, with a receding hairline and a long bushy beard and sideburns. She asked God for forgiveness in case he had heard her judgmental thoughts about his servant. "The women, who are they?"

There was a slight delay. Everybody in this village seemed to linger in thought before answering a question.

"This sculpture was before my time, but the official story is it was commissioned by a heartbroken husband on the death of his wife during childbirth. The artwork is titled 'Faith', the woman standing over her is pointing towards heaven."

"The official story? Are there alternate opinions to the artwork?" Rather than stare at the vicar, trying to detect subtle signs of lying, she thought better of it and admired the white marble once more. The curves of their bodies, the expressions on their faces, they seemed so real, so full of emotion.

"It is not for me to comment on the beliefs of others." He clasped his hands in front of him. "God has given us free will. The ability to choose our own path in life. Make our own decisions and inferences."

Catherine had to look in his direction. His smile seemed genuine. This comment, that we chose our own path, had thrown her off balance a little. She had always believed in fate, a predetermined future, and even if one rebelled, became lost or knew no better, events would happen beyond our control, forcing us onto the correct pathway. However, he was correct, God had given us free will, which made sense when interpreted in this way. Without free will, God would be a dictator.

"Faith, fate, freedom. Remarkably interesting concepts," said Catherine.

The vicar laughed, "I rarely hear people say my words are interesting." His eyes almost disappeared when he smiled.

"Who commissioned this piece? The cost must have been phenomenal."

"This is from the 18th century. As far as I know, the husband of the woman, and father of the child, lived in the castle, and he had this sculpture created in their memory. To always have 'Faith' even through adversity."

"Such a sad story. The castle you speak of, are you referring to Carlisle?"

"No, the one on the other side of the river. The one with the waterfall."

"That is a castle?"

"Yes, it appears to be quite bland from this perspective. No castellated battlements to see, or towers or portcullis. I can assure you it is more pleasing to the eye from the front façade."

"What else can you tell me about the church?"

The vicar, who was only an inch taller than Catherine started walking along the left side of the church. "This window here is dedicated to the memory of St Constantine."

"Hence the name of your church." They continued walking. "And this window?"

"St Helena, St Constantine's mother."

Catherine had never heard of these saints before. Her thoughts were interrupted.

"Are you visiting or staying around here?" asked the vicar.

Now it was Catherine's turn to pause before answering. "I am staying temporarily at Rose Cottage. I …" She stopped herself from admitting the truth, then decided to say it anyway. "I was in the lunatic asylum. I'm here on a trial basis, to see if I can live a normal life again." There, she had said it out loud, instead of feeling ashamed, she felt this was therapy. If she acknowledged her difficulties, she could confront them.

His eyebrows raised, "Well, I must admit, I was not expecting this revelation, but I am grateful for your honesty. You know where to find me if you need to talk."

Catherine walked towards the door. "As we are being honest, I have something on my mind which is worrying me." In truth, she had numerous questions and worries but she did not want to bombard this pleasant gentleman on their first meeting. "I have heard there are cells around here. Have you heard of them?"

The vicar smiled again. "Please do not worry. The cells you have heard people talk about are the cells of St Constantine. They were part of the Monk's Priory. Some believe that the cells were for the monks to hide in. Others believed the monks stored treasures there, to keep things safe from the king's men, traitors, thieves, raiders, Border Reivers, etcetera. When I say treasures, this may have been food, potatoes, wheat, grains. I have heard no stories of actual treasure such as gold or jewels but who really knows? We are theorising about history spanning three or four centuries before our time."

"So where are these cells?"

"There is a walk through the woods, the path forks to the left. Steps downhill lead to a metal gate, behind the gate are the cells."

"Oh, the caves? I found the metal gate the other day. I thought the gate guarded the entrance to caves. So, there are no prisoners there?"

The vicar confirmed that to the best of his knowledge, the caves or cells had never been used as gaol cells.

Catherine smiled, "Thank you for the pleasure of your company. This has been a most interesting and informative conversation."

"Likewise, I'm sure we will meet again." He followed her to the church door. "I would be delighted to see you at one of our services. They are stated on the noticeboard in the church yard. Sundays are always popular."

"I would like that, thank you." They shook hands. "Catherine Fawcett."

"Reverend James Thornton."

As Catherine made her way back home, she felt so alive, almost back to her old inquisitive self. The vicar seemed amiable, he had answered her questions and was knowledgeable about the area. She would have to bide her time, but she would definitely visit him again to glean more information on the history of the village. Edenvale was certainly an intriguing little place.

When she got back home, she found some paper and a quill from the drawer in the downstairs dresser. She sat at the small round dining table by the window and started creating a list. The circumstances to her being there meant she wanted to keep busy and refrain from idle thoughts. This would keep her mind engaged and focused on a daily task.

Where did Mr and Mrs Kavanagh go?
Who was the gentleman who had jumped / was pushed from Suicide Point?
Who had resided at Rose Cottage previously, specifically, who may have written The Story?
What is the agenda at Oak Bank Hall? Who frequents there?
The orphanage, why does the house feel creepy and who owns it?

Catherine paused to refill the quill once again. Her mind went blank, there were other questions, but she had forgotten them at this moment. She wished she had written them down at the time of thinking. *The Story,* she contemplated writing a sequel, as an aide-memoire to her investigation.

She put the quill down on the table and went into the kitchen area, stoked up the fire and put the kettle on. That was the last of the water. She would need to refill the pail. After making herself a pot of tea, she sat down at the table. She added more questions to her list.

Who is the benefactor funding Rose Cottage?
Is this cottage used for asylum patients?

Do people in the village regard me as a lunatic?

With conviction, she scribbled the last question off the list. Catherine mulled over the conversation with the vicar.

The squared area with the round column base, what was once there?
Why was St Constantine honoured so much in this village?
What did St Constantine and his mother do to deserve becoming saints?
The white marble sculpture, Faith, why something so elaborate and expensive in such a simple village church?

Sipping her tea, she did not know where to start in finding the answers to her questions.

Chapter Fifteen

The sun had chased away the chill in the air and the afternoon was promising to be pleasant. The arduous task of collecting water from the well was beckoning. Catherine decided to go whilst the weather was decent.

She changed out of her best clothes and put on her cream and brown checked dress with the higher waistline. The dress was comfortable for physical work with its loosely flowing skirt and plentiful sleeves, but it was now looking a little shabby. Smiling, she pretended she did not care.

The well was a ten-minute walk away and she pondered on whether she could carry two pails of water. As it was sunny, she decided to try and carry both, knowing she could stop and rest at any point along the way.

When she turned the corner signposted for St Cuthbert's Well, her initial reaction was to sigh, thinking there was a long queue for the gently bubbling spring water, but it was in fact the children from the orphanage. Each child had some form of receptacle, relative to their size, to carry water. The smaller children carried bowls, bottles and jugs whilst the older ones had pails of different sizes. Overseeing the task was a slender, young lady dressed in blue. Crooked was the best description, with her wonky nose and missing teeth.

The guardian spoke gently to her wards, "Children, please stand aside so this lady may collect water." The children parted like a biblical scene.

"Oh, please do continue, the smiles on the children's faces are a joy to behold," said Catherine.

"Thank you, you are most kind," said the guardian.

The children continued to fill their items, they were being careful, respecting the site and appreciating how precious, clean water was, but the inevitable happened and water would run down their forearms and drip onto their clothes. Overall, their giggles confirmed their joy in the simplest of tasks.

Catherine noticed a girl with curly blond hair, wearing a calliper on her right leg. She wondered if this was the child from *The Story*. The book had stated she was four or five years old. This girl was perhaps six or seven at a guess. *The Story* could have possibly been written one, two or three years ago.

"I believe you are residing at Rose Cottage?" The guardian initiated conversation.

Catherine felt uneasy. She remembered the feeling of being watched by a dark shadow from the tower window of the spooky house. "It is a temporary arrangement, for rest and recuperation." At least this was not a lie.

"How are you finding the village?" The lady asked the question but then her attention was drawn to a boisterous water fight. Apart from being wet, the children in her care were immaculately dressed and looked well nourished. She intervened in a calming manner and the children quickly settled. The lady floated with grace and her gentle tones were caring despite her crooked face. Her skin was flawless, creamy with a rose hue, and her shiny dark hair provided contrast.

When the lady returned, she asked her question once again, to which Catherine replied, "There is plenty to see, places to explore and certainly lots to research, it's a fascinating place."

"I quite agree." The lady paused and looked at each child in turn, eighteen of them, now all carrying water. She moved her hands together to form a V shape and the children formed an orderly line without her saying a word. "I'm sure we will meet again."

Catherine nodded, "Your children, they are so well behaved and the smiles on their faces have brightened my day. I would have loved to have children."

The lady acknowledged the sad confession by placing her left hand on her heart. Her navy gloves complimented the brighter blue ruffles of her coat. "The Lord works in mysterious ways."

Aware the lady was wanting to leave, Catherine nodded and moved aside, allowing the children to walk past with their treasure. Some children smiled, some appeared quite shy, one cheeky boy stuck his tongue out at Catherine, at which she reciprocated and they both chuckled. One child waved and the last little girl, the one with the calliper, stopped to give Catherine a hug. Despite her stiff knee, the girl marched to catch up with the others resulting in water splashing everywhere. Catherine's heart was melting.

After filling her pails with water, Catherine struggled back to the main road, frequently having to stop due to the weight of the load which occasionally spilled over. It was always surprising how heavy water was to carry. Hands on her hips as she rested, she suddenly realised she did not know what day it was. From now on, she would buy a daily newspaper to remain orientated and keep abreast of current affairs, especially if Doctor Wainwright was to question her again.

As she passed the store, she decided not to buy the newspaper now for it would most likely become wet and crumpled.

Relieved to have made it home, she struggled down the side entrance and dumped the water by the back door. Her skirt and boots were saturated, and her arms were burning with the sustained effort of fetching and carrying. She decided to go to the shop whilst still in her outdoor attire, rather than get changed and head back out.

As usual the bell above the door announced her presence but unusually, there were two other people in the shop. The space felt uncomfortably crowded, even more so because one of the other shoppers was the man from behind the bar at the Wheatsheaf.

"Why, hello again," he beamed.

As much as she tried not to worry about her appearance, she regretted her decision not to change into more suitable attire. She asked, "Are you on your way to work?"

He nodded, "Unfortunately, yes. Did you find Vincent?"

"Unfortunately, no. The plot thickens. Mrs Kavanagh is also missing."

"Oh." He paused for a little while. His mouth came in close to her ear, she could feel warmth emanating from his body and his breath. He whispered, "They weren't married."

It was Catherine's turn to say, "Oh." She wanted to say more but this meant she would have to lean in closer to him. Plucking up the courage she whispered, "So they were living in sin?"

Once again, he whispered in her ear, "Rumour has it they were brother and sister."

"No!" said Catherine with a shocked tone. Mrs Dawson and the other customer stared at her.

He leaned in close, "Please, come to the bar later, I would love us to chat more."

Catherine wondered why this handsome man was even remotely interested in her. He appeared much younger than her, with barely any wrinkles or lines suggesting age. He was perhaps in his early thirties. Then she felt foolish, there was no evidence he was interested in anything other than friendship, and despite his charming looks, he was knowledgeable and interesting. He could be a good friend.

As she came in close once more, there was a radiance between them, "I am aware we did not introduce ourselves the other day. My name is Catherine."

"Solomon." Their smiles reached their eyes as they continued to chat in whispered tones.

Engrossed in their conversation they had not realised the first customer had left the shop. Mrs Dawson demanded to know what he wanted. Solomon politely gestured for Catherine to go first but she declined his kind offer with a shake of her head and her hand. Solomon gave Mrs Dawson a written list and she silently packaged the goods together, giving him more time to converse with Catherine. He winked on leaving the shop, "Come in around three ish?"

Catherine nodded with a shy smile as he walked out of the door. For the first time in a while, she felt sad and alone, but tried to remain positive at meeting with him again later that afternoon. What a handsome young man he was but he was mischievous, his eyes twinkled, he would be trouble, she could sense it.

To take her mind off intimate thoughts, she changed into more suitable attire and then sat in the armchair by the fireplace and perused the newspaper she had purchased from the shop. Her stomach churned when she saw the headline:

A GREEK TRAGEDY

There was little factual detail to the story, other than the death of Alesandro Demetriou at Suicide Point. He had been staying at the Lawson's Lodging House and his belongings taken to aid the police in their investigation. The journalist had surmised why someone with Greek documentation would have come all this way to fall to his death at Suicide Point, a notorious spot for those wanting to take their own life. History had shown that people had in fact travelled a fair distance to jump from this place, knowing their death would be certain and make headline news. Catherine doubted that Suicide Point in Edenvale would be internationally renowned in this instance though.

So, if not suicide, this meant the man had been hauled over the cast iron railings. She questioned who had pushed him over and why. A stranger from Greece, who had potentially travelled for weeks if not months, who happened upon this pretty village, is murdered within a short time of his arrival. It did not make any sense. Catherine was beginning to feel chilled to the bone.

On collecting wood from the kitchen, she built up the fire in the living room and sat down in the armchair. Other than the headline story, there was little else of interest. Having read the newspaper from start to finish, she contemplated what to do next. The clock briefly chimed for half past three. She stepped outside and locked the front door behind her.

Chapter Sixteen

Three of the Inn's regular customers Len, Ken and Tommy were sitting in their usual corner, drinking their usual tipples. The dirty glasses pushed to the end of their table suggested they were already consuming their third round of drinks. Jimmy was missing from the group. As last time, their banter stopped when Catherine walked into the bar. Ken and Tommy nodded their heads as an acquaintance then resumed their conversation in more muted tones.

Two men were sitting at the bar puffing on pipes, whilst Solomon topped up their glasses with red wine. He had three other customers waiting to be served. When he raised his head and caught her eye, he could not help but smile. With a nod and a gaze, he suggested she sit at the far end of the bar. After a battle with her skirt and petticoats to ascend the wooden stool, Catherine felt exposed and awkward with sitting so high. She tried to keep her mind busy by taking in her surroundings.

The polished bar was gleaming. Sparkling glasses were aligned according to size on the shelves behind. Like a semi-circular amphitheatre, spirit bottles were displayed on tiered supports and precisely turned for reading their decorative labels. Solomon seemed at ease behind the bar. Conversation flowed with the punters. His dexterity in handling fragile glasses and bottles was remarkable and he moved with such confidence as if fluid with his surroundings.

After serving the other customers, Solomon poured Catherine a glass of wine and gave her a wink on refusing her offer of payment. Conversation flowed in a simple way with general pleasantries about the weather and how she was settling into the village but then questions became more personal.

"So how come you're in Edenvale, for it's not the most exciting of places?" asked Solomon.

"I think that is the general idea, some peace and quiet. I've been out of sorts for a long time so I'm here for rest and recuperation."

Solomon's eyebrows gathered in disappointment, "You're staying for a while though?"

"I'm not sure, another month or two hopefully." The terms of the contract had stated up to three months, but she was beginning to enjoy living in Edenvale.

His forehead relaxed and the smile returned to his eyes on hearing this news. "Do you know anyone here? Relatives? Friends?"

All these personal questions, maybe she should not have come. Thinking quickly, she needed to ask him a question in return and deflect the attention from herself. "I'm here because it's a pretty village, the houses are either quaint or grand and there are plenty of scenic walks on the doorstep. The fresh air, being away from the hustle and bustle of town, the water seems better here, the food is tastier somehow. There are many reasons to want to stay. Are you from the village?"

"Not originally, we moved here a couple of years ago, after my mum died. Dad couldn't cope with the memories."

"I'm so sorry to hear that. Do you and your father live together on the road to the station?" She saw the quizzical look on his face, and she blushed. "You turned left out of the store earlier."

His face relaxed, "Yeah, dad does a few odd jobs here and there to make ends meet. He coordinates the deliveries from the train and brings them up to the village on his cart. If there's any post, he takes it to the store. You've seen the Lawson's place?" Catherine nodded. "Well, he helps out there with general maintenance, gardening, that sort of thing. He tends a few of the gardens around here as well."

"And is this your only employment?"

"Yeah, I guess so."

Solomon revealed his dream of becoming a reporter for one of the local newspapers. He loved people, he loved chatting, he felt energised around others. Most importantly he loved listening. Laughing as folk recalled funny incidents, feeling heartbroken as people told their sad tales, and hearing people detail their daily struggles just to exist, he wanted to appreciate and understand different perspectives on life. Every day without fail, he bought the Carlisle Journal from the store and read the newspaper from cover to cover.

Catherine wondered if she should confide in him, share her theories about some of the happenings in the village for he would probably enjoy investigating her concerns. Aware she was possibly being paranoid, for she did not want to become one of his articles, she decided to wait as she had only become acquainted with this gentleman. "I wish you well with your career ambitions. Although the headline in today's paper was indeed tragic.

Do you know anything else about the Greek gentleman's death or why he was here?"

Solomon admitted that he thought the death was not suicide. His eyes penetrated deep inside her own as if searching for the truth, "Please do not tell this to anyone else, promise me!"

"I promise, hand on heart."

He looked around the bar to ensure no one was close by, he lowered his tone, "My father collected the man's belongings from his room at the lodging house."

"Was there anything of interest, to confirm either murder or suicide?" Catherine naturally found herself leaning towards her new friend, mirroring his behaviour.

"The usual stuff, clothes, a comb, that sort of thing." Another brief glance around to check no one was within the vicinity. "But there was a leather-bound notebook crammed with little pictures, diagram like clues, little hand drawn maps and loads of written notes."

"How interesting, about what?"

"Dad couldn't say, it was all in Greek." He laughed, then jokingly said, "Shhh … but the guy was obviously looking for something in my humble opinion."

"Were there no clues as to what he was searching for? The maps, the diagrams, anything we could investigate?" She felt so animated and alive with suddenly having a purpose.

Their conversation was interrupted when they heard the door open. Cool, fresh air wafted into the room, diluting the stale, smoky atmosphere. A skinny man with a large paunch walked up to the bar.

The three gentlemen in the corner gave a low mumble. "About bloody time," shouted Ken.

Len then insisted, "Get the drinks in mate, the usual," then coughed with audible secretions heavy on his chest.

"That was bad timing," said Jimmy, "Gan on then, otherwise I'll never hear the end of it." Jimmy did not need to place the order as Solomon expertly poured the drinks. Jimmy searched his pockets, knowing the exact amount required, and passed over the coins for the round. "There ya gan lad, keep the change."

"Cheers, Jimmy. Appreciate that."

Solomon helped Jimmy carry two of the drinks over to the lads, then collected the numerous empty glasses piling up at the end of the table.

Returning to Catherine, Solomon asked "Now, where were we?"

"The Greek gentleman's notebook and possible clues as to what he was searching for." Catherine daintily sipped her white wine, feeling a little heady with her rare consumption of alcohol. Her face felt flushed by the fruity tones.

"Oh yes." Solomon described what little information his father had gleaned from the notebook. There were religious references, dates, some sort of triangular interlinked symbol, XX VV and written in English, Edenvale. They were desperate for more detail but that was as much as his father could glean. Mrs Lawson had been too upset to collect the deceased's belongings, so she had sent Solomon's father to the room. With the police questioning Mrs Lawson about the Greek gentleman, he did not have time for a more detailed search.

Catherine continued the conversation, "I am none the wiser. What do you think he was looking for?"

Solomon shook his head. "My concern is, we have a murderer in the village."

Catherine shuddered at the thought and took a sip from her glass, giving herself time to think about possible suspects when the realisation of what had transpired at Sam's house, Fernleigh, popped into her mind. How had she forgotten the murder? For a moment, she time travelled back to 1845.

Solomon broke through the darkness, "Not you, is it?" Catherine nearly choked on her wine. Before she was able to reply, Solomon started laughing, "Please forgive me, I'm so sorry for the tease."

Laughing was the last thing she wanted to do but it seemed the only appropriate response to his tease without appearing guilty. He was correct though, they had to consider the possibility of a murderer in the village. A ghost of a question appeared in her mind, sending chilling tingles along her upper limbs. Could she have been involved in the Greek man's demise? She had murdered before, so could she have committed another crime without remembering? Quickly, she dismissed the notion, how silly to even contemplate such a ridiculous suggestion. Not wanting to dwell on the past and the state of her mind, she subtly changed the subject back to the notebook and Solomon agreed that he would ask his father if he could recall any further detail.

Thankfully, customers approached the bar giving Catherine an excuse to leave, as she felt uncomfortable with the sudden resurrection of her suppressed memories: murder, dead bodies and skeletons. Would these fleeting apparitions ever find peace, or would they torture her for eternity? She carefully descended from the bar stool and thanked Solomon for her drink. He blew her a kiss goodbye, seemingly oblivious to her discomfort although to be fair to him, he was now busy with customers.

The pleasant day had left a chill in the air and dusk was settling in for the night. Walking down the hill towards the cottage and feeling slightly woozy with the wine, she remembered why she had originally ventured to the

Wheatsheaf Inn, to get information on the Kavanaghs being brother and sister, but the turn of events with the death of the Greek gentleman had dominated the conversation. Approaching the bend in the road, swirling smoke from the chimneys and faint flickers of light emerged from the shadows of Oak Bank Hall. The residence was alive, the windows were like eyes watching her from the protective cloak of deepening darkness. She needed an excuse to visit there.

Chapter Seventeen

The morning sun bathed the village in a hazy gold and the cool blue sky smiled upon a perfectly tranquil landscape. The grass was lush with thirst-quenching dew. Shiny red berries contrasted against the backdrop of the evergreen shrubs. In the garden, even the feathers on the lone starling seemed imbued with rich purples, decadent greens and warm orange tones. Only the sweet, happy tunes from hiding birds broke the peace of the dawn. This was going to be a good day.

Once up and about, Catherine made her way to the store to buy a newspaper, which was now a daily routine. She was pleasantly surprised to find she had received a letter. Excitedly, she walked home with a spring in her step for she recognised the handwriting.

My Dearest Catherine,

You can imagine my joy on receiving your letter and hearing the good news, that you are deemed well enough to leave the asylum. Your father is expected home on the 13th of November and therefore I give you advanced notice of our arrival on Saturday 14th.

I love you my darling and to be able to see you and hold you in my arms once again will be such a blessing. Therefore, please do not make a fuss by tidying, preparing food or going to too much trouble. I know how hard you try to create a good impression and I admit, this may be through no fault of your own, but I have also witnessed the chaos you create in the kitchen if not supervised. Having lost money, pride and status, it is only now I realise these things do not necessarily create happiness. Seeing you well is all I ask for and all I need.

As requested, I have packed you a trunk full of your belongings. I have also managed to squeeze five hats in your hat box. Before he left, your father gathered a few books, ones he thought you will like.

So many people have been asking after your welfare and they are overjoyed that you may soon come home. Father has been working extremely hard these last few days. Hearing your good news seems to have given him a new lease of life. We are hoping that we may be able get out of this dire financial situation. This is in strictest confidence; your father has not been well since you were admitted to the asylum. He was devastated in having to request your admittance to that place. I am hoping he can finally be at ease knowing he made the correct decision, that after all these years you are once again happy. I implore you, please do not show shock or concern at his gaunt appearance.

Until the 14th, take care my beautiful child, the most precious gift I have ever had the pleasure of receiving, a gift from God, from which I am truly blessed and grateful.

All my love,

Mother

The letter brought tears to Catherine's eyes. After all these years, her mother had stated that she accepts her, a mentally ill failure of a daughter and admitted to loving her. Her parents, locking her in that room, she shuddered at what they had endured together and apart. The days, weeks, months and years of solitude. Neglect was never an issue, each day her mother had brought her food and water but the isolation, the conversations had been through a closed door. With the gift of hindsight, she could reflect on why her parents had treated her that way, they had no other choice. Catherine had become violent, had taken to cutting herself with sharp objects or hitting herself with heavy objects to create pain and physical suffering to portray her internal agony.

Her parents had then confiscated most items from the bedroom to minimise risks but this void, this bleakness, created more intense isolation and Catherine took to smashing her window and cutting herself to escape her physical and mental prison. Shutters were added, beckoning a deeper darkness from the world. Catherine could not harm herself anymore.

As the years ticked by, she became more withdrawn, more subdued, life slowly slipping away from her tortured body, mind and soul. Her parents tried to bring her back into the home, but she struggled to deal with the harsh reality of life. Catherine had frequently lashed out, taking all those years of pain out on her parents. In the end, her father had said, 'Enough is enough!' She could still clearly see his face that day, the anger had gone, the love had gone, the fight had gone, he no longer cared, he had been pushed to his limit. He locked her in the bedroom that day and they forgot about her, other than for food and water. The shuttered room was her gaol.

When the lunatic asylum officially opened its doors in 1862, Catherine had been one of two hundred patients to be admitted. Two men had opened the door to her bedroom and grabbed her, each holding an arm. The bruising, where they had held onto her so tightly, the memory of the pain was still clear in her mind. Catherine had wriggled, kicked, shouted and screamed but they calmly carried her out of the house and into a waiting carriage. Once they were out of sight of her parents, the men bound her wrists and ankles tightly together with buckled leather straps.

Arriving in the estate grounds, she remembered the ominous cawing of the crows hiding amongst the trees. The awful sound, as if they were mocking her mental decline.

Brooding in the failing light, the dark stone structure of the asylum was oppressive by its sheer size. Her heart had truly broken that day on realising how many other lunatics were locked within those vast walls. Having lost the will to fight, she cooperated silently as the men guided her down a long corridor decorated with sickly green tiles. Everything was sterile and cold. She had been taken into a room and warned that if she were to show any signs of violence or try to escape, she would be strapped to the chair. After a few minutes, two doctors entered the room. The two burly men who had brought her to the asylum retreated to guard the door, watching her every move.

The doctors took it in turn to ask her questions. She remained mute. They searched her hair for lice, used implements to look inside her ears, nose and mouth, shone a light into her eyes and forcibly spread open her legs to internally examine her private parts. Catherine could not stem the flow of silent tears running down her face as she closed the door to reality. The doctors chatted amongst themselves for a few minutes then confirmed she was in fact crazy. After they signed the paperwork, she was officially admitted to the asylum. Since that day, she had never seen her parents again.

The letter she had received from her mother dropped from her shaking hands which brought her back to reality. Her mind was falling into a downward spiral. She needed to stop dwelling on the past and concentrate on the present day. She folded the letter and placed it in the right-hand drawer of the dresser. Fresh air was required to blow the stale thoughts away.

The church seemed an obvious destination. Serenity and prayers were required, to be thankful for the small mercies. Health, food on the table, money to survive, a warm roof over her head, indeed, on reflection she felt rich.

As she walked down the street, the Kavanagh's yellow house on her right and Oak Bank Hall on her left, there was little to note in either dwelling, both eerily quiet.

On reaching the gate to the church, she walked under the wooden porch and then paused to admire the beauty of the old building. The octagonal tower had a castellated roofline and the double entrance doors had medieval decorative ironwork, almost like crossbows and arrows. Movement caught her attention and she turned to see a lone robin redbreast hopping across the grass. The tiny bird made her smile.

As she opened the door to the church, she prayed for solitude. As she looked around, her wish had thankfully been granted, only the white, life-size figures of the statue 'Faith' were present in the room. On approaching the altar, she knelt before the beautiful stained-glass window beyond and to the crucifixion of Christ in front of her. Her forearms leaned against the smoothness of the wooden rail. She closed her eyes, offered prayers of thanks for the many wonderful things in her life, then made the sign of the cross over her body. Not wanting to move, she remained kneeling for a little while, gazing up towards the wooden figure of an innocent man, made to suffer for other people's sins. Sam's gentle face smiled down at her, a hazy vision after all these years, his features vague, she was struggling to remember his beautiful countenance. Not wanting to dwell on her past, she once again diverted her thoughts to others. Jesus Christ, on the cross, nailed by his hands and feet, the prolonged agony, hours of torture in the same position, in the heat, thirsty, hungry, the pain, the humiliation, the thorny crown prickling his skin, blood trickling from his wounds. How this man must have suffered. She questioned why the Romans hated him so much. Jesus was trying to be good, trying to help people, trying his best but for some, this would never be good enough.

The church did not provide the comfort she was seeking, she was now sobbing, crying for both Jesus and Sam, the suffering they endured through no fault of their own. Paying for the sins of others. Life was not fair. One of Doctor Wainwright's therapy sessions came into her head, the five 'A's: acknowledge, accept, analyse, action, advance.

Catherine could hear his voice: 'One must reflect on the past and acknowledge its existence. There is no long-term advantage in internalising or hiding feelings such as disappointment, regret, sorrow, humiliation, anger, fear or sadness.

'On acknowledging these emotions, one must then accept them. The past has happened, no one has the power to change this. However, one has the power to control their emotions. Emotions may be appropriate, or applicable at the time, but do not let them fester or linger for too long.

'Analysis is important. Why did this happen? Could this have been prevented? Could this have been handled differently? But do not keep analysing, do not keep overthinking the same things, time and time again. That is when the craziness, the anger, the hatred takes over our thoughts.

'Action or acquire. From your analysis, learn. This may be new skills, new ways of thinking, ways in which to relax, strategies to cope, but please do learn something, and I don't mean only from negative experiences, we can learn and acquire new skills from positive experiences too.

'Advance. Catherine, for you this is the key to overcoming your troubles. To dwell, to stagnate, to obsess time and time again over things that cannot be changed is a futile undertaking. Let these feelings, these emotions be a driving force for good, to succeed, to motivate, to prove yourself worthy. Do not allow the past to be a dead weight, dragging you down, drowning you, suffocating you, a heavy burden to carry on your shoulders, limiting your progress and creating more pain. Advance with new hope, the future beckons.

'Everything is about perspective. Black or white, good or evil, light or dark, it is the same scale, from one extreme to the other. Decide where you want to be. However, the scale is never constant, you will slip and slide throughout life, for the world does not stand still. Like the weather, day and night, the seasons, earth cannot stagnate, it is constantly evolving and changing and so must you.'

Laughter and voices broke her thoughts when three men emerged from the vestry, Reverend Thornton and two other gentlemen. Catherine tried to stand on seeing them there, but her knees had seized, and the heels of her boots became entangled in her petticoat, she appeared unsteady and in pain. The men rushed to her aid and saw the tears in her eyes.

The first man to reach her wore simple, loose clothing, tied in the middle with what appeared to be no more than rope. His face showed great concern as he supported her by the elbow and aided her to stand. In broken English he asked, "Is there anything we do to help you?"

"I'm fine now that you have helped me to my feet, thank you."

Reverend Thornton was now on the other side of Catherine, "Miss Fawcett, if my memory serves me well?" She nodded.

The third man had a warm glow to his skin, as if he had been toiling in bright sunshine. Although appearing to be the youngest, he was not as agile as the other two men for he had limped his way over to the scene with the support of a mahogany cane. He wore a smart, blue suit.

She attempted to walk but her feet felt numb, affecting her gait.

With a hint of a foreign accent, the gentleman in the blue suit said, "Take your time, please do not leave on our account."

"I was leaving anyway. I've said what I needed to say." Catherine continued to hobble.

"Nabil is staying at Oak Bank Hall and heading there now." The vicar nodded to the man in the blue suit with the stick, "I'm sure you can help each other up the hill."

Nabil looked down at his left leg and shrugged his shoulders, "For me, it would be an honour." He subtly bowed.

The vicar continued, "Rebu and I are required elsewhere." They eyed each other. "We will see you later Nabil, as we agreed." All three men nodded their acceptance.

Escorted by Nabil, the uphill climb felt like summiting a mountain, but the feeling eventually returned to her feet. As they chatted, Nabil revealed he was from Syria but was rather vague in his reasons for staying in Edenvale, stating it was, 'A lifelong Christian mission to travel the world.'

Catherine smiled to herself when she was just as vague with her answer as to why she was also in Edenvale, 'I needed some me time.'

Nabil was charming and interesting, having travelled through the Ottoman Empire and into Eastern then Western Europe. He was sad when he admitted that this was the furthest destination of his journey and that he would be heading home, via a different route, in a couple of days.

By the time they reached the railings around Oak Bank Hall, she was walking independently. "Thank you so much, Nabil, I must admit, I would have struggled with the ascent were it not for your assistance."

Nabil smiled, "May God be with you, Catherine." He turned to walk into the grounds.

"The service on Sunday, at the church, will you be there?"

His head turned, "I will indeed."

"Then I may pluck up the courage to attend."

"See you then." He waved goodbye and carefully made his way over the gravel in the grounds of the grand house. This gentleman had helped her up the hill when he was suffering with his own infliction. His knee seemed to be the problem, tending to remain in a fixed position.

A tinge of guilt crept through her thoughts. Secretly, she hoped Nabil would reveal clues on what went on in that residence if she befriended him. And why, after travelling through all those fascinating countries, exploring places such as Constantinople, Transylvania, Salzburg, and Bruges would his final destination for this leg of his journey be the sleepy village of Edenvale?

Chapter Eighteen

In preparation for her parents' visit, Catherine tidied the house from top to bottom. When she dusted the books on the shelf, she realised she had not read *The Story* in a couple of days. There it was, on the mantelpiece, in plain sight but she had somehow forgotten about it, she had been so busy with her thoughts.

Having completed her tasks, she decided to boil some water, have a well-deserved cup of tea then read some more of *The Story,* but a knock on the door changed her plans. She was surprised to see Solomon standing there, she did not know whether to invite him in or not. The decision was quickly made, "Would you like to come in?" She was excited yet nervous.

Two people in the cottage made the room feel small. Solomon's height made the low beamed ceiling feel oppressive. She invited him to sit on the sofa and he seemed so broad compared to the cosy surroundings. He took off his cap and placed it on the arm of the sofa. He rested his interlocked fingers in his lap, his legs comfortably wide. She made the excuse of preparing a pot of tea to give herself time to calm her nerves.

Catherine was shaking as she walked across the room and placed the tray on the small table by the window. She poured the tea though the strainer into the cups. Her hands were trembling as she carried the cup and saucer over to him.

He took a sip, "Blimey, you make a grand cup of tea." He pulled a sour face after looking at the bland colour in the cup. "I like it weak." A glimpse of his cheeky smile emerged at the right-hand side of his face.

With Solomon observing her every move, waiting for the tea to brew had been too much to contemplate. "I have to admit, I feel a little flustered by your presence here." They smiled at each other. Solomon had such lovely warm eyes.

He tried to ease the obvious tension, "I asked my dad about the Greek man's diary and got a few more details from him." He pulled a single piece of paper from his pocket, which was folded with perfect symmetry. "He drew this symbol." Solomon leaned towards Catherine to offer her the drawing but instead, in a brave move, she decided to come and sit on the sofa next to him. Warmth radiated from his body. A subtle magnetism drew her closer to him as they studied the drawing together. At the top of the page was the first attempt, which his father had started, made a mistake, then crossed out. The second attempt was neater. The third attempt was refined. Overall, they concluded the design was like three leaves from a birch tree intertwined at a central point, but the line was continuous, the pen did not need to leave the paper to complete the symbol.

A symbol of infinity, thought Catherine.

Solomon continued, "Dad's been asking questions when he's been out and about in the village. Apparently, the symbol is called a triquetra."

They looked at each other and shrugged. Catherine felt shy at catching his eye, "I have never heard of it, have you?" Solomon shook his head. "What do you think it means?" she asked.

"Dad said he asked Miss Montgomery when he was tending the gardens at the orphanage. Nobody else knew what it was. She said she'd noticed a few of these symbols scattered around the village. She didn't know if they held any significance though."

"I must admit, I cannot say I have seen any around here. Have you?" Catherine wondered whether she should remain by his side or move to the armchair. Her blood was racing, for this man created such intense physical reactions throughout her body. Even if she had chosen to move, she did not think her legs would be able to carry her gracefully over to the chair.

"We could look together, that is, if you'd like?" He lowered his head, yet his eyes remained shyly focused on hers.

"I would take great pleasure in that suggestion." *Catherine Fawcett,* she told herself off for being so flirtatious, but for that moment she did not care. The feeling was wonderful.

"I'm on my way to work now but how about tomorrow?" His eyebrow raised in question.

"My parents are visiting me tomorrow and they did not state a time." How sad he looked, he obviously thought she was making excuses. "And on Sunday, I thought I may go to church." His shoulders seemed to droop. "But we could meet on Sunday afternoon?"

"Catherine, you have made me a happy man." They each smiled but then feeling embarrassed, they quickly turned away to look back at the piece of paper. "So, this was the other symbol that he saw frequently dotted throughout the notebook." He pointed to the bottom of the page where the letters XX VV were neatly written.

Catherine voiced her rambling thoughts, "Roman numerals? Ten, ten, five, five? Twenty ten? Thirty? A time or date perhaps? Twenty something? Ten something?" She shook her head, devoid of further possibilities as to the meaning of the capital letters.

Solomon shrugged his shoulders once more. "Interesting though, eh?"

"Most definitely. I'm loving the mystery, the intrigue after so ..." she realised what she was about to say, *After so long in the shuttered room and lunatic asylum.*

Solomon neatly folded the paper and put it back in his coat pocket. "Sorry about the other night at the Wheatsheaf, it suddenly got busy, didn't it? We never really got to say goodbye."

"Yes, I was sad to leave," Catherine's face tingled with a cosy warmth, "It was only on my way home that I realised you never told me about the Kavanaghs."

"What about them again?"

"We were in the store, you told me they weren't married and were in fact siblings."

Solomon quickly remembered, "Oh yeah, well from what I've heard, they were brother and sister, nobody ever said they were married."

"But you don't actually know?"

"Well, I suppose not."

Catherine told him about Mr Kavanagh turning up at her door appearing lost and anxious, "So when I asked him about his wife, he said she had died, or he thought so. Then ..." she took some time, a quizzical look on her face, "Actually, now I think about it, Mrs Kavanagh was at the door. So, I asked him if this was his wife and home and ..." Another brief thought, "But no, Mrs Kavanagh said they had had four children but after their last little girl had died, sorry I cannot recall her name, they stopped trying."

"I'll question my dad, see if he knows anything." Solomon stood from the sofa.

How sad she felt at his imminent departure. She stood to see him to the door, "One more thing, Miss Montgomery you say, the lady from the orphanage, is she the young, elegant lady?"

Solomon took a few seconds to think about it, "Yeah, I guess so, in the way she moves. Why?"

"Strange question, she seems so graceful yet her face ..." Catherine was trying to find tactful words.

"Looks a bit rough with her wonky nose and missing teeth?" Solomon smirked, "Please, I'm no Lord or Sir and I like honesty. Just be yourself, I won't judge. I like you as you are." Now it was his turn to blush.

"Well, I was thinking along the lines of she has seemingly suffered some sort of tragedy or adversity. However, your words are more succinct and certainly hold no ambiguity." They both laughed. "Do you know what may have happened to her?"

"No, but I'll put it on my list of questions." He walked to the front door and checked his pocket watch.

Catherine sensed he needed to leave but couldn't.

He paused, then turned around to ask her, "I've enjoyed our chat today, have you?"

Catherine nodded, "Indeed I have." Her eyes twinkled, she felt so alive. She tried to suppress her heaving heart. "So much so that I cannot wait for Sunday."

"Me too," he said, then winked and sadly opened the door to head for the Wheatsheaf Inn.

Chapter Nineteen

The Fawcetts left their rented terraced property in Carlisle just after ten o'clock in the morning. With the magnificent cathedral and unique St Cuthbert's Church as a backdrop, Blackfriars Street had wonderful views but supposedly the dwellings were built on the graveyard for the victims of medieval plagues. The street was grimy, the houses black with soot but the name originated from the cloaked Dominican Friars who lived nearby.

Devoid of transport, the Fawcetts had borrowed an old hag of a horse and a rickety cart from a dubious acquaintance who called himself a rag-and-bone man. Mrs Fawcett hoped the weather stayed dry for the trip as the ripped bench seat was open to the elements.

The journey was tediously slow, and the cart extremely uncomfortable but Mrs Fawcett tried not to complain. She bit her lip to physically stop herself from moaning about their circumstances. The occasional glances over at her husband did not clarify his mood. Sometimes he seemed to be smiling, other times she sensed he was gravely troubled. Not that she could see much of his hair at present, for he was wearing a rather worn top hat, but he was thinning on top, and the grey outnumbered the dark strands on the sides. His once round face, that proud and chubby picture of wealth and excess, had now faded to a gaunt and tormented soul.

Neither of them had ever heard of Edenvale, and everyone they asked shook their head, so they only had Catherine's letter and the address from which to work. Catherine had enclosed the hand drawn map from Doctor Wainwright.

"We'll try down here," shouted Mr Fawcett as he used the horse's reins to force a right turn. A wood and metal representation of the crucifixion of Christ marked the corner. The track continued through a tunnel of trees, making this section of the journey feel dark and oppressive. A smell of dampness hung in the air. As they rounded a corner, they were stopped in their tracks.

"Bother!" shouted Mr Fawcett. He got down from the bench seat and walked a few feet to a lone workman. "What's going on? Can we not pass?"

"Sorry, sir, the new water pipe is being laid and all the ground is dug up." The man was weathered looking, with rough skin, bulbous nose and red ears.

"Can you confirm where this road leads?"

"To Edenvale."

"So how do we get there?" asked Mr Fawcett, proud that he had chosen the correct path but annoyed by the diversion.

"You'd have to go on a detour through Scotby village, then on to Cumwhinton, then a left to Edenvale."

"How long will that take?"

The workman pondered on the question, "Not sure but I'd say at least an hour."

"Thank you. Good day to you." Mr Fawcett tipped his hat and retreated to the cart.

Mrs Fawcett asked, "So what did he say?"

Mr Fawcett ranted and raved for a few minutes whilst turning the horse and cart around. His face was red and fuming. Mrs Fawcett decided to let him get his anger off his chest.

In different circumstances, the journey would have been pleasant, for the day was quite still and autumnal colours clung onto the trees. For many a year, the Fawcetts could not have afforded any transport, so had rarely ventured far. Even though the cart they were now travelling in was borrowed and decrepit, they were both secretly thankful for the temporary freedom this provided.

"Surely, we must be there soon, Dickie. My posterior is most certainly bruised from this constant hard pounding."

Mr Fawcett glanced at his wife with a look of disdain, "Well I for one will not be inspecting your bruised derriere. You promised you would not moan today."

"Honestly, I have sat here in silence for nearly two hours. My insides have been shaken like a sack of potatoes on the back of a farmer's cart." She folded her arms to show disgust when their rickety, old cart hit a bump in the impacted dirt road. She reached out to grab her husband to save herself.

"Potatoes would at least provide some sort of amusement." He pulled his arm away from her grasp.

"While your entertaining repartee consists of swearing, huffing, puffing and passing wind." She sneered at her husband, "From both ends, simultaneously!" She turned away from him with her head held high.

"Can you even begin to imagine what I have had to endure, living with you all these years, watching you eat, like a pig in a trough, wanting the finest truffles." He snorted a couple of times.

95

"You are deplorable, wasting all our money on fine whiskeys and imported cigars, thinking you were so hilarious, well you have no friends now you're skinny and poor."

The cart suddenly stopped. They had again reached a roadblock. "For goodness' sake, can nothing be straight forward?" asked Mr Fawcett with immense frustration. Once again, he climbed down from the seat to ask for information.

After chatting with the two workers, he returned to the cart. "We'll have to leave the horse here and walk into the village. They are laying a new road."

Mrs Fawcett got down from the cart and could barely walk. Her bottom was painfully sore, but she dared not complain. Taking pride in her appearance, she straightened her skirt, hoping she was presentable. She had owned the once fine dress for nearly twenty years but had been forced to adjust the material after losing so much weight.

Mr Fawcett tied the horse to a nearby fence post near the grass verge and collected the trunk and the hat box from the back of the cart. They started walking into the village.

"I'm never venturing anywhere with you again," said Mrs Fawcett carrying the hat box, "It's always a disaster, as if you magnetise trouble."

"For goodness' sake, woman, stop whining. I should be bloody knighted or sainted for tolerating your taunts, your negativity, for you're a bloody Jonas." Carrying the heavy trunk crammed with possessions was taking its toll. Sweat beaded on his brow.

"Blame me, as you always do, and I suppose you blame me for Catherine's situation?"

"She's been living in a bloody madhouse for years. No wonder she flipped, having to live with you. At least I could escape. That's why I worked away so much, to get rid of you." Under his breath he muttered to himself, "Damn nuisance." He marched ahead, leaving his wife trailing behind.

Mr Fawcett found Rose Cottage. With apprehension, he knocked on the door, expecting to see the haunted, skeletal soul of the girl he loved but had failed. When he saw his daughter standing there, so beautiful, so healthy, so happy, if perhaps a little older, he broke down crying. "My goodness, my angel!" He dropped the trunk and hugged his girl.

Mrs Fawcett finally made it round the corner. On seeing them hugging, she too broke down in tears, "My gorgeous girl, oh how I've missed you, my darling."

All three were smiling and hugging each other.

The Fawcetts chatted animatedly about the last few weeks and months. Although not officially stated, everyone avoided talking about the past, specifically the shuttered room. Mr Fawcett was flabbergasted when he checked his pocket watch against the clock on the mantelpiece. Many an hour had seemingly disappeared.

"I cannot believe my own eyes for the time has flown so quickly. Therefore, your mother and I must unfortunately make headway home but before we do, I have some final good news of my own."

He stood up from the sofa and walked over to the window. He straightened his waistcoat and cleared his throat, as if about to make an important announcement. Suddenly, Catherine was reminded of the speech he made many years ago on her eighteenth birthday when he had announced her engagement. Palpitations made her feel faint. Jeremy Fisher, her intended, was an heir to a vast fortune, a very handsome and charismatic gentleman in polite society, but he had turned out to be some sort of sexual deviant when in private. Declaring his love of debauchery, such as orgies, he admitted he wasn't fussy about his liaisons, as long as everyone indulged in the most depraved acts known to man. He had called her a bitch when she had scorned his advances. Her stomach churned at what her father was going to say.

"As you will recall, we have tried to sell our once beautiful home, Petteril Bank House, on several occasions over the years, but we have failed to find a buyer, the house being too expensive for these parts and sadly, it does now require a fair number of repairs. For this reason, the present occupier does not wish to renew the tenancy. I have therefore taken it upon myself to market the house and its contents for sale. For the last few days, I have travelled extensively across Northern England, to whichever rich town or city the train has allowed me to visit." He cleared his throat once more. "I think we may have a potential buyer for our home."

Catherine and her mother were thrilled to hear this news, then Mrs Fawcett appeared concerned, "But we will lose the rent in the meantime. How will we survive with no income at all?"

"Do not worry, my dear Isobel. I have faith that the sale will go through quickly once the tenant has departed."

"How can you be so sure?" asked Mrs Fawcett.

"If only he had become our son-in-law, we would never have been in this mess anyway." Mr Fawcett raised an eyebrow at his daughter.

Catherine and her mother stared at each other in disbelief.

Proudly, Mr Fawcett announced, "Jeremy Fisher has kindly made us a cash offer to buy our home."

Anger rose from the pit of Catherine's stomach at the thought of Jeremy Fisher being in her life once again. The pompous, arrogant, sarcastic, depraved – oh there were insufficient insults to describe his abhorrent, deluded, and vile personality. How ghastly, she had never told her parents why she had called off the engagement. They still thought he was wonderful, a distinguished gent, whose family had royal connections. She had to avoid Jeremy at all costs, otherwise, he would subject them all to abject misery.

Chapter Twenty

Seeing her parents again was a blessing after months of confinement at the asylum, but to hear the name of Jeremy Fisher after all these years felt like a curse. Her father had arranged the marriage back in 1844. The Fishers were rich beyond the comprehension of most people, but Jeremy Fisher was the worst kind of snob. He pranced around expecting everyone to be at his beck and call. He used people: for pleasure, for entertainment, for gain, for the sake of it. Catherine would not pander to his perverse demands and the shock reverberated throughout their social circles when she refused to be associated with this rogue. Her decision resulted in their richer acquaintances ignoring the Fawcetts and banishing them from the inner circle. Her father lost all his trade contacts as a result of her ditching Jeremy Fisher. The money soon ran out.

She was still shaking at the implications of him being in their lives once again. However, she tried to remain positive as this meant her parents would be able to sell the house and its contents and hopefully sort out their dire financial situation. This also raised questions about where Catherine could live if her parents were financially stable. She thought about Sam's home, Fernleigh, and that maybe she should sell the house. The dead body raised its ugly head. If the new owners were to find the skeletal remains, the repercussions were not worth the gamble.

Sam, he had always been on her mind whilst she was incarcerated at home and in the asylum when it dawned on her that being in this village with its strange goings on, that he had rarely been in her thoughts. This created feelings of sadness and guilt, but she tried to turn this into a positive and she decided it was about moving on and advancing into the future, not living in the past. This also reminded her that she was supposed to write to Doctor Wainwright with her progress as part of the contract of living in Edenvale.

As the evening was drawing in, the room had become quite chilly and she shivered, believing someone had walked over her grave. She had wanted the house to feel warm and welcoming for her parents, a way of reassuring them she was healthy, happy and coping with living on her own, but she was now running out of both kindling and coal. Trying to be sensible, she put aside the remaining fuel to prepare a meal and a drink for tomorrow. She had also spent all her money on a few special items at the store for her parents' visit: cold meats, cheese, fresh bread, a cake, scones and some little pots of preserve and cream. Her money woes would not be going into the letter to her doctor. If she was frugal with the morsels of food remaining, she could last until Monday when she would hopefully be paid again.

To keep herself warm, she unpacked all the belongings from the trunk. Initially, she was happy and smiling at the garments but then with each passing dress, bodice and skirt, memories of her past life, good and bad, came flooding back. Not wanting to reminisce at this time, she quickly tidied her belongings away and proceeded to the hat box. As her mother had stated in the letter, she had expertly squeezed in five hats diminishing in size to fit in the box. At last, she had some variety of colour and design, although she deemed them all old fashioned.

Her father had obviously been back to Petteril Bank House as some of her favourite books from the library were also in the trunk. She cried, so many memories were bound within the pages for he had packed some of her medical books. She pondered on her time at the House of Recovery, the hospital for contagious diseases down Collier Lane. Razed to the ground to make way for the new railway station in Carlisle. How young and naive she was then. At the time, she had felt somewhat ashamed by her wealth. Her clothes were colourful and embellished with detail, expensive fabrics, the height of fashion, clean. Wealth had not brought her happiness but neither had poverty. She had been a fool. Surely it was better to be wealthy and sad than poor and sad. Doctor Wainwright had said acknowledge, accept and analyse the past. If she had learned anything from the experience it was to be grateful for what you have.

All the possessions her parents had brought were now neatly put away and again the chill in the air made her want to go to bed. It was only eight o'clock and she thought about walking up to the Wheatsheaf Inn as Solomon would be working there. She imagined his warmth, his smiling eyes, the glow from the fires, the comforting noise of friendship and general chatter. Then she realised she had no money and would feel embarrassed sitting there with insufficient funds to purchase a drink. Her heart was telling her to go and see Solomon, but her head was telling her not to for she may be considered an easy woman, God forbid, a disorderly woman frequenting public houses on her own.

Solomon, she did not even know his surname. She closed her eyes and smiled at the vision before her. He appeared strong, wearing a pristine white

100

shirt with his sleeves neatly rolled up above his elbows, ready for work. Braces and a flat cap completed his look. He wore no jacket despite the chill in the air. His eyes were warm enough to melt away any icy stare.

She shivered at the thought, she needed warmth. She imagined his protective arms gently wrapped around her, but she had to suffice with going upstairs to bed for the comfort she craved. After checking the doors and windows, ensuring everything was safe and secure, she blew out the candles around the room except for one which she intended carrying upstairs. Peeking from behind the curtain, she had a little look outside. All was quiet. This village did not even have gas lights, it truly was behind the times. The only light was from individual homes. The night sky was dark, no moon, no stars, only blackness.

As she ascended the stairs, the wood creaked and groaned under her weight. The same noise she frequently heard from next door but at least she had not heard the growls recently.

She placed the single candle on the bedside table and went over to the upstairs window in order to close the curtains. With being away from the candlelight, and as her eyes adjusted to the darkness, she looked over the village green once more. Mesmerised by Oak Bank Hall, she could see shadows in the windows, people were obviously moving around, as if they were raising their hands in the air, but it was hard to tell with certainty. Movement from the right distracted her. A couple strolled arm in arm around the corner, straight past her house and continued along the street in the direction of the store. From what she could see, they appeared to be in love, and she heard animation in their voices as they passed below her window. They turned down the road on the right, heading towards the railway station.

Moments later, she saw a horse and carriage coming from the same direction. This village was generally quiet, and carriages were rarely seen, for there was nowhere to go as both access roads were currently closed. The road to the southwest was blocked due to laying a proper road and the northeast road was closed due to the laying of the new water pipes. She pondered on where this contraption had come from and where it was going to. She thought about the Lawson's Lodging House and the stables behind but every time she had passed, they had been empty. Only today, her parents had confirmed that both roads to the village were impassable by carriage.

When they had chatted the other day, Solomon had recalled seeing a horse and cart outside of the Kavanagh's house in the dead of night, onto which their belongings had been loaded with urgency.

She strained her eyes to see if she could see who was in the carriage, but it was too dark. However, there seemed to be a struggle going on in the back and she could hear muffled protests. The couple who had headed towards the station, she wondered if they were locals or residents of the lodge.

101

Perhaps they were departing. Strange though, to leave the village at this time of night in complete darkness on rural roads. They had appeared so happy, their body language and laughter indicating a tender intimacy, so why were they now arguing, possibly even fighting in their carriage?

Catherine once again considered writing her own version of *The Story* but the chill in the air was too much to bear and the bedcovers beckoned her to seek refuge in their warmth.

After preparing herself for bed, she got under the covers which were freezing, and she wished she had a warming pan to take the chill away. With her teeth chattering and goosebumps spreading like a contagious disease, she wriggled and moved to try and warm herself and the covers. Finally, she felt more comfortable and commenced reading *The Story*.

22nd May

Thirty-two minutes past twelve

Rev. Thornton and a foreign looking gentleman have walked up the hill and are now heading into the grounds of Oak Bank, the door has been opened for them, they do not even have to knock.

Twelve forty-two

A gentleman on a horse has now arrived at Oak Bank. Once again, the door is opened in preparation for his arrival. He presents as quite distinguished.

A man comes from around the back of the house and takes the horse. This man may not have the money or the attire, but his muscles are very well defined, even from this distance.

Three minutes to one

A well-to-do couple have just passed by my window, they are also heading to Oak Bank Hall. There is obviously some sort of event there today. This couple seem so much in love. The way she looks adoringly into his eyes. He seems so protective of her.

Three twenty-eight

Finally, one of them has left. The distinguished gentleman. His suit is impeccable, his shoes are gleaming, catching the sunlight. His horse is not there though, oh he is walking out of the grounds. Rather than walk over the green, he is skirting around the periphery, I wonder where he is going. Oh my, I think he is coming here. He is crossing the street. His handsome face, I feel giddy at his presence. His smile, he is an angel, far too perfect to be from this world. Blast and bother, he has walked past my garden gate. No way! He is calling at my neighbour's house. I do not believe it, that miserable cow from next door of all people. The number of times I have been out in the garden and tried to make eye contact or exchange a few friendly words, nothing, I get nothing, I have stopped bothering now.

My ear is to the wall, and I am trying not to breathe. Blast, I cannot hear what they are saying. That stupid boy, I can hear his grunts though. My legs are hurting, I sit back down by the window.

Thirty-seven minutes past three

An older gentleman has now left Oak Bank, I am sure I have seen him before, his beaky nose, fluffy feathers of speckled, grey hair fluttering in the gentle breeze, escaping the confines of his top hat, he reminds me of an emu. Oh, I do believe he is going next door too! He is, what on earth is going on today?

Thirteen minutes past four

The men leave together, they are smiling, they wave back at the house, I cannot see but assume the woman or her man-boy must be seeing them off at the door. It has been a while since I have laid eyes upon him, but I hear him occasionally through the walls, the growls, the grunts. The men walk back to Oak Bank. Waiting in the grounds is the muscular gentleman and the beautiful stallion. I will not divulge here how I know but it is blatantly obvious, even from this distance that the horse is male, or is it his tail? I really should not jump to conclusions. His coat is so shiny, such warm browns in the sun. The handsome gentleman climbs on his steed. He is utterly masterful in his ways. The horse canters off.

Four twenty-eight

Seven guests are now standing on the steps to Oak Bank Hall. They are obviously saying their goodbyes. Kissing, embracing, that sort of thing, they appear at ease and close to one another, as if they really care. Yet from what I see, different people come and go all the time.

Quarter past five

Mr Smith is pulling his hand cart along the road, he's had a lovely day for gardening, not too hot, not too cold, he must be heading home now. I am correct, he's heading down the hill. He's such a lovely gentleman, very kind and thoughtful.

Catherine stopped reading when a guttural sound emanated through the walls from next door. Then a loud crash, a woman's scream, then she shouts, "Don't you dare, no!" Another crash, then silence. Catherine looked at the time, just before ten o'clock. Having stayed in an asylum, silence could be good or bad, depending on the circumstances. She prayed it was the former.

Chapter Twenty-One

Dewy spider webs sparkled in the morning sunshine as Catherine made her way to the Sunday service. Meekly, she entered St Constantine's Church and was thankful to find a seat at the end of one of the rear pews. She was surprised that most of the congregation were strangers to her. She recognised Len and Jimmy from the Wheatsheaf Inn and assumed they were with their spouses and children. The young man from the blue and white cake house was in the middle row, she assumed with his mother and his grandmother. They had similar postures, with sloped shoulders of the same degree. Then she spotted Nabil and Rebu, sitting in the front row to the right.

Reverend Thornton conducted a typical church service until he announced the theme of the sermon was to be war and peace. Catherine was rather shocked, she had always thought being a good Christian was about forgiveness, love and understanding rather than fighting. Her ears pricked up in preparation for what he was about to say, and her posture suddenly seemed more upright and animated.

Reverend Thornton referenced passages from the bible, "According to Ecclesiastes 3:8, everything has a time. There is a time to love but also a time to hate. There is a time for peace and therefore there is a time for war." His deep soothing tones filled every corner of the church, easily reaching the listening ears of his congregation. There was no malice to his voice and no aggression in his mannerisms. There was a longer than necessary pause, as if he was giving his audience time to reflect on the words. His voice dropped to almost a whisper as he offered, "The key is to choose wisely. Like the holy hands on a celestial clock, God will show us the way and guide us at the correct time."

Swooping like an eagle, he paced the front of the church, his parishioners unable to settle as he imparted his insightful wisdom as to the problems in society, whilst his talons captured their guilty souls. With the stealth of a black panther hunting prey, his mesmerising words encircled his audience into submission. Then, like an elephant stomping around and calling for his herd to charge against a potential threat, he rallied his troops into fighting for God and upholding holy laws. "The Ephesians 6:11 promise God's armour will protect us so we can take a stand against the devil's schemes. Armour is not necessarily metal, chain mail, helmets or spiked gauntlets. Our armour is God's love, our faith, evidence of his miracles, our enduring love for one another.

"The Ephesians confirm we are not fighting in the physical realms of flesh and blood against our brothers and sisters. No, we are fighting against dictators, self-proclaimed rulers, false authorities and dark forces who want to divide us, to make us weak and vulnerable. I sense you are shocked. I see the fear in your eyes, but when the bible says fight for your rights and your beliefs by brandishing your sword against evil, it means your words, your presence here, being kind, thoughtful, spirited, unnerving in the face of adversity. Love is like a sword in the side of the devil. Your laughter is a laceration, your smile a stab, your goodwill a gloved fist in the face of evil. And remember, the book of Revelations states we will inherit the world if we care to be victorious."

With his back to the congregation, Reverend Thornton stood below the crucifixion of Jesus Christ. He extended his chest and abducted his arms to create the sacrificial position but instead of bowing his head, as Jesus did on giving up the ghost, Thornton stood there with his head extended, gazing towards heaven as if praying for salvation. The villagers were silent, watching the spectacle, wondering what was going to happen next. His movements almost undetectable, the vicar returned to a normal stance. He turned and surveyed the room, all eyes were upon him, he had captured his audience.

"To make this absolutely clear, I am not calling for blood-stained fields of death and destruction, killing those who oppose or suppress us. Fighting could mean discussing, arguing, standing firm, debating the theory of war and peace. Thornton slowly climbed the steps of the pulpit.

"Love and hate, war and peace, it is all about perspective. Killing someone, maiming another human being is wrong so can it be justified in any way? Bear with me. Imagine those predatory animals we read about in the deserts, in jungles, on the plains, stalking their prey. Do they do this because they hate other animals? Do they kill because they are scared? Do they kill those animals because they are so different to themselves? Do they kill because they can, because they want to, because they exude power over weaker and smaller animals? What about fearing those who may do them harm? Or put simply, do they kill because they are hungry, an instinctive fight to survive, to live another day?"

107

He leaned forward, resting his hands on the pulpit. "We kill animals because we are hungry. We kill animals because we are frightened, those hairy spiders," he shuddered with exaggeration, then made a scurrying move with his hand and fingers along the wooden frame. A small titter was heard from the congregation. "How about people killing people? Over the centuries people have gone into battle for all those reasons: for hate, for hunger, for fear, for differences, for fun. Yet some people have gone into battle for completely different reasons: for love, to protect, to defend, to prevent devastation, to maintain peace, to ensure freedom, to stop the spread of evil. War is horrendous. Killing is horrendous. But if undertaken for the right reasons, for love and peace, then maybe it is a sacrifice we should be willing to make."

On witnessing his silence, the congregation clapped. He said, "Let us conclude with a hymn."

Catherine mouthed the words, for her breathing was too shallow and uncertain to perform, as all she could think about was murder.

As the congregation sat down and listened to the vicar's closing words, she was reminded of Sam's final statement at the gallows, about doing the wrong things for the right reasons. Fear. Survival. Love. Protection.

The vicar's words, justifying murder, a bizarre notion that a man of God could find reasons to kill, but the way in which he had presented his sermon seemed logical and sensible. Catherine felt as if he had directed the meaning to her alone, that he knew about her history and what she had endured.

There was sudden chatter amongst the congregation. The service had ended. People were leaving the church. Catherine was aware of her isolation and the awkward situation she found herself in. She had been in a daze, reflecting on the past.

Quickly, she stood and adjusted her clothes, giving herself time to gain her composure. To appear busy, she walked over to the south wall and started reading some of the dedications but always with a peripheral eye on the crowd. She wanted to speak with Nabil. Eventually, he appeared from the crowds, and he smiled on seeing her standing by the door.

"I'm thankful I managed to see you, I just wanted to wish you well for your journey home."

"Dear Catherine, yes, I am hoping to make haste this afternoon. A different route home, so many things to see, so many wonders to experience."

"I cannot begin to imagine the many wonders of the world you have already seen. I am intrigued as to why Edenvale would be your destination for the outward leg of such an epic journey?" Inside, she grimaced, hoping her questioning was not too soon or too obvious.

His eyes twinkled at the question, and he smiled whilst laughing through his nose, "Edenvale is an intriguing village with a fascinating history. To

108

outsiders this may seem idyllic, hidden away from prying eyes, a secret worth keeping but to me, it is about my ancestors."

"Your ancestors were here? The other day, if I remember correctly, I believe you said you were Assyrian?" asked Catherine.

"This was all to do with the Roman Empire. My ancestors were barely able to read or write and even if they could, they were too poor to afford writing implements. But as a family we were close. Our family history has been passed down over the centuries through storytelling and carvings in wood. Some of my ancestors were taken by the Roman Army, for they possessed fine carpentry skills. They were kidnapped by soldiers in the middle of the night and forced into slavery. But one, considered too old and weak by the soldiers, well he volunteered his services for he wanted to protect the younger generations." Nabil retrieved a handkerchief from his pocket to wipe his nose. "They became part of the Roman Army, traversing many a distant land until finally being stationed here in Carlisle or Luguvalium as it was called then. Their skills were admired in the building of mighty forts along Hadrian's Wall, so they were moved to Uxelodunum which was the largest fort on the Wall, housing a thousand strong army. They were the ultimate fighting force and known as Ala Petriana. My family and their ancestors built fine accommodation and furniture for these elite cavalrymen."

"This is truly fascinating history, I never realised this area was so important, that people would come from far and wide to retrace the steps of their forefathers, for now there is little to see other than crumbling walls. And I must admit, I thought the Roman Army were all Italian, as if from Rome."

Nabil laughed, "You are not the only person to hold such a misconceived idea. The Roman Empire was in fact a diverse army, with soldiers from Syria, Libya, the Moorish regions of Africa and so on. I cannot speak for everyone but some, like my family, were forced into slave labour whilst others volunteered to join. I do not know if they wanted to join to be part of an elite powerful force or because they felt safer, being on the strongest side."

"And did you see what you wanted to see? Hadrian's Wall, any evidence of your ancestors?"

Nabil suggested they sit on a nearby pew. "I visited the site of Uxelodunum, but sadly there is little evidence today of the fort's existence. There is the bridge abutment where the Wall crossed the River Eden, some remains of the Roman bath house, some foundations of the perimeters of buildings but nothing to see with respect to the carpentry skills of my ancestors."

"Even so, the emotions this voyage must have created, your heart, your mind, you must be so proud, so fascinated by their story."

"I have many stories to pass onto my children, to God I am thankful for this opportunity to serve him. There is one special place, here in Edenvale that I wanted to visit. Near the cells of St Constantine, there are inscriptions from the Twentieth Legion my ancestors served in. They are inscribed in the rock formation on approach to the cells. My eyes searched for a while, for the inscriptions are now quite faded with centuries of wind, sun, rain all weathering the stone, but I found the words, evidence of their existence, building Hadrian's Wall, such a feat of engineering, to be part of such a massive slice of history. Whether forced or by volunteering, I am proud of my heritage, of my family's history. To build the final frontier of the Roman Empire."

"Nabil, I must find these inscriptions for I would love to share in this amazing history. It is such a shame you are leaving so soon. I would have loved to share in your travels, I'm sure you could enlighten me with so many wonders."

Nabil made to stand, "Dear Catherine, I must make haste, it has been wonderful making your acquaintance. I wish you a wonderful life blessed by God."

"You too, Nabil, a safe trip home to your loved ones."

He nodded his head and made his way over to the church door. Swinging his cane freely, his knee was moving with ease and his limp barely noticeable. The other day he was struggling to bear weight. He turned, waved and was gone.

There were still a handful of people in the church but no one that Catherine recognised. She headed outside into the sunshine although the air remained chilled. The hands of the church clock were nearing twelve and she was excited about meeting up with Solomon.

As she walked through the grounds towards the lychgate, she saw a small group of people congregating around the strange stone formation, the square base with the round column with nothing on top. They did not appear to be just standing there chatting, they genuinely seemed to be intrigued by the stones. The church bells rang, sounding twelve chimes.

As she headed up the hill, her heart was straining with the steep climb but then she saw him, and the beating momentarily stopped. Standing there by her gate, he looked so handsome yet broody, appearing deep in thought. His eyes were shadowed by his broad flat cap. His long coat hung just below his knees and his upturned trouser legs were placed at a perfect height to his brown leather boots. His hands were clasped in front of him as if on guard. He seemed anxious, distracted. Even when he saw her, he did not smile. With urgency, he grabbed her in his arms and held her there, as if he had not seen her in a thousand years.

Catherine could barely breathe. She sensed something was wrong but did not want to say or do anything to disrupt the moment. If Solomon needed this, she wanted to help, sensing his upset. He released her from his hold, his body suddenly weak. They stared into each other's eyes.

"What's troubling you so much?"

He covered his face with his hands.

"Something is obviously amiss. Please, Solomon, just tell me." She placed her gloved hand on his forearm.

His fingers dragged down his face like melting candlewax. "My Dad, he's disappeared … he's missing."

Chapter Twenty-Two

"Your dad is missing?" Catherine wondered if she had heard Solomon correctly. Minimally, he nodded his head. "Come inside, I will make us some tea and you can tell me what has happened."

"Part of me just wants to keep looking for him. I can tell you on the way, if you don't mind?"

Trying to appear positive she stood upright and with an air of conviction she said, "Let's go! Where shall we start?"

As they walked, Solomon told her he had already been to Suicide Point and there was no evidence of his father on the train tracks, the station or the viaduct below. He had called into the Lawson's Lodging House, but the proprietors had not seen his father that morning, which was not unusual as Sunday was his day off.

Solomon had walked home in the early hours of Sunday morning after finishing his shift at the Inn. He had quietly opened the front door and had ascended the stairs on his tiptoes, not wanting to wake his dad. Saturdays were always late nights at the Inn, and he had arrived home just after one in the morning and went straight to bed, shattered.

He had naturally woken up at around nine, lounged in bed for a bit, then got up to make some breakfast. Everything was tidy and normal, apart from his dad not sitting in the chair reading a book, or outside tending to the garden. Shadrach was a man who liked to keep busy, but he was homely, he liked pottering around the garden and keeping a tidy home.

Solomon had started feeling uneasy. He had knocked on his father's bedroom door, preparing to see a dead body in bed, just like what had happened to his mum, dying in her sleep. He prepared for the worst.

"So, what happened? What did you find?" asked Catherine.

"His bed was messy, crumpled, he had obviously been there, and he is always so organised and tidy, he would always make his bed, then pull back the covers to air the sheets for a while."

"Do you think he's wandered off somewhere?"

"I'm just thinking about what you said with regards to Mr Kavanagh, that he seemed to disappear. My dad wasn't a wanderer though he was completely sound of mind."

Catherine felt uneasy, an instinct that this did not appear to be normal. "You wanted to go in search of him, so where are we heading?"

"I thought down to the river and through the woods, look at the cells."

They made their way along the riverbank, past the waterfall from the mouths of dragons and into the ancient woodland. They arrived at the fork in the path. Solomon stopped and awkwardly held Catherine by her shoulders, "I'm so grateful for this, being here with you, I'd be driving myself crazy with the worry, my dad, he's everything to me with mum ..." his voice failed, unable to complete the sentence.

They looked into each other's eyes and held each other's gaze for longer than friends would do. "We'll do our very best to find him," said Catherine with a reassuring smile.

Solomon led the way, helping Catherine navigate the worn steps. Partly wanting to search the rock face for the Roman inscriptions but also wanting to remain completely focused on looking for clues to Shadrach's disappearance, she quickly gazed along the wall. There were numerous inscriptions, some professionally chiselled, others probably scratched by bored children, and some were obviously etched by lovers, an eternal reminder of their enduring love. There were so many drawings, letters and numbers to consider, and without knowing what she was looking for, happening upon Roman inscriptions from centuries ago seemed an impossible task.

Various years were carved into the rock, 1782, 1672, 1849, then she saw remnants of XX VV surrounded by harder to decipher words, possibly in Latin. Solomon had said his father had seen XX VV written in the Greek man's leather notebook. The letters or Roman numerals had to have significance.

When in church, Nabil had mentioned the Twentieth Legion and Catherine wondered if the XX, as in ten ten or twenty, was the sign for this group of Roman Soldiers. If XX was possibly the Twentieth Legion, then what did VV stand for? Five five representing ten, the Twentieth Ten Legion? It did not make sense.

She glanced over at Solomon. He was standing by the metal gate which blocked the way into the cave. He started to climb the metalwork, hauling himself up on the slightest bit of leverage which his fingers and toes could latch onto and he scaled the high gate and wall. Catherine's stomach was churning like the river flowing forty feet below. Solomon jumped down on the opposite side of the gate and disappeared into the cells. With her insides flipping, she carefully leaned over the sheer drop to look more closely at the promontory on which the caves stood. There was no sign of a body. If Solomon's father had indeed fallen or had been pushed to his death from this point, it was possible that his body would have carried along the fast-flowing river. She prayed that he had not met the same fate as the gentleman from Greece.

Catherine gasped with joy when Solomon reappeared from the cells and he climbed the gate once more, safely landing with a thud. She desperately wanted to hug him, thankful he was safe and standing next to her once again, as if this was where he should be.

He spoke gently, "There's nothing in there, just three separate cells cut into the rock. They are full of windswept leaves, looks like the rooms haven't been used in ages. One of them has a fireplace but it was cold. No signs of recent activity." A pause. "Where shall we look next? The Priory grounds?"

"Yes of course, but there's something I would like to show you first for it may be relevant to our search." Catherine gazed at the sheer rock face once more but could not find the letters and numerals amongst the maze of digits. For a moment, she thought maybe she was crazy and had imagined the whole thing. Paranoia, delusions, mania, whilst in the asylum she had seen too many patients with mad ideas, hearing non-existent words and seeing non-existent apparitions. As her search became more frantic, she told him what she was looking for. She desperately needed to find those inscriptions, to confirm her lucidity.

Amongst the carvings, Solomon finally found the XX VV etchings. Like Catherine, he was unsure if they were letters or Roman numerals, but he confirmed those were the digits written throughout the notebook, according to his father.

They retraced their steps and continued along the woodland path for a short while. They climbed out of the shadows of the bare trees by going through a wooden gate then strode the short distance along a track to the ruined priory and entered the grounds through the stone archway.

As Catherine had found previously, the door on the right to the small sanctuary was unlocked. Cautiously, Solomon pushed opened the door and they ventured inside. On the shelf was some food and two bottles of ale. The wooden sign, detailing the conditions of asylum, continued to hang on the wall. What she had not seen the first time was the emblem of the … she could not recall the name. Shadrach had drawn the symbol from the Greek man's diary on a piece of paper. A three leaf design joined in the centre by a continuously drawn line. Triquetra, that was the word. There it was, on top of the sign. Miss Montgomery from the orphanage had told Shadrach this symbol was common throughout the village, but this was the first time

Catherine had noticed it. She contemplated its possible meaning then brought Solomon's attention to the wooden board.

"Do you think it's all connected?" asked Solomon. "The Greek man's death, the leather notebook, my dad's disappearance, the triquetra signs, the XX VV?" His whole demeanour was on edge, his eyes scanning everywhere for clues to the whereabouts of his father.

"It's all so complex, I really cannot say but let's have hope. We will find him and solve the mystery."

They left the claustrophobic room and stood outside the arch of the gatehouse. "Solomon, does anyone live in this building?" She pointed to the door on the other side of the archway.

"Not that I'm aware of. As you can see, the place is falling apart."

He strode over to the door on the left and pounded the old, splintered wood with his fist. Not a sound from inside was heard. Solomon tried the door handle, it was locked. He put his large hands either side of his nose and mouth and shouted up towards the tower, "Dad, can you hear me? Are you in there?" They stood still and listened, but the only sounds were flutters of feathers and some cooing from the birds sheltering in the rotten rafters.

"I think it's empty," suggested Catherine. She turned around with the intention of walking amongst the ruins of the monastery to look for possible clues, but a sudden bang made her jump and she turned back towards Solomon. He had broken the lock on the door with a large stone.

"Oh my goodness, Solomon, what on earth are you doing? You are not going in there, surely?"

He did not stop to answer her questions but went inside.

Catherine stood there, unsure what to do. Her sense of adventure wanted to follow him, but she was worried about trespassing. Then she had the idea she should stay outside and be a scout, a sort of ship mate, keeping a look out for possible dangers and approaching enemies. Everything was quiet. After a few minutes, she became restless, wondering if something dreadful had happened to him. Against her better judgement, she ventured inside.

The door immediately led to a spiral staircase which she climbed with some trepidation for the stones were worn in the centre and her dress was so bulky with its layers of pleats and petticoats. She could not see her feet, so each step was precarious. Her right hand held onto the central column as she ascended clockwise.

In front of her were two choices, to leave the stairs and venture left or continue up the spiral. The left beckoned.

The hall was rustic with exposed timbers and stone walls. Six throne-like chairs upholstered with red velvet surrounded a medieval-looking rectangular table. Two armchairs faced the large fireplace. There was a basket full of kindling and the usual fire implements, including a poker and shovel. The hearth was cold but there was ash in the grate. To the right, a large mahogany dresser displayed a variety of metal plates and jewelled goblets.

On the wall hung a colourful tapestry depicting a bloody battle. Knights of the realm were brandishing lances whilst on horseback. Foot soldiers wielded swords and carried shields. At the centre of the scene was a rearing horse, its eyes wide with fear. Protected by spiked gauntlets, its front hooves were ready to trample a terrified enemy as he lay wounded on the ground. For some reason, she thought the rider of the horse was the legendary King Arthur for he held aloft a mighty sword.

Displayed on the other wall was a small, wooden crucifix. Standing beside this was a suit of armour, the arms fixed to hold a sword and a shield. She heard footsteps above. As she gazed up at the ceiling, the slats were so old and crumbling that there were numerous gaps in between and through the creaking floorboards she could see someone walking.

"Solomon?" she asked in such a whispered voice that she knew he had not heard.

With evidence to suggest that the tower was still used, she desperately wanted to leave.

Someone was descending the stairs. With a pounding heart, she bravely waited at the uneven junction. The footsteps were louder, getting closer. Recognising the brown boots and the brown upturned trouser legs, she relaxed knowing it was Solomon.

"Mother of God, holy ..." Solomon nearly jumped out of his skin on seeing her standing there.

"Sorry to startle you."

They both laughed even though Solomon was clutching his chest. "You frightened the ... never mind, at least we are both safe."

Surprisingly, he gently placed his hand around the back of her head and kissed her bonnet. Even though she could not feel his tender kiss, the gesture made her tingle inside.

The stairwell was too narrow for them to pass, so Solomon asked her to return to the room. "There's something I want to show you." Once in the hall he led the way. "In here, there's a rope, a whip, a knife, and a pistol." He opened the top drawer of the mahogany dresser to reveal the items. Catherine peeked inside and grimaced.

"And over here ..." he made his way to the tapestry and pointed to the saddle of the rearing horse where XX VV could clearly be seen.

"And look at the king's shield ... the triquetra symbol perfectly centred."

Taking hold of her hand, he then led her over to the fireplace, "And there, look." He pointed to the large stone mantle which was also engraved with the triquetra symbol. "What do you make of it all?"

116

As much as she wanted to explore the gatehouse in more detail, she also wanted to leave, for a wave of apprehension and sense of despair was starting to mist her mind. "Can we leave and discuss this outside, please? I'm beginning to feel anxious, this space, the tower, I'm feeling hemmed in as if there is no escape, as if the walls are closing in on me." She retrieved a handkerchief from her embroidered purse and held it over her nose and mouth, feeling quite nauseous.

Solomon helped her descend the spiral staircase. As she blindly navigated the tricky steps, he held her hand, but she could not hide the tremor as her anxiety increased. Finally, they made it outside and her whole body slumped with relief. Rather than take her time, she insisted on leaving as soon as possible, she just wanted to leave the tower with its suffocating presence.

With the priory gatehouse now out of sight, their pace slowed to a more manageable speed. As interesting as the exploration had been, there was no evidence of his father having been in any of the places they had explored. However, the situation had created an unease, an undercurrent of despair and damnation.

Still rather pale and breathless, Catherine managed to say, "But it's a priory, a monastery, where holy people lived. I cannot comprehend why I would feel that way in such a place."

"I sensed it too, the oppression, the malice. It didn't feel holy."

The church sermon she had witnessed on the morning. Love and hate, war and peace, neither had she expected this discussion to take place.

On reaching the end of the track, they were surprised that two men were working on the road, even though it was Sunday. They asked the workmen if they had seen anyone pass by fitting Shadrach's description. The workmen shook their heads. Catherine looked at the length of the road, she was convinced that nothing had changed since the first day she had arrived in Edenvale. She made a clear note in her head that the last row of cobbles was level with the silver birch tree on the left. Catherine and Solomon said their thanks and walked away.

Feeling pain in her heels, Catherine asked if they could briefly stop off at the cottage and she would change into more comfortable footwear.

Once home, she made her way upstairs to freshen up, leaving Solomon pacing the room downstairs.

By the time she had changed, he was standing by the window and looking out over the green. "I've got an awful feeling that something has happened to him because he was asking questions about things he had seen in the leather notebook. The symbols, the Roman numerals, the maps, and Edenvale. I'm sure he mentioned something about river formations too, or something like that. Do you think he's been silenced? He could be meeting a similar fate to the Greek gentleman."

Continuing their conversation from the kitchen area she said, "Solomon, please, we need to stay positive. Yes, I can understand why you think those things, but we have no evidence to suspect sinister undertones to his disappearance." She offered Solomon some milk to drink but he shook his head. "However, I do think it would be prudent, to watch what we say and do when in public."

He nodded his head, "Can we go back to mine after this, just for a minute or two, to check he hasn't returned home? If he's not there, I would like to go down to the well and then onto the water works. See if those workmen have seen him walking around."

Catherine enquired, "The laying of the road, where we asked the workmen if they had seen your father, how long have they been laying the cobbles there?"

Puffing out his lips in thought he eventually replied, "Dunno really, I'd guess about two years."

"And is the road any further along?"

"Well since I've been here, they were all the way back to Cumwhinton, so they have done a fair bit."

Instead of skirting around the subject, she decided to come straight out and say what was on her mind, "I know I may be paranoid, but I am thinking the workmen may be either stopping people from entering the village or stopping people from leaving."

After apologising for laughing, Solomon said, "But you came to the village, I came to the village, you said your parents visited yesterday, the Greek man got into the village, the Kavanaghs have seemingly left the village."

"I guess so and at church this morning they had a gentleman who had come all the way from Syria."

"I reckon the workmen are just slow workers. Honestly, they've done loads on the road since I've lived here."

Having rested a short while, they headed downhill towards the railway station and to Solomon's house. It was semi-detached and quite grand from the outside. Etched into the glass above the door was, *Wood Grange.* The front garden was small but immaculately kept with a topiary bush in the shape of a bird as a focal point. Catherine stood at the gate.

"You can come in if you like, I promise I'll be good." It was the first time she had seen the cheeky Solomon she met by chance the other day. Gracefully, she walked down the path, aware that prying neighbours may be observing their every move.

The house was clean and tidy. There was little evidence of personal belongings, no pictures or paintings, only a couple of ornaments but plenty of flowers and plants. Everything in the room was functional. The overall theme was green with dark wood panelling. Although she had never met Shadrach, from what Solomon had said this house seemed to fit his personality. A practical man who lived a simple life, kept busy, liked to potter, a general handyman. Even the colour scheme fit with his passion for nature. However, Catherine felt sad that he loved his wife so much, he could not bear to have any reminders or mementoes of her existence. Seeing her or being reminded of her was too much to endure. Catherine wondered if Solomon looked like his mother in any way. Maybe Shadrach could not cope, seeing her likeness in their son.

After a few minutes, Solomon returned to the sitting room, shaking his head, "Still no sign, and the bed is still unmade. It's just not like him." He slumped into the green armchair and rested his head back against the leather and closed his eyes.

"Let's keep searching, let's not give up just yet."

They left the house and headed towards the well from which she had regularly collected pails of water since arriving in the village. Catherine stopped to examine the signpost. Carved into the weathered wood was, *St Cuthbert's Well*. She was unsure if this was relevant, but a small village having numerous dedications to saints seemed a little excessive. St Martin was etched into the glass above her front door, the church and cells were dedicated to St Constantine, St Helena, his mother, was portrayed in stained glass in the church and St Cuthbert had a well in his honour. She looked at the sign again. Although faint, the triquetra symbol was just visible. "Solomon, look, it's here again." She pointed to the sign.

As the well came into view, there was no sign of Shadrach, only two people conversing. Solomon approached the villagers to enquire about his father whilst Catherine remained higher up the hill. On returning he said, "Neither of them have seen my father today. The tall, spindly gentleman with the impressively fat moustache is Mr Lawson from the lodging house. The smaller, muscular gentleman smelling and looking like a horse is Frank Butterworth from Oak Bank."

A smile emerged on Catherine's lips. Despite Solomon's matter of fact tone when commenting on his acquaintances, his down to earth descriptions matched her own thoughts although she was thinking Frank Butterworth's features were equine, rather than horsey which somehow seemed less offensive.

"And another thing, that three-leaf design thingy symbol is on the well too."

119

The gentlemen were still chatting, although occasionally they eyed the young couple, and they seemed less animated now. Rather than wait for Catherine to see the symbol, they decided to move on.

Catherine had never ventured down the other road, having been told the way was blocked by the water works. More beautiful houses lined the way. Grand designs, probably from the 1700s were dotted here and there but some newer residences had been built in between the detached older properties. All the houses exuded wealth and architectural beauty.

They were stopped in their tracks as the road was completely dug up with a sectioned clay pipe sunk in the depths of the earth. It was an impressive sight to see. Two workmen were standing in the trench. Solomon gave a description of his father, but the two gentlemen shook their heads.

"What do we do now? We have exhausted all options. I cannot see my dad walking anywhere else, he's really fit physically, I cannot imagine him falling or jumping in the river or coming a cropper somewhere, and yes, he is depressed by mum's passing, but he gets on with things. He keeps himself busy as a distraction. He's not one for friends. I cannot imagine he would be round someone's house having a cuppa and a catch up. I've no idea where he could be." He sat on a nearby rock, took his flat cap off and ran his fingers through his hair. The weak sunlight detailed warm, golden tones.

"There is something, but it could be nothing. I didn't want to say this earlier because I did not want to worry you unnecessarily. Last night, I was getting ready for bed and was about to close the curtains when I saw a young couple walk past my house. They were chatting and laughing, and seemed enamoured with each other. They were heading in the direction of your home. A moment later, a horse drawn carriage rattled past my house. It came from your direction, I mean, from the direction of your home. There was a struggle of some sort in the back of the carriage, as if they were holding someone against their will. They headed up towards the Wheatsheaf Inn. I thought it odd as no one seems to have a carriage here and both roads into and out of the village are impassable. At the time, I wondered where they were going and how they would get past the road works in a carriage."

Solomon seemed to age, his breathing quickened, his fingers opened and closed slowly, his knuckles cracking with the pressure. "This is not good news. I feel sick to my stomach."

"It may not be anything to do with your father though, it was too dark, I could not see. Maybe I shouldn't have told you for I do not know if—"

"What time was this?"

"I was really cold last night. I couldn't get warm for I had no fuel for the fire, so I made to go to bed early to get some warmth. It was maybe nine by then, around that sort of time. I was standing at the window, about to draw the upstairs curtains when I saw the couple, seemingly so happy, then the commotion in the carriage."

Catherine sat next to Solomon on the rock and gently placed her hand into his. His tension eased slightly, and he sighed. Neither of them knew what to do next.

Chapter Twenty-Three

For the first time, Catherine felt uncomfortable being on her own in the cottage. Since arriving in Edenvale, there had been growls and groans from next door, a possible murder and the disappearance of two of her neighbours. With Shadrach Smith having vanished, her anxiety levels were rapidly rising.

Catherine sat in the armchair by the fire and looked at the questions she had scribbled down about her concerns. The first two questions were about the Kavanaghs. She still did not know what had happened to them. They had lived in the village for years, seemed to be well respected and involved in village life yet suddenly they disappeared, and no one mentioned this fact.

The next question related to the gentleman at Suicide Point. She now knew his name, Alesandro Demetriou, but other than some clues in his notebook, which Shadrach Smith had divulged to his son, she knew little else about the man. The villagers had never mentioned him since, he had seemingly been forgotten.

The history of Rose Cottage and who had written *The Story* were also on her list. Catherine was still unsure whether she wanted to know the answers. She wondered if she should confide in Sam and tell him about *The Story*. A sense of dread froze her entire body. Her mouth gaped open, unable to move or say anything. Sam, had she subconsciously said Sam in her thoughts? Sam, Solomon, Shadrach, their names all started with 'S'. That was it, a slip, a blip in concentration. She knew Sam was ... she wanted to say dead, but the word had dreadful connotations. Thinking his soul had passed to a higher dimension seemed less final.

Solomon, Solomon, Solomon, she questioned whether she should confide in Solomon and tell him about the book. If she told him about the diary, then maybe he would mention who had lived in Rose Cottage previously. Unsure whether she wanted answers at this time, she wondered why she felt slight unease about asking him the questions. He seemed genuine, she could sense his feelings, she felt the same way about him but something, that little voice in her head, kept warning her to be careful.

Oak Bank Hall and its residents were the next question on her list. She had met Schubert the butler when he answered the door that day. She had met Nabil who was staying there. She could not remember the man's name, but Solomon had mentioned him at the well today, the man with the equine features, Butterworth, Frank Butterworth was the name. He had a long face and big, buck teeth but very muscular. In *The Story,* the author had mentioned seeing Mrs Kavanagh at Oak Bank Hall on a few occasions.

The next question related to the orphanage but a knock on the door paused her thoughts. Shaking with fear, she did not want to answer. Creeping closer to the door, she jumped when another knock was heard. "Catherine, it's me."

A sigh of relief escaped her lungs. She opened the door, still with some trepidation, but there he was, Solomon, standing there looking all cosy in a warm thick overcoat. "It's ..." she looked over to the clock, "... nearly seven o'clock. Is everything all right?" She looked around the village green to see if anyone was watching but not a soul could be seen.

"I was worried about you. Everything we did today, chatting to the workmen, breaking down the door to the priory, my father and his disappearance, I thought ..."

"You thought they may take one of us next? I must admit, the thought did cross my mind." Aware that he was still standing on the doorstep, she invited him in.

"What if one of us is taken during the night, like my father? I have been unable to stop worrying about my dad ... and you." A sad smile briefly appeared on his face.

"Do you have any suggestions, to make things safer?"

"We could stay together?" He genuinely said this with a worried look on his face, the cheekiness, the twinkle in his eyes, long since gone.

"Solomon Smith, I ... do not know what to say to such a proposition. I ..." She knew it was the safest decision but to sleep under the same roof with a gentleman, she imagined what the neighbours would think.

"Honestly, Catherine. My intentions are honourable. I could not bear to lose you, even though it has been such a short time, my feelings, I cannot explain the urgency."

Since her time in the asylum, she had flitted between worrying what people thought and desperately trying not to care. On this occasion, her head and heart were saying stay together and forget the repercussions or the chatter of others.

"What are the specifics to this suggestion?"

"I know my dad was taken from home, but I could sleep in his bed and you could sleep in mine, but I am also wary of staying there. They know where we live. If I were to stay here, the accommodation …" he looked around the tiny room, "I'm not sure how it would work."

Her heart was now racing. Jeremy Fisher, the man she had been forced to engage with all those years ago briefly came into her head, recalling the time they had stayed under the same roof, and he had tried to barge his way into her room. Putting the thought quickly aside, she suggested, "You could sleep on the sofa, but it is small. Your feet may dangle over the edge, but we will at least be together."

Solomon smiled. "The sofa it is then."

The reality of this agreement suddenly dawned on Catherine. They now had to entertain each other for the evening and the house was so cold and she had little food. She asked, "Have you eaten today?"

He shook his head, "With what has happened, I really cannot face the thought of food."

"Earlier this evening, I followed a recipe from a book I found on the shelf and baked some bread." She walked into the kitchen, "And as you can see, it did not go according to plan." She brought the loaf through, "I'm sure if you cut off the black bits, it may be perfectly delicious underneath." They both laughed at the charcoaled brick.

"I certainly won't be marrying you for your cooking skills." He winked and for that split second, he was back.

"There is a reason why I cannot really cook or bake, but maybe that's for another time." She took the blackened bread through to the kitchen.

"So, what *shall* we talk about?" asked Solomon.

"I can see you are worried about your father but if you wouldn't mind answering a few questions about the village, it may take your mind off your current predicament."

"I've never been interrogated before." His body was beginning to sink into the comfy sofa. "Go on then."

Taking a deep breath, she blurted out, "Who lived here before me?" There, she had asked the question, there was no going back now.

The furrow between his eyebrows deepened, "It was a bloke, not sure of his name. Rarely saw him. Thin chap, bushy beard, weird hair and a small monocle."

"And do you know when or why he left?"

"Sorry, I don't. He never frequented the Wheatsheaf and with my hours, working late at night, I just don't know."

"As an approximation though, has the cottage been lived in recently?"

"I would say I probably noticed the place was empty about six or seven months ago, but it could have been longer than that." He stretched his long legs out and put his hands behind his head.

"Did he leave voluntarily, or did he seem to disappear?"

124

Solomon pricked up at the question. "Excellent question but sadly one I cannot answer. You'd make a great investigative journalist you know." He winked. "Definitely better than me."

With a shy smile, Catherine started to relax into her armchair. "My neighbours, do you know anything about them?"

"Felicity and Jonathan. Mother and son. They rarely venture out. I think he has some sort of condition, his face, his limbs, he has deformities."

"How sad for them both." Catherine was aware they may be listening by the walls. "I think it prudent that we lower our voices." She nodded over to the wall and put her hand behind her ear.

Solomon cottoned on to her meaning, "You could always come and sit here, so we can chat with lowered voices?" His voice raised as in question. Catherine could not read his body language, wondering if this was a ploy to bring her closer, or was he really concerned about eavesdroppers. Either way, she so desperately wanted to sit beside him, even if just for warmth.

"You take up most of the room, Mr Smith," she said shyly, for Solomon was now relaxing with his arm over the back of the sofa. Such a warm smile, so loving, he stared at her with complete adoration.

"Ask me another one then."

"A what?" She felt flustered, her concentration waning.

"Another question."

"Oh yes, silly me. Ah, the next question, right, yes." Honestly, she was convinced he must think her a fool, for he seemed so relaxed and at ease. "Do you know who owns this cottage?"

"No idea." His smile was getting bigger.

Aware of his amusement at her flustering, this exacerbated her nerves. "Do you know anything about the church?" Now her heart was racing, she could barely bring herself to look at him.

"Not a thing." He shook his head and even though she dared not to look, she could sense he was gazing at her. He leaned forward from the back of the sofa and rested his forearms on his thighs. "Catherine." She lifted her eyes to his. "I can see you are uncomfortable. I could always leave, this situation, it's strange for both of us."

"No, or yes, whatever you think. I'm sorry if my questioning was too boring. I … I've been on my own for so long that maybe I find it hard to—"

"Relax around people?" His head cocked to the side.

Tears were on the verge of falling. All she could do was nod her head in agreement.

"Catherine, you perplex me. You are so refined, yet you walk around in muddy boots with your skirt an uneven quarter way up your legs. Your voice, you seem so ladylike, yet you spend your time with me, knowing I work in a public house." He opened his arms and looked down at his simple attire.

"You are so intelligent, so aware, so knowledgeable about so many things. You use big words that I can only guess their meaning. But somehow you seem so innocent, so sheltered. You are an enigma, a mystery, I've never met anyone quite like you."

Their eyes lingered lovingly, neither could speak, their hearts were pounding with the feelings they held for each other. Neither of them moved, too afraid to show their true feelings when all they wanted to do was hold each other in their arms.

Solomon broke the silence, "Why are you really here in Edenvale, Catherine?" Slowly, he rose from the sofa, his eyes not wanting to break the spell. He held out his hands, to which Catherine responded. Mirroring his moves, she slowly raised from her armchair. Solomon gently wrapped his arms around her. The moment was magical, the much-needed warmth from their bodies, sensing each other's heartbeat, he tenderly touched her cheek, then stroked her hair. So soft and silky.

As if nursing a wounded sparrow, his finger ever so softly lifted her chin, so their eyes once again made contact. So as not to frighten the scared and delicate soul, he slowly moved towards her, until their lips tenderly touched. Neither of them flinched or fluttered away. The sensation was intoxicating. Solomon's heart was flying high and swooping low with sheer delight.

He asked, "Where have you been hiding all my life?"

Calmly, she said, "The lunatic asylum."

Chapter Twenty-Four

Solomon had left Rose Cottage in the early hours of the morning. Exhausted but unable to sleep, Catherine remained under the covers, their conversation playing on her mind. The consensus amongst the masses was always that honesty is the best policy but when the truth hurts people you love, maybe lying should be considered virtuous.

Working at the House of Recovery, the hospital for contagious diseases, the attack, the murders, being an undertaker, Sam's arrest and incarceration, Catherine had told Solomon nearly everything. Some things she could not bear to speak of again, so she had not been completely honest, but neither had she lied.

Her ensuing madness, the shuttered room, being imprisoned at home, a life devoid of anything sharp or hard; she exposed her broken heart to Solomon. Her admission into the newly opened lunatic asylum in 1862 had been a humiliation for her parents but with hindsight, the experience had turned things around within the year. The gentle approach of the nursing staff, the kindness shown, the daily tasks, the talking, the fresh air and exercise had pieced her together, the cracks barely visible at a glance.

Solomon had listened and had asked appropriate questions. He had seemed devastated yet fascinated by her story. His whole demeanour was of disbelief, not that he did not trust what she was saying, but he could not comprehend how someone could suffer so much heartbreak and be so strong.

When there had been little else to say, Solomon had invited Catherine to seek refuge in his open arms. Exhausted, she had fallen into his warm embrace, their bodies perfectly aligning, finding comfort as they had cuddled in silence on the sofa. Her head had rested on his broad, muscular chest. Tenderly, he had placed a kiss on her hair. His strong hands so gentle on her skin, a sweet, caring touch. Finally, she had felt at peace, content to just slip away, afraid of never feeling this much love again.

Drained by the intensity of the revelations, Catherine had felt drowsy, her eyes heavy as she had listened to the calming beat of Solomon's heart. The rhythm had been soothing, deep and true. The beat never faltering, she had felt reassured and safe in his loving arms. Her body heavy, she had started to relax, her breathing slowing in time with his. So peaceful, she felt like she was drifting, comfortable in his—

Suddenly, Solomon had moved, guiding her to the side. He had stood up from the sofa and gave a little shake of his limbs. She apologised for his obvious discomfort, worrying that she had somehow caused his apparent pain. He had reassured her that it was only his arm that had 'gone to sleep' but he then suggested in the circumstances that it seemed best if he returned home. He had left so abruptly, especially since he had been so adoring moments before.

Alone in her bed, she reminded herself of Doctor Wainwright's theory of the five 'A's. Analysing the situation at this time in the morning was futile, she was too tired. She quickly acknowledged and accepted what had happened and decided she needed to take action and that was to sleep. She would deal with the repercussions in the morning.

As she closed her eyes, she prayed that they may both be safe from harm. Solomon had turned up unannounced that evening, concerned for their safety, worrying that they may be forcibly taken if they slept alone, just as his father had mysteriously disappeared in the night. Yet he had seemed to just suddenly dismiss this notion, like it no longer mattered. Continuing with her prayer, she asked God that he was not gone forever, in more ways than one.

Chapter Twenty-Five

Incessant knocking on the front door roused Catherine from her eventual slumber. Half asleep, she could not see the time on the clock by her bed. When her eyes focused sufficiently, she jumped out of bed in a state of panic, ten thirty! She had barely slept, possibly only drifting off to sleep at around five or six o'clock. The knocking continued, but louder. Whoever was at the door was persistent. A smile appeared on her face. Hopefully it was Solomon and he had forgiven her of everything she had admitted to last night.

Her hair was a mess, she had not washed, her teeth had not been cleaned and she was barely presentable. The knocking continued, pressurising her to answer the door. She put on her dressing gown over her long white nightdress.

She opened the bedroom curtains and light flooded into the room. The uncomfortable glare made her blink. The knocking stopped. Up against the windowpane, she could not see anyone standing at the front door, perhaps they had gone, or worse, she had imagined the whole episode and was indeed insane. Her state of mind became a concern. The knocking recommenced and she breathed a sigh of relief, they were obviously still there but standing close to the door.

With a spring now in her step at seeing Solomon, she descended the stairs and opened the front door. Her eyes, her mouth and her hands were wide with surprise as Nurse Jones stood there in her uniform.

"So, you *are* in."

"Why yes, of course I am, I …" Catherine struggled to string a coherent sentence together.

"May I come in?" asked the nurse politely.

"Of course, yes, please do. Here. Have a seat, there, yes, I'll put the kettle on, but I'll need to light the fire first. Oh, I cannot, I haven't got any … Oh, sorry, as you can see, I've only just got up and your presence here has rather—"

"Catherine ... breathe." Nurse Jones demonstrated a slow inhale through the nose and a slow exhale through the mouth.

"Yes of course, breathe." Catherine copied the nurse's movements. "I'm so sorry, the state of me, I was up very late last night, until approximately 3 a.m. and then I could not sleep."

"Come on, we will make the tea together and you can tell me all about it." Nurse Jones took off her cape and walked into the kitchen area as if she was at home.

"I'm sorry but I may not have sufficient fuel for the stove, but we can try."

Together, they got a small fire going and soon they were chatting about general things.

They sat down together at the small dining table. "I must admit Catherine, when you opened the door, I was most shocked at your appearance. You were always so presentable on the ward, taking pride in your appearance."

Catherine could at least laugh, "I agree, I must look like a scarecrow." She tried to comb her hair with her fingers. "Like I said it was a late night."

"You can tell me about that later but for now, I will tell you why I am here." She opened her bag and retrieved a notebook. "As part of the agreement for you staying here, you were supposed to write to Doctor Wainwright at least once a week, detailing your general physical and mental health, how you were coping financially, how you were managing to interact with the villagers, etcetera."

Like the rising sun, it dawned on Catherine that she had completely forgotten about the asylum's contract, as if that was the darkness and she was now in the light. However, the mesmerizing rays had blinded her, leading her on a merry dance around the village. The reality of failing to fulfil her contract may result in her being forced back to the dark place.

"I've been so busy here. I've met so many wonderful people. Writing letters, I completely forgot. The asylum, Doctor Wainwright, surely it's a good thing it wasn't on my mind?"

"In one sense yes, but how were we to know those things? When you didn't write we were worried about you. You may have been confused, wandering, not eating, crying and this is why I am here now. To ascertain your wellbeing. You stated you have met some wonderful people, so tell me who they are. Who are you friendly with?" It seemed an innocent question from the nurse.

"The Kavanaghs, Mrs Dawson from the store, Solomon from the Inn, the vicar from St Constantine's church, Mr Schubert from over the road, Miss Montgomery from the orphanage. Everyone is really lovely." Omitting the full truth was better than complete honesty, as she thought about how three people had gone missing and how one had been murdered or possibly committed suicide.

"And how have you engaged in village life? What are you doing to keep busy? That sort of thing." The nurse had a brief look out of the window.

"I have ... become involved with the church. I attended the service on Sunday. I have … undertaken some research into the history of the village. It's quite a fascinating little place."

"And have you met anyone of your own age? Engaged with someone on a personal level?" The nurse maintained full eye contact with Catherine.

Catherine could feel her face flush. This conversation felt like an interrogation, with the outcome determining her freedom or further imprisonment. Her teeth were furry, her hair felt like a bird's nest, she was still in her night attire, and she wrapped the loosening gown around her body. This was not a favourable situation.

"Solomon, together we have been researching the history of the village. We stayed up last night until the early hours. He works long shifts at the Wheatsheaf Inn, just up the road." She pointed in the general direction.

With a look of disdain, the nurse asked, "Are you describing a public house?"

"Yes, I've been there a couple of times just so we can talk."

"And they allow you to frequent this establishment without any … hmm … judgement?"

Catherine realised what the nurse was insinuating but she remained calm and gave the pretence of innocence to avoid that particular line of questioning. "The locals seem nice; they have all welcomed me to the village."

With a sigh, the nurse moved on, "How are you coping with money, with preparing food, shopping?"

"Well as you can see, I'm still here, I haven't wasted away, I think I am doing considerably well."

Nurse Jones eyed Catherine up and down, "You certainly seem well, if not a little bedraggled but I can understand why given your explanation. But routine, a good night's sleep, it helps with the body's internal clock, with normality. The body knows what to expect so experiences less stress, less surprise."

"Honestly, last night, I can put my hand on my heart and swear that I cannot remember ever staying up so late."

"Catherine, it was a pleasure having you in the asylum and I will write a pleasing report for you but please, do not let me down, do not let yourself down. I cannot be seen to lie for you. Your dishevelled appearance today, I will let it go, but next time, I cannot keep covering for you."

"Honestly, this is the first time. I am normally up and about by seven or eight most days. I'm loving being here, the village, the people, the history, the intrigue, people watching. I promise, this opportunity is doing the most amazing things for my confidence, my mind, my soul. I cannot bear to let this go."

"Then write, every week, every day if you have to. Put the date to show orientation, present beautiful calligraphy to show pride in your work. Try and detail excellent presentation and grammar which will reassure Doctor Wainwright, and your benefactor, that you are of sound mind. Doctor Wainwright will pick up on the slightest tremor, the slightest disorientation, a mundane or melancholy sentence may create worry and concern from his perspective." The nurse came in close. "I am forbidden to tell you this, so please do not divulge this information to anyone else but I really want to help you with your recovery. I believe there is someone in the village who feeds information back to the asylum. I wanted to warn you, but I don't want to scare you either. Just be vigilant, be yourself, be free but be careful."

"Thank you, honestly, I will. I do not want to jeopardise my progress."

"Then I will depart. The carriage is waiting at the road end. Doctor Wainwright just wanted to know you are safe having not heard from you. Take care, Catherine. Look after yourself."

"Rainbows after the storm," said Catherine.

The nurse smiled, "They are certainly a magical mystery."

Catherine escorted her to the door. They waved goodbye and the nurse closed the garden gate behind her. Once out of sight, Catherine closed the door and leaned against the wood with a heavy sigh. She shuddered with embarrassment at her appearance. A creeping chill invaded her body at the thought that someone in the village was watching her every move and feeding back information to the asylum. From now on, she had to be extremely careful.

Chapter Twenty-Six

The unexpected visit from Nurse Jones had depleted Catherine's enthusiasm and she had not left the cottage all day. Solomon had not called in on his way to work either, so she feared the worst, that she had scared him away by telling him the truth about Sam's hanging, her spiralling madness, the shuttered room and her admission to the lunatic asylum. She had been honest but hesitant to divulge everything. If he could not handle those aspects of her past, then there was no way she was going to reveal the darkest aspects of her history, that she was a murderer and had allowed Sam to take the blame. For around eighteen years, she had tortured herself with the guilt. Like a flesh-eating disease, the remorse had almost consumed her. By the time she was admitted to the asylum she was nothing more than a walking skeleton.

Recognising her destructive thoughts, she gave herself a shake and stopped herself from spiralling into the depths of gloom.

Cold, ravenous, and with little else to do, she picked up *The Story* to distract herself by admiring the beautiful pages of calligraphy, interspersed with colourful drawings of flowers. For a few days, there was the usual drivel of times and sightings with nothing of any interest. She contemplated whether the author was in a similar situation to herself, for he or she seemed obsessed with the goings on in the village, as if they were always on the lookout. Did they also know they were being watched? There were sightings of locals that Catherine knew or recognised. There were descriptions of strangers, with details about clothing, sometimes ridiculing their attire, their gait and their demeanour. Catherine could not understand why the author had this obsessive need to document every person walking past the window unless it was to protect themselves or provide evidence in case they disappeared.

The Story did not have printed page numbers, but the author had added their own. On page 72, the writing became more like a scribble, as if the creator had a tremor or had possibly rushed the content. Whatever the reason, the comments took a more sinister tone.

Fourteen minutes past eleven

There are numerous strangers milling around. They are looking over here, seemingly taking an unusual interest in this cottage.

I have yet to find the hidden treasure, but I am so close. I am praying these people haven't beaten me to it. Years of research, years of accruing debt, of people chasing me for payment. I know I am obsessed with finding it but what price must I pay?

Eleven thirty-two

The first journal is with Hodder, Stretton and Puddifoot solicitors situated on The Crescent in Carlisle. If anything happens to me, please enquire there, say you have concerns for my welfare.

The Order of the Priory
The Twentieth Legion of Valeria Victrix

I feel it tingling in my bones, in the pit of my stomach, my hairs stand on end, it is definitely hidden here yet I cannot find the strength to write down the words, admitting what I have been searching for. This secret has almost destroyed me, torn me from my friends and family. I should have heeded their warnings.

There are too many people from afar. We are all possessed. The madness is obvious in our eyes. The obsession is real. The lengths we go to, to find, to prevent, to obscure the truth with lies and deceit. I am not wrong in my judgement, in my thinking. I fear for my safety. The Order have protected the secret for centuries of time. They will not let me or others get in the way.

A man in a dark suit is walking down my path,

The Story stopped abruptly, that was it, a scrawled name at the end, written in haste, on an angle, the nib appearing to have torn the textured paper. Rushed, thick ink blots as if scribed in a panic, the perfect art of the author's calligraphy had vanished. Catherine's heart was pounding, the signed name at the bottom. It could not be, surely it was a coincidence.

Sam

The author had signed off *The Story* as Sam. Could be male, could be female, Sam, Samson, Samuel, Samantha, it could not be her Sam, or could it? Her Sam was dead, hanged for crimes he had not committed. The Sam who had written this story was a different Sam, it had to be.

Her lungs needed more air, her bosom expanded with each forced breath. Was this his way of warning her, a message from the grave perhaps? No, this was impossible. She had analysed all options and the conclusion was it had to be a different Sam.

Catherine re-read the last few pages of *The Story*. Sam, someone was after him or her. Sam had been meddling, searching for something hidden in the village. Like the Greek gentleman, he too seemed to be hunting for something important. Had Sam met a similar fate? Was he alive, dead or suicidal? Had he mysteriously disappeared like others in the village?

The Order of the Priory. The Twentieth Legion of Valeria Victrix. Solomon had stated that when his father had been tasked with collecting all the belongings from the Greek gentleman's room, he had seen images of crosses and Christian symbols throughout the leather notebook. Was the treasure something biblical?

Lost as to what to do next, her only option this evening seemed to be perusing the cottage for hidden clues and tomorrow she would try to head into Carlisle to find Hodder, Stretton and Puddifoot situated on The Crescent, to retrieve the previous storybook.

She searched every nook and cranny of the cottage but to no avail. Next, she painstakingly picked every book off the shelf, opened its cover, turned the book upside down so the pages fanned and gently shook the leaves. Nothing fell out other than specks of dust.

Of all the books on the shelves, *Hadrian's Wall: The Final Frontier of the Roman Empire* seemed to be the most used, for the spine, covers and pages were creased and dog-eared in comparison to the other books, some of which looked pristine. Catherine scanned the contents page then flicked through the book. At first glance, The Roman Empire appeared to be a fascinating subject.

The book detailed the Roman Army's invasion of Britannia in A.D. 43 under the leadership of Emperor Claudius. Some aspects were underlined or starred, and some areas had added text. Catherine's eyes skipped to the highlighted sections.

The Romans arrived in Carlisle, or Luguvalium as it was known then, in A.D. 72-73. They built a wooden fort on the site now occupied by Carlisle Castle. Each chapter detailed the continued conquest of the island. Emperor Agricola was appointed Governor of Britannia in A.D. 78 and pushed forward with his plans to occupy the northern territories. Publius Aelius Hadrian became Emperor in A.D. 117 and envisaged building a wall to confirm the final frontier. In A.D. 122, his dream became a reality, with the building of a border wall to protect The Empire. The wall stretched from the east coast to the west with towers, milecastles, forts and ramparts. The wall followed the rugged undulation of the land and crossed three significant rivers.

Engrossed in the history of the Roman Empire, Catherine did not notice the shadowed stranger walking down her path.

Chapter Twenty-Seven

Catherine was unaware of the solitary figure walking down her path. The strong knocking on the door made her jump and she lifted her head out of the book. Quickly, she noted the time. She had been reading about the Roman Empire for over an hour. Another bout of knocking. She remembered about *The Story* and how Sam had feared for his safety when strangers had approached the cottage. The curtains were open, she could not hide, the person would have seen her as they walked down the garden path to the front door. Her thoughts jumped to Nurse Jones, how she had warned about being watched by someone in the village. Catherine did not want to open the door with so many people disappearing. The knocking became insistent. There was no hiding place.

"Hello. May I ask who's calling?"

"Just open the bloody door!" A man's voice.

"What do you want?"

"Catherine, just open the door!"

There was a curt, irritated tone, an angry quality, but the voice sounded familiar, and he had used her name. Unsure whether this was a good or bad sign, she opened the door by a fraction. A man stood there, his face shadowed by the deepening night and by the brim of his black top hat. His oxblood shoes reflected the weak candlelight from the cottage and his clothes were of an expensive, tailored fit. Catherine's eyes again tried to take in the gentleman's face. He tipped his hat further down, concealing his face in deeper shadow. His right hand held onto the velvety brim. Beguilingly, he took off his hat, keeping his face obscured for as long as possible, building the tension. Speckled with grey, his thin hair was tied in what could only be described as a low and limp pony's tail, which ended level with his heart. His skin was ashen, his cheeks sunken, his eyes encircled by darkness. With a handkerchief, he dabbed the weeping scabs around his mouth.

"Do I need to invite myself in?" A familiar, arrogant smile surfaced on his face, then his left eyebrow raised in question.

Catherine felt horrified when she finally recognised the stranger, "Jeremy Fisher?"

"At your obedient service, young lady." He bowed deeply, his head almost on his knees.

"What on earth are you doing here?"

"Your father is selling Petteril Bank House. Word got to me when I was back in Cheshire, so I offered to buy your home. I viewed the dwelling today. Compared to when I was there with you, our first acquaintance I do believe, the house is now in a bit of a sorry state. However, I have formally made a reasonable offer through my solicitor." He fidgeted his weight. "Are we going to stand here all evening?"

"Indeed we are, Jeremy. Our last meeting involved you drunkenly trying to force your way into my bedroom. You called me a bitch if I remember correctly, for declining your lecherous advances." A defiant stare formed on her face.

He laughed out loud, "Ah yes, the joys and perils of young love. Catherine, you always were intriguing. You were the one that got away. The only one resistant to my charms. To think we could have been blissfully married. What would it have been, eighteen years or so? We could have had children, little bambinos running around. With my brains, dashing good looks and money, and your insufferable piety, how conflicted they would have been."

"On behalf of my parents, I am most grateful for your generosity in offering to buy Petteril Bank House but for now I need you to leave." Her fingers were turning white as she held firmly to the door.

Shaking his head with a cheeky smile on his face he said, "Catherine. Catherine. Catherine. I can sense your anger. Indeed, I do believe your animosity towards me means you are still without the pleasures of intimacy. After all these years, still moody, still sexually frustrated."

"Goodbye, Jeremy!" Catherine tried to close the door, but he wedged the intricately carved cane he was holding into the door frame.

"What are you now, nearly forty years old and still a spinster of this parish?" He laughed as he shook his head. "Catherine, even after all these years you remain a mystery to me."

"Remove your cane from my front door, please!"

"Oh my, a sexual innuendo, perhaps?" A snort of humour escaped his nose. "For this evening, I'm staying at the godforsaken Lawson's Lodging House, but for what it is worth, I might as well be sleeping in a stable for they have straw on the floor." He tutted his disgust then put his top hat back on his head. He leaned in closer, "So you know where I am if you wish to

138

partake in carnal pleasures. Depravity, extreme euphoria, ecstasy, hedonism. Let yourself go, be free, you'll feel so liberated. It will help your mental health too." He winked.

Catherine could not think straight. Jeremy was constantly bombarding her with the pleasures of intercourse. His personality and behaviour had obviously not changed in all those years but physically he was a shadow of his former self. In 1844 he had been strong and commanding, yet now he appeared frail and gaunt. His hair and eyes once sparkled with vitality, now they were dull and grey.

Within a few minutes, he had once again insulted and offended her on so many levels yet the thing which hurt the most was the comment about her mental health. She really hoped her father had not betrayed her confidence.

Jeremy turned and limped down the path. He stopped to close the gate and blew her a kiss. The man was so bloody facetious, and within minutes he had also made her swear, even if it was only in her mind. The bloody arrogance of the man. He made her skin crawl, like an irritating rash she could not cure, a fever making her overheat with his nasty and patronising ... oh ... she slammed the door shut.

Fuming, she was just about to go and make a cup of tea, but she realised she had no fuel for the fire. Wine, ale, gin, she craved something stronger than tea to help her calm down. Never in her life had she been intoxicated. She had tried a few different tipples over the earlier years but always in polite company and never to excess. The tingling merriment of liquor she liked. The stupor she had witnessed in other people she disliked. This evening she needed the stupor, something to distract her from her thoughts. This day was certainly cursed.

Solomon, she closed her eyes and imagined his sweet face. He had a cheeky smile, but it was filled with love, with adoration and shyness. Then again, last night, this morning, he looked close to tears as he walked away after their heart-to-heart about her sufferings. Like Jeremy, he too had stood to close the gate but when he did, he stared longingly, lovingly but with such sadness in his heart. Was she his siren, luring him into dangerous seas, suffocating him in the depths of her depression, her delusions, her paranoia? Her honesty had maybe been a warning sign, the light in the darkness, keeping him at bay.

Desperate to see Solomon, she could not wait any longer even with the threat of strangers watching her every move. Doctor Wainwright had said in their therapy sessions she had to acknowledge, accept, analyse, action, advance. There was little point in worrying about something when she could quite easily face her worries and concerns by taking action and speaking with him.

With her newfound determination, she got herself ready, locked the front door, closed the gate behind her and marched up the hill to the Wheatsheaf Inn.

Chapter Twenty-Eight

The moon provided light to the dark streets below, creating silvery shades of grey. As Catherine climbed the hill in the direction of the Wheatsheaf Inn, a lone figure came round the corner and headed towards her. She put her head down, fearing conversation at this time of the evening but some inner instinct made her look up. Solomon stood there, watching her walk the last few steps until they met in the street. Fate had thankfully intervened.

With hearts racing, they chatted shyly about their day and Catherine enquired about any news on his father. Sadly, Shadrach was still missing but Solomon was thankful that there had been no further confrontations at his home.

He said, "I've managed to get a couple of hours off work as I wanted to see you."

Catherine's heart was exploding at the news and a smile emerged on her lips, "And I was hoping to see you, even if from the other side of the bar."

"We could go back in there as it's relatively quiet, if that's what you'd like, have a drink?"

After a few seconds pause, Catherine suggested, "Actually, now I'm here, I'd rather we had some privacy. I've been in the house all day. Maybe we could go to yours?" Her heart had spoken before her head had engaged. She was shocked by her own suggestion of being alone with him.

Solomon could not hide his surprise. With eyebrows raised he responded with a slightly too high a pitch, "Oh, of course!" His arm extended forward as if implying for her to turn around and head back down the hill.

Occasionally, the clouds obscured the moon, but the light was sufficient to navigate their way. Catherine watched Solomon open his front door and being a gentleman, he stepped aside and let her pass. Standing in the dark hallway, she waited for Solomon to light the lamp and then followed him into the living room. Catherine's body was alive with tingles, her breathing all haphazard, making her feel flushed and giddy.

"Sorry, I know you like tea but all I have is some milk or some ale. Shopping has been well down my list of priorities in the last couple of days." Solomon seemed awkward, as if lost, even though he was in his own home.

"Honestly, I'm fine thank you. I just wanted to see you, to discuss things from last night when I said where I'd been."

A quizzical look appeared on his face, "Where you've …" His voice tailed off, having remembered how they had parted. He had intended kissing her when he said something like, 'Where have you been all my life?' The lunatic asylum was not the answer he had been expecting to hear. A forced smile emerged on his face.

"I guess I wanted to chat with you, to gauge your reaction and know your thoughts. It was quite a revelation for you to hear. In fact, it was quite a revelation for me to admit." She pursed her lips and tried to breathe out calmly to settle her ever increasing nerves.

"I must admit, initially I did not know what to think or feel. I feel terrible for walking out, for leaving you alone, especially with my father having possibly been taken."

They stood there awkwardly like distant acquaintances, the moonlight and single oil lamp only a drop in the darkness. Catherine broke the silence, "I'm hoping we can still be friends."

Solomon removed his flat cap and threw it on the sofa. He ran his fingers through his hair. As he walked towards her, he slowly removed his heavy coat and flung it over the chair arm. Without saying a word, he continued walking towards her, his eyes never leaving hers. She felt unsure of the situation, wondering what was going through his mind. He stood in front of her, their noses almost touching. Her bonnet was tied under her chin. Solomon delicately pulled on one length of the pink ribbon, resulting in both ends falling away and hanging loosely down her beautiful pale neck and onto her bosom. Carefully, he lifted her bonnet away, revealing beautiful curls of auburn hair, allowing them to cascade over her shoulders. Catherine closed her eyes, finally breaking their visual bond as she inhaled deeply. A contented sigh escaped her moist lips as she felt his hands unbuttoning each delicate rosebud button on her coat. With tenderness, he slipped her coat from her shoulders and with a slow backwards extension of her arms, the coat slipped away, falling to a heap on the floor. Their eyes intense, their breathing heavy and synchronised, the alchemy between them palpable.

Noises outside, deep voices, they both turned to look out of the front bay window. Two men walked past, deep in conversation. Catherine could barely breathe, convinced one of the men was Jeremy Fisher. The moon was momentarily bright outside, a silver cane handle shimmered in the light. Within seconds they were out of sight and Catherine and Solomon turned to face each other once again.

Solomon smiled, "Where were we?"

With a slight clearance prior, Catherine found herself incapable of lying, "I do believe you were going to kiss me."

Her hair framed her face and Solomon gently took hold of one of the ringlets, wrapping the silky strands around his finger. With such adoration, his fingertips surveyed the warm contours of her skin, taking in her beauty, her perfection, her femininity. Her red and white dress was low cut, with off the shoulder detailing, revealing her toned shoulders and perfect cleavage. His fingertips continued to explore her soft skin, all the way down to the brooch placed centrally on her bodice, just above the line of her breasts.

Catherine finally managed to breathe and gasped at his touch. Unable to resist his loving embrace, she reciprocated by placing her hands on his chest. His muscles were defined, and she wondered how such strength could be so tender, creating tickles of pleasure through her body. Feeling confident, her hands explored further, spreading out to his shoulders, feeling the contours of each defined muscle bulk. Following the lines, her hands ran across his biceps and down to his wrists, culminating in them holding hands which quickly turned into a passionate hold.

Taking her by surprise, he started singing sweetly to her, creating beautiful musical tones. Solomon gently swayed his body and together they moved to his rhythm, easing the sensual tension. Unable to remember the next verse to his song, he mumbled and then sang a few silly words that rhymed. Catherine giggled, resulting in Solomon singing a fast, entertaining number and he swept her around the room. They were so happy, each of them smiling, enjoying the closeness, the intimacy and the friendship.

Dizzy with spinning, Catherine flung herself onto the sofa and landed disgracefully in a heap. Solomon pretended to be dizzy too and did the same silly flop onto the couch. They both laughed and sighed with contentment. Even though no words were spoken, they looked at each other and laughed again as they held hands on the seat.

Catherine made three attempts to get off the large soft sofa, needing to use momentum with legs in the air. Solomon placed his hands on her bottom to aid her ascent. They giggled like children.

Breathless with the frivolities, Catherine suddenly became serious, as if all the energy and magic they had created had disappeared with the forming mist. Solomon could not help but copy her solemnity. He sat forward on the sofa and with pleading eyes, looked up at her face, trying to read the sudden change. Worried, he stood from the sofa and held her hands, "Is everything all right, dear Catherine?"

Almost crying, she could barely speak, "Everything is wonderful, and I'm so scared of never feeling this way again." Her nervous smile squeezed her eyes, forcing tears to fall. Solomon lovingly wiped them away.

"Marry me, Catherine. Please make me the happiest and luckiest man alive in this entire world. I know we are newly acquainted but since the first time I saw you, I don't know, I cannot find the words, the right words, beautiful words, ecstatically happy words to describe the feelings I have for you." He wrapped his arms around her, and they embraced with such unconditional love. As they smiled at each other, Solomon grabbed her up into his arms, lifting her off the floor as if to show her he would protect and care for her, carrying her over any troubled waters. Catherine was aware she had not answered his question. Literally and figuratively, she was being swept off her feet. She wrapped her arms around his broad shoulders.

"Catherine, I love you, your beauty, you smell of spring flowers, your shiny hair, your energy, your kindness, your thoughtfulness, your craziness, your intrigue but what I love most of all is your cooking skills." They both laughed.

With a reversal of roles, Catherine had a cheeky and mischievous look on her face, "Solomon Smith, I think we need to continue this conversation in more comfortable surroundings." Her eyes looked up towards heaven.

In disbelief, Solomon clarified, "You want me to carry you up the stairs?"

Biting her lower lip in a nervous way, she was unaware of the emotional and physiological effects of how irresistibly alluring this small gesture was to Solomon. Barely perceptible, she nodded her head.

With a combination of total adoration and pure lust, Solomon leaned towards her, and their lips passionately embraced. Pulling apart, he asked once again, "Are you sure upstairs?" Now it was his turn to look up towards heaven, indicating his bedroom.

"I'm sure," nodded Catherine.

"Then I'm bloody ecstatic because my arms are aching." He pretended to walk as if he was carrying a baby elephant.

"You are in so much trouble, Mr Smith," laughed Catherine.

"I hope so, Miss Fawcett." With a wink, he then carried her up the stairs into the comforting darkness.

Chapter Twenty-Nine

Consumed by their earlier lovemaking, they lay breathless but content in each other's arms. Catherine's head rested perfectly in the contours of his muscular chest and shoulders. Solomon was tenderly stroking her hair when he suddenly panicked. He rolled her over like a felled log to free his arm, grabbed the clock on his bedside table and waited until his eyes adjusted to the dark. "Bloody hell! I was only supposed to be gone a couple of hours."

Rushing around the bedroom, trying to find his abandoned clothes in the waning light of the moon, he tripped up and lost his balance as he tried to put his trousers on in the dark. Catherine could only giggle at the sight. His body, so utterly perfect, muscular yet tender, she felt so … alive, happy, passionate. She also dared to admit to feeling desperate … for more.

"I'm so sorry to rush off like this but Mr Scrogg, he'll be livid."

"Don't worry, I'll see myself out. Go on, before it's too late." Catherine shooed him out of the room.

"But I don't want to leave you." He poured clean water into a bowl, washed his hands then splashed water over his face. "And you never answered my question."

"Hmm, now which question was that?" Catherine was enjoying the tease, knowing fine well what he was referring to.

"Tell me now, before I get fired."

"No."

"No? Is that the answer?" Solomon looked as if his world had come to an abrupt and disappointing end.

"I meant I'm not telling you now."

He sat on the end of the bed to put his boots on, "Tell me your answer now or I'll have to tickle you until you say yes."

With an air of nonchalance, she teased, "I like tickles."

"Right, that's it!" He pounced on the bed and started to tickle her, she squealed and screamed with sheer delight.

"I surrender, you win, the answer is yes!"

"Truly?" asked Solomon, breathless from all the fun.

"Yes, Solomon, I will marry you. I have known from the very first day that I love you, that I could happily spend eternity with you."

"I don't want to leave. I want to hold you in my arms, oh you have made me so very happy my darling wife to be."

"Go, before you get fired." Catherine winked at him. How content she felt in his company.

"Stay if you want, come to the Inn if you want, otherwise I will see you tomorrow, my love. Until then." Solomon reluctantly made his way over to the bedroom door then paused, "I truly cannot bear for us to be apart."

Catherine blew him a kiss. With a heavy heart, Solomon walked out of the door. She could hear his footsteps bounding down the stairs then the bang of the front door.

She smiled, laughed, then blushed as she recalled the fun they had had over the last two hours. She adored everything about him and did not want to leave his room, feeling close to him there. For a few more minutes she lay in his bed, still happily exhausted from their lovemaking.

Once dressed, she dared to explore his bedroom which was filled with books, newspapers, various quills and inks. His writing desk was laden with papers. Drawings too, sketches of flowers, landscapes, people.

One sketch stood out amongst the others. A portrait of a beautiful woman, slim, elegant, the feeling from the picture was of love, her eyes gently smiling, her lips peaceful, as if there was nothing left to say, content with everything. A presence oozed from her, as if her eyes were following, seeing, sensing, accepting. Catherine became uncomfortable, wondering who this mysterious young woman was who had captured his heart. Trying to place the papers and drawings as she found them, she gathered the rest of her things and despite her hair being a mess, she placed her bonnet and was ready to leave.

Solomon had left her his father's key to lock the door behind her. As she walked down the small path to the gate, she saw two men walking down the hill towards her. Her heart nearly stopped beating when she realised it was Jeremy Fisher heading towards the Lawson's Lodging House. She had nowhere to hide.

"Well, well, well, Catherine Fawcett, out at this time of night." Jeremy raised his lantern to her face. "Why, I do believe you have the undeniable flush of fornication." He sniffed the air. His mocking laugh commenced, "And the scent of intimacy." He looked towards his companion and winked.

The friend eyed Catherine up and down, "Such a sweet delicacy, I can understand anyone wanting to feast at this table." He bowed as if his words were a beautiful compliment. His blond curls climbed like ivy over the brim of his top hat.

"We will escort you back to your home," said Jeremy.

Not wanting to engage in conversation, Catherine ignored their inappropriate taunts and tried to walk gracefully so as not to show her fear. The men followed her at an uncomfortably close distance, their shoes crunching the loose grit underfoot, Jeremy's cane stabbing the ground with purpose. Her chest was heaving with angst.

"Is she a lady of the night, Jeremy?" enquired the friend, making no attempt to whisper or disguise his question.

Jeremy laughed, "If this was the case I would sincerely die from shock."

"You know her well?" asked the friend.

"I presumed I did. We were to be married, I forget when, but alas her frigid ways were not palatable to my diverse tastes."

"She seems to have gotten her just desserts now." The men laughed.

"I believe the lunatic asylum has been her abode for the past year. On the breaking of our union, she spiralled into a miserable existence and her family lost everything in the aftermath."

"How bothersome, to lose such an influential husband, high society, and all that."

The two men gossiped about her all the way, so Catherine was relieved when she reached the sanctuary of her home. As she opened the gate, she wanted to explode at them and shout like an old fish wife, but she refrained. Instead, she turned and with dignity said, "I volunteered at the House of Recovery, a hospital for contagious diseases, dealing with yellow pus-filled wounds, green phlegm, red skin rashes and black buboes. Jeremy, by your walk, your stance, your gaunt face and your scabby mouth, I would diagnose you have syphilis and have been taking mercury as the cure. This has fuddled your miniscule brain, leading to profound and untreatable stupidity. The only cure for the severity of your ailments is complete isolation from society, so you cannot sprout and spread your vile vitriol to innocent and vulnerable victims of your depraved ways."

With an ethereal grace, she floated down the garden path and unlocked the front door. Oozing regal superiority, she turned around and stood there for a moment to revel in the glory of shocked faces. "Thank you for escorting me home, after I have had a most pleasurable evening with my fiancé, but now I must bid you goodnight." A minimal wave with the back of her hand preceded a shrug of her right shoulder before she stuck out her tongue and slammed the door.

Jeremy forced a laugh but inside he was fuming, pondering on how a lunatic could know the pain he was suffering.

Chapter Thirty

Lying on her right side, with the various sheets and blankets tucked under her chin for warmth, Catherine had gone from experiencing sheer bliss with Solomon to feeling sheer hatred for Jeremy. If only he would somehow accidently strangle himself with his long hair. His snidey comments, time after time trying to humiliate her, as if he took pleasure in goading her and winding her up so tightly until her mechanism broke.

With a huff, she rolled over in bed. Her father then became the focus of her anger. How dare he tell Jeremy of her predicament, that she had been incarcerated in a lunatic asylum for nearly a year. Maybe it was to gain the pity vote so Jeremy would sign the deal for the purchase of Petteril Bank House. Whatever the reason, it was unforgivable that her father would reveal such personal information about her to Jeremy Fisher of all people.

She tried to think of Solomon and the fun, the laughter, the intimacy, the all-consuming passion that had evolved and overwhelmed them both. She smiled, trying to re-create the wonderful feelings but then all the vitriol from Jeremy, the taunting, the jibes, oh how she hated him.

Desperate to distract herself from her thoughts and to make herself sleepy, she went downstairs to retrieve a few books off the shelves then made her way back upstairs to bed. She skimmed through the pages finding snippets of potentially useful information, and made mental notes.

The reasons were unclear as to why the Roman Empire decided to build Hadrian's Wall where they did. One suggestion was the barbarians further north had stopped their progress, so this really was as far as they could go. The theory sounded plausible until one questioned how simple tribes with little weaponry or armour were able to fight off elite Roman soldiers.

Another possibility was the Romans found nothing of interest further north, but scholars had questioned why the Romans would go to such extreme lengths of conquering foreign lands to suddenly stop. Why not explore the fertile lands and discover more precious metals and minerals in the wild and rugged hills?

A different argument put forward was the wall was built to act as a trading post to control the movement of goods as a way of raising taxes. Even without reading the explanations, Catherine knew in her heart this was not the reason why the wall had been built over a thousand years ago. None of the stories quite rang true. To go to extraordinary lengths to build a stone wall, extreme both in height and width, just to trade some grains with Neanderthals. There had to be another reason why they chose this particular area.

The next book was about William the Conqueror. Victorious against King Harold's army in the Battle of Hastings in 1066, the then Duke of Normandy declared himself King of England and was crowned on Christmas Day. Plagued by threats from foreign invaders, in 1086 he requested a list of all the English territories he owned. The list became known as the Domesday Book. Carlisle was the only English city not to be included in the list. Some scholars thought the omission of Carlisle from the Domesday Book was simply an error, with the writers believing Carlisle was in Scotland. Other evidence pointed to the fact that Carlisle was under the control of a local warlord named Dolfin and belonged to neither territory. Whatever the reason, whether a deliberate or foolish omission, Carlisle was not included in the book. William the Conqueror then sent his son, William Rufus, to the Anglo-Scottish border to investigate the city. William Rufus, so called for his ruddy complexion and red hair, claimed Carlisle for his father and commissioned the building of the castle to protect the city. William Rufus became King William II on his father's death.

The next few books detailed the history of various kings and queens of England. In the early 1300s, King Edward I briefly made Carlisle the seat of Parliament. He died near Hadrian's Wall and the fort of Aballava.

In 1482, just before being crowned King Richard III, the then Duke of Gloucester was appointed Warden of the Western March and resided in Carlisle Castle. His role as Lord Warden was to secure the border between England and Scotland and conserve the truce between the opposing countries.

During the House of Tudor, King Henry VIII fortified Carlisle's defences, strengthening the castle, the medieval walls and the citadel towers to the south. Academics had questioned why the south would be fortified when all other historical fortifications were always to the north. Some historians interjected that the south was fortified when Henry VIII denounced the Catholic Throne, to stop any potential threats from the Catholics further south, for example from Spain, France or Italy.

None of the information she had read made sense, for Kings of England to go to such expense and extreme lengths to protect a tiny city of very little importance. According to the book, Carlisle's population was around two thousand at the time of Henry VIII's reign.

Reading was not making her sleepy. In fact, she was fascinated by the history, and she wanted to keep researching the evidence, to try and piece together the reasons why Carlisle and the hidden village of Edenvale were so important.

Just after one in the morning, there were gentle knocks on the front door. Catherine initially froze, wondering if an inebriated and angry Jeremy had come back to taunt her. Then she remembered how Jeremy had knocked on the door, as if he was demanding the immediate payment of a debt. She concluded it must be Solomon. She tiptoed out of bed and peeked out of the bedroom window. Solomon was standing back from the door and looking up at her, he waved.

Catherine skipped down the stairs and opened the door. An aroma of stale ale and smoke tickled her sense of smell, but she did not care. They lovingly embraced, as if centuries of time had separated them.

In silence, Catherine took hold of his hand and led the way upstairs. Warmth still lingered in the bed sheets but having been outside, Solomon's hands and feet were so cold that Catherine was squealing by his touch. The chill soon dissipated by their antics.

Lying in the hook of his arm, her head on his chest, Catherine enquired about his father but there was still no news. Over the last few days, Catherine had refrained from telling Solomon about *The Story* for she did not know if she should trust him, but with everything that had happened over the last few hours, she felt it appropriate to confide in him.

She sat up and turned to search the pile of books on her bedside table. She retrieved *The Story* and showed Solomon some of the more important diary entries. He could barely form any words as he read the last few pages.

Catherine suggested, "I think Sam was taken to, for being too nosy, investigating something relating to this Order of the Priory."

"Like I've said, my dad would never have upped and left without saying anything. I think he was taken too, for asking questions about things he had seen in that notebook."

"So, if that's true, who has taken him, the Order of the Priory? I'm thinking they are linked with Oak Bank Hall. There are numerous people coming and going, day and night, it all seems very secretive."

Solomon flicked through the diary, "Yeah, seems a bit strange, doesn't it? I reckon if we can find Sam, we will find my dad."

"I've been doing some other research. The numerous books downstairs, I'm not sure if they were left by Sam or already there. *The Story* was hidden amongst them. Carlisle has been an important city since the Roman Empire. Now, as much as I love Carlisle, and will not hear a bad word said against it, it just does not seem the type of place to be so interesting to the Romans and Kings of England, yet history seems to suggest otherwise." She gave him a general overview of the research she had undertaken.

"There's got to be something more." He passed her the diary to place on the pile of books on the bedside table.

"*The Story* mentioned the solicitors in Carlisle. Maybe we should try there?" suggested Catherine.

"I don't start work until one tomorrow so we could go in the morning if you'd like?"

"But how would we get there?"

"Leave that to me." He rolled over and propped himself up on his elbow and gazed adoringly into his future wife's eyes. Their passion was palpable, breathless for each other, sensitive areas tingling with anticipation. Catherine turned to blow out the flame, but Solomon was insistent, "Let the candle flicker. I want to see you. I need to see you, for I adore everything about you"

Chapter Thirty-One

Waking up together felt wonderful yet weird. They barely knew each other but the feelings they had for each other were immense. Last night, their love making had been gentle and loving, passionate and frantic, taking the time to enjoy each other in so many ways. Yet this morning, with the sun's rays penetrating through the curtains, Solomon asked about her scars.

"They were ... erm ... hmm ... when I was not myself, at home, locked in my room, I started to hurt myself, torture myself, trying to physically feel the pain, show evidence of the scars that were inside me." Catherine's breathing was erratic, echoing her thoughts.

Gently running his fingertips over the raised lesions, like horizontal train tracks over her tummy and thighs, he wiggled down the bed and kissed her tenderly over the larger indented scar just above her hip bone. With mixed feelings, Catherine allowed him to explore the marks she had hidden from the world for so many years.

Solomon kissed his way back up her body and finished with a lingering kiss on her lips. "Catherine Fawcett, I hope you are healing inside."

"Solomon Smith, your medicine needs to be administered daily."

"I will always be here for you, don't ever hide away, never suffer on your own, to do this, I can't imagine how hurt you were inside. I will heal your wounds and together we will be stronger."

Content, Catherine allowed herself to dream of a future filled with peace and tranquillity.

As the clock approached eight, they forced themselves out of bed. All the menial chores of getting washed, dressed and making food somehow seemed magical today, as if fun could be found in anything when sharing the task with the person you love.

"Why don't we go and see the vicar and book a date for the wedding," suggested Solomon.

On hearing this suggestion, Catherine nearly choked on her shocked inhale. With her coughing bout settling, she asked, "Why the hurry? I'm happy, I'm loving this, spending time with you, getting to know you, I don't want to spoil anything."

"I know, but I cannot explain it, the thought of losing you, I want you to be mine."

Clouds started to form in her head. The warm glow was changing to laden grey. "I've been honest with you, but not entirely."

This remark tweaked his interest, with a subtle straightening of his posture.

"I may have been discharged from the asylum to live here, but not completely discharged from their care. I am under a review process. I am to write to my doctor with my progress, my worries, my concerns, my happiness and my wellbeing. If I can prove to the doctor that I can live an independent and safe life, then I will be free."

"But you are well, you are wonderful, you are saner than me."

"I feel well, at least I think I am, but I do not want to rush into anything. Partly to protect me, but I'm thinking more about you. I do not want you to be lumbered with some madwoman, for if there is any chance of my sanity deteriorating to the depths I was in before, I do not want to burden you with my troubles." Catherine looked out of the window to try and distract herself from negative thoughts. Solomon did not deserve to be saddled with her past or her secrets. She toyed with the notion of cooling things off, to protect and distance him from her bad luck. She had told him nearly everything. If they were to be married, she would need to confess her two darkest secrets before they made their vows in front of God. She prayed that Solomon would not judge her as malicious or evil. Her thoughts were interrupted by Solomon.

"Then how about we go to this solicitor's place in Carlisle? Heady, Teddy and Footy or whatever it was called."

"Hodder, Stretton and Puddifoot, but how will we get there though? As far as I am aware, we are too far away to walk from here into Carlisle."

He leaned forward and raised an eyebrow, "Can you ride a horse?" Catherine shook her head. "Then we pinch one horse and ride into town together." A cheeky wink sealed the deal.

"From whom?"

"The Dawson's farm, they'll never know."

"No, we couldn't possibly—"

"Stop there, we can, and we will."

"Solomon, I really do not have the words to describe you. You are leading me astray and I'm loving it." Catherine blew him a kiss across the table.

They were soon out of the house and walking up the road towards the Wheatsheaf Inn. Solomon had instructed her to walk on ahead, past the road works and he would divert around the back, over the fields to fetch a horse.

Catherine strode confidently past the workmen, noting the landmarks she had set and finding that very little work had been achieved. "Morning!" she shouted so the workmen could hear.

"Morning, miss, you off somewhere nice?"

"Just a brisk stroll."

"There's not much of any interest down there and it's miles to the nearest village."

"Yes, I know, I just need a good long walk and make the most of this beautiful, sunny day."

"Take care then, miss."

Catherine continued to stride with confidence. This feeling, this strength, this naughtiness, all those years of denial, the limits of pride, virtue, the opinion of others, morals. How utterly boring and droll. As planned, she walked out of sight and sat on a large boulder by the wayside. Not a soul could be seen.

A while later, she heard a galloping horse. She stood from the cold, grey stone and instead stepped on its height. Solomon slowed the horse to a canter then stopped in front of Catherine.

"I am here to rescue you, my princess." Solomon beamed from his brown steed.

"I beg your pardon, but I am no damsel in distress. I am a mighty warrior, on a mission to steal a horse and flirt with a handsome stranger until he is under my spell." Her cool, blue eyes were mesmerising, as if she truly wanted to exert her magical powers over him.

"I have stolen the horse as you commanded."

With a perfectly serious expression, Catherine said, "Then I shall mount the beast between your legs."

Solomon's eyes nearly popped out, "Well, I don't know how to respond to that comment."

They both laughed.

Catherine's first few attempts to mount their swag were hilarious. Solomon's stomach was aching as he suppressed the urge to laugh. She had as much grace as a sack of coal being thrown on the back of a cart. A rug on a washing line waiting to be beaten was his next description. On one attempt, she nearly dived headfirst over the other side, but ever the gentleman, he persevered in helping her mount the horse. Having stolen their ride, the horse was neither saddled nor bridled but thankfully Solomon was an experienced rider. He wrapped his arms around her and held onto the horse's dark brown mane.

154

"Gently squeeze the horse with your inner thighs so you don't fall off. This will not hurt the horse, if anything, the horse will feel better with a weight that moves fluidly with him, rather than against him." Catherine nodded, a discreet tremor to her respiration.

The journey started with a gentle walk to Cumwhinton village and with increased confidence the horse and riders coped with a trot.

As they turned right and headed towards Carlisle, Catherine panicked as the asylum came into view. Whether it was her instability or paranoia, she doubted Solomon's integrity. He was escorting her back to the asylum. He was the unknown conspirator, feeding information to the board members. They had obviously requested her return to the asylum, for being a loose woman and sleeping with a man out of wedlock. His arms were wrapped around her, guiding the horse. She had no means to escape. He had lied to her, betrayed her, used her. Tears were about to fall.

The stone walls of the asylum were ever closer as the horse cantered down the track. She closed her eyes and heard the cawing of the crows nesting in the bony trees. She squeezed her eyes tightly, her face distorting as she tried to block out the memory of the screams.

The horse was slowing down, the soporific clip-clopping was inducing a state of drowsiness, making her feel as limp as a rag doll. Briefly, she wondered if Solomon had medicated her morning tea, a little something to dull her senses, make her more compliant. Time was slipping away; she was waiting for the moment when everything stopped, and her life changed forever.

Solomon was saying something, she could hear muffled sounds, a question perhaps. Mustering all her strength, she opened her eyes. Disorientated, she wondered where she was, as memories of her past life flickered by. London Road, so close to her family estate at Petteril Bank. Gallow's Hill, a site for public hangings leading to thoughts of her Sam. His sweet face, so gentle, but so serious, he was caring, thoughtful, kind but ...

The asylum was not one of those memories. They had cantered past the mental institution. Those cold, stone walls were now behind them as they headed towards the centre of Carlisle. She scolded herself for doubting Solomon's sincerity and prayed for God's forgiveness. Even now, there were times when she doubted her sanity, paranoid about people's intentions, hidden agendas, their secrets and lies.

She squeezed his strong and protective arms. A contented smile formed on her lips, thankful for finding love once again, a different kind of love, a happy, funny love. Someone she could trust.

The horse trotted up Botchergate towards the town centre. It had been nearly twenty years since Catherine had seen Christchurch, the shops and the banks. Coming into view were the large defensive citadel towers fortified by Henry VIII to strengthen the south side of the city from attack.

As she looked to her left, the House of Recovery had been razed to the ground to make way for the train station. She sighed, wondering how different her life may have been were it not for that fateful night down Collier Lane and the murder.

On her right was the crescent row of grand terraced houses and they spotted the sign for Hodder, Stretton and Puddifoot. They dismounted and left the horse in front of the east tower of the citadel. Breathless with the unknown, Catherine and Solomon crossed the busy street, avoiding the steaming manure, rickety carts and grand carriages.

As they opened the door to the solicitors' office, a seated woman at a desk raised her head to look at them. "Good morning, how may I help you?"

Catherine had prepared many approaches to the questions she wanted answered. At the time, they had sounded appropriate in her head but standing there now, she did not know what to say and she really did not want to lie.

"I am hoping you can solve a mystery as to the whereabouts of a person we know." Solomon had said the last person to have stayed in Rose Cottage was a man, so they took a gamble on Sam being male.

"Of course, I will do my best to help you, but I cannot breach the confidentially of any of our distinguished clients." The lady was petite, with tightly pulled back hair which seemed to take up the looseness of her skin.

"He lived, or was staying I suppose, in Rose Cottage, Edenvale. He wrote in his journal that he had given you information, a book I believe, with personal research he had been undertaking." Catherine knew she appeared shifty.

The woman hesitated for a few seconds and eyed them both from top to bottom. She forced a helpful smile onto her face, "And the gentleman's name?" She cocked her head to the side whilst waiting for the answer.

"Sam," said Catherine.

The woman dipped her quill into the ink and wrote Sam on the paper, "And his surname?"

The pause was uncomfortable. Solomon chipped in, "He had a bushy beard and wore a monocle."

The woman put down her quill, "Are you actually acquainted with this gentleman?"

Solomon continued, "He was staying in the village and was a neighbour of mine and then he suddenly disappeared. He left this journal, saying to contact yourselves should anything happen to him."

Catherine got *The Story* from her bag and opened the page at the solicitors' address and then showed the woman the last entry.

"May I have a closer look?" asked the woman. Reluctantly, Catherine passed her the book. The woman studied the cover. She flicked through the pages inspecting the content, the pictures and the writing. With a raised eyebrow, she seemed to notice the change from the beautifully written words to the scribbled notes at the end, the blotches, the mess, with Sam writing his name on the angle.

The woman opened a drawer on her right side and pulled out a large ledger, with neatly written names and addresses. She perused the list. "And you have no other information on this gentleman?"

"I saw him around the village regularly at first. I assumed he liked walking as he was always out and about. Then he rarely left the cottage. From *The Story*, we now realise he was not well and was confined to the house. I kind of forgot about him then, out of sight, out of mind kinda thing. Then one day, I realised the house was empty and then Catherine moved in about a month ago."

"Why do you doubt that he did not leave of his own accord?"

Catherine answered the question, "There were no personal belongings as such, but his books were left on the shelf. He had made notes in a few of them and underlined some of the information." Catherine did not want to give too much away. Maybe she had already admitted too much, and this woman would demand the man's books be returned to them. "He seemed interested in Carlisle's history." Trying to justify things was creating more questions rather than closing the topic. She tried not to expand on what she knew.

For a few moments, no one spoke. The sparrow like woman trolled through the numerous clients in her ledger but then, whilst keeping her lips tightly closed, she lowered her jaw which sucked in her cheeks, giving her a very pompous appearance.

With a patronising tone she stated, "I believe I have found your missing person, living at the said address."

"He stated in the book you hold details of the research he had been undertaking. Will you be able to help us by sharing this information?" asked Catherine.

"For now, I can assist you no more. I will discuss this with the partners of this establishment and will try and locate Mr ..." she hesitated, aware she was just about to reveal the surname.

"Thank you so much. If we come back tomorrow, could we maybe have more information or at least look at the research?" asked Solomon.

The woman extended her lips which made her look more like a duck, "I do not think so. Our client's information is strictly—"

Solomon interrupted, "Please, my father and two other vill—"

Now it was Catherine's turn to interrupt as she did not want Solomon revealing more details.

He obviously realised her concerns by the change in his countenance. He grabbed Catherine's hand and led her to the door as he whispered, "We are wasting our time here."

"Thank you!" shouted Catherine as she was being dragged out of the door.

By now, Solomon was fuming, "She was never going to give us information, and we cannot blame her, she is only doing her job."

"It is not worth getting het up over some stranger. We still have information, the notes in his books, his—"

Interrupting, Solomon said, "But this is about my dad, people disappearing, possibly being murdered if the Greek bloke's death wasn't suicide. I need to know what is happening."

He dragged Catherine across the road by the hand. The horse they had stolen was happily chewing on some grass, so they headed further into town.

"I will apologise for what I am about to say. You must think me awful, some kind of petty thief but my dad, he was my world, *is* my world. Until you came along, he was my everything. And if I need to go the ends of the world to find him, I will."

Catherine laid her hand on his arm and felt the tension in his muscles. "Why do you have to apologise for loving your dad?"

"I wasn't apologising for that. I am apologising for what I have done and am about to do."

The lines deepened on Catherine's forehead.

"You must think I'm some sort of petty criminal, some lowlife scum from the middens. I can assure you it is purely through desperation."

"But what specifically do you need to apologise about?"

"Pinching the horse, breaking down that door at the priory gatehouse, breaking into the solicitors' office."

Catherine looked around, nobody was close enough to hear their conversation but still, she started to whisper, "You are going to steal the man's file?"

"When that scrawny woman was looking through the ledger on her desk, she paused at the name Samson Cohen. One way or another, I will break into that office this evening and retrieve that file."

"But they will know it was us. She has too much information."

"Yes, I thought about that, but she does not know our names."

"Yes, but she knows I'm living in Rose Cottage."

Solomon paused for a moment, then heaved a sigh of frustration. "Then we need to get someone else to do it for us, whilst we have tight alibis. You need to be with someone this evening and I will go to work as usual."

"Solomon, you are crazy, and I think that is one of the many reasons why I love you." After glancing around, he pulled her down Packhorse Lane and passionately kissed her. Being naughty felt amazing.

Chapter Thirty-Two

Catherine and Solomon arrived back in Edenvale just before midday. Ravenous, they headed to Solomon's house. He insisted Catherine sit down whilst he prepared some buttered potatoes and bags o' mysteries bought fresh from Mrs Dawson's shop.

When in Carlisle, Solomon had called in to see some of his friends on which he could call a few favours. Catherine deliberately did not go, so as not to be associated in any way to these people: ignorance more convincing than lies. He told her that she needed to arrange an alibi for this evening. She assured Solomon that she would figure something out but would not divulge her plans, so if questioned, he would not need to lie either.

In a rush for Solomon to get to work on time, they devoured their lunch and quickly tidied up. Solomon locked up the house and walked Catherine to her door. They discreetly blew each other a kiss, and off he ran around the corner to the Inn.

Catherine sighed with bliss, as if she was making up for the eighteen years she had lost to the sadness, isolation and darkness. In a daydream, she fumbled in her bag looking for her front door key when she heard animated voices from next door. People were obviously still living there.

Reluctant to stay inside on such a still day and wanting to be seen out and about by as many people as possible, she gathered a few items from the cupboard under the stairs with the intention of sweeping the path, cleaning the windows and tidying the garden. She even contemplated polishing the front doorstep and windowsill.

Edenvale had always seemed so quiet, with hardly a soul wandering, but with being out in the garden, she had seen a few more villagers pottering around and a few even stopped to say, 'Hello,' complementing her on how tidy the garden looked.

The effort had been worthwhile but now she was beginning to tire. Her clothes were filthy, her knees and back were aching, and her hair was falling from its ties. There was one strand which was particularly annoying and with having dirty hands, she did not want to touch the rebel curl, so she kept blowing it away with the side of her mouth.

Standing in the garden admiring her hard work, the paved path was no longer overgrown, the weeds between the shrubs had been removed, the collection of fallen leaves and dead twigs were now in a neat pile and the door and window frames were spotless. The neighbour's front door opened diverting her attention. Jeremy Fisher stepped over the threshold. Catherine was astonished to see him next door and tried to fathom a reason for his visit. He was supposedly in the Carlisle area to purchase Petteril Bank House and in Edenvale to see her, so why was he visiting her neighbour? Was he fishing for information? He was saying his goodbyes to Felicity and Jonathan then flinched when he saw Catherine standing there.

"Hello!" he said, his tone a little too high.

Felicity briefly poked her head around the door. With stunning copper hair, fair skin and rosy cheeks, she smiled at Catherine, said goodbye to Jeremy, then closed the door on him.

Sheepishly, he grinned at Catherine and with a handkerchief wiped some drool from his mouth. "Can we talk?"

"If we must but not here though, somewhere public."

"Why don't you escort me over to Oak Bank Hall? I was just on my way over there."

Her heart momentarily faltered. Oak Bank Hall had been a mystery and she was desperate to know what went on there. "I thought you were staying at the Lawson's Lodging House?"

"A better description would be the Lodging Sty or Stable. Oak Bank did not receive my letter in time and my unexpected arrival was most unfortunate as all the rooms were taken. So, will you be joining me, or must I beg?"

"I would love to join you but ..." she looked down at her filthy attire. "Would you allow me the hour to change and freshen up? As you can see, I've been busy tending to the garden."

Astonished that she would even give him the time of day without any sort of sarcastic or caustic comment, he genuinely smiled, "Then I shall inform Schubert of your soon to be presence and he can prepare us some drinks. What is your fancy, wine perhaps?"

"How very considerate of you. I would indeed like to partake in a drink. Not wine though, surprise me with something more exotic."

"Splendid, sounds divine. I shall indeed look forward to our rendezvous." He tipped his top hat and limped over to the hall.

Once inside the cottage, she leaned back against the front door and questioned her sanity. This was sheer madness. She was jeopardizing her future with the possibility of being deemed a mad woman by this frivolous,

161

adventure-seeking stranger she was becoming. However, no matter how hard she tried to resist, she was being dragged along by the turbulent current. She needed an alibi, she needed to be seen by a variety of people, to corroborate her story if required.

Forty minutes later she was fresh and smelling like flowers. She wore an old but still refined blue and white dress which she could put on independently with a struggle.

With her teeth chattering nervously, she skirted around the edges of the green and had a quick look across to the Kavanagh's house. There were no obvious signs of habitation.

The impacted dirt road became a gravel path when she reached the grounds of Oak Bank Hall. As she approached the stone steps, the front door magically opened. Mr Schubert greeted her with a smile, "Miss Fawcett, please do come in."

"Thank you. I am hoping you are expecting me." Out of politeness, she maintained her focus on the gentleman because what she really wanted to do was look around for clues. *The Story* had mentioned the goings on at Oak Bank Hall, the Order of the Priory and the Twentieth Legion. She desperately wanted to search for information but did not want to appear too obvious too soon. She had imagined Oak Bank Hall being the headquarters of some sort of religious sect or cult.

Mr Schubert led her down the hallway and into a drawing room. With dark wood panelling and furniture inlaid with red leather, the space felt oppressive. Everything else was in shades of gold. Strong, bold designs with masculine lines, no softness, only hard edges. Jeremy was bathing in the sliver of light coming in from a large window. He stood on seeing her enter the room. Mr Schubert bowed and closed the door behind him, leaving them alone.

Awkwardly, Catherine sat down as indicated by Jeremy. With a roguish smile he said, "I'm pleased you kept your promise this time."

"I have questions which I would like answered," she replied with a new-found confidence.

His eyes never leaving hers, Jeremy picked up a large tumbler glass containing a golden-brown liquid of perhaps brandy or whiskey and gulped a large quantity. There was a knock at the door. Mr Schubert walked inside on Jeremy's command, carrying a silver tray laden with two crystal glasses and two decanters. "Your drinks, sir, miss."

"Thank you, Schubert. Please do not disturb us from now on unless you are called."

"Very good, sir." Schubert bowed and left the room.

Jeremy lifted the crystal stopper from the decanter and inhaled deeply, taking in the aroma of the red liquid within. His eyes opened wide, and his throat tickled with the strong scent. He poured the concoction into the glasses and offered Catherine the drink. He raised his glass in the air, "To civility amongst enemies and friends."

"To civility." She stared provocatively. "Now please can we drink, I'm desperately thirsty after my gardening efforts."

Jeremy was impressed and each drank from their glasses.

The strength of the concoction made Catherine catch her breath, "Wow, my head is spinning already." She finished the sentence with a cough.

"Indeed, now you shall understand how you have made me feel these passing years." He lounged back in his large comfy armchair, "You were always a tease." He stared as if he was trying to penetrate the depths of her soul.

With a coarse voice she asked, "Shall I start with the interrogation?"

Jeremy raised his arm with an upward palm, "The floor is yours, but please be kind, I am at your mercy." A smirk formed on his lips.

"Why are you really here? In Carlisle, in Edenvale, in Oak Bank Hall?" Catherine also reclined into her chair, feeling a little faint with the concoction's after-effects.

"Carlisle, because of your father and the sale of Petteril Bank House. In Edenvale because I wanted to see you." His smouldering eyes were trying to hypnotise her, the stares, the slowness, channelling some sort of power over her.

"And Oak Bank?"

"Simple, I own this hall."

Catherine took a sharp intake of breath, "You own Oak Bank? How? Why?"

He leaned forward to fetch his glass, "I built the hall a few years ago. You knew I wanted to be an architect and have travelled the world studying architecture and design."

"But why here?" Catherine sipped from her glass, trying not to cough as she swallowed the warming fluid.

"For a short time, the railway viaduct here over the River Eden was renowned amongst architects and civil engineers for being the largest viaduct in the world. Dixon's chimney is currently the tallest chimney in all of Europe at 305 feet and I should know as I worked on the project with Tattersall, an amazing architect from Manchester. My dear friend Worthington, another architect from Manchester, won the commission for building the church at the lunatic asylum. I worked with him too. I have many reasons for being here. Including seeing my son."

Catherine's eyes would have fallen out if they were not wedged in place, "Hold on! There are too many tangents for me to follow." She took a breath, "Let's finish what we started with, architecture, so you built Oak Bank Hall and are you also saying you helped build the church at the asylum in Carlisle?"

He nodded. "And that is how I came across you."

"Jeremy, this is all too much to absorb. I do not know which line of questioning to take. I want to know everything yet somehow; I know I would be happier in the shadows of ignorant bliss." She took another mouthful of the red liquid and coughed at its strength. "Tell me about your son, although I think I may have already guessed."

"Jonathan, next door to you. He is my son."

"And his mother, you and her?"

Jeremy laughed, "Felicity. Enemies, friends, old acquaintances, I seem to have this effect on people, they either adore me or loathe me with seemingly equal measures. I cannot understand why people don't fall for my dazzling charms." He interlocked his fingers and rested his chin on the bridged support, as if waiting for her reply.

"And you said something like, 'You came across me,' what did you mean?"

"As you probably know, the asylum's church was not quite ready when they opened the doors to the lunatics. I was working with Worthington on the finer details of the interior when I saw you working in the fields one day."

The concoction she had been consuming threatened to resurface, so she swallowed hard to keep the bad taste away, "My father did not tell you about my incarceration?"

"Good Lord, no. He admitted to his financial difficulties but did not mention your personal predicament."

"I feel terrible now. I thought he had given away my secrets, telling you about my troubles, as maybe some sort of perverse way of making you feel sorry for us, to buy our home."

"Your father is many things, but he utterly adores you, he would fight for you, die for you. He never betrayed your confidence." Jeremy made a little pyramid with his fingers and tapped them together as if in contemplation.

There were so many questions. Catherine asked, "So, what happened then?"

"With your father?"

"No, after you saw me at the asylum." She sighed with a combination of frustration and confusion.

Jeremy could see Catherine was overwhelmed by the numerous convoluted pathways, so he started from the beginning.

His interest in Carlisle resulted from his arranged marriage to Catherine, when their fathers had arranged their first acquaintance back in 1844. In preparation for a wedded future, Jeremy had sourced business contacts and furthered liaisons with architects in the whole of the Northwest region of

England, with a view to making some sort of compromise with regards to his wish to explore the many wonders of the world but still fulfilling his own needs and earning an income. After Catherine called the wedding off, Jeremy had continued with his grand ideas. With considerable wealth and an already impressive property portfolio, he set out on a quest to become a Duke or Lord of Cumberland, just without the official title. His desire was to own as much land as he could. Cities like Manchester, Liverpool and Chester were already competitive, but the northern counties such as Cumberland and Westmorland were collections of sleepy, little villages with cheap land prices but had swathes of potential due to their natural beauty, mountainous landscapes, barren locations and wild coastline.

He bought vast quantities of land, from Keswick to Carlisle, and in collaboration with his architect friends and business associates, they set out on a quest to create architecturally different homes, set in pretty villages, with beautiful views.

For Jeremy, it was not about wealth, he already had countless bags of the stuff, it was about prestige and respect, the fame of being a renowned architect, but more than that, he wanted to be some sort of impresario of the architectural world, an entertainer of life, an entrepreneur to promote beauty in nature and design. He wanted to relish in admiration and glory.

To allow Catherine time to take in all the information, Jeremy rang a bell and Schubert soon appeared with the silver tray, this time laden with appetizers to nibble on and a decanter filled with a yellow concoction. Jeremy topped up Catherine's glass, the fluid turning the red remains into a fiery setting sun of which shepherds would be delighted. He continued with his story.

Jeremy admitted to owning most of the property around Edenvale and this included Rose and Bluebell Cottages, now occupied by Catherine, Felicity and Jonathan.

Felicity was originally from Liverpool, the fourth daughter of a poor man who queued for daily employment down by the docks. Her life had been in essence murky shades of brown, from the hand-me-down clothes she wore, to the food she ate, and to the filthy items her father retrieved from the Mersey. Despite her dire situation, Jeremy had been mesmerised by her innocence and beauty. He needed to know her secret, in where to find so much joy and happiness whilst living in abject poverty.

In disbelief that such a handsome and wealthy man such as Jeremy would seek pleasure in her company, she had quickly fallen for his charms and their clandestine liaisons had led to the birth of Jonathan. The scandal of an unmarried mother and illegitimate son made Jeremy move them to a house on the outskirts of Chester. Jeremy was not directly involved in their lives, but he ensured they were catered for financially. Sadly, it soon became apparent that the boy had deformities and was an imbecile.

Jeremy had continued with his building work in Edenvale and when Bluebell Cottage was ready, Felicity and Jonathan had moved in. The boy was now sixteen and no longer allowed to board at the school, but he still had his challenges to live a normal life.

"Catherine, what you said to me yesterday, about syphilis, was like being knifed in the chest. I felt blood pooling in the pit of my stomach, congealing into a lump of sorrow, for your accusations are true."

Moved by Jeremy's honest words and seeing this brash and annoying man subdued by age and ill health, her hatred for him slightly mellowed. She held out her hand across the table. "Jeremy, I am so sorry to hear this. Please forgive me, I would never have wanted this dreadful disease to be inflicted upon you."

Jeremy reached across and placed his hand on hers. "I do wonder how our lives would have been had we wed."

Catherine pulled her hand away. "It would have been purgatory for us both." In synchronisation, they laughed at the comment, knowing it to be true.

"I do believe we have finally found common ground." Jeremy raised his glass, Catherine reciprocated, and their crystal glasses clinked creating a pleasing sound. "I am trying various medicinal concoctions and searching for a cure but alas, despite my wealth and contacts, health forsakes me." He paused to take another shot of his drink. "Anyway, enough with the doom and gloom.

"I recall the first time I saw you after all those years. You were working in the asylum fields. It was a sunny day with a gentle breeze. Your hair was tied back but loose strands were caught in the flow and occasionally you would rest to move those annoying strands. I distinctly remember the contrast of your glowing auburn hair against the whiteness of your bonnet and apron. You were dazzling, like the sun emerging from dull clouds. Your vitality, you were smiling despite your predicament. I was amazed how you could find pleasure from hard labour in a dirty field. I vividly remember being enthralled, bewitched by the simplicity of your natural beauty. The way you moved, so free, so … hmm … not constrained by corsets and all the paraphernalia with all those blasted undergarment thingies."

Catherine confirmed, "They can be most restrictive and uncomfortable."

"I would gladly unburden you of your underwear." His smile narrowed his right eye to a wink.

"Keep with the story please, Jeremy."

He shrugged his eyebrows in frustration then continued, "Worthington and I completed the interior work on the asylum chapel and by then I had forged a close friendship with the governors on the board. I so wanted to help you. I offered my services and became a private benefactor to the asylum."

Catherine suddenly fathomed the unsaid meaning, "Oh, so you are my benefactor?"

Jeremy nodded, a smugness appearing on his face.

"I am shocked. I am ... both grateful and ... I'm not sure." Her tone changed to one of paranoid inquisition, "Have you been spying on me?"

Jeremy laughed, "As fascinating as you are, watching you read some medical drivel about elbows or causes of scabs is not my idea of entertainment." He swigged the last of his drink.

Annoyed with Jeremy but furious with herself for finding his humour intriguing in a strange sort of way, she found herself warming to him. "Thank you, Jeremy. I owe my sanity to you, being here, in Edenvale, in Rose Cottage, I cannot thank you enough."

"Over the years, pleasure has always been about me and my insatiable demands. Whether with increasing age, or this blasted curse," he dabbed his mouth, "I am finding pleasure in the simplest of things, by making other people smile."

An awkward silence then ensued, and Catherine became increasingly uncomfortable as Jeremy could not take his eyes off her. She had to say something. "Tell me about Oak Bank." Now quite tipsy, Catherine slurred her words but with a newfound confidence in her manner she said, "But not the dull, architectural stuff." She flicked her hand as if brushing aside trivial information, "I want to know what goes on here, the interesting stuff."

"I haven't a bloody clue as I'm rarely here, but I will tell you what I know." His mouth dry from talking, he poured himself another glass from the decanter. He downed the unknown concoction and nearly choked on the dregs in the bottom of the glass.

They laughed, but he continued to splutter, resulting in Catherine coming around the table to pat his back to alleviate the choked cough. Tenderly, she gently massaged between his shoulder blades until his breathing calmed down. On regaining his composure, Jeremy stared at Catherine for a fraction longer than was comfortable. He grabbed her and pulled her onto his knee.

With a coarseness to his voice he said, "That man you are with, the ragamuffin with sackcloth half-mast trousers, what fascinates you so?"

Catherine tried to raise from his lap but found herself being held too firmly by Jeremy's hands. "The ragamuffin you refer to is my intended. We are soon to be wed at St Constantine's Church." She tried once more to stand.

Jeremy would not let her go. "You are the bane of my life, Catherine Fawcett, the one person I could not have. Everyone else I have used, for personal or professional advantage. For pleasure, pain, humiliation, reward,

167

furthering a cause, as a step towards my ambitions, sheer lust, whatever." He went to pick up a drink and was annoyed that both of his glasses were empty. "Yet you. You drive me crazy. Such beauty yet, so bloody annoying. You read me and I find this unnerving, as if you know me better than I know myself, yet you will not even give me the time of day to prove your theories."

Wriggling, she escaped his hold. "It is simple, you scare me."

"I scare you?" His hands gripped the chair arms, as if he needed a firm hold on reality.

"Your strength and ambition, you are so driven to fulfil your dreams, so self-assured, arrogant, focused, powerful. I really could go on."

"Why does that scare you? Surely, they are attributes to admire?" He raised a questioning hand.

She had to smile at his lack of insight despite such intelligence. "No, Jeremy, they are frightful. You plough through fields, churning everything in your way, trampling on feelings, using people for gain, taking what you need, searching for this holy grail, this perfect world full of ecstasy and wonder, whilst leaving everyone and everything in your wake in a muddy mess. I doubt you will ever be genuinely happy. It is an impossible dream resulting only in disappointment. You achieve your goal, find it is not what you expected, then you plan for the next thrill, with each task becoming more complex and challenging."

Silence ensued as Jeremy digested the information. Catherine took a moment to explore the room. There were stuffed creatures, plants in various pots and paintings of landscapes: of sea, woodland hills, lakes and rivers. A large floor to ceiling bookcase with an inbuilt ladder housed many an ancient text, with one section dedicated to various religions from around the world. She wished she had more time to take in the books, wondering what vital information they held in their pages. Next to the bookcase was a large globe with a wooden surround depicting astrological, astronomical and celestial bodies. There was symbolism everywhere, on the walls, carved into panels, above the fireplace, but no triquetra design. She had to ask, "The Order of the Priory, does this mean anything to you, Jeremy?"

He shook his head, "Are you seriously implying I am religious and believe in that drivel?" Desperate, Jeremy leaned across the table, grabbed Catherine's glass and slugged the last of her drink. "You know my sexual preferences, Catherine; I would be damned to hell for my sins."

She walked back to the table and sat down opposite Jeremy. "You annoy and intrigue me with equal measures, Mr Fisher. I believe in fate and in God's work, that he weaves this mysterious web, this intricate and impossible network of silken threads to guide us on our way. For some reason, our paths have crossed too many times, you are part of my life and in many ways, I am thankful for your intervention. In a strange, convoluted way you are my

168

saviour. You are fascinating, like an annoying character in a book. A character I detest, yet one that makes the story more interesting. A sad character that I cannot help but feel pity for, but one that hopefully finds peace in the end."

"Then marry me, Catherine. How's that for a happy ending to our story?"

Chapter Thirty-Three

Seven o'clock and Catherine was checking her appearance in the mirror. Even though her dress was old in terms of years, she had rarely worn it due to her ensuing madness, so the material appeared like new. With dark blue intricate lace over-layering the front panel of the bodice and skirt, it was one of her most daring outfits. Jeremy would certainly approve. The simple tapering of the sleeves was edged by more of the beautiful dark lace. In a richer blue material, the bodice curved down around her bosom gathering at her waist to then fall into the layers of her skirt. She felt like a princess waiting to attend a royal ball.

She had agreed to accompany Jeremy for dinner, half past seven at Oak Bank Hall. He indicated it was an exclusive event, with renowned architects, influential doctors, respected solicitors and successful merchants. Preoccupied with pride, recalling the many pretentious events her parents had organised in the past, she tried to remember how to behave. Posture, speech, deportment, etiquette, she wondered if times had changed regarding the expected behaviour of a single, young lady in society. Then she remembered she was nearing forty years of age and was engaged to be married. The mirror suddenly reflected a sadness, a troubled face, with lines of worry and dark shadows. She no longer felt royal.

She summed up her life. Poor, then rich, a volunteer nurse at the House of Recovery, her work as an undertaker, her involvement with the police during the spate of murders, her forced engagement to Jeremy, the incident at Fernleigh, her engagement to Sam after he proposed when in gaol, the birth of their baby, the death of their baby, her instability, paranoia, delusions, depression, the harming, she was deemed insane. She was liable to scream and crumple at the slightest annoyance. The asylum, Edenvale, poverty, her engagement to Solomon after only knowing him for a few weeks. A lot to consider. The evidence alluded to an unstable mind.

She thought about Doctor Wainwright's advice: acknowledge, accept, analyse, action, advance. She had advanced, she had moved on, but had skipped through the other four stages, too much to bear, but she kept reverting, wanting to analyse the past over and over again which made her run further down the rabbit hole, becoming lost in the warren. She found herself struggling to accept what had transpired.

Now feeling depressed, she made one final check in the mirror. She could do no more. The worries, the doubts, the ugliness within, murder, lies, death, imprisonment, the acceptance of a flawed life, she was a failure. Tonight, she needed to act, pretend she was a lady, to entertain her host and present as a confident woman who had experienced life and survived. She walked down the stairs feeling a fraud.

Jeremy said he would knock on her door at twenty past seven and escort her around the village green so they could arrive together at Oak Bank Hall. Therefore, the knock at the door was no surprise. The clock showed five past, he was early, so she was thankful she was ready. Heading down the stairs, she ruminated on everything they had chatted about earlier in the day, he had been so kind in many ways, and she toyed with the idea of inviting him in. Then she remembered how he acted when they were younger. How he had tried to force his way into her bedroom to lay with her. His admission of orgies, enjoying intimacies with men and women, his debauched nature, cruelly taunting her with graphic details from his past. The fine hairs on her arms prickled. She had to keep her distance.

She opened the door expecting to see Jeremy but when Solomon was standing there, a surge of guilt flowed through her body. Drinking mysterious intoxicating concoctions and teasing with Jeremy earlier in the day, she had barely thought of Solomon since their canter into Carlisle on the morning. Their adventure seemed a long time ago.

"Wow, you look amazing!" Solomon was overcome with pride. His soon-to-be wife was stunning. Her hair was heavenly as if angels had fluttered their wings and created perfection. In the candlelight, her auburn hair glowed like the setting sun and the rich fabric of her dress shimmered like the darkest of oceans in moonlight, she was divine.

"Solomon, I was not expecting you." She hoped he could not hear the loudness of her heartbeat. "Lovely to see you though."

"I said I would take a half hour break from work. Wow, just wow." Solomon leaned forward to kiss her open lips. "My heart is overflowing with pride."

Catherine was flattered by his reactions but wanted him to leave. Trying to think of appropriate words to say, she responded with, "I thought we were trying to keep apart, to have alibis for this evening. I am going to a dinner at Oak Bank Hall. I need to be there. You should leave."

"Yeah, yeah, of course but I find myself dreaming of you day and night. You are eternally in my thoughts. You are so ... oh you do these crazy things to me." He scooped her up into his arms and with ease, lifter her off her feet and carried her inside.

"I need to go now, and I need you to go too." She was now uncomfortably wriggling in his arms, so he tenderly placed her on her feet.

"Catherine, you drive me crazy." He kissed her once more.

She subtly pushed him away, not wanting Jeremy to lay eyes on him. "You'd best go now, quick, for we do not want to be seem together. We both need alibis, remember? We can't be seen to be cavorting or conspiring in public."

Solomon tried kissing her again, "I love you so much, that's what I want you to remember."

"I love you too, now go. Shoo!" Suddenly, she wondered if those words were true as she ushered him out of the door.

Intoxicated by love, he swayed down the path, blew her a kiss whilst closing the garden gate and then disappeared around the corner on his way back to work.

Catherine sighed, relieved he was gone. Arguing with herself, she clarified her meaning, that she was thankful he did not encounter Jeremy as that would be awkward. Aware of the path this line of thinking was taking her, she busied herself with a few menial tasks around the cottage.

Nearing half past, she put on her coat, pinned her hat in place, placed her dainty silk gloves on her hands and waited. The only sound was the ticking of the clock on the mantlepiece.

Twenty minutes later, there was a couple of hard knocks on the door. Her body came alive, tingling with excitement and fear. Catherine was hoping it was Jeremy and that Solomon was now safely tucked away at work. She reprimanded herself for thinking such thoughts. Shaking, she opened the door and saw Jeremy standing there. "You're late!"

He checked his pocket watch and shrugged his right shoulder but then he properly saw her. "Words fail me." His eyes could not stay still, taking in every little detail of her being. "Indeed, you are a beautiful lady." He held out his elbow. "Would you do me the honour of escorting me to the ball?"

"Thank you, kind sir. I would be delighted." Catherine stepped outside of the house and linked his arm. Together, they strolled around the green. The dark sky twinkled with distant stars whilst the world stopped breathing, admiring the dazzling display. A perfectly still evening. Subtly, Catherine looked up the road to see if Solomon was there, but the street was deserted.

Mr Schubert opened the door of Oak Bank Hall as they climbed the stone steps to the arched entrance, "Good evening to you both. Such a wonderful couple, you complement each other exquisitely." He bowed in their presence.

"Stop licking my balls, Cedric," said Jeremy.

"As you wish, sir," responded Schubert as he winked at Catherine.

She nodded in reply, "Good evening, Mr Schubert."

Instead of turning left as they had done earlier in the day, they were escorted straight ahead along a grand hallway and were announced into the ballroom. Decorated in shades of gold, the room was magical, shimmering in the flickering flames from lamps, chandeliers and candelabras. Around the edges of the room were eight circular tables, each with ten place settings.

All eyes laid upon them. Catherine wanted to shrink away with embarrassment.

Jeremy was the main event. People swarmed around him, vied for his attention, wanting to be near him, fawning over him, delighted to be in his company. With each physical brush off, being ignored or discreetly cast aside, Catherine shrunk away, leaving Jeremy to glow in the limelight of his admirers but he would soon pull her to his side and introduce her as his guest. There was never a moment when he did not include her, engage her in conversation and he assertively controlled the evening's events.

For hours, they dined on fine food, chatted with distinguished guests, and drank copious amounts of intoxicating fluids. The room was bursting with energy.

Jeremy turned to her and asked, "Dance with me." He discarded his cane and held out his hand.

"But your leg?"

"Be my support. You have propped me up all evening and been my rock." His gaze was intense. "I want to dance with you."

The orchestra played lively music. People were merrily engaging and having an immense amount of fun. Laughter and frivolity filled the room. Catherine was worried because Jeremy struggled to walk, never mind dance.

As everyone continued with the expected choreography, Catherine and Jeremy stood on the periphery. He held out his arms in which Catherine slowly aligned herself with his body and they embraced. Their bodies fitted together perfectly. The muscle tone of his youth had gone, to be replaced with a leaner physique but he exerted a strength from within, firmly pressing his hips against hers and they swayed in synchronisation with each other, oblivious to the music and the crowd.

"You have enchanted me this evening, Catherine. Everyone has paled into the background. I can think of only you."

They continued to move to their own tune, "Being with people again after such prolonged isolation, the silence I have endured, these crowds, the deafening noise of joy. I have had butterflies all evening, but you have comforted and included me. I appreciate your protection."

"It is not protection, it is love."

They continued to sway to their own rhythm, "Please do not make statements like that. I am engaged to another."

"Yet he is a pauper, a simple man. I believe he serves drinks in a public house and lives in a rented property."

"He is a kind and honest man who loves his family."

"He wears a flat cap, rolls up his sleeves and smells of manure."

"Jeremy, I am warning you. I love him for who he is." They continued their slow embrace, "And you know he doesn't smell of manure, so stop with the exaggerations and lies."

"Given more time, can you not love me?" They momentarily parted and Jeremy held her at a distance so he could study her face. Catherine looked away but seemed to be considering an answer.

As they continued to dance, Jeremy lowered his hand to the gentle curve of her back and eased their hips together. Placing his other hand on her exposed neckline, he silently persuaded her to extend her spine, her bosom now raised, pressing into his chest, their hearts racing. She was moulding to his demands, hypnotised by his masterful moves and compliant to his touch. Each taking pleasure from his dominance and her subservience. As his hands explored her body, moving from her hips, exploring the contours of her waist and the sides of her breasts, he was so close to kissing her neck, intending to make his way up to her—

The music suddenly stopped, and the musicians announced they were now to have an hour's break. Everyone on the floor departed, except for Jeremy and Catherine. They continued to sway. "I cannot bear to let you go," admitted Jeremy.

"But you must," insisted Catherine.

Reluctantly, Jeremy freed her from his hold, his eyes trying to hide the dejection. She had to admit, she was warming to his contrary ways. Kind yet cruel, powerful yet vulnerable, he was an enigma, a challenge, an unwanted distraction. She made an excuse of freshening up.

Annoyed with herself for admitting even a slight fascination with Jeremy, she immediately focused on the evening's events. Her alibi was certainly secure, there was no doubting her presence here, too many witnesses. The five courses had been exquisite; she had forgotten how important food could be in general wellbeing and happiness. Jeremy, he had been divine in looking after her, including her and making her feel at ease with the people she had encountered. *Bother*, she was thinking about him again, she had to remain focused. The other guests, they certainly did not appear to be religious fanatics or involved in an occult sect. They all seemed like normal people from different walks of life.

She made her way back into the hall. Jeremy was chatting to a group of women. They were hovering around him, drawn to the delights of sweet honey. Catherine froze, not wanting to impose on the group. She could sense the simmering tension, the smiles, the chemistry, they were all flirting outrageously with Jeremy. The thought of home was calling. She had consumed too much alcohol; it had initially settled her nerves and gave her courage but now she felt woozy. As she made her way out of the room, a hand on her elbow prevented her from leaving.

"Please, I want you to stay." Jeremy was standing there, pleading with his eyes. "Don't leave."

"Jeremy, I—"

"Just for this evening, please." His hand was not going to let her go.

"Can we go somewhere else then? Being locked away for such a long time, the isolation I've endured, I am quite overwhelmed by this evening's events."

Jeremy led her to the drawing room they had enjoyed earlier in the day. He drew the curtains and proceeded to light the fire. "The thought of you leaving is filling me with dread. As if part of me will die."

Catherine laughed, "Please, stop teasing me."

"Honestly, this evening there are young nubile ladies who are desperate for me, begging for my attention but I am not interested. I have been propositioned by men, young, old, rich, poor with grand ideas, I am bored by their suggestions. You give me grief, you question me, you completely go against everything I say. You are the only one I cannot control. I need you in my life. I want you to *be* my life. I will treat you like the goddess you are, who you deserve to be."

"Forgive me for laughing but I am completely flawed. I am a horrible person. I have done awful things and I certainly do not deserve a happy ever after. They are just in fairy tales."

"We could be so amazing together. You would want for nothing."

"I am not sure what I want."

"But surely you do not want poverty and hardship?" When there was no reply, he grabbed her hands. "Together we could rule the world."

"I'm not sure I want to rule the world. I just want to be part of it, enjoy it, be in awe of it."

He threw her hands away in frustration, "Honestly woman, you are a bloody impossible fortress, that despite numerous attempts, I have failed to penetrate." With this statement they stared at each other with frustration, then laughed. A defeated man, he asked, "Dance with me once more." He held out his hand. "Please."

With some reluctance, she tenderly placed her hand on his and together they danced in the silence of the room. The mood, the drinks, the feelings, they fluidly intertwined, and Catherine was taken in the moment, resting her head on his chest. She could hear rhythmical beating, confirming he did have a heart. They moved slowly in synchronization with each other.

"I cannot let you go, Catherine. For the first time in my life, being here with you, holding you in my arms, I feel … I don't know what I feel. I think it is … peace. A sense of belonging."

"Really?"

"Yes, honestly, I feel complete, as if you are the missing piece to my puzzle."

Catherine did not know what to say. For many a year, she had detested him. Her skin would crawl at the mention of his name. Yet here they were, nearly twenty years later, finding solace in each other's arms.

Jeremy broke the silence. "I am to sign the documents for the house sale tomorrow. Would you like to accompany me to the solicitors' office and see your home one last time?"

The implications were immense. Part of her rehabilitation was to advance, move on and not dwell in the past yet Petteril Bank House, it would be lovely to see her beautiful home one last time. But spending time with Jeremy, this was too much, it was encouraging him to think there was some sort of friendship, a possibility of their relationship developing, she did not want to encourage such thoughts. And Solomon, what would he make of all this? Sadly, she declined his offer.

"Fantastic! I will call round at ten in the morning. Unfortunately, we cannot get the carriage from here, but our ride will be waiting at the road end."

"Jeremy, I said no."

"I know you did but I think no means yes, in your heart."

"No means no in my mind and heart."

"Ten o'clock precisely, Catherine." He winked.

"You never listen to me. You always just do your own thing. I'm going home now, Jeremy."

"Great, I'll walk with you. I think I need some fresh air." He gathered her things and guided her across the room.

"Are you pushing me out of the door? I thought you said you couldn't live without me?"

"I can't, but you're a bloody pain sometimes, but I will be calling for you in the morning."

Linking arms, they walked down the hallway and Schubert seemed to appear out of nowhere. "Good evening, Mr Fisher, Miss Fawcett, it has been a pleasure serving you." He helped them put on their overcoats.

"Likewise, Cedric, if I may call you that?" asked Catherine.

"Of course." He bowed slightly as he saw them to the door which he closed quietly behind them.

Arm in arm, Catherine and Jeremy strolled around the green, their footsteps synchronised to perfection. The darkness was captivating as two souls wandered in its shroud. Almost everyone in the village appeared to be in bed for there was little permeation of light from the surrounding houses.

As they stood at the door to Rose Cottage, Jeremy suggested, "Catherine, I know the trial period in the contract was only for three months, this was Wainwright's suggestion, but if you would like more time, I would gladly extend the contract. I want the best for you. I want this to be your home if you are happy here."

Jeremy had a knack of provoking extreme feelings. One minute she detested him for his crudeness, the next she adored him for his thoughtfulness, or she was irritated by his selfishness, then shocked by his kindness and warmth. "Thank you, I appreciate your generosity and I must admit, this cottage is beginning to feel like home."

"I shall also increase your allowance. Otherwise, if there is anything I can do, anything you need?"

"By buying Petteril Bank House this will completely restore my parents' sanity. I cannot thank you enough. With hindsight, I wish we had spent more time together. I am afraid I made rash judgements based on initial impressions. I was wrong to judge you so soon."

"Likewise, although I do believe you were absolutely correct in your assertions. I was a complete cad. Without a doubt, you did the right thing at the right time for I would have destroyed you, hurt your heart in so many ways with my indiscretions. Only age and infirmity have softened me."

Jeremy opened his arms and they embraced, lingering in the moment. Then, there was an almighty crack, forcing them apart. Solomon had punched Jeremy on the cheek, knocking him sideways. As he fell, he hit his head on the cottage door, leaving a blood-stained smear along the wood grain as he slumped to the ground.

"You've knocked him out!" cried Catherine as she knelt to help Jeremy. Blood stained her blue gloves.

"Well, the bastard was fondling you. You had your arms all over each other," insisted Solomon.

"He is a friend of the family from many years ago who happened to be in the area." She stood up but lowered her tone. "This was part of my alibi, old friends, getting together etcetera. You've probably obliterated all knowledge of me now."

On Catherine's insistence, they lifted Jeremy to his feet, but he was still out cold. Fumbling between them, they carried him inside and laid him on the sofa. Catherine got a clean towel and dipped it in the bowl of fresh spring water from the well. She wrung out the cloth and tenderly wiped away the trickling blood. Jeremy's eyes were beginning to swell and bruising was appearing on his face.

"Solomon, I am appalled by your behaviour this evening."

"Tit for tat. Whatever. Your behaviour has shocked me. Cavorting with another man. Then again, with his long hair he's ugly enough to be the backside of a horse."

"Oh, for goodness' sake, you are being ridiculous!"

"*I* am being ridiculous? We are soon to be husband and wife, yet I find you in the arms of another man, woman, animal, whatever." Solomon paced the room.

"I have known him for nearly twenty years. If anything was to happen, it would have happened by now." Catherine sat on the edge of the sofa, ensuring Jeremy was comfortable, monitoring his vital signs from what she could remember from her nursing days.

Solomon was fuming, his body tense, unable to stay still. "Maybe we have rushed into this. I hardly know you at all."

"Maybe you are correct. Please just leave and take some time out to think about your actions and their consequences."

Solomon continued to pace the room like a caged animal, obviously wanting to stay but feeling like he should leave. "Catherine, how would you feel coming across this situation? Imagine you found me with my arms wrapped around another woman, holding each other close. Anyway, I heard him say something about hurting your heart."

"Solomon, please just leave. We can discuss this another time when—"

He interrupted, "When you're not drunk? What on earth have you been doing this evening? It is well after one in the morning."

Annoyed by his insistence in prolonging the argument, she pulled him into the kitchen area and lowered her voice, "Stop with the interrogation, please. We were supposed to have a cast iron alibi for this evening. You are ruining things. We are not supposed to even be in contact with each other. Just leave, go home and trust me. We cannot be indicated in this. What if the police come tomorrow, asking us questions about the theft at the solicitors' office? People may have heard all the noise. The neighbours may testify we were arguing. Is your friend definitely breaking in there tonight?" Solomon nodded. "Then go home. I will see you in the morning."

As he walked past Jeremy, who was now snoring on the sofa, Solomon's face distorted in anger. "Please, don't hurt or lie to me because I truly do love you." His eyes were pleading, his posture had lowered, he had surrendered.

"Trust me, Solomon."

In silence, he walked over to the door and slammed it behind him.

Catherine flinched at the noise. She checked on Jeremy again and quietly made her way upstairs. From the chest of drawers in her bedroom, she found a couple of blankets, carried them downstairs and placed the folded layers over Jeremy's frail body. As he slept, she noticed a rash on the palm of his upturned hand.

The first time they met, she recalled how dashingly handsome he was and felt melancholy at how time and disease ravage the features. He had admitted having syphilis. How sad, that his carnal pleasures over the years were now causing his pain.

As she said one final goodnight, she prayed he would not be knocking on her bedroom door in the early hours of the morning as he had done nearly twenty years ago, or worse, be knocking at the pearly gates of heaven or shackled to the blistering railings of hell.

Chapter Thirty-Four

Following the consumption of too many unknown potions at last night's soiree, Catherine woke up feeling disorientated and dreadful. There was a little man in her head, hammering away at her skull. Another little man was tanning her stomach from within, and her mouth was so dry she was convinced a third little man had attempted to cure her insides with salt.

She remembered that Jeremy was sleeping on her sofa, having been knocked unconscious by Solomon's punch from the right, then hitting the left side of his head on the door. Wondering if Jeremy was dead or alive, she tiptoed down the stairs but to her surprise he was gone. In many ways she was relieved but admitted to feeling a little sad by his departure. She wondered if he would reappear at ten o'clock, as he had suggested yesterday evening, in order to view Petteril Bank House. Her options were to dress accordingly, just in case he did turn up, to remain in working clothes as an excuse for not going with him or to get her walking gear on and leave the house so as not to have to deal with his assertiveness. Her heart really wanted to go with him, to see her old house, to walk along the hallways, inspect the rooms and see the gardens one final time. The books in the library, she wondered if they were included in the sale. The anatomy books that Jeremy had bought her for Christmas of 1844, she wondered if she should cheekily ask for them back if they were still there. Imprisoned in the relative darkness of the shuttered room, she had lost track of who was renting the house and whether any of its contents remained or had been sold.

Yesterday, Jeremy had been quite the gentleman, being attentive and thoughtful. He had mellowed over the years but still had grandiose ideas. Then she remembered how he had teased her the other day about being a virgin, resulting in her seeking out Solomon and ending up in his bed. Jeremy was a bad influence, humiliating her about the scent of sexual intercourse. She hoped that it was a tease and that he could not really smell the bedroom encounter. She was mortified by the thought.

Jeremy created turmoil, heightened her anxiety and threatened her dignity. As much as her heart wanted to accompany him into Carlisle, her head won the argument and she decided to go for a walk to avoid further confrontation. Seeing the house again may unravel the progress she had made with her treatment at the asylum and her respite in Edenvale.

The time was nearing nine thirty so in case of an early call, she left the cottage and walked briskly in the direction of the river. Despite the chilling winds, a few people were milling around the village. Over at Oak Bank, Cedric was saying goodbye to two house guests who were looking a little worse for wear.

As she walked down the hill, she saw the vicar chatting with a gentleman she had seen at the church service. When Reverend Thornton spotted her, he waved, and the other gentleman turned and smiled. She reciprocated.

Making her way along the sandy banks of the river, she strolled along the well-trodden pathway, past the waterfall, climbed the convoluted pathway through the ancient woodland and headed back round to the priory gatehouse. She noted the door had been fixed from Solomon's desperate search for his father.

As she returned to the village green, she smiled when she saw the children from the orphanage putting on a show. They were dancing, singing and playing music. Catherine's heart started to jump with innocent joy. A few of the other villagers stopped to enjoy the spectacle and everyone cheered at the finale. In one sense, Catherine enjoyed seeing them smile, perform and entertain but on the reverse, she felt sad that her own child had been cruelly taken away.

With wisps of dark hair, she had named her beautiful girl Genevieve after Sam's grandmother, but the baby's limbs were limp and mottled grey. The silent bundle was quickly taken away whilst Catherine was left to clean up the bloody mess in her room. Afterwards, her parents had told her Genevieve was stillborn, that they had tried to revive her, but the little girl had never taken a breath and must have died in the womb or through birth.

Other than pain, she had felt numb. Catherine remembered her parents bringing her a metal bath to soak in as a kind gesture for what she had been through. She remembered the clean warm water turning red. Genevieve had been a sickly grey, a colour that still haunted her thoughts to this day. Sam would have doted on his daughter; she had been perfect, with a cute nose and rosebud lips. Weak and trembling with the aftershock of bereavement, Catherine had cried for days in solitude.

Her melancholy thoughts were interrupted by distant, muffled words. Someone was shouting at her, not angrily, but as if they were deaf. Their image was hazy. Catherine focused her mind. An elderly woman stood beside her. Her white hair was striking against the redness of her cheeks and her shoulders were stooped as she bore the weight of layers of warm clothing. "Wish I could run around like those bairns," she shouted.

Catherine recognised her as Mrs Humphries from the beautiful blue and white house. "Indeed, such joyful innocence."

The old woman continued to shout, "My grandson, he met his wife through this. She was an orphan too. Molly Montgomery as she was then. They wed this year and are now living in Carlisle. Molly's sister is the main governess at the orphanage."

"You know the children well?"

"Hell? Yes, indeed, must have been purgatory for them all. Can't imagine what those poor bairns have been through."

"So, Miss Montgomery and her sister were orphans?"

"Yes, but I don't think they would be bothered. Their mother used to beat them up and make them work. Their father was a waste of time. The mother used to beat him up too, I think he was a simple man."

"So, what happened to them?"

"The mother took on other babies, sold herself as a wet nurse, a bit of a baby farmer, she had about eight of them to make ends meet." She coughed. "Not sure of the exact details on how she died. Molly has never really talked about it. Everything else I've heard is just hearsay."

"Molly and her sister created the orphanage then?"

"They did, but this one's full of love. Molly is a lovely girl, a free spirit, seeing joy in life. Unlike the older sister though, I think she's been tainted by the experience. She's suspicious of people, always looking on the dark side but I can't say I can blame her. Yet she is so good with the children. She hides her secrets well."

"I think I may have got the wrong impression of Miss Montgomery. I thought her quite aloof, yet I can understand her distance is a protective mechanism."

"It is indeed." Mrs Humphries started to hobble, "Oh, I've stood yapping for far too long my legs have seized up."

"Here, I'll escort you back home." She held out her forearm. "I'm Catherine by the way."

"Daphne?" she sought clarification with her hand behind her ear and her eyes screwed up.

"Catherine," she said with exaggerated lips movements.

"Call me Ada. Mrs Humphries makes me sound like an old fuddy duddy."

They laughed, "Ada it is then."

As they slowly walked towards the cake house, Catherine asked about the neglected house next door.

"It's an eyesore, it really is." Ada stood at the gate, staring up at her neighbouring house.

Catherine felt uncomfortable in case someone was home, "Does anyone actually live there?"

"A man comes to stay occasionally. Maybe a weekend here and there. A week at the most. Look at the state of the house though, it's filthy. His front doorstep hasn't seen red in a year and it's a wonder he can see out of the windows. Honest to God, some folk have no decorum."

The old woman looked serious, but Catherine tried to hide an amused smile, "I'm just thankful I cleaned my windows and polished my step yesterday." They looked at each other and laughed.

"My eyes aren't very good nowadays, but I know where you live. It's a lovely cottage but just be careful lass. For a small village, there seems to be a lot of comings and goings with folk. Here one minute then puff, gone the next."

They started walking once more and arrived at the sweet blue gate. "Now look at that, a cobweb on my gate, you'll think I live in a midden."

They laughed once again, "It has truly been a pleasure, Ada, I'm sure we will talk again." Catherine watched her walk down the path until the old lady was safely inside.

On her way home, the pounding in her chest alerted her to potential danger. A policeman was standing outside her home. For a moment, she toyed with the idea of diverting her path and trying to evade potential questioning. Thoughts of the solicitors' office popped into her head, wondering if the paperwork had indeed been stolen by Solomon's friend. As she walked cautiously towards him, the children from the orphanage started crossing the road to head home. Catherine paused, allowing the children to cross a distance from her, giving her space and distraction from the policeman.

One young lad had a withered leg that failed to touch the floor, so he hopped with the aid of a crutch under his arm. An older girl stared at the floor, her upper limbs hanging limply, her gait a shuffle. The girl with the calliper smiled at Catherine as she staggered past. As the final little lad crossed the road, she recognised him as the cheeky one who had poked out his tongue when collecting water from the well. Before he was able to, Catherine poked her tongue out at him. He laughed and then pulled a funny face, sticking his tongue out to the side and making himself go cross eyed. They both laughed. Miss Montgomery was the last to cross the street. She glided with such grace, almost ghostly. The ladies made eye contact and they each nodded politely.

"A beautiful performance by the children," called out Catherine.

"Thank you," accepted Miss Montgomery and she continued up the driveway to the gothic house.

When Catherine looked at her cottage once more, the policeman had gone. A lead weight had been lifted from her already depressed shoulders, yet she could not rest. Maybe something dreadful had happened for a policeman to be calling at her door. She was beginning to regret avoiding him, for now she was worried, the uncertainty would continue, and she would never know the minute he would return. Did he have questions? Did he have answers? Maybe it wasn't to do with the solicitors' office at all. It may be about her parents or some other concern regarding the Kavanaghs or Shadrach Smith or the Greek gentleman. The policeman could have been standing there for a number of reasons.

Jeremy popped into her head. Maybe he had died, a latent result from his injury. Maybe something had happened to him when travelling into town. Then horror slapped her in the face. What if he was going to Hodder, Stretton and Puddifoot to sign the documents and deeds for the house sale but the paperwork was missing due to a theft? Maybe the sale would fall through, and her parents would continue to be at the end of their tether in financial despair. The repercussions were awful.

What if the visit was about Solomon? She felt guilty for him being at the end of her worry list. Had something happened to him? Had he suddenly gone missing in the dead of night like his father? They had parted in rather a foul mood after last night's events. She hoped he had refrained from doing anything stupid. Maybe Jeremy had pressed charges against him, and the police were after an arrest. There was only one thing to do, she had to find the policeman. Worry through ignorance was worse than knowing the truth.

Chapter Thirty-Five

As Catherine opened the heavy door to the Wheatsheaf Inn, the smell of tobacco and stale beer was nauseating. She wondered how anyone could find pleasure in these pursuits.

Solomon was behind the bar, polishing the woodwork. A gentle smile formed at the corners of his mouth on seeing her approach. After the incident with Jeremy, she was unsure if they were still friends, so his smile, however small, settled her nerves. Conversation was awkward at first, discussing topics such as how busy the bar had been but then he rested his forearms on the gleaming woodwork and whispered, "Someone has been in here today, asking about your whereabouts."

"A policeman?"

Solomon looked a little surprised, "I take it he found you then. What did he say?"

"As I was walking home, I saw him by my front door, I panicked, then avoided the confrontation."

"I think I know why he was after you." Blood increased its pace through her veins. He leaned in closer. "I've got the book."

She wanted to squeal with delight, but the misty shadows of men in the bar stopped her from celebrating. Unable to contain her excitement, she asked, "Have you read any of it yet?"

Solomon gave a quick overview of the morning's events. He had once again borrowed the Dawson's horse and headed into town to meet up with his friend. By the time he had returned to Edenvale, it was time to get ready for work. "So no, I've not read anything, and I'm not telling you about my mate or how he got it, or what happened because I didn't ask."

Catherine was disappointed but she could understand why it was better not knowing. "Do you think that's why the policeman wanted to see me?"

"Let's not talk about it. Might not be about that anyway."

Catherine briefly thought about Jeremy, hoping he was well but praying he was not planning his revenge.

Perusing the room to ensure no one was nearby, she asked, "Where's the book now?"

Solomon stood upright and from his waistcoat pocket produced a door key, passing it over the bar to Catherine, "The book is underneath the chest of drawers in my room. Remove the bottom drawer. You'll see a false floor. Lift the wood and the book will be hidden under there."

"Thank you," she mouthed, "but I'll wait for you, we can look together."

"I can see how desperate you are to read it." He winked, "Go on, before you burst with excitement."

With a subdued squeal she grinned from ear to ear, "Thank you, Solomon. I'll come straight back with the key." She blew him a subtle kiss. Solomon smiled and with fingers from his temples he saluted her departure.

Wanting to run down the hill, she suppressed her desire by acting ladylike. Her breathing slowed, her spine lengthened, and she daintily made her way along the dirt road so as not to arouse suspicion from other villagers. As she turned the corner, her excitement completely disappeared when she saw the policeman standing at her door. Desperately wanting to go to Solomon's house to retrieve the book, she knew she would have to confront this situation first, otherwise this officer would hound her for eternity.

"Hello, may I help you?" She forced a smile, hoping she appeared innocent and friendly, as guilt bubbled inside.

"You live here?"

"I do indeed, and you are?"

"Officer Jenkins." Frowning, his eyebrows merged over his close-set eyes. A thick moustache concealed his lips. Catherine concluded he was not smiling beneath the combed parallel hairs.

He continued, "Rather than conduct serious business in the street, can we go inside?"

"Of course."

The officer moved out of her way, allowing her to open the front door. She walked inside and quickly glanced around. Thankfully, she had tidied all the books away, but her notes were still visible on the table. She smiled, "Would you like some tea?" She thought this an excuse to clear the table of the items.

"No, but thank you." Without waiting to be asked he sat on the sofa. "Where were you on the night of the 24th?" Obsidian eyes devoured every tell-tale sign.

She clarified, "Of November?"

He nodded slowly, appearing unimpressed.

"Erm … that was yesterday, Wednesday, wasn't it?" She knew it was Wednesday, she knew it was the night of the ball, but she was trying to appear as if she was thinking about it. She was convinced he could hear the cogs of her mind jarring. "I was at a party at Oak Bank. Over there." She pointed to the impressive hall across the green.

"How very convenient."

Nerves affected her voice as she questioned, "Pardon me for asking, but what is this about?"

"On the 24th of November, you and a rather dowdily dressed gentleman went into the offices of Hodder, Stretton and Puddifoot. You enquired about a book belonging to one of their clients. As if by sheer coincidence, a fire has destroyed swathes of documents, and lo and behold, there is no evidence of the information you desired."

Fuming at his description of Solomon's clothes, Catherine suppressed a cutting retort. Uncomfortable silence ensued and Catherine felt obliged to say something to slice through the atmosphere.

"How ghastly, I'm hoping no one was injured."

"A policeman involved in fighting the fire was badly burned."

"This is such sad news. I do hope he will make a full recovery."

"I doubt it, the skin of his face and hands were burnt off. He is crying with the pain. He is unrecognisable, even to his family."

Catherine no longer needed to act, she was genuinely horrified, "I will pray for him and his family."

The officer stared at Catherine. He broke the gaze by getting off the sofa and walking over to the bookshelves. "What was so intriguing about the book you so eagerly desired?" He continued to explore the room, looking at the various books until he stood immediately in front of Catherine. He stared down at her as she sat in the armchair.

"I believe he lived in this house before me, and he left a book here saying 'they' had come for him and were taking him away. He said whoever found the book to go to the solicitor and enquire about his welfare." Not wanting to appear guilty, she maintained eye contact.

"I have done some research of my own. The gentleman who resided here is currently alive and well, residing in the Cumberland and Westmorland Lunatic Asylum. Everything in the book will have been his fantasy, the mutterings of a madman. The people he refers to in the book were staff from the asylum. 'They' had come to take him away because he was delusional. This house of yours seems to attract nutters. You are seeking refuge here too, residing in an idyllic village but everyone knows you're a freak. They all know you are mad too, Miss Fawcett."

Horrified by this revelation, she could not stop the fire rising to her cheeks which were burning with humiliation, "Then I am truly sorry for wasting your time." She put her head down, now wanting to avoid further inspection.

"It's obvious you didn't start the fire or take the book, but if you have in anyway been an accomplice or involved in this criminal offence, I will return to arrest you. Next time it won't be the men in white coats coming for you …" He walked towards the door. "Remember, people here are watching you." By the look on his face this appeared to be a threat rather than a warning. He opened the door and saw himself out.

Wanting to cry but desperately trying not to, Catherine busied herself with menial tasks. She wiped down the surfaces with a damp cloth. She hung the rug over the washing line and beat it vigorously. She swept the floor with the broom. The kitchen was sparkling after receiving an intense scrubbing. Flitting from one job to another, she was trying not to think, undertaking laborious tasks to distract herself from going crazy.

She washed a few smaller items of clothing and hung them on the line. Thoughts rattled around inside her head. Who knew about her history? Which villagers knew her secret? She grimaced, wondering if everyone knew. Realising she was thinking again, she cleaned out the fires in the living room and bedroom and prepared the logs for later.

Taking a break from her chores, she looked out of the window. All was quiet. From this angle she could just see the adjoining house to where Solomon and his father lived. Even though she desperately wanted to read the book, she dared not go to Solomon's house in case the policeman was still making enquiries.

She studied the numerous books on the shelves either side of the chimney breast. When Doctor Wainwright had first offered her the option of staying in Rose Cottage, he had been honest in describing the house as cosy but reassured her that all necessary items would be provided. She had assumed that the books on the shelves were part of the package provided by the asylum. The books were a source of information and distraction which was good for a recovering mind. There were educational publications, historic titles, fictional novels, books on mastering a new skill and books on homemaking. Now that Jeremy had admitted to owning Rose Cottage and being her benefactor, she wondered if he had provided the books. Another option was that Samson Cohen owned some of the books, adding to the collection that was already there. Whoever owned them, Jeremy and the governors at the asylum had obviously failed to read what was written inside.

Catherine retrieved a few of the books that Samson had made notes in. His writing was beautiful even though he was only making brief points. He did not seem like a man who was insane. With his detailed notes of all the goings on in the village, she questioned whether he was realistic, paranoid or obsessive. He appeared to be an informed gentleman, had obviously

188

stumbled upon something of historical importance and had enough gumption to follow through on his findings.

Three hours later, after reading every underlined text and page in which Sam had made a note, she felt like a chicken in a coop. She needed to venture outside. The hidden book was calling, enticing her with its mysterious content.

With the light fading, she held her head high, and like an actress on stage, she gracefully made her way to Solomon's house. The only person she encountered on the way was an old gentleman shuffling along the road with a cane. Apart from the orphans, nearly all the residents in Edenvale were middle-aged or elderly.

The gate to Solomon's house swung open without complaint. The key turned easily in the lock. After closing the front door behind her, she heaved a sigh of relief and allowed the wooden support to take her weight. Her shoulders slumped and all the worry drained from her body until she thought about locking the door behind her. With a tremble in her hands, she quickly secured the door and sighed with relief once more.

Walking along the hallway, a sense of foreboding prickled the fine hairs on her arms. As she peeked in each room, everywhere was a mess. Plant pots shattered, cushions ripped apart and crockery pulled off shelves, leaving broken fragments everywhere. Her boots crunched underfoot as she explored each room.

Scared, but needing to know, she made her way upstairs, cautious that someone may still be lurking, ready to pounce if she confronted them. Catherine now regretted locking the front door behind her in case she needed to escape with haste. With trepidation, she checked each bedroom, but no one was to be found.

Feeling slightly more at ease, she tiptoed over to the chest of drawers in Solomon's room. None of the drawers were properly closed and the trespasser had obviously rummaged through the contents, for items of clothing were scattered in the vicinity. Catherine swiped the discarded items to the side and pulled out the bottom drawer, revealing the base of the frame. She tried to lift the false base from its resting place, but the wood was a snug fit. With caution, she quietly made her way back downstairs to retrieve a knife and a long-handled spoon. Back in Solomon's bedroom, the angle of the spoon handle worked perfectly in leveraging the false base out of its grave, revealing a book entombed inside the chest of drawers. With her hands in prayer, she rested her fingertips on her pouting lips for she now had choices to make.

Tidying up was the first option. Leaving the house and its contents the way she found it was the second option. She contemplated involving the police but in the current situation this was possibly a flawed option. She would need to tell Solomon, but she wondered whether she should tell him now about his house being ransacked or wait until his shift was over. What she really wanted to do was go into hiding and read the book, but this posed another dilemma. When not reading the book, she considered whether she should hide it somewhere safe or carry it around with her. There were too many choices and if she did carry the book around with her, a stronger person could easily overpower her and take the book from her. She concluded that she needed to go and tell Solomon the news. He needed to see his home as she had found it and any further decision should be his or theirs together. With a struggle, she wedged the pages into her corset and tightened the ribbons to secure her treasure.

Outside Solomon's house, she kept her head held high and did not dare look around. She was convinced everyone was looking out of their windows, peeking behind the curtains, laughing at her misfortune. They probably thought she was insane with all the ideas she had about the place: murder, suicide, kidnappings, religious cults, creepy orphanages, hidden meanings and symbols around the village. They must find it all rather amusing, the ramblings of a madwoman.

As she walked along the road, the corners of the book were stabbing into her torso, so she decided to head home first, hide the book, then proceed to the Wheatsheaf Inn to tell Solomon the devastating news. When she got back home, she had no idea where to store the book. Having seen Solomon's house, the trespassers had pulled everything out of the cupboards and flung everything off the shelves to complete a thorough search. She needed a hiding place like Solomon had found, but this house was too small. There was barely any furniture or space, everything was of a simple design, there seemed no obvious hiding place.

As she looked around the room, she had the idea of hiding the book in an obvious place, as Sam had done, placing the book amongst the others on the shelves. However, whoever was searching for this book now knew of its existence, so the shelves were no longer an option. Her nose was right in front of her eyes, but she could hardly see it. She needed to place the book somewhere obvious but easily accessible and quickly concealed.

Catherine made her way into the kitchen and started a fire to boil the water in the kettle. The hard edges of the book pierced her abdomen as she pottered, but she could not risk leaving Samson's diary lying around in case someone forced their way into her home. She had to create a hiding place. Waiting for the kettle to boil, she searched the house, but a hiding place was elusive. Like Solomon, she had to create somewhere new.

After making the tea, she carefully placed the cup and saucer on the small table by the window. Although sitting was uncomfortable due to the book digging into her tummy, she sipped the steaming liquid and thought about a hiding place. It was then she had the idea of hiding the book under the table. All she would need was some material and a few nails. Like a small pouch, the book could be easily and quickly placed inside. The table was so small and thin, that no one would think that a book could be hidden underneath.

She raced up the stairs and rummaged through her wardrobe, looking for the shabbiest material. After cutting a few sections of thick cotton from one of her petticoats, she fashioned a large enough sling to hold two books side by side.

Skipping down the stairs, she collected some nails she had spotted earlier when she had been cleaning out the kitchen cupboards. She had another sip of her tea then moved the cup and saucer from the table to the mantlepiece. The small table was easily turned upside down and she forced the nails into place with a pan. She turned the table upright. She loosened the ribbons of her corset and wiggled out the book. Retrieving *The Story* from the shelf, she placed the books into the cotton pouch and checked its effectiveness to secretly house both journals. From the top, the books were hidden from view, but when she sat on the sofa, she could see the white material sagging underneath. "Bother," she said out loud. Having flipped the table, she pushed the books apart and placed two more nails at the centre of the fabric to create two smaller pouches. She sat on the sofa then the armchair to check for tell-tale signs. The white cotton pouch and the books could not be seen. Retrieving the lace tablecloth from the armchair, she threw it over the table. "Perfect," she admitted to herself.

With all the hammering, she suddenly heard growls and moans from next door. Jonathan was probably upset with all the noise. She briefly thought of Jeremy and his proposition of marriage and quickly dismissed the thought.

She had to go and tell Solomon about his house, but she also wanted to flick through Sam's book. Too excited to wait, and Solomon had said to go ahead and peruse the pages, she removed the books from their hiding place and placed them side by side on the tabletop. Like twins, the books had the same dimensions, spine and bindings, just different colours, burgundy and blue.

Although only briefly scanning the pages, there were maps, descriptions and symbolism, XX VV and the triquetra sign, just how Shadrach had described the Greek man's journal. Catherine knew these men were not mad. Samson Cohen and Alesandro Demetriou had stumbled onto something interesting and potentially deadly.

Chapter Thirty-Six

After hiding the books, Catherine headed towards the Wheatsheaf Inn. The place was heaving, and she felt awkward making her way through the crowds. The noise was overwhelming. People were chattering away happily. Two older men nearly fell off their bar stools as they snorted with amusement at something funny.

When Solomon saw her approach, a big smile formed on his face. "Hi!" he mouthed then nodded for her to sit on the solitary stool at the end of the bar where the dirty glasses were piling up. Feeling rather anxious, she wanted to leave the oppressive atmosphere but felt obliged to tell Solomon about his home.

For well over half an hour, Solomon was too busy to chat. The punters were queuing for drinks, two deep at the bar. A few drunken men gave Catherine a lecherous stare, but Solomon quickly intervened and warned them off. Thankfully, Mr Scrogg appeared behind the bar, looking rather tipsy with his bleary eyes and flushed face but he gave Solomon a hand. Once everyone had been served, he allowed Solomon a quick break so he could talk with Catherine.

"I've been desperate to come over and talk with you, young lady."

Young lady, with everything she had been through she felt ancient. Solomon suddenly seemed so young, animated and happy. There was no easy way to tell him what had happened. Whatever she said the smile would disappear from his sparkling eyes. "I have some bad news."

His face completely changed, "About my dad?"

She shook her head, "No, sorry, I have no news about that." She paused for a moment, "I came here to tell you that your house is a total mess."

"Cheers for that," he laughed it off but looked offended. "You been in the kitchen again?"

"No, I apologise for that did not sound right, I mean your house really is in a mess, like it has been ransacked, broken glass and crockery, everything's lying around." She took a deep breath, "I think they were looking for the book."

Len approached the bar, intending to get a round in for the lads and two more men walked through the door. Mr Scrogg gruffly called Solomon back to work, "Come on lad they're dying of thirst in 'ere."

"Sorry, but there's an emergency back at home." Solomon disappeared into the back and returned with his coat within a few seconds, "I'll be back as soon as I can."

The punters moaned, but Solomon was having none of it. He grabbed Catherine's hand to leave. Striding home, Catherine was almost running to keep up with him. On passing her house she suggested, "Let me go and get the book, I've hidden it, we can then perhaps read through it together for clues."

"Hurry up then, I'll stay out here, I don't want to know your hiding place."

Catherine had a quick look around the house to check everything was in order, retrieved both books and locked the door behind her.

"Sorted?" asked Solomon. She nodded.

Without saying a word, they walked at a more amenable pace to his house, Wood Grange. Once inside, Solomon could see the devastation the trespasser had caused. Catherine could see his eyes narrowing, his brow furrowing and his shoulders rising. He was like a wolf, snaring, ready to pounce on a victim. Solomon and his father had few belongings to start with, so to see everything broken and twisted was heart-breaking.

Each room the same, everything pulled out of place and scattered, as if searching frantically for something.

"Jesus Christ, forgive me, but I'll kill the bastards who have done this. If it's the same bloody scoundrels that have taken my dad, then I'll kick their bloody arses into the depths of hell."

Seeing such anger and hatred not only in his face but the tension in his entire body, he looked ready to explode. Slightly scared of the power he possessed, Catherine kept quiet and allowed him to vent his frustration.

His search continued upstairs, "No! The angel ornament smashed to smithereens." His shoulders slumped. "Dad bought this for mum when she was poorly, like a guardian angel watching over her." In a rage, he threw the fragments to the floor, creating even smaller fragments.

"How can I help you?" Initially there was no reply, only more huffing and swearing under his breath. "Please, let me help. Do you have a basket or something we could put all the broken things in?" Solomon did not reply. "Or your clothes, I could re-hang them or fold them, put them back in your—"

"Just leave everything, *please!*" His fists clenched and his top lip tightened.

With tears glistening, she turned and was going to walk away but Solomon saw her upset. "Sorry, sorry, sorry, it's just seeing all this, honestly, I'm truly sorry for speaking to you like that."

"It's fine, I'll give you some space. I'll wait at home."

"No, I apologise profusely once more, I'm devastated, I'm not thinking straight, my family are my world. You mean the world to me too. I'm angry, but not angry with you."

"I'll wait downstairs then, I'll read the book. Take your time, you know where I am if you need me." They smiled awkwardly at each other.

Trying to be dignified, she slowly descended the stairs and cleared the sofa of various items. She placed the diary on the small table beside her and began reading the first journal. She had to read the first few lines a number of times as the banging and swearing from upstairs was distracting, but once she got into the details, her concentration was taken into a whole new world.

Chapter Thirty-Seven

Plodding footsteps descended the stairs. Solomon appeared weak and defeated. His skin tone was ashen, his limbs were limp and his demeanour broken. He threw four torn fragments of paper into Catherine's lap then slumped on the sofa next to her. Having pieced them together, caring eyes of a young woman stared back at her, the portrait she had found in his bedroom of the beautiful girl.

"Who is she?" asked Catherine, unsure if she wanted an answer.

"My mother. Dad drew this on their first wedding anniversary or so he told me."

"Oh Solomon, I'm so sorry this has happened. She was beautiful, and your dad is a very talented artist."

Solomon rested his head against the back of the sofa and closed his eyes. Catherine placed her hand on his thigh, then copied his posture. Only the sounds of their occasional weary sighs were audible. The once reliable ticking of the grandfather clock had been silenced, broken in the search for the book.

Aware she was drifting off into sleep, Catherine made an effort to move. She looked at Solomon, who must have sensed her movement, for he opened his eyes and turned to face her.

"Let me make us something to eat or drink. What would you like?" asked Catherine.

He shook his head, "I can't face anything, but thank you for offering. Just help yourself to whatever you can find in the mess." He closed his eyes again.

Catherine dared to ask, "Did you managed to get everything sorted upstairs or do you need a hand with anything?"

Solomon sat upright on the sofa, "Look, about before, I can't apologise enough for shouting at you. All of this," he perused the messy room, "It's just too much."

"All is forgiven, I was worried about you that's all, I just wanted to try and help."

"I know and that's why I feel so wretched. I was shouting with anger and frustration at them for doing this, not shouting at you."

"Honestly, there's nothing to forgive, I cannot image how you are feeling, having to deal with the loss of your father and now this."

Close to tears, he changed the subject, "Did the book reveal any clues, anything that may help us find him?"

"First of all, I'm insisting we have something to eat and drink."

"I suppose you're right, and it's getting dark. I'll light the lamp and some candles, and you make us something." A hint of amusement formed on his face, "On second thoughts, you sort the lighting and I'll make us something to eat and drink." Catherine smiled at the subtle dig, openly admitting that cooking and baking were skills she did not possess.

Walking around the house with a candle, trying to find and then light other candles, she heard commotion from the kitchen.

"Damn, they've broken nearly everything, the basta…" His voice tailed off.

Catherine made her way along the hallway and saw a lost man leaning on the kitchen table, physically and mentally exhausted by events out of his control. In a sudden rage, he swiped all the broken items onto the floor. Dewy droplets of red splashed onto the jagged fragments of glass and porcelain.

Unnerved by his power, and on seeing the blood dripping from his right hand, Catherine tried to coax him away from the devastation, "Come on, let's head over to mine and we can sort this out tomorrow, when the light is better and …" she quickly refrained from saying, *and when you've calmed down.*

With no energy left to fight, he nodded in agreement. He reached for the white towel, seemingly the only item still in its original place, hanging over the handle of the stove. He wrapped the cotton material around his hand a couple of times, the blood soon seeping through the cloth.

His demeanour changed. "We'll take this." Lying on the floor was a fish which he grabbed by the tail. He shook the scaled body to get rid of the broken glass and crockery. "I caught it this morning down by the river and …" he looked around the kitchen, "… and I pinched this potato from the basket out the front of the store." He winked.

Feeling slight unease at his labile mood, she tried to make light of the situation, "I hope you are teasing me, Solomon Smith."

He winked once more, "No questions, no lies."

They both smiled for the first time in many an hour and headed over to Catherine's cottage.

After a delicious meal, they sat on the sofa. Solomon was not in the right frame of mind to read Sam's journal, so he asked her if she would summarise the content of each page of the book she had read so far.

"The story starts with Samson Cohen and his fascination with trying to prove the existence of the artefacts associated with the Lord Jesus Christ."

"Like the goblet from which they drank wine at the Last Supper? Or his burial shroud?"

"Yes, exactly, all those sorts of things but soon he concentrates on only one item. The cross, the actual wooden cross on which Jesus Christ was crucified."

"*The* cross?" asked Solomon. Catherine nodded. Solomon sighed out of ballooned cheeks. Catherine continued with the story.

"Samson Cohen was living within a Jewish community in Germany. Everyone else at the time was looking for the real treasures, such as the said goblet, thinking gold, silver, jewels, priceless artefacts, whether religious or not. Samson only wanted to find things for his love of Christ. A pilgrimage of love, purely for devotion and protection. He made a list of all the items mentioned in the bible and attempted to do some research, but others were doing the same. He then realised that no-one was looking for the cross on which Christ had died. The cross was not decked in jewels or made from gold, so he surmised that nobody was interested as it was only made from wood and held no material worth. Anyway, it seemed to have disappeared. He read the scriptures detailing the landscape of the area where crucifixions were said to have been undertaken. He read about how centuries later, Constantine and his mother Helena also started researching what had happened to the cross. Anyway, to cut a long story short, here are the main facts. One, Samson Cohen believes the cross is hidden here in Edenvale. Two, that the Romans brought the cross with them to Carlisle and for a while, the cross was hidden and protected by the elite fighting force, the cavaliers known as Ala Petriana. They were based at Uxelodunum, the largest fort on Hadrian's wall. Some believed the Romans had taken the cross so very far away as people from all over the world were coming to the original site of the cross. The Romans hated that people travelled so far and wide to kneel and pray where Christ had died. The Romans had tried to burn the cross, bury it, chop it but they were mysteriously defeated at every turn. Their only choice was to take the cross far away, to the final frontier of the Roman Empire, as far away from Jerusalem as possible with the force of the Roman Army to prevent any further worship or martyrdom." She paused for a little while to get her breath and focus her thoughts. Solomon remained quiet, enjoying the peace and distraction her story was bringing.

"So, where was I? Yes, the cross was brought to Carlisle by the Romans. Roman Emperors throughout the occupied centuries came to Carlisle and

Hadrian's Wall, specifically Uxelodunum because of the cross. The XX VV or in other words the Twentieth Legion of Valeria Victrix assisted in hiding and protecting the cross."

"Ahh, we thought XX VV was twenty ten or a continuation of roman numerals. When in fact the VV stood for Valeria Victrix."

"Precisely, it was a victorious fighting force, the strongest army there was to protect the cross. The emperors thought they were hiding and protecting the cross from the Jews and Christians, preventing their pilgrimages. Little did they know XX VV were secretly formed to protect the cross from the Romans."

"Like a double lie?" asked Solomon.

"I guess so. As with every other secret, word somehow spread. Now please remember these are Samson's written words not mine, so do not be offended thinking this is me saying this."

"Go on."

"Samson thought Carlisle sounded a rather boring town, so he questioned why Roman Emperors, Kings of England and holy saints would be fascinated with the place. History books explained the fascination was to do with mighty battles between England and Scotland, with Carlisle Castle being one of the most besieged castles, but at the time of Christ and the Romans, England and Scotland did not exist. Samson believed the fighting and fascination was to do with the cross. William the Conqueror conquered England in 1066 and sent his son to Carlisle to investigate the city. By then, Carlisle was like a no man's land, run by a local warlord named Dolfin. That was why Carlisle was not included in the Domesday book, Carlisle was not in England or Scotland as we know it."

"You've lost me now. This is too much information to take in." Solomon had slipped down the sofa and was properly relaxing.

"I'm trying to summarise but maybe I've over simplified things or over complicated things, I'm not too sure. I think Samson was implying that even William the Conqueror knew what was going on and was trying to protect Carlisle from scrutiny, hence why he did not include it in the Domesday book."

"But what's the Domesday book?"

"Hold on," she scrolled back through the journal, "William the Conqueror compiled a list of all the land he owned in England, and this became known as the Domesday book."

"So, he didn't want people knowing about Carlisle?"

"According to Samson, yes. But then William the Conqueror sends his son, William Rufus to build a castle in Carlisle on the former Roman fort of Luguvalium."

"As an extra deterrent to fight for and protect the cross?"

198

"From what Samson has written, yes." She flicked through the pages to remind herself of the kings who had fortified the city of Carlisle, "Henry I, King David of Scotland, Edward I, Richard III, Henry VIII etcetera, they strengthened the castle's defences and fortified the city's walls. Samson Cohen suggested they did this to protect the cross from invaders."

"So, for many a century, the cross was in Carlisle. But where is it now?" asked Solomon.

"The ultimate question. Samson believes it's in Edenvale. His reasons are so detailed that I cannot remember them all, but I'll try to give an overview. Edenvale is situated on the River Eden. He believes this is a play on the Garden of Eden. This was based on biblical descriptions of being in an area with four tributaries. Around Carlisle Castle, the Rivers Caldew, Petteril and Eden converge."

"But he said there was supposed to be four tributaries?" enquired Solomon.

"The River Lyne is now north of Carlisle and Samson stated there is evidence that the river was forced to change its course over time."

"That man had too much time on his hands!" Solomon shuffled to sit more upright. "No wonder he's in the asylum."

"Honestly, he goes into immense detail about Faith, Hope and Charity. In the church there is the statue of 'Faith'. Have you seen it?"

"No, never been in."

"It's on the left-hand side. A woman stands over a mother and her child. Samson questioned whether she is pointing to heaven or if she is pointing to Jesus on the cross. The grieving woman who is lying down is supposedly Mary Magdalene."

"And who is the child?" asked Solomon.

"Samson reckons the child may be born from Mary Magdalene and Jesus Christ. She is mourning his death but the woman or angel standing over her is pleading with her to have faith."

"What? Hmm, this is all getting a bit too far-fetched for me. I'm not too sure about all of this. These assumptions could be from a madman. That policeman who came to your house, you said the men from the asylum had taken Samson away."

Catherine did not admit it, but she had come to the same conclusion at one point but there were just too many coincidences.

She continued undeterred, "The stone seat by the River Eden, you must have seen that?"

"The one with the angel wings?"

Catherine nodded, "Samson wrote that the seat represents 'Hope'. One can sit there, admiring the beauty of nature with protective arms wrapped around you, like your own personal guardian angel."

199

Solomon mocked, "Yeah, whatever."

Slightly annoyed she continued, "Charity, the small altar area in the priory gatehouse. Offering asylum and food to anyone needing help. You must admit, it is all fitting into place."

"Yeah, but how is this gonna help me find my father? How is he involved in this? Why has my house been ransacked?"

After a few minutes of silence Catherine continued, "I think people get too close to the truth. They start searching, asking questions and are killed, or taken somewhere, but if we continue trying to work things out, it may lead us to him. Your dad saw the diary, the information from the Greek gentleman then he started asking about the triquetra symbol and XX VV. They must have been watching."

"This *Order of the Priory* sounds like they are evil, to do this to people, I can't get my head around why." He scratched his scalp, as if his brain was itchy with the exertion.

"I know, it just doesn't quite make sense. We need to find the cross. I'm sure the people at Oak Bank are involved with this. I haven't told you about my alibi and neither will I at present, but I was told the Order were 'one of the deeper layers of cells within a society of secrets', whatever that means, and I'm convinced they must be part of this."

"So how do we find out?"

"I know you won't like this, but I need to talk further with Jeremy."

"That snob who was all over you?"

Catherine did not immediately respond, needing time to think about possible reactions to what she might say.

Solomon leaned forward, resting his forearms on his thighs. Following a big sigh, he said, "If it means finding my father then do what you need to do, but don't tell me. The least I know the better." His palms slapped the top of his thigh and then he stood up sharply, "I'm going home. I need to sort things out."

"If it's all right with you, I'd like to stay here and finish the rest of this book. It may reveal a few more answers." She followed him to the door.

"Take care, you know where I am if you need me."

She nodded, feeling sad that he was going.

As if reading her mind, he said, "I find it hard leaving you."

"You too, I love having you around the place."

They embraced tenderly. Solomon distanced himself from her and held her at arm's length. "I love you, Catherine, and again I'm sorry for …"

Pretending to be annoyed, she ushered him out of the door, "Stop saying you are sorry, or you *will* be sorry." She started laughing. "But I am sorry you have to go."

He turned, as if unable to leave but knowing that he must, "You will be in my dreams this evening." He blew her a kiss at the garden gate and walked along the street without turning around.

Catherine felt so alone. Having Solomon around was a comfort. She had been so strong for such a long time, functioning in complete isolation and now she had the opportunity to be part of something, to share the burden with another. Solomon looked after her, cared for her, would probably do anything for her and she would reciprocate for him.

This evening, even though he only had the use of one hand, he had prepared the fish which she was thankful for, because there was no way she could have dealt with its eyes. Despite his injured hand, he had prepared the stove, cleaned out the grate and lit the fire, all whilst his own house was a ransacked mess. How dear he was to her, yet she did not want to admit her growing feelings for Jeremy.

He was cocky, he pushed boundaries, he was wild, unpredictable and horribly mean. Yet in complete contradiction, he was interesting, extravagantly kind and thoughtful, allowing her to stay in this quaint cottage and funding her expenses. Oh, but he was so annoying, she wanted to hate him but found herself ... she stopped short of saying loving him.

To distract herself once more, she prepared everything ready for a comfortable read in front of the fire. She picked up Samson's journal and did not stop until she had absorbed every haunting word.

Chapter Thirty-Eight

To avoid unannounced visits and further questioning, Catherine fulfilled her side of the contract and penned a letter to Doctor Wainwright, informing him of her thoughts, activities and achievements since being in the village. This seemed a simple task, but she questioned every word on the page, wondering what he would deduce from her scribblings. In the end, she decided not to worry, for she had been so wrong when he asked her to visit Sam's house, Fernleigh. She had thought Doctor Wainwright knew about her secret and was wanting her to confront her past, yet he was only wanting to know if she could live there.

Day by day, Fernleigh featured less in her ruminations, and she once again considered whether she could sell it. The house had been so beautiful, with pleasing patterns of brick work, fancy wooden fascia, stained-glass windows in the front door and beautiful tiling around each fire. She sighed, Sam's dream slowly turning into a nightmare: the rotting porch, the peeling paint, the overgrown garden.

The proceeds of the sale would certainly help the financial situation for her and her parents but hopefully Petteril Bank House would soon be sold to Jeremy, and she would not have to think about Fernleigh anymore. The thought of someone moving in there and living with the ghosts of the past would not go down too well. It was not worth the risk.

With the letter finished, Catherine took her time in precisely folding the pages and writing Doctor Wainwright and the asylum address on the front. She donned her outdoor attire then walked to the store to post the letter. She contemplated knocking on Solomon's door but decided against it, knowing that he just wanted to be alone to sort out the house and find some quiet time. As she retreated her steps, the orphans came out of the spooky house with their instruments and Catherine decided to wait and watch them play.

The governess, Miss Montgomery, orchestrated the most beautiful songs. The angelic children engaged with the haunting music they were creating from their simple instruments. They appeared to be consumed by the melodic notes, their expressions fluid with the musical journey.

Moved by the magical performance, Catherine felt transported to a spiritual realm where emotions were heightened with such intensity that she had to suppress the urge to cry. The delicate hairs on her forearms created goosebumps and she shivered as the music came to a crescendo.

As if snapping out of a trance, the children carefully placed their instruments on the village green then ran around with such joy as if the last few minutes had been an illusion. They rolled in the grass and down the banks. Miss Montgomery looked perturbed at the state of their clothes.

Catherine approached her. "You have such talented children."

"They have all suffered in some way, yet they are like flowers, blooming despite adversities. It's a small blessing they have each other and can find a release for their emotions through their music." Miss Montgomery stood tall and proud for such a young woman, yet she seemed to carry such a weight, her eyes heavy with sorrow.

"Thankfully, they appear to be happy now," said Catherine.

The women stood and watched the children play for a few moments.

Catherine continued, "If I may be so bold and I apologise now for my directness, but who funds the orphanage? You are so young, and you have so many children, and you live in this grand house, I was wondering …"

"Initially I did not know. I was told they wanted to remain anonymous. When my parents died, my siblings and I, we had nowhere to go and my mother had been working as a wet nurse, looking after other children for money."

"I am so sorry to hear this news. You must have been devastated by their loss. How did you all cope?"

"Our landlord kicked us out as we had no means to pay, so we were made homeless. We slept on the streets and scavenged for food. Thankfully, it had been a warm summer and we coped by huddling together under a bridge. A sympathetic policeman found us close to death, we were skin and bones by then. He took pity on us and took us to the workhouse by the castle. I genuinely believe he thought he was doing the right thing in caring for us but the conditions in the workhouse were dreadful. The wardens beat us and locked us in the dungeon for bad behaviour. The children weren't being bad, they were only playing, but the proprietors were strict and devoid of humour. They made us work until our hands or knees were bleeding."

Catherine's heart was close to breaking at the sad story, trying not to think about the details, "How on earth did you escape and come to be here?"

"I assume you know him for I have seen you chatting and walking with him. Jeremy Fisher is our proprietor."

203

Catherine struggled to suppress her shock. "Jeremy and I are acquainted from years ago, and I'm surprised he funds an orphanage. He never wanted children of his own. I would even go as far as saying he detested children."

Miss Montgomery paused to reflect, "Time changes us, I guess. Our priorities evolve. Jeremy has acquired a fair amount of land in these parts. He built this grand home and offered to house us. His children both have deformities, and he pays me to take in those children who are different."

Again, Catherine was flabbergasted. "I was only aware of Jonathan, so he has another child?"

"It is no secret, so I know I am not breaking his confidence. He adores her, but his lifestyle means he is never around much. Her mother died when she was only one year old. He paid for a governess to care for her, but the child was lonely and bored."

Catherine reflected on her own childhood when they moved to Petteril Bank House. A grand home, set in acres of land, overlooking the River Petteril, the location was wonderful, but the isolation was depressing, with only a tutor for company.

Miss Montgomery continued, "Her name is Angela, but he calls her Angel. The little girl with the silken ringlets, the one with the calliper on her leg."

Trying to find her, Catherine's eyes darted around the green in search of Angel. It was the same little girl that had caught her eye. The same little girl that Samson had written about in his book. As she played on the green, she appeared slow and clumsy compared to her friends, but she was smiling and chuckling and having a wonderful time. The sight was sheer joy.

"She's so pretty and happy." Emotion seemed to crowd Catherine and she suddenly felt overwhelmed. The rush of feelings made her cry. "Many years ago, I lost my little girl. I nearly died too through losing so much blood. Not a day goes by that I do not yearn for her, wondering what she would have looked like, her personality, wondering what her interests would be." Catherine dabbed her eyes with her handkerchief. "Please ignore me, how embarrassing, but seeing the children so happy. My heart is finally grieving for my baby girl."

"Children are truly a blessing, lent to us by God. I thank him every day for taking care of us and him bringing us such joy, knowing one day he may take them away, so every day is precious and not to be wasted."

Catherine recovered her composure. "What I said before, I have never told anyone. Please, if you can keep ..." She hesitated.

"Your secret is safe with me, if that is what worries you." The lady smiled. "Everyone has their dark and mysterious side."

Feeling relieved, Catherine smiled once again. *Thank you*, she silently mouthed. For a few more minutes they watched the children play. Billy was the oldest child, born with a cleft palate and had speech difficulties, but he was a lovely lad and always willing to help the younger children. Jimmy was the second oldest of all the children, but he was their natural leader. He liked rules and order and liked to line up the children as if they were soldiers. Prunella was the clown of the group, always pulling faces and doing funny things. Her laugh was contagious, when she started giggling, she could not stop, resulting in all the children laughing then eventually crying, ending with them all exhausted and sighing. Then laughing again.

Miss Montgomery clapped at a steady pace and the children on hearing the familiar rhythm knew it was time to line up and go home. Jimmy counted the children until he reached little Angel at the back of the line with her heavenly curls and cherubic face. He then took his place at the front of the queue.

Miss Montgomery offered, "It has been a pleasure chatting with you."

"Likewise, if you ever need help with the children, or just someone to talk with, you know where I am."

"That would be lovely, thank you." Miss Montgomery slightly bowed her head.

As the children crossed over the dirty road and headed home, the women noticed Jeremy Fisher leaving Oak Bank Hall. He waved at the ladies then headed towards them. Jeremy was on his best behaviour, acting like a true gentleman, kissing the back of their hands. Miss Montgomery and Jeremy chatted for a few minutes about the children, with Jeremy ensuring their every need was catered for. He mentally made a note of the few simple but necessary items they required. Catherine was in awe of Jeremy, with how thoughtful and caring he was of his adopted wards. As her mind drifted, wondering how life may be with Jeremy, she was aware of a voice talking to her.

"Catherine, are you well?" asked Jeremy. His forehead was furrowed.

"Sorry, yes, I am fine, thank you. My mind was drifting. You were saying?"

Miss Montgomery repeated, "I asked if you would both like to come inside for some tea?"

"But yes of course, I would be delighted," said Catherine, her whole body beaming with happiness at the invitation.

"Before we do, I need to have a word with Miss Fawcett in private if that is agreeable?" Jeremy looked at them both.

"Of course," said Catherine.

"I'll head inside and tell the children you will be here shortly." Miss Montgomery nodded, stepped backwards and then made a slow dignified climb up to the house.

"Am I invited into your home?" Jeremy raised a cheeky eyebrow.

"Are you going to be cordial?" asked Catherine, she too raising an eyebrow.

"I won't make promises I cannot keep."

She sighed, "If you must come in then do so, but please, no sexual references."

"I'll be discreet, you won't even know I'm in there." He winked, laughing to himself.

Catherine was oblivious to the subtle innuendo. "I'm so sorry about the other night. Your face, the bruising, the swelling…"

"Shh, do not worry yourself, I'll survive."

She smiled.

Once inside, he dropped himself onto the sofa and lounged freely, his legs spread wide. "Small but cosy, I love this little cottage." He perused the room.

"I hope so, you built it." Catherine took off her hat and her gloves. "Tea?"

"We'll be having tea there. Do you have anything stronger?"

After first tutting, she scolded Jeremy, "It is still morning."

"Never stopped me before," he grinned. His surname was appropriate. He would throw the line, she would bite, and he would slowly reel her in. "Relax, Catherine. You are always so on edge. At the ball, I saw the real you. Charming and delightful."

From the kitchen, Catherine shouted through, "That was the copious amounts of intoxicating beverages I consumed."

"Then I suggest you drink more often." A smug smile appeared on his lips, waiting for a sarcastic reply.

Catherine arched backwards so she could see him, "Actually, we did have fun, didn't we." She smiled.

Jeremy was not expecting that reply, "You were dazzling, you captured my heart, my mind, my soul. You drive me crazy, you tease me, you say the most hurtful things to me." He feigned sad eyes.

"And you deserve every morsel for your intolerable ways, Mr Fisher."

"There are hordes of girls more beautiful than you, more intelligent too, with a palatable dress sense. I have them throwing themselves at me, even with this visible infliction. I'm a killing machine yet they still drool over me. Money, that's it. That is all they crave. As for you, you are mediocre at best, but you excite and interest me in a way others do not. You are so very different." This time he feigned a serious look. "You say you detest me, but I know deep in your heart you lust after me." His lips lifted to the right, his eye wrinkling with mischievousness.

Trying not to smirk, for her acting skills were not as finely tuned as her guest's, she carefully carried the tea tray through. "Your kind words truly flatter me. I am honoured to be described as mediocre by such a highly influential character as yourself." She placed the tray on the small table and opened the teapot to stir the leaves. "Lust is maybe too weak a word for my obsessively salacious desires. You are my sordid secret." She poured the tea.

"I knew it. No man or woman has ever resisted me before. My charms are infinite, able to penetrate the hardest of exteriors." His left arm cradled the top of the sofa, and he had a look of sheer contentment on his face.

"Is this why you needed to speak with me? To pick away at my defences until I succumb?"

"No, my dearest Catherine. Today I am as sober as a vicar just before he devours the sacramental vino. Once again, I will ask for your hand in marriage. If I had the opportunity to whisk you away somewhere romantic, a beautiful landscape such as Rome or Paris I would but I know you would refuse such a notion. So here I am." Despite the pain and discomfort, Jeremy got down on one knee and from his pocket he produced a ring, a petite gold band housing an impressive oval ruby surrounded by sparkling diamonds. "Will you marry me, Catherine?"

The silence was awkward.

Jeremy continued, "Ever since we parted Christmas 1844, I have missed you dearly, wanted you, cried for you, you have never left my thoughts. Believe me, I have searched Europe, Africa, Asia but no one compares, your beauty, your divine soul and I mean in here and here." He touched his head and then his heart, his hand remaining there.

"I'm going to have to stand, my knee is killing me." He got up with some assistance from Catherine. He continued to hold her hands. "It is official, I have purchased Petteril Bank House from your father, but I have put your name on the deeds. The house is yours, dear Catherine. Do what you wish with it. An orphanage, like Mary has achieved here, or a school, a specialist hospital, whatever you would like to do, the choice is yours."

"I am truly lost for words Jeremy." She could barely breathe.

He gently tugged on her hands to get her attention. "Look at me!" She did as she was told. "I am not trying to buy your love. I love you. I always have. You never realised this, but I have watched you from afar since the day we parted. I know this sounds creepy, and I did not want to admit this, but I know everything about you. Initially, when my father announced we were to marry, I rebelled. I did not want an arranged marriage at that age. I was having too much fun. Yet, since the day you walked away, I have never met anyone who I would even contemplate marrying. Like I said, this is not about money, this is about love. The house is yours anyway. Whether you marry me or not. The only thing you cannot do is sell the house without my permission. If you survive me, then the house fully becomes yours, to do with what you see fit."

So many words and thoughts yet no sensible sentence would form. Jeremy had been watching her from afar, what on earth did he mean by that statement? Her mind flitted to the opportunities, what she could do with the house, her parents, the people she could help. Jeremy, he was suffering with this infliction. The craziness of his youth had gone, he was successful, powerful, admired. Her mind was fuddled, too many things to consider.

Her thoughts turned to Solomon, he always seemed to be last on her list of considerations. Now feeling awful that the lovely gentleman was the least in her thoughts only made her feel worse. She tried to justify her thoughts by thinking he was last on her list because he was well, he did not need sympathy or financial help or support. He was strong and reliable … but then she realised he did need support. His father was missing, and his house had been destroyed by thugs. For a split second she wondered if Jeremy had orchestrated these events.

His voice broke her garbled thoughts, "So, will you marry me, Catherine?"

"Jeremy, I am eternally grateful for your kind offer …"

"I sense there is going to be a *but*."

"Your generosity is amazing. You are so kind and thoughtful. My heart is racing at the thought of going home to Petteril Bank, after all these years. I cannot thank you enough."

"Yes you can, by marrying me."

"Jeremy, please."

"I'm still waiting for the *but*."

She deliberately did not say *but,* "However, I cannot accept."

"The house or my hand in marriage?"

"Neither, both." Her eyes glistened with sadness.

With a smirk Jeremy said, "You are so predictable."

He put the ring back in his top pocket and walked towards the door.

"I'm truly sorry, Jeremy." Her heart deflated at the prospect of him leaving.

"No you're not. Come on. We will go and see the children. You know about Jonathan, I would also like you to meet my daughter, Angel. And as for your hand in marriage, you know I will never give up."

Chapter Thirty-Nine

Mary Montgomery gave Catherine and Jeremy a grand tour of the orphanage. They started in the grounds, admiring the tidy fruit and vegetable plots, although at this time of the season, there was little colour. From a large oak tree dangled a swing, made from ropes hooked over a sturdy branch and tied to a log for the seat. At the bottom of the garden was a crooked tree with knots and gnarls plus many levels of low-lying branches which Mary admitted was a magnet to the children for climbing.

As the tour continued inside, Catherine could see the house was well cared for. The spooky, gothic exterior was a misleading façade for a warm and welcoming interior. There were a variety of toys such as rag dolls, painted wooden trains, metal soldiers and miniature houses with miniscule furniture. There were some interesting wooden puppets including a king, queen, jester and a witch and an expertly constructed mini theatre with red velvet curtains. There were plentiful books and the children had access to quills and paper.

With three of her friends, they found Angel playing with an old wooden wheel as she tried to run alongside it as she rolled it down the long corridor. She was so pretty with blond ringlets, fair skin and bright blue eyes. The only imperfection being her right leg, but with support from the calliper, her impairment failed to hinder her fun.

The love demonstrated between father and daughter was a joy to witness. They both beamed on seeing each other. With an abnormal run, she jumped into her father's arms, and they hugged for ages. He spun her around and kissed her all over her hair to which she giggled and squealed with delight. He gently lowered her feet to the floor and ensured she had gained her balance before he let her go. From his inner coat pocket, he revealed a shiny penny. Angel's eyes shone bright at the gleaming coin. Her father clicked his fingers and the coin suddenly disappeared. Angel could not hide her shock; her eyes and mouth open wide with wonder. Jeremy tickled her behind the ear, making her laugh and the coin magically re-appeared in his hand. Her innocent eyes were as wide as the penny. By now, most of the younger children were queueing up so they too could retrieve a magic penny from behind their ear. Jeremy did not discriminate, he entertained them as much as his daughter. They were a family.

When all the children were rich with coins, Catherine, Jeremy and Mary climbed the stairs to the tower room. Framed pictures and poems adorned the walls, the artwork seemingly created by the hands of the children. One picture stood out amongst the others. There was a big round face, with swirls of black hair sprouting out of the top, then cascading like the branches of a willow tree. There were scary black dots for eyes. The caricature had a big wonky nose and an unfortunate ink blot, creating what looked like a gangrenous wart at the tip. The face had one big tooth at an angle.

Jeremy noticed Catherine admiring the picture. "Exquisite don't you think? Angel has captured Mary's likeness so eloquently. The tones, the shading, the experimental strokes, remarkable as she was only four years old when she created this masterpiece."

"I quite agree, her talents should not be ignored." Hoping not to offend, Catherine gazed over at Mary who was rolling her eyes but then she smiled.

Jeremy intervened, "For a long time I have wanted you two to meet. You girls are my world and with Jonathan and Angel and the other children, I'm the luckiest man to have ever lived."

The ladies looked at each other and smiled in amusement. Jeremy continued, "In many ways, you have been part of my life. I have helped you both, but more importantly, you have helped me. Drinking, money, socialising, entertaining, extravagant balls, blah, blah blah, with hindsight, so superficial, so boring. At the time they were amazing, heaven or should I say hell knows how much pleasure a man can have." He closed his eyes and smiled, as if re-living his finer movements, then sighed. The ladies once more glanced at each other and rolled their eyes. "But I have a confession. You are not here by sheer coincidence, a stroke of luck or by chance. I was unsure who to confide in first, so I have decided to tell both of you at the same time."

He raised from the chair and paced the room before settling to look out of the tower window. This was probably the highest point in Edenvale, with magnificent views over the village green and to the countryside beyond. Jeremy turned and rested on the window seat, his face now partially shadowed. "You both know me well, devoid of tact, heartless some would say, so I'm just going to blurt it out."

The ladies were no longer smiling as they held their breath, waiting for the revelation.

"Catherine, this is your daughter. Mary, this is your mother."

The women glanced sideways at each other to gauge a reaction.

"Catherine, your baby did not die. She was taken away by your parents and left on a doorstep. Mary, sweetest Mary, I look on you as my own daughter, I am so proud of you, but Catherine is your birth mother. The woman you called mother was a baby farmer, a paid guardian, she was not your kin."

The ladies were silenced by his admission. Catherine's eyes glistened with tears, her bosom heaved with a racing heart, her hands shaking by his confession. Mary was stoic, her emotions frozen.

Catherine broke the ice first, "Jeremy, please tell us the truth, I hope you are not teasing us."

When Jeremy did not immediately reply, Mary said, "I sincerely believe he has never lied to me, other than omitting to tell me the truth about my family." They looked towards Jeremy, waiting for answers.

"Catherine, you had been poorly for such a long time. My heart was breaking, knowing you were incarcerated in that room, but I ensured you and your family, along with Mary's family had sufficient means to survive all these years, without me directly being involved in your care."

They chatted for what felt like hours, with Jeremy recalling information from over the years that the women knew to be true. Catherine was unravelling. Her face was writhing, trying to stem the screams, the anger, the grief, her body trembling. Mary kept herself calm and composed, almost emotionless. Jeremy gave further examples of the times he had intervened, how he had provided money, a means of escape, why nasty people had mysteriously disappeared from their lives.

"Why keep this information to yourself for so long, knowing how we have suffered at the hands of others?" asked Mary.

He shrugged, "Life, right or wrong, secrets, knowing what to do for the best, fate. I've made many mistakes, but the time seems right to tell you both the truth."

"All those years I could have been with my daughter, but you kept her from me. All those years locked up, screaming, sobbing, hurting myself, tormented by pain. You could have saved us both from a torturous life." Catherine was losing her sanity. She could sense her regression into the dark place, her hands were restless, tense, fidgeting, destructive.

"I tried, honestly I did, but your parents, they took Mary away, leaving her on the doorstep of a childless couple who loved her, bringing her up as their own. Mary was so happy and thriving. Within a couple of years, the husband took ill with some sort of respiratory illness and the wife could not cope. They passed Mary on, not because they did not love her, it was because they could not provide for her. They thought they were doing the right thing. They found a woman who had taken on other children who seemed happy

211

enough. The woman was paid a fair price, the last of their meagre savings, to look after the child. The woman wasn't deliberately cruel, just hardship turned her that way. When her husband died and she was on her own, she completely lost it."

Mary added, "And that was the day she repeatedly hit me with the broom for dropping an egg on the floor. For breaking the shell, my punishment was a broken nose and teeth."

No longer able to suppress her emotions, Catherine hurried over to Mary and held her lovingly. "Even though you were only briefly in my arms before you were taken away, I named you Genevieve."

"Now, I didn't know that!" said Jeremy. He raised from the window seat and moved back to the armchair to be closer to the ladies, fascinated by the heightened emotions, in awe of true adoration and unconditional love.

"Jeremy, is all this really true?" asked Mary. The ladies clung onto each other's hands.

"All I can do is apologise for not telling you sooner."

Catherine and Mary gazed into each other's eyes. Recalling a portrait Sam had shown her of his mother nearly twenty years ago, she sensed the resemblance, a certain *je ne sais quoi*. "If my memory serves me well, your paternal grandmother was from France, and you look so much like her, elegant, fair skin, blue eyes, dark hair. Your father was called Samuel Thompson, or Sam ... oh dear ... there is so much to tell you about him. He was so wonderful, so caring but ... oh I'm sorry for rambling and being vague but so much time has passed yet the memories are still raw. Anyway, if I remember correctly his mother was from Brittany."

"Strange you should say that as I have been teaching some of the older children French. It's a beautiful language, romantic and poetic yet complex, with mysterious pronunciations."

"That's because they are inherently lazy and can't be bothered to speak properly, slurring their words after drinking too much wine" said Jeremy sarcastically. The women ignored his flippancy.

"So where do we go from here?" asked Catherine, as she dabbed her eyes with a handkerchief.

Jeremy held up his hands, "It is for you to decide. For many a year I have ensured you have both had a roof over your head, food and clothes. You are now able to decide what each of you want to do. However, I love you both for different reasons and I pray you will allow me to be part of this family, our family, whatever your decision."

Chapter Forty

The life she had known was collapsing like 'The Tower' in a pack of tarot cards. Racking her brain, Catherine recalled the card signified something like destruction, upheaval, ruinous circumstances but leading to liberation by escaping figurative and literal gaols. It was a churning cycle of events, but she placed her faith in God by daring to dream of happiness.

Slumped in her armchair, trying to remain physically calm to counterbalance the dizzying effects of her tumbling thoughts, Catherine went over the revelations in her head. Eighteen years ago, her daughter had been born grey in colour but covered in blood. Her parents had lied to her, deceived her all these years, insisting they had done everything possible to save the poorly bairn. On reflection, the blood had probably been her own, from the trauma of childbirth, a life changing event she had suffered on her own. The silent baby probably only needed her nose and mouth clearing or a few rubs or pats to her back to get her lungs filling with air. The house had been eerily silent. Catherine had never heard her baby cry, the shrill little sounds of dependency, there had been nothing to suggest her baby had survived the birth.

Since that day, Catherine had endured years of isolation, tears and sorrow for there had always been something missing from her life. She had always sensed Sam was close to her, for a long time denying he was even dead, holding on to those treasured moments of happiness. Strangely, she had never sensed her baby, putting it down to having never had the chance to bond, to feed, to smile, and to say, *I love you.* The memories were only fleeting, often doubting they were even real, with no evidence of her little girl having ever been born. After yesterday's revelation, she understood why. Their daughter was alive, with no sign of Sam's deformities, and even if she had developed a hunched back, Catherine would have adored her just the same because she was born out of love.

Little Genevieve, supposedly renamed Mary after being abandoned on a doorstep of strangers, was cared for in the first two years of her life, but callously disfigured years later by the very person paid to protect and look after her. Catherine's heart was close to breaking.

All those childhood years lost. All those years Catherine could have held her baby in her arms and watched her grow. She could have taught her to read, write, and play the piano. She wanted to cry once again. Instead of cheering at the news that her daughter was alive, celebrating how fabulous life was, she instead wanted to cry, to rip the curtains down, shred the cushions, tear down the walls. She wanted to take out her frustration on something, to mirror the devastation and pain inside. She felt she had been cheated, her life in tatters, shredded by the selfish cruelty of those who supposedly loved and cared for her. Jeremy, her parents, they had kept this secret from her all those years.

Doctor Wainwright's advice popped into her head. Acknowledge the past. She had to accept it. There was nothing she could do to change it, but she screamed out loud, mimicking the desperate cries she had heard in the asylum on many a dark night, expressing the pain and torment required to create such a blood-curdling sound. A scream so dark that nothing could escape from its hold. Her blood churned with anger, the very people she trusted, how could they be so cruel. Her own parents, giving their only grandchild away.

Jeremy had said it was mainly due to embarrassment, that the child's father was a convicted murderer, hanged in public for all and sundry to see. Money, they had none, or very little by this stage. They could not afford to feed another mouth. She had asked Jeremy why he had not intervened then, by giving them money. His excuse was he had observed from a distance, not wanting to be seen, but to be there, to do the best he could without interfering directly with fate. Her parents had also worried about Catherine's mental health, that she could not even look after herself, never mind a defenceless child. The cutting, hitting, biting, all self-inflicted, they had worried that she may harm the child. On first hearing this admission, she felt she wanted to die, that her parents would even contemplate the idea that she would harm her own child, the shared flesh and blood of the man she had grown to love.

Jeremy had not deliberately forced the women apart, but the events of the last few months, seeing Catherine in the fields of the asylum, the opportunity to help when her situation was discussed in the case review. It had seemed like fate was showing him a way.

He had once again confessed his love, reiterated he wanted her hand in marriage. She thought about his proposal and how her life could be. Mary, her daughter, Jeremy, her husband, Jonathan and Angel, his children. Life would be complicated, but it was a family. The children at the orphanage, she wanted to be part of that family. Her own life had been so boring, losing all her friends when they moved to the grand but isolated Petteril Bank House. Forced into pretending she was a lady. Her parents prayed she would attract a rich husband. They had succeeded there with finding Jeremy.

As wonderful as life was in their impressive home, the embroidered dresses, silk slippers, dazzling jewellery, a private education, countless books, a comfortable carriage, she had felt empty inside, as if luxuries were meaningless. Then the guilt, how she had felt so ungrateful, as if wealth and comfort was something to cast aside after her father had worked so hard in accruing his fortune. Compared to others, she must have appeared to be a spoilt brat, as if the world was insufficient to fulfil her needs, always wanting more, never happy with her lot.

She had wanted for nothing, then suddenly she craved excitement, wanting to forge her own path in life, to be free to engage with others, make friendships, to be a little rebellious but in a good and decent way.

Samuel Thompson, he was so gentle, such a beautiful soul. She remembered sitting at the table in Fernleigh when the police turned up to arrest him. The desperate weeks he spent in the rat-infested gaol awaiting his trial. She hadn't felt well in a while, but she put it down to his wrongful arrest, the dread of fate dealing him the wrong card. She had been sick with worry, her appetite diminished and as a result she had lost so much weight. Little did she realise morning sickness was exacerbating her symptoms. Sam never knew about his baby.

She cried endlessly thinking of how everything had gone wrong the day he died. Reminiscing about the past was exhausting and finally she fell asleep in the chair.

A knock on the door of Rose Cottage woke her but she remained in a daze. She did not know the time of day. It was dark outside. Feeling awful with a blinding headache, she closed her eyes once more and could feel their tightness, swollen by tears for the death of a life barely lived. She thought she may just leave the door but when she heard Solomon's voice calling for her, she knew she had to answer. Dread swamped her.

Opening the door, she kept her head low and hoped that the darkness of the night hid her face, "Sorry, I'm not feeling too well at the moment. Can you come back later?" she suggested.

"Good grief, you don't look well at all. Is everything all right?" His hand gently held onto her arm.

"I just need some time on my own." Her head remained low, avoiding all eye contact.

"Yes of course but your face, have you been crying?" He tenderly touched her cheek and tried to wipe away the tear stains.

"Please, I just need some time." She kept him by the door.

"You're frightening me, Catherine. I know something's wrong. Please let me help and let me in. No one has threatened you or harmed you, have they?"

Shaking her head, she said, "No, nothing like that, I just have a really severe headache and I feel under the weather. I need to go and lie down." She tried to close the door, but Solomon insisted that he came inside. He lit the fire for her and some of the candles. He made her some tea and pulled together a few nibbles from the meagre provisions she had in the kitchen. "Have you eaten today? There's hardly anything here." She could hear him rummaging in the cupboards.

Her heart was breaking. He was so lovely and caring despite his own troubles. All the information she held inside, she was a mess, he deserved better. "I'm fine, honestly."

He brought through the tray. "Here, hopefully you'll feel better with this down your neck."

Her appetite had diminished, she felt sick at even trying to nibble the small piece of cheese and stale bread, but she smiled at Solomon and thanked him for his trouble.

"Any news on your father or your home?" She thought it best to distract from her problems.

"Mr Scrogg has given me a couple of days off from work, unpaid unfortunately but it's worth it. The house is almost back to normal apart from a few bits and bobs." He sat down and leaned forward, interlocking his fingers, "Nothing about my dad though."

Even though she did not feel like talking, she felt he deserved to know. "I finished the rest of the book that Samson Cohen wrote. Like I've already told you, he was convinced the cross of Christ was brought to Carlisle by the Romans, maybe in the mid-300s or so. The cross was brought to Hadrian's Wall nearing the fall of the Roman Empire. Everything is in that diary. It all makes perfect sense. I think he is correct. However, anyone found searching for the true cross seems to meet an unfortunate end. Samson refers to suicide, murder or going missing. The Order of the Priory is a secret society that watches over the cross and anyone with intentions of revealing the whereabouts of the cross meets an untimely end. This explains why Sam had started to write everything down in miniscule detail, the times, the people, the places. If anything were to happen to him there would be some sort of evidence."

Solomon puffed out his cheeks on realising the implications, "So, are you saying that my father has been a likely suspect to the Order of the Priory?"

"He had started to ask about the symbols, the triquetra, the XX VV around the village. They have obviously been monitoring him."

"I can't see how this helps me find him though?" He shook his head.

Catherine was blinking repeatedly, her eyes gritty and heavy with the swelling. "If you find the cross then I believe you will find your father, but you will need to be on your guard at all times."

Scratching his emerging stubble whilst thinking, he started to shake his head, "I cannot risk anything happening to you, to us. That sounds like a bad idea."

"I am deliberately withholding information from you at present, Solomon. For now, I have too much to think about. I am no longer getting involved with the book, Samson's story, the Order of the Priory, the crucifixion, I'm exhausted by it all." She placed her thumb and middle finger on the bridge of her nose hoping supportive pressure would ease her symptoms.

"Catherine, you are scaring me." He got off the sofa and knelt before her, resting his head on her lap. "I'm here for you. Your worries are my worries, but I cannot help if you don't let me in."

She stroked his head and felt pity for him. "I will but for now I cannot, I need some time."

"Can I see you tomorrow? We can discuss locations for the cross and where it might be hidden?"

She shook her head subconsciously but tried to show signs of hope, "I cannot promise anything. The news I had today, I'm shattered, I need time to think."

"Please, I'll call round tomorrow morning. I remembered you saying it was your birthday on the 6th. I want to spend the day with you."

She had forgotten all about her birthday. Feeling guilty, she reneged, "All right, come over tomorrow. I'm sorry about this evening. Hopefully, I can explain everything tomorrow. I need to sort things out in my head." She leaned over and kissed the top of his head.

He got up off the floor. She was reminded that Jeremy had also been on his knee, offering her Petteril Bank House and asking for her hand in marriage. It was all too much for a fragile mind to consider.

"You're not listening, are you?" asked Solomon when he received no reply following his question.

"Sorry, please forgive me. I've had a rather exhausting day." Her posture was slumped, the sleeve of her dress almost sliding off her right shoulder. "What were you saying?"

Feeling sad, nevertheless he smiled, "It can wait." Catherine followed him as he walked over to the door. "You know where I am if you need me. Sickness and in health, night or day, rich or poor or something like that." He went to kiss her, but she was still too dazed to notice. The kiss landed awkwardly on her cheek.

"Yes, something like that. Goodnight, Solomon." After seeing him out with barely a glance, she closed the door and immediately felt like crying again.

After checking everything was as safe as could be, she made her way upstairs and got ready for bed. No washing, no brushing of hair, only a clean of her teeth and then she got straight into bed. She had a decision to make. Marry Solomon, a caring soul who would do anything for her but with limited resources. Yet he had ideas, he wanted to be a journalist, a reporter, highlighting travesties and inequalities in the world. But they were only dreams, he had done nothing about his desires, instead he worked in a public house, helping people to waste their hard-earned money by washing their sorrows away.

The alternative was to marry Jeremy, a seemingly mean and cruel acquaintance who had interfered in many aspects of her life. When engaged, he had tried to force his way into her bedroom, calling her a bitch when she had declined his advances. His sarcasm and arrogance, his brutal honesty, even admitting his sexual preferences knowing sodomy was a sin in the eyes of the law. Yet he was thoughtful, the rare anatomy books he had painstakingly sourced and given her for Christmas 1844, such a perfect gift. How he had kept an eye on her and her family, helping them out in the bleakest of times yet never asking for glory or praise, happy knowing he had secretly helped former friends. Jeremy had offered her Petteril Bank House, wealth, comfort and above all a family, children and a purpose. He had given her a free reign on how she could utilise the house, whether for personal gain or as a charitable cause to help poor souls. Maybe his reasons were egotistical, but this was still better than doing nothing at all. However, she truly believed she had been wrong about Jeremy, that beneath that arrogant exterior beat an altruistic heart. She fell asleep still undecided about who to marry, if at all.

December 1958

"Are we nearly there yet?" asked Joyce.

"I'm not too sure, I'd guess another three hours or so," offered John.

His wife sighed. "Really? It's already been hours."

John's back was aching, but he did not want to complain. "Well by my reckoning, we should be hitting the new Preston bypass shortly."

Joyce did not respond, other than to open her handbag. She found her compact mirror, checked her teeth for lipstick and gave them a clean with her tongue. Her blond curls remained in place, but she still gave them an unnecessary tweak.

John continued, "I'm hoping it really is open. That's why I wanted to travel today. We will be literally one of the first few people to drive along this new stretch of motorway, what an honour."

"What *are* you on about?"

He explained about the new M6 motorway and the years of speculation and planning to build a road with two or three lanes the length of England, bypassing all the cities and towns, making travel up and down the west side of the country easier and quicker.

Bored, she responded with, "I was hoping we would get there earlier, so can try again."

"You on about sex again?"

She nodded with an air of nonchalance.

"For goodness' sake, why can't we just have sex without it being about babies? Why can't it be about us making love and enjoying the togetherness like it used to be? By the time we get there, I bet we'll both be too knackered to do anything tonight."

She tutted her annoyance.

They continued along the A6 in silence. Vans, cars, bicycles, tricycles, motorbikes, so many people with somewhere important to go. The journey from Derby had been tediously slow.

"There's definitely more cars on the roads nowadays." He sighed but then suddenly perked up, "Joyce this is it, the road, look! It's opening up."

John was fascinated by the architecture, the bridges, the sloped embankments and the physical barrier to the south bound road. "Wow, this is amazing! Shall I overtake this truck?" He put his foot on the accelerator and the car built up speed in the outside lane. He pulled back over to the left-hand lane having overtaken the truck and three cars. He was almost bouncing in his seat with enjoyment. "Crickey, that felt so fast, and the road is so smooth."

Joyce sighed, "If you were this enthusiastic and excited about impregnating me, we wouldn't be in this situation."

"For once in your life just enjoy the ride."

With a smirk Joyce replied, "That is exactly my point." She adjusted her neck scarf.

In awe and with sheer pleasure, John continued weaving in and out of traffic with relative ease along the first stretch of motorway, ignoring the sarcastic comments and digs from his wife.

Following a few minutes of silence John said, "Ha, I can't believe it, we are just about to overtake a Rolls Royce. The first one we have seen on the road in months, here on the bypass, on today of all days." They glided past the beautiful ghost. "A 1938 Wraith. What a stunning car."

"How come we haven't got a Rolls Royce?" asked Joyce.

"Because they are too expensive."

"Could you not get a staff discount, or get one as a company car?"

"Well, there was a staff discount, but the cars are still too expensive. Then again, I am getting a huge pay rise with this new job." They continued bombing along the road, "Anyway, our little Austin Cambridge has done us proud today." He patted the steering wheel.

"You still haven't told me about this new job." Joyce opened her handbag once more and took out a nail file. As she shaped her nail, the filings dropped on her skirt, and she brushed them onto the floor.

John grimaced but refrained from starting another argument. "Like I have already told you, I'm not at liberty to tell anyone about my new job." He started sweating under his tweed jacket despite the Christmassy scene outside the car. The reality of what he would be tasked with played on his mind. Too late questioning his decision now, but the money on offer had been too enticing.

"I'm not just anyone though, I'm your wife. We've often said to each other, 'Don't say anything to anyone else but ...'"

"Yeah, and then you say to your friends, 'Don't tell anyone else but ...'"

"I do not!" insisted Joyce.

"Yes, you do," corrected John, "and that is why I'm not telling you anything. Not at the moment anyway." He wound the window down to get a blast of fresh air.

"Then you can at least tell me who your employer will be."

"I can't tell you that either, it's all top secret, classified information etcetera." His stomach churned at the prospect of his potential creation and the impact on humanity. "I just don't want to be sacked before I've even started, that's all."

"Poppycock!" said Joyce.

John wound the window back up for he was now shivering and not because of the bleak wintery scenes outside.

Chapter Forty-One

Howling winds rattled through the roof timbers and rain hammered against the windowpane, waking Catherine from a troubled sleep. Not a good start to her birthday. Her bones ached with lethargy, her muscles drained of life and her entire body felt heavy with worry. She tucked the covers under her chin, attempting to block the uncomfortable physical and mental chills.

By the dreadful sounds outside, the weather was causing chaos. Creaking, battering, scratching, smashing, crashing, groaning and then a sickening scream. Catherine jumped out of bed, put on her dressing robe, moved aside one curtain and witnessed the devastation of the storm. Bare limbs severed from tree trunks, grey roof slates slicing through the air, debris rolling across the village green, Mrs Dawson's hat swirling in the raging tempest, her hair possessed by demons as she fought her invisible enemy. As if looking through an enchanted mirror, the weather reflected Catherine's mind, so she closed the curtain and went back to bed.

As the minute hand approached the vertical, she mentally prepared herself to get out of bed. The clock chimed ten, but she could not find the energy to rise. Ten minutes later, she crawled her way out of bed and made her way downstairs. The house was freezing, and a cold draft was wafting from underneath the back door. She shuddered and pulled her robe in tighter.

After lighting the kitchen fire and making herself a brew, she opened the curtains in the front room and was shocked to see a distorted face staring back at her through the watery windows. The white face was melting, disfigured by the storm when a hand suddenly appeared on the windowpane. Catherine's legs were fragile and about to give way. She heard a muffled voice.

"Catherine, are you well?" Solomon's caring tones. "Open the door!" His hand attempted to wipe away the water on the misted glass as he peered through the pane. "Catherine!" He was drenched through.

Shocked by his appearance, she quickly rushed to the door to let him in. "You scared me, literally I was frozen to the spot. What on earth are you doing standing out there in this weather?" She retrieved a towel from the small dresser and handed it to Solomon.

"It's your birthday so I didn't want to wake you if you were still sleeping. I thought after yesterday you needed the time to rest and to think." He patted himself down and dried his face, but his cap continued dripping water onto his nose. After taking off his cap and his jacket, he looked around for somewhere to hang them, aware they were sodden with rain.

"I'll hang them from the hook in the kitchen. It's a little warmer in there now the fire's on."

Solomon nodded but continued to shiver. Without being asked, he cleaned out the living room grate and started a fire, the small front room quickly warmed through.

"Happy birthday!" he finally announced and out of his pocket appeared a beautiful gold ring with a small, square emerald and even smaller round diamonds either side. "It was my mother's mother's engagement ring. I hope you like it. It is the only precious thing I have to remember her by." He got down on one knee. "I know I have asked you this before but today I want to make it official. Will you marry me, Catherine?" He offered her the ring.

Her past, present and future, swirled in an endless downward spiral. She felt like she was falling into a dark place. A place from which she could not escape. The deeper she fell the more she could not breathe. The air was dense, choking, too thick to inhale, clogging every breath she tried to take. The blackness crept up on her, extinguishing all light.

She woke up on the sofa, disoriented and anxious.

"Hello you." Solomon was sitting in the armchair, reading the diary penned by Samson Cohen. He closed the book and made his way towards her. He sat on the cold, hard floorboards and held her hand in his. "You fainted, just take your time, I'm here for you."

She wanted to turn away from him and cry. His handsome face, his toned body, his caring nature, he personified an angel, yet she wanted to recoil away from him. Disturbed by her thoughts, she wondered if she was possessed by a demon. "I don't deserve you, Solomon."

"Don't be silly. I love you. I'm worried about you. I just want you to feel better."

"I'm a mess."

"You are just a bit under the weather, and I bet you haven't eaten much. I don't know what happened yesterday, or the day before, but whatever it is, was, I'm here for you." He gently squeezed her fingers then tenderly kissed the back of her hand.

223

"You don't deserve me. I've done things, awful things. I have secrets, I tell lies. The asylum, I'm trouble you do not need in your life."

He paused for a while, as if taking everything in. For the first time, a shadow of doubt cloaked his face, probably wondering what secrets she kept locked in her heart. "But I love you, Catherine. I cannot begin to imagine what you could say to me that would make me change my mind." With sorrowful eyes, he longingly gazed into the depths of her soul. "Tell me what troubles you. What are you hiding from? This belief that you are somewhat crazy or evil. What could be so bad that you cannot tell me?"

Catherine wanted to blurt out everything: the murders nearly twenty years ago, disposing of the body, to having Sam's baby out of wedlock, to hearing yesterday that the baby had survived and was now a governess of an orphanage and living two doors away, the proposal of marriage from Jeremy and their growing relationship and admiration for each other. Money, Petteril Bank House, the opportunities he had offered her. The list seemed endless.

"You would no longer love me if I told you."

He paused before answering, "Then maybe it is for the best if I know. Although with the way I feel about you, I cannot imagine there would be anything that could turn my heart cold other than you admitting you kidnapped my father."

Catherine gently pulled her hand away from his and made to sit upright on the seat. "I feel so dizzy, perhaps a drink will help."

"Well, you've been out cold for a few minutes." Before she could even attempt to stand, Solomon had jumped to his feet and was in the kitchen filling the kettle with water. He was soon back in the front room and sat next to her on the sofa waiting for the kettle to boil.

They sat in silence as they sipped the hot tea. Catherine was desperately trying to predict possible outcomes depending on how much information she divulged. Ultimately, she loved Solomon, and did not want to hurt him. However, for some inexplicable reason, she also loved Jeremy. He teased her, cruelly made fun at her expense, humiliated her in front of his friends yet he was always on her mind.

She knew Solomon would conclude this was all about money if she decided to marry Jeremy. However, she had been rich previously and this did not make her happy. If anything, money and pride had been her downfall. She did not love Jeremy, but she found him interesting and exciting. Now she was contradicting herself, saying she loved him yet did not love him. For some bizarre reason, she wanted him in her life, despite his sarcasm and rudeness.

Solomon, she loved him so much, he was caring, loving, thoughtful, kind, funny but … but she could not fathom what it was that was missing, and why Jeremy filled that elusive part. Reversing her thoughts, she questioned what advantage Solomon would gain by marrying her but for once her mind was devoid of any thoughts.

"The cogs were spinning but now they've stopped."

Hearing Solomon's voice brought her back to reality. "Sorry, I was in a daydream."

"And have you come to any conclusions?

"I will tell you something but not everything, at least not yet. I'm sorry but I need more time to come to terms with something that has only just been revealed to me."

Solomon adjusted his seat position so he could see Catherine more easily. "Go on."

Catherine took a deep breath in and sighed, "I have a daughter."

With strigine eyes, Solomon bit his bottom lip as if trying to stop himself from reacting.

"You've heard me talk about Sam and my reasons for being in the asylum. Well ..." Catherine took a large inhalation and allowed the air to escape. "On one occasion, we ..." Again, she sighed in an attempt to calm her nerves. "We slept together, resulting in a pregnancy."

Now it was Solomon's turn to sigh, but he refrained from commenting.

"Sam never knew about the baby. Before I was even aware, the police had arrested him and he was sent to gaol, awaiting trial for the murder of numerous people. Wrongly arrested I might add."

Solomon nodded but still did not speak.

"I have already confided in you about my incarceration, the self-inflicted hurt, the isolation but I did not disclose the reality of having a baby. I gave birth to her in that shuttered room, with only a mattress and straw on the floor. I was bleeding, I was barely alive, my daughter she was covered in blood and all I remember is the grey, she was so very grey. My mother had been watching from a peep hole in the door. When she saw me hold by daughter in my arms, she came in, snatched the girl from me, told me she would clean her up, bathe her and things, but an hour or so later she told me the baby had died. I believed her because I had heard no cries, no screams as newborns usually do."

Solomon could see the tears welling in her eyes, she was swallowing hard, her voice trembling, her hands shaking, she was close to breaking. He held open his arms and she fell into his embrace. He kissed her hair and held her close. He slowed his breathing, hoping she could sense his calming heartbeat. He tickled her back, gently stroking her body, trying to dampen the shaking and spasms from her laboured breathing. After a while she slumped with a large final sigh.

"You were in love, you made love, you had a child out of wedlock, so what? It sounds like you would have married given the chance if it wasn't

225

for Sam's wrongful incarceration. Honestly, I am shocked but these events, as heart-breaking as they were for you, they are in the past. You have moved on. You have faced your many demons and are here to tell me the tale."

"There is more." She lifted herself away from his chest and comforting arms and for the first time since she started her story, made eye contact with Solomon. "Not only did I find out my daughter had survived, but she is still alive. My daughter is Mary Montgomery from the orphanage."

Solomon was shocked, his body recoiled, not in revulsion, but in sheer surprise, as if an almighty force had destabilised him. He regained his equilibrium, "Catherine, I'm …"

She finished the sentence for him, "Speechless?" He nodded. "So, can you see why I have kept this from you? I need time to come to terms with this … this lie, this … whole other life which has been kept secret from me all these years."

"Catherine, I want to reassure you that none of these concerns change how I feel about you. Your fragility and strength, you amaze me, I am completely disorientated by the extremes you endure but I still want to be here for you. Even more so now."

She started to cry, "Please don't be so kind, it only makes me worse."

"Then come on you silly beggar, no more sympathy." He crossed his arms and legs in an exaggerated manner.

"That's better." She laughed and snorted at the same time. "Oh my goodness, look at the state of me and I don't have a handkerchief to hand." She kept her hand over her nose.

Solomon reached his arm out to her, "Here, use my sleeve." They both laughed. "Honestly Catherine, stop trying to fight all your battles in solitude and fear. I'm here to share life's dramas with you."

She retrieved a handkerchief. "Solomon, I really don't deserve you." She walked over to the window and gazed outside at the wind battered trees and shrubbery as she cleaned herself up.

"I love you and that is all that matters." Solomon stood from the sofa, walked over to where she stood and wrapped his loving arms around her.

They stayed there for a while, holding on to each other, soothing away their troubles, with eyes protectively closed and hearts open to hurt but hoping to heal. Her head rested comfortably on his chest, the sound of his heartbeat providing a perfect rhythm in which to unwind and start the healing process. She felt comforted being in such strong and protective arms. Rain suddenly pelted against the window, giving them both a fright and making them jump apart. On hearing the noise, they both looked through the melting windowpane. They each saw a different distorted image. Solomon saw battle weary souls fighting an invisible enemy that was attacking and swirling from all sides. Catherine saw Jeremy leave Oak Bank Hall and her heart made itself known, winning the sound war against the storm.

Chapter Forty-Two

Alone on her birthday, she felt guilty for asking Solomon to leave, especially since he had offered her the beautiful emerald and diamond ring whilst down on one knee and asking for her hand in marriage. She had been unable to give him an answer. Even worse, she had requested time to think about various aspects of her life and being the gentleman he was, he had sadly left to face the pouring rain outside.

She wondered if there had been any mail from her parents, but the storm was a good excuse not to go to the store to find out. If her parents had sent a letter or a parcel, she did not know how she would feel, knowing how they had kept her daughter, their granddaughter, a secret all those years. Better not having to deal with the situation, especially on her birthday. Anyway, the store was probably closed after seeing Sally Dawson braving the weather earlier and heading in the direction of home.

Her daughter Genevieve, or Mary as she was now known, would be unlikely to know it was her mother's birthday. Catherine thought about the girl's features, she certainly had Sam's dark hair. Jeremy could be pretending they were mother and daughter for some sick thrill, but she knew in her heart he was genuine and telling the truth. A mother's instinct perhaps. The subtle signs were there if one looked closely enough for them.

Solomon, how dear he was, too perfect in fact, he was besotted with her, she could see love and devotion in his eyes, detected a tenderness in his heart and adoration oozed from his touch. She so dearly wanted to love him.

The beautiful engagement ring, it meant the world to him, passed down through generations of his family, he had said it was the only thing of worth, probably meaning emotionally as well as financially. She could not betray his devotion, yet she could not tell him how she really felt, that there were aspects of love from other sources. For the daughter she thought she had lost and for Jeremy, a somewhat flawed guardian angel whose kindness seemed to hold no bounds.

Money, she felt guilty even thinking about it. Money had been the bane of her life when she had it. Now it was the bane of her life without it. She denied Jeremy's wealth was a reason for loving him but now she had to ask herself if his fortune *was* a factor in her indecisiveness. How she hated herself for even thinking about money. Her daughter Mary, the orphanage, together they could make small changes, not enough to solve every problem but enough to change the lives of the poor children. She wondered if Solomon would want to be a part of this. She wondered if Jeremy would allow Solomon to be part of their family. When Jeremy asked for her hand in marriage, he had intimated that due to his infliction, the syphilis that was ravaging his body from the inside out, he knew that their relationship would not be physical. She pondered on whether he would be jealous of Solomon and refuse to allow him into their lives. Would Jeremy support him financially, allowing him to study and be the journalist he wanted to be? She could analyse all day long, but this needed action, she needed to speak with Jeremy.

Solomon had remembered it was her birthday and had waited outside in the pouring rain with an ensuing storm, allowing her the chance to lie in on her special day. He had given her a beautiful ring holding so many personal memories. It was all he could give. As she put on her outdoor attire, ready to face the storm, she wondered if Jeremy had remembered her birthday. Even after all these years, she had remembered his birthday, the 29th of March.

She closed the door behind her and went in search of Jeremy. The first place she stopped was Oak Bank. She had seen him leave but had not seen him return. Mr Schubert confirmed that he was not in residence and was unsure when he was due back. He did not know of his intended destination.

Catherine roamed the village for an hour, with no signs of Jeremy, but she had spotted his carriage on the outskirts of the village, so she knew he had not gone far.

Two workmen were sheltering from the rain under a tree. The road had made a little progress since her last visit, maybe one or two more rows of stones. A quick calculation revealed approximately one stone had been laid every other day. She knew they were up to something and wondered if they were part of the Order of the Priory, watching and reporting on any visitors to the village who may have plans to find or reveal the location of the cross.

She smiled at the workmen, and they reciprocated. She walked down the road, and by now she was soaked through. She remembered the last time she was this cold and damp, the day of Sam's hanging and the long walk to his home, resulting in increased confusion and a temperature. She needed to stay sane.

As she approached the priory gatehouse with its castellated roofline, she saw a flickering glow from the middle window. Walking through the stone archway, she turned to her left. Needing to use both hands, she twisted the heavy, ringed handle to open the thick medieval door. Not knowing what to expect, she climbed the stone spiral staircase with caution. Her long, flowing skirt made the ascent treacherous for she could not see her feet or the steps, and each stone was worn away with centuries of visitors.

As she opened the door to the hall, six men were sitting around the rectangular table feasting on the copious amounts of food. Two of the men jumped up from their seats, revealing the decorative wooden thrones upholstered in red velvet. The men were obviously prepared to fight as they stood there with a jewelled dagger in their hand. Jeremy was sitting at the far side, with a clear view of the door. A pistol lay on the table within hand's reach. In his usual laid-back way, he leaned on the chair arm and crossed his legs. He raised his left hand as if to command the two standing men to stop and he slowly patted the air as if suggesting they should calm down or sit down. On seeing him smile, they acquiesced the motion.

Jeremy was the first to speak, "Catherine, your bedraggled appearance suggests it is still raining heavily outside. Do come in and warm yourself by the fire. Lawrence, get the lady a chair, come on, be a gent."

A giant of a man, with blond hair and a gingery Viking style beard, Lawrence was the first to ready himself to fight at the sight of her entering the room. He retreated to the fireplace, keeping his eyes on Catherine and turned one of the armchairs around.

"Thank you, Lawrence." Catherine sat down with grace and adjusted her drenched skirt.

A gentleman sporting weaved hair in precise rows directed his question towards Jeremy, "Can you introduce us to your acquaintance?" He sat taller in his chair and straightened his striped, purple jacket.

Jeremy nodded, "Zeb, she may look a state now, but this is the lady I wish to marry, yet twice she has refused my proposal. I fear she does not think me worthy of her hand in marriage." He bowed in subservience to his object of desire.

"Well, I can't say I blame her," said a man with an unusual accent, a sort of brusque, clicking rhythm to his words. Draped in layers of a rich bronze material, and wearing numerous pieces of jewellery on his body, the other gentlemen tittered at his humorous response and continued with their jokes at Jeremy's expense.

"Yohannes, my dear friends or maybe not as dear as I thought …" he played the room with theatrical exuberance, enjoying the banter and retribution for his sins, "… this is my darling Catherine." He limped over to where she sat and delicately kissed the back of her hand, prolonging eye contact with her, his eyes twinkling with desire.

A chubby gentleman scraped his throne-like-chair across the wooden floorboards to observe the interaction. He smiled when they made eye contact, his receding hairline and bushy eyebrows instantly recognisable. "Dearest Catherine, welcome to the Order of the Priory."

"Doctor Wainwright?" Despite her best efforts, Catherine could not hide her surprise. "You are part of the Order?"

"Indeed, I am. In fact, my official title is Grand Master of the Priory. We have been watching you with interest. You have surprised me with your intellect and insight. I'm afraid I underestimated your capabilities."

The six men were staring at her. The room started pulsating, from feeling tall and wide to suddenly closing in like bellows. A snap from the fire made her jump and brought her back to reality.

"Truly, I'm sorry about everything. I did not deliberately unearth your secret. I do not know where the cross is. I will never tell a soul. I promise." She placed her hand on her heart.

"Good grief, we are not some freaks to be feared. I dread to think what preconceptions you hold of our Order." Doctor Wainwright picked up a rather large goblet and gulped at its contents. "What *are* your thoughts by the way?"

"I'm ... not really sure to be honest. I was only looking for Jeremy."

He beamed with pride. "I knew she could not resist me forever. Persistence always wears them down eventually." The other men jeered, laughing at his arrogance and adding further insults.

Catherine was a little perturbed by their actions, "It's my birthday today and I needed to speak with him about something personal."

"I hope you did give many treasures upon her my kind friend?" said a man with a different foreign accent. She had heard the others call him Mayeso.

"The world would never be enough for my darling Catherine." Jeremy waved his hand loosely by the wrist.

Catherine did not know why she was shocked at Jeremy's cruelty for she had witnessed it numerous times before.

Doctor Wainwright could obviously sense the tension, "Now then Jeremy, we know Catherine has been through immense misfortune."

Lawrence joined in the conversation, "Let's stop skirting around the point. Do we need to deal with her?" He had a gentle voice for such a mammoth of a man.

The men looked at each other and all seemed reluctant to commit. They waited for Doctor Wainwright to conclude. "Catherine, would you agree to us asking you some questions? You have stumbled upon a centuries-old secret which we want to keep that way."

"You have nothing to fear from me," but she sensed she had something to fear from them.

"Then let's begin," suggested Doctor Wainwright.

"Hear him, hear him," the other men chanted.

As if being tried by jury, Catherine sat on her own in the dock with six men watching her every move. They questioned her on her mental health, her religious beliefs, her research into the Order of the Priory, her thoughts on the whereabouts of the cross and asked about her life in general. Jeremy had obviously confided in Doctor Wainwright about her daughter as he asked specific questions on her thoughts relating to this information. How dare Jeremy divulge personal secrets.

They questioned her on Solomon and what she was hoping to achieve by all of this skulduggery.

"Honestly, I just want to be happy. I have no answers. I try my best. I just want my family to be happy. I want to keep busy. I have always been fascinated by the world we live in. Researching about the cross, it was a distraction. I meant nothing by it. I happened upon its existence by accident."

The accuracy and fluency of Mayeso's English was not as smooth as the others, "And why shall we believe you, Catherine? Doctor Wainwright tell us you have only just got out from a lunatic asylum."

"I would do anything not to go back there." Catherine sat taller in the chair, not wanting to appear intimidated by their probing questions.

"Like burning down the solicitor's office? Like breaking down the door to gain access to this hall?" asked Zeb.

Catherine tried to remain calm, "I never did any of those things."

"But you know who did it, yes?" asked Mayeso, struggling to turn his head, seemingly devoid of a neck.

Catherine sat there, nearly in tears. "Please, I mean you or your cause no harm. Your secret is safe with me. Just as all other secrets are safe when I have been told them in confidence. I am weighed down by secrets, tormented by secrets, of my own and others. I will not be the one to disrupt your cause." She looked towards Jeremy for support. He appeared sly, leaning back in his throne-like-chair, watching her every move, listening to the other men with glee. He could surely sense her discomfort, see her pain, yet he did nothing to ease her suffering.

"Zeb, what do you think?" asked Doctor Wainwright.

Twiddling a gold button on his purple jacket, he finally offered an opinion, "I believe her to be no threat to the Order or cause."

The other men nodded except for Jeremy. He narrowed his eyes, "I'm not convinced. I think she needs to be kept busy. She needs to marry me, and I will ensure she keeps her word." His thumb supported his chin, his middle finger protected his lips, and he supported his head along the length of his index finger. He stared at Catherine for an uncomfortable age.

"Then I will instruct Reverend Thornton to read the marriage banns. Jeremy and Catherine will be married in the New Year." Doctor Wainwright drummed a beat on the wooden table and the large goblets wobbled with the vibration.

Deep voices murmured their acceptance of the plan.

Yohannes raised his goblet, "To Jeremy and Catherine, may the Lord bless and protect this union."

"To Jeremy and Catherine," repeated the others, their goblets now all raised in the air. They all took a swig of their drink.

"No, I'm sorry but I will not accept this … this grotesque display of male dominance. I will marry for love and for no other reason."

"She loves me, she just won't admit it." Jeremy winked at Catherine, "To my soon to be wife, a toast!" He held aloft his goblet. "Until death do us part."

His comrades joined in the celebrations once more, holding their goblets in the air. They each leaned across the table and clinked their support, red wine spilling everywhere.

"To Jeremy and Catherine, may you finally tame and make an honest woman of her!" Lawrence gulped the remaining dregs of wine from his goblet. He spluttered and coughed; the liquid having gone down the wrong way. "Monks' toenails," he managed to say as he pounded his broad chest with the thumb and finger of his fisted hand.

Raucous laughter reverberated around the room, except from Mayeso who admitted, "I no get why amusing."

This statement made the other men guffaw.

Lawrence wiped tears of laughter from his eyes, "The medieval monks would make their wine by crushing the grapes with their bare feet." From his seated position, he demonstrated an alternate stomping movement on the floorboards. "Sometimes you would get a bit of hard skin and toenails in the mix."

Everyone looked at Mayeso. His face contorted with disgusted amusement. He raised his goblet once more. "Anyone fancy a beer?"

The men snorted with laughter, their jaws and bellies aching with the frivolity of it all.

Catherine intervened, "Call yourselves Christians, do you? You are a disgrace."

Jeremy replied, "You are quite correct, we are a disgrace to the god we serve. When I first met Albus through the asylum, he asked me which god I worshipped. Obviously, everyone worshipped me at that stage but when pushed to pick one it would have to be Satan. His followers seem to have so much more fun than the others. A little bit of chaos here and there, anything goes, debauchery, orgies, you know me and my tastes, Catherine. That was why you refused to marry me the first-time round. But the problem with Satanists is it all gets a bit boring after a while. World domination, subterfuge, creating doubts, even questioning science. It was all very tedious in the end."

Yohannes directed his question to Jeremy. "What's so important to you about protecting the cross when you don't even call yourself a Christian? I thought we were all Christians here."

"An excellent question. Christians have far more elaborate secrets. I like secrets, they give me a sense of power over people. Knowledge, knowing something others do not puts me on a higher level, a feeling of superiority which I love.

Catherine sensed this was a reason why he never told her about her daughter.

On hearing the men continue their discussion, Catherine got out of her chair and with her head held high, left the grand hall of the priory gatehouse. Wanting to scream with anger, she would not give them the satisfaction of seeing her unravel in front of their sneering faces. Silence showed mental resilience, physical control and emotional mystery. Doctor Wainwright and Jeremy could not use any outburst as evidence of being insane, or a threat to herself or others. As she descended the spiral stone steps with caution, she had a moment of clarity; that maybe she *was* insane, for contemplating a life with Jeremy. How foolish and naïve she had been.

December 1958

The journey up to Carlisle had taken much longer than expected. They had come all this way without incident, then got lost trying to find the village. By then, they had been travelling for over eight hours and tempers were short. John was too stubborn to ask someone for help and persevered in reading the map even though it was now dark outside. In the end, Joyce wound down the car window and asked for directions from a passing stranger.

A sense of relief overwhelmed their weary souls when they found Rose Cottage. The amber glow from the streetlight created a warm welcome in the bitter cold. Hard to tell in the wintery darkness but their cottage appeared to be at the heart of the village, overlooking the green. Opposite the cottage was a rather grand country house hotel, The Killoran. John wondered if the hotel was open to non-residents as that would be handy for a few beers after a long shift.

On entering Rose Cottage, they both shivered as a deep chill swirled around their exhausted bodies. Joyce opened her mouth to complain but stopped on seeing her breath condense in the icy atmosphere. On finding some matches, John knelt before the rustic fireplace and got to work on lighting the neatly prepared logs in the grate. Joyce found the immersion heater switch in the kitchen. Watery rumblings commenced.

With chattering teeth, Joyce could not refrain from moaning that the rented cottage was far too small. The living room only had room for a two-seater sofa and an armchair. The kitchen was a square box with barely any cupboard space. Already, she had concluded that the open staircase would lead to all the heat escaping to the upper floor. She climbed the wooden steps. John could hear her walking around upstairs and he concluded that he could still hear her complaining despite them being on separate floors. Was she talking to herself? She was moaning about the wardrobe which would not house all her clothes and that the bathroom was built for a leprechaun. She stomped back downstairs. Trying to remain calm, John reminded her that it was only a temporary measure and that as soon as their house sale went through, they would contact local estate agents and buy their perfect home.

Although they were tired, they forced themselves to empty the two suitcases and boxes from the car. In silence, they placed their personal items around the cottage. Joyce must have been exhausted as she refrained from complaining about having insufficient coat hangers when she had to triple up on some of her blouses and tops. She didn't even moan about the musty aroma. She just sighed and wearily threw her underwear in the drawer.

The bathroom was too small, so they took it in turns to get ready for bed. The cottage was now quite cosy and within minutes of heads touching the comfy pillows, they fell asleep, completely shattered by the journey.

*

John woke with a jump having dreamt he was flapping his arms and flying high through the mountainous terrain of the Lake District before everything stopped and he somersaulted to the ground in a death spiral. He was sweating, then he realised the central heating was still on. He looked at the alarm clock, of which the numbers and tips of the hands were glowing in the dark, eleven minutes past one or 111. Joyce frequently reminded him this was a sign. A sign of what he did not know.

Nervous about his job, he could not get back to sleep and thoughts swirled about tomorrow's induction. He corrected himself, today's induction in what … eight hours. Doubts crept into his vulnerable mind, the state of purgatory between being sleepy and dismissive to the brilliance of dreamy imagination and infinite possibilities. He had been offered a once in a lifetime opportunity, to create something so powerful, but that was the problem, its use could be lifechanging in both a good and bad way. Warnings … screams … push the button … panic … blood … apocalypse.

*

Six o'clock in the morning and the alarm was ringing. He quickly pressed the button to avoid waking Joyce. John felt like he had only just fallen asleep after hours of restlessness. Joyce murmured but drifted back to sleep. Exhausted, he forced himself to get out of bed and get ready for his first day at work. With the stealth of a ninja, he toileted, brushed his teeth, shaved and bathed. With the towel wrapped around his waist, he ventured downstairs, found the ironing board in the understairs cupboard and ironed his shirt. With precision, he created crisp lines along each sleeve. His grey suit had been hanging up in the car and then the bedroom doorway overnight so remained sharp. A blue silk tie with subtle white diagonal stripes completed his sleek look. With a comb, he tweaked his hair to perfection.

Breakfast was a meagre affair of a limp, corned beef sandwich from yesterday's provisions and a black cup of tea. Arriving so late, they did not have time to go shopping for fresh milk and food. He scolded himself for being lax and disorganised. He couldn't leave anything to chance with his new job. Every detail had to be precise. Every problem anticipated. Every error needed a solution otherwise there would be catastrophic consequences. Learning from this mistake, even though it was only seven o'clock, he decided to leave the cottage and give himself plenty of time to find his new place of work.

John had placed every correspondence in a lockable briefcase. Every letter he had received had re-iterated the importance of confidentially and was stamped with TOP SECRET. With his new role as chief engineer, he felt he could justify owning a briefcase, even if it did only hold a day-old sandwich.

A bright but frosty morning greeted John. The village green could be more accurately described as white. Covered in a sprinkling of frost, the scene was very picturesque, and the surrounding houses were either grand, quaint or interesting.

Sat in his car waiting for the windows to clear, he unlocked the clasps of his briefcase which was sitting on the passenger seat. He found the letter detailing the address and location of the place. He was unsure what to call it … factory … compound … maybe facility was more appropriate than office or place of work. He would know what to call it when he saw it.

Following written directions, for the location of the facility was not detailed on his map, he headed through Brampton and continued along the A69 towards Newcastle. He remembered that he had to take the first turn left after the steep, long climb. At the brow of the hill, he saw the turn and indicated left. The view was amazing. He felt like he was in the middle of nowhere. All he could see were fields and rolling hills, covered with a slight sprinkling of icing sugar.

For what seemed like miles, he drove through a desolate landscape. Boggy fields covered with a thin film of ice, surrounded by boring conifer plantations. His workplace, the facility, really was in the middle of nowhere, but that seemed appropriate for what he was about to create. His line of work carried a very high risk of serious injury, even death. It was then he saw the sign to confirm he was on the correct path:

**MINISTRY OF DEFENCE. THIS IS A PROHIBITED PLACE
WITHIN THE OFFICIAL SECRETS ACT. NO UNAUTHORISED
PERSONS. RISK OF ARREST AND PROSECUTION.**

The sounds from his shuddering heart reverberated throughout his body.

Winding through marshland, the road suddenly felt spongy, so he slowed the vehicle's speed. Already unnerved, as he turned a corner a pocket of mist obliterated his view, and he disappeared inside its shroud. The car crawled at a snail's pace as he navigated his way through the cloaked landscape. Through the mist, a barbed wire perimeter and a small wooden hut came into view. As if by magic, the security gate opened as John's car approached the entrance. He clocked a surveillance camera on top of a long pole. Unsure what he should do, he drove inside the grounds and waited for the perimeter gates to close behind him. Too late to back out now, he proceeded cautiously and stopped at the security hatch for further instructions. John wound down his car window. Was he here on the right day? Were they expecting him? Was his name on the list of visitors? Would they search the car? The guard lifted his sash window.

John rested his forearm across the frame of the car's open window. "John Stone to see Wing Commander Sherrard." Palpitations made him feel anxious.

"Hello, Mr Stone. Welcome to Spadeadam. Just follow the road around and you'll see the car park soon enough. Mrs Briggs will be waiting for you."

John said his thanks and wound up the window. Rather nervous, he put the gear stick into first and continued along the winding road. There were various wooden huts and bricked buildings of differing sizes, all of little architectural significance. Following the road around, the site continued to reveal its secrets. Tiered, concrete monstrosities, like utilitarian pagodas, emerged from the ground, inviting alien spacecraft to land. Sloped bunkers with reinforced steel doors were the backdrop to tall functional pillars. Metal pipes of various sizes snaked between buildings. Not that he had ever been to Russia or China, but he imagined this would be the type of communist government facility to … he stopped himself from making judgements.

When he saw a car park, he puffed out his cheeks having finally arrived, *at the place.* He was still unsure what to call it. There was no obvious signage to confirm this.

A middle-aged woman with a slim torso but ample hips and thighs appeared from a simple wooden doorway. Her navy suit was smart, tailored to her curves and her red hair was coiffed, obviously sprayed into place as the crosswinds from the isolated location did not catch one strand. With a welcoming smile, she stood with her hands clasped in front as she watched John walk towards her. He straightened his jacket suit and adjusted the cuffs on his shirt sleeves. This suddenly felt real.

"Good morning, Mr Stone. Are you trying to catch us off guard or trying to impress us with your early arrival?"

"Can I be honest and say I just didn't know where I was going, so I set off early?"

"I admire honesty. Come on in and I will show you around."

Mrs Briggs introduced herself and guided John into a small reception room where she offered him a drink. She handed him a folder containing a list of introductory measures, an itinerary for the day and a map of the facility for him to peruse whilst she prepared the tea.

According to the map, there were numerous buildings dotted around the ten-acre site. He quickly flicked through the rest of the file. At the top of each page was an emblem of what looked like a stag's head in front of a shell and scribed underneath was the motto: Si vis pacem para bellum.

Mrs Briggs returned with a tray. She poured out the tea, added a pinch of milk and two sugars as John had requested, and handed him the cup. She sat on the chair opposite him.

John thanked her for the tea, took a well needed sip, then asked, "The motto, I'm guessing Latin, what does it mean?"

"If you seek peace, prepare for war."

"How very apt," said John.

"Indeed."

Mrs Briggs went through the specifics of the day's itinerary and tried to explain how best to use the map. There were various sectors such as accommodation blocks, general administration areas, finance offices, design workshops and construction facilities. John would mainly be located in C3, Spadeadam's testing zone. C3 was built into the land, with facilities overhead but housing a couple of underground tiers. The subterranean levels were to improve security from threats externally as well as internally.

Having finished their tea, Mrs Briggs led John on a mystery tour of the site. The administration and finance rooms were dreary and functional, but the staff who had arrived early seemed cheery and welcoming. The security team were housed in a brick building with metal window frames affording 360-degree views over the bleak countryside. One windowless room housed a wall of monitors, relaying real time information from security cameras positioned strategically around the site. Teddy, the current officer on duty had dark bags under his eyes. He looked exhausted, as if watching TV all day was hard work. He shook John's hand with gusto and admitted he had spotted his car arriving from miles away. Teddy joked that John needed to try harder next time to evade capture. Teddy and Mrs Briggs laughed, which put John at ease. He already felt at home. No fuss, no airs, just plain-old friendliness which he was not expecting on his first day but had secretly been hoping for, especially considering the task he was going to be undertaking.

As they walked across the site towards the design workshop and construction facility, people were beginning to egress from coaches. Like worker bees, they swarmed across the site to their place of work. The site was coming alive, the atmosphere buzzing.

Continuing with their exploration of the facility, John's heart rate increased on seeing the vast workspaces filled with gadgets and gizmos galore. John was thrilled and excited by the hive. As if in honeycombs, staff were switching on computers, tools were being calibrated and engines were being primed. Steel carcasses were large enough to walk through.

"As with everything here, you are not at liberty to divulge any information to anyone outside of this establishment. We are dabbling with so many secrets that this rule is imperative for everyone's safety." They left the building. "Even within the reinforced walls of C3, different people have different clearance levels, so you must be on your guard at all times. No holding doors open for people or leaving files laying around. One needs to be vigilant, always. We are exploring various ways of physically protecting these secrets. For instance, we are trialling electronic keypads."

They were now approaching one of the tiered concrete monstrosities. Mrs Briggs pressed a sequence of numbers on the keypad and the light changed from red to green. The door made an unlocking sound and she quickly pulled on the large metal handle.

"You are one of only a handful of people to have full clearance to the entire site. Unfortunately, not everything here is technologically advanced. We still have many rooms and buildings which have to be opened in the old-fashioned way." She passed him a metal ring which was approximately the circumference of an apple. "This is your set of keys."

"Not exactly easy to carry around," said John, feeling like a jailer. He placed the set of keys in the inside pocket of his suit jacket. The bulge from the outside appeared interesting. They both laughed.

"One can never sneak up on people while carrying these." She jangled her set of keys. "Hence why I like the keycode entry system. Hopefully, we will get around to converting all the locks at some point. I hear they are considering fingerprint and retinal scanners. Technology is expanding at a rapid pace. Absolutely amazing! I can't even begin to imagine what we will achieve in years to come."

They continued their tour. There was a large open plan staff area with various seating and dining areas. There was a kitchen and bar area. Mrs Briggs explained that all refreshments were heavily subsidized and for him to enjoy the hospitality on offer as a way of de-stressing from the demands of the job. "I have to admit that sometimes testing goes wrong and we have to re-schedule timetables and go into what we call a 'holding position'. Sometimes you may have to stand down for an hour or two at a time until the situation has been classified as safe."

John's anxieties were not easing.

They descended two flights of stairs. Off a corridor were various rooms. "These are sleeping quarters for the top dogs. As chief engineer, you have been gifted a room. Find T2 on your key ring."

John found the required item. Without being asked, he tried the key in the lock and opened the door. The room was simply furnished with a single bed, wardrobe, bedside table, desk and chair. "Interesting." He did not know what else to say. The room felt claustrophobic without any windows or natural light. "I imagine this is like being in a submarine."

"Indeed, Mr Stone, but this is to keep you safe from harm. You are surrounded by reinforced concrete and steel." She walked a little way down the corridor. "I do believe submarines are being talked about as part of Rolls Royce's new defence programme?"

John nodded but was unsure. His role had been with aircraft and rocket engines.

Along a different corridor was a door with a sign, *John Stone, Chief Engineer.* Mrs Briggs asked him to locate the key and John opened the door to his office. The space was bigger than the entire footprint of Rose Cottage. There was a large desk. In the far corner was a round table with capacity to hold a meeting for six people. There was so much to take in, wooden shelves, built in cupboards, metal filing cabinets, a large computer. Every other office he had seen so far had been bland and functional. This was relatively plush.

"Wow, Mrs Briggs, I was not expecting this."

"You are vital in making this project work, Mr Stone. The government and allied agencies appreciate your worth." She prompted him to leave his briefcase and to pick up some headphones, which were on top of one of the filing cabinets, in case he needed them as they continued the tour. He did as he was told as he was presently dumbstruck.

Further down the corridor they were greeted by a bald man with a wrinkly forehead. Of average height and build, he had wide set eyes, thin lips and large ears. John was reminded of a sphynx, the cat with no hair only loose, pink skin. When the man introduced himself as Wing Commander Sherrard, John hoped his new boss was oblivious of the rising heat and discomfort that was showing on his face. Mrs Briggs wished John the very best of luck then said her goodbyes.

Sherrard marched John along the corridor as he explained, "I am employed by the Royal Air Force but my role here is to coordinate and liaise with the various stakeholders such as Rolls Royce, de Havilland, the Department of Aviation, The Ministry of Defence and our alliances abroad in the United States of America, Australia and so on. As Wing Commander, I have ultimate authority for this station."

"So, do I report to you with any concerns, any findings, reports?" asked John.

"No. That would be Mrs Briggs."

John's face turned crimson. "Mrs Briggs is my line manager?" Sherrard nodded. "I feel awful now. I thought she was your secretary, or personal assistant, something along those lines. Like a receptionist would, she gave me some tea, then gave me a tour of the place, I thought she was just showing me around until I met you."

Sherrard laughed, "She always plays that game. It's her way of seeing how you engage with the staff. There may be a hierarchy here, but we must all work together to make this project work. One must never assume. Like you, Mrs Briggs has degrees in mechanical and electrical engineering and has worked her way up to board level in companies such as de Havilland and Hawker Siddeley."

"Wow, total admiration as I know first-hand how competitive the market is. So, what *is* her role here?"

"She's the project manager, bringing everything together, health and safety, budgets, meeting targets, testing, reporting to government …"

John blew out his cheeks in respect, "So, she's kind of your right-hand man?"

"Precisely. Anyway, let's get down to the main reason you are here."

Wing Commander Sherrard stopped abruptly by some double doors. He placed his hands on the handles and pushed down. He turned to John and said, "Welcome to the Blue Streak Project." The doors swung open on his command.

The control room had shoulder to shoulder computers. There were various panels with switches, buttons, levers, red, amber and green lights, visual display units and auditory monitoring systems.

"What are these hanging from the ceiling?" asked John. He was referring to horizontal handles attached to vertical poles.

"Periscopes. When we test the rocket, or certain components, everything is recorded remotely but we can observe via these periscopes as it's too dangerous to watch at close range, although we do have observation stations which I'll show you next. At present, Morris over there is our sequencing officer and he coordinates each test. That's when you'll need your headset. Everything is operated manually at present, but we are hoping for this to be all controlled digitally someday. Less margin for error." Sherrard offered an open palm. "Go on, have a look."

John held onto the handles of the periscope and slowly approached the eyepiece. He was speechless at the sight, his mouth opened wide.

Sherrard could see his reaction, "Come on, I'll show you the rocket from one of the viewing platforms, a bird's eye view as they say." He checked with Morris that no testing was scheduled then they made their way outside onto the roof of the building.

Like a giant soldier standing to attention, the Blue Streak Rocket was a metal beast, nearing a hundred feet tall and about ten-feet wide. Compared to the German V2 missiles from the second World War, the Blue Streak Rocket was an absolute monster. The rocket was standing in an area known as 'the bucket', a concealed and reinforced area to ward off electromagnetic blasts, soaring temperatures and possible radiation leaks. Being in the bucket also meant the rocket was hidden from ground view. Sherrard was describing the different components, but his words were carried away in the breeze as John could not help but stare at the demon. A rising acid created pain in his chest as his stomach churned at the potential devastation this beast could cause on impact if fired or worse, exploded right here through his negligence. Propulsion bay ... tank bay ... ...guidance bay ... separation bay ...nuclear warhead ... John had to focus on Sherrard's words.

"... so your specialist skills with Rolls Royce are crucial in developing this ballistic missile. We are aiming for an intermediate range of say at least two thousand nautical miles, but more if possible."

"Are we aiming for anywhere in particular?"

Sherrard hesitated, "Russia, places like that. That sort of radius. The rocket currently has two Rolls Royce engines, RZ2s. When combined we classify them as RZ12 and together they produce a thrust of about three hundred thousand pounds."

"What kinda speed does that create?"

"I think they are estimating about eight to nine thousand miles an hour so it would reach its target within minutes."

John puffed out his cheeks.

"We need you to work on various aspects such as target accuracy once deployed, the stability of the warhead for our safety when stored, fuel efficiency to increase range etcetera. We have the British Oxygen Company on board, or BOC for short, who are currently building a facility next to this compound in order to provide us with all our fuel needs, which is currently liquid oxygen and kerosene. As the new chief, I expect you to coordinate all these aspects of engineering to create a safe but effective nuclear deterrent should the need arise."

"And what would that need be?"

"I'm sure by now you have seen our motto, Si vis pacem para bellum. If you seek peace, prepare for war."

"Protecting people, places, our freedoms," suggested John.

"Exactly, to name a few. Classified information, secrets, gold reserves, treasured artifacts, we have so much to hide, spanning centuries of time."

"Mrs Briggs said I have full clearance. Do I get to know what we are protecting?"

Sherrard laughed, "Nice try sonny, you certainly have full clearance to the site, but not full clearance for information outside of these walls, at least not yet. Mrs Briggs doesn't even know the secrets we try so hard to protect or the threats we receive from foreign regimes." Sherrard's forehead wrinkled creating deeper worry lines, "A few of us regularly meet in the Killoran Country House Hotel. It was a former gentleman's residence, Victorian, very grand, and we have a private room there, somewhere we can meet in secret. Perhaps you can join us for a few drinks one evening. You can meet the others and chat about things, all confidentially of course."

"How very odd. I am renting Rose Cottage which is opposite that very establishment."

Sherrard winked, "I know, nothing ever happens by chance around here."

Chapter Forty-Three

Catherine was fuming as she slammed the door of the priory gatehouse. How could she have contemplated involving Jeremy in her plans; this really did confirm she was insane. Recently, she had warmed to his eccentric ways, had detected glimpses of compassion and saw evidence of generosity. For goodness' sake, she had even considered marrying him. How foolish to fall for his promises. She had been bought by his random and rare acts of kindness which had blinded her to his true debauched nature. How despicable he was, having humiliated her in front of his friends.

The disagreeable chatter of those men in the gatehouse. Detestable examples of human beings. And Doctor Wainwright of all people, he had probably been spying on her every move. Deceit and lies at every level. Supposedly, he held a position of responsibility, caring for the mental wellbeing of his patients, when in fact he was a manipulator and schemer. A conspirator in protecting a centuries-old secret, she considered what extremes he would go to, to suppress this shrouded information.

She stormed up the hill towards the village green, livid by the Order's revelations and actions. Solomon came into her mind; how truly sweet he was. She had been so foolish in doubting him, or them as a wedded couple. He would lay down his life for her, fight to protect her, do anything for her, she sincerely believed this now. She prayed that she could hold everything together for them to be married as soon as possible. However, she worried that Doctor Wainwright would insist on her re-incarceration at the asylum as punishment for her actions relating to her investigations into the whereabouts of the true cross.

Like a streak of lightning in stormy skies, she was hit by the repercussions of Solomon finding out that she had briefly considered marrying Jeremy instead of him. The devastation this would cause was too ghastly to contemplate. She was driving herself crazy, too many thoughts swirling in her head. She needed peace. Her dreams were to be settled with Solomon, to be blissfully happy and content, to support her daughter in caring for the poor little mites at the orphanage and to be well. A flash of light, she dared to dream of having another child of her own. Solomon would make such a wonderful father, but she was nearly forty, too old to consider starting a family now.

Catherine slowed her pace. Her heart was pounding with the climb up the steep hill but now there was pounding of a different kind. The noise was unnerving, as if the world was imploding. A cataclysmic event. Like a biblical intervention, God's wrath was being unleashed on Edenvale. The chilling sounds reverberated through her flaming body, calming her down, neutralising her anger, forcing her to a stop.

People were starting to collect around the stone monument perched high on the edge of the green. The women were obviously scared as they were holding on to each other for comfort. The few men who had gathered were more elderly and they looked perplexed as to what to do for the best. There was one small child who was grabbing onto her mother's skirt, hiding her face in the flounced fabric but occasionally sneaking a peek at the unfolding events.

At the centre of the commotion was Solomon. He was wielding a large pickaxe in an attempt to destroy the grey monstrosity. If anyone approached him, he warned them with his eyes, flared nostrils and the raising of the glistening blade.

Time and again, he swung the axe with all his strength, breaking up the grey monolith and its plinth. Some of the women observing his berserk behaviour became too afraid to stay. They hurried back to the safety of their homes.

Having been momentarily frozen to the spot with confusion, Catherine saw her daughter walking down the pathway of the orphanage. Catherine ran the last few yards up the hill and made her way through the gathering crowd.

She got as close as she dared. "Solomon, it's me."

He didn't stop to look up, recognising her voice, "The cross, it's hidden in here, I know it is. I read the rest of that book." He took another large swing at the plinth with his axe.

"What if you are wrong? Please Solomon, put the axe down, you could hurt someone with it, including yourself."

Solomon ignored her pleas. The axe continued picking off fragments of stone.

"This isn't worth it. Please Solomon, come home with me. We need to forget about the cross. There are things I need to tell you. Some things have changed."

He continued to chip away at the almost impenetrable stone until he revealed an opening in the plinth. A quick glimpse inside and then with renewed vigour he pounded away at the monument's base. The opening was now wide enough for a small chimney sweep to fit through. Solomon stopped swinging his axe and properly looked inside the hole. He could not believe what he saw inside. Finally, he looked at Catherine with a beaming smile on his face.

"It's true, it's there." His eyes welled with tears, "The cross on which Jesus Christ was crucified." He dropped the axe and fell to his knees, unable to hide his emotions. His hands were shaking, and blood trickled from his blistered palms. Tears of relief started flowing down his cheeks.

Feeling a little safer, Catherine cautiously approached him and placed her hands on his shoulders. He accepted her touch and moved aside to let her see down the hole. She lowered herself onto her knees as if praying and peeked inside the hollow he had created. Her eyes opened wide at the surreal sight. The green was not just a pretty mound of soil and grass at the heart of the village, but an underground cavern, a crypt carved out of the stone walls.

To the left was a medieval door with thick iron metalwork, probably leading to Oak Bank Hall via an underground passage. To the right, a spiritual image was to behold. The aged wooden beams of the cross stood proud within the simple surroundings. The warmth of the wood shimmered in the flickering candlelight, making the cross appear to levitate. Near the ends of the crossed timbers were stains, dark patches of … Catherine paused at the reality of what she was seeing … the dark patches could only be blood, for at the centre of each stain was an indentation, as if something sharp had been forcibly hammered into the grain. Further down the cross was a small platform, maybe to bear some weight and a similar dark stain with a precise indentation.

Nailed near to the top was a wooden sign, different in colour and texture to the cross. Three different languages were chiselled into the timber. Unable to read the words, but recalling her biblical studies as a child, she recalled one of the languages being Hebrew. The second language was probably Latin for she recognised the word 'Rex' meaning 'King'. The third language could possibly be Greek, or maybe a local language, as the letters were more like symbols. Trying to think back to her religious studies, the sign stated something like, *Jesus of Nazareth, King of the Jews.*

Overwhelmed by the historic find, Catherine flung her arms around Solomon, "You found it! I had every faith you would." Oblivious to the growing crowd, they enjoyed a lingering kiss, thankful they were sane. Both were consumed by the passion.

Their joy was minimal. Two men witnessing the destruction of the stone monument suddenly pounced on Solomon and knocked Catherine sideways, resulting in her banging her head on fragments of chipped stone. Solomon fought the men off momentarily, but they clung to him again, forcing him to the ground. A third man ran and grabbed the axe. He swung it deliberately, catching Solomon on his ankle, the sharpened spike piercing his flesh. Blood emerged from the wound.

Catherine hauled herself up into a sitting position and felt her temple. Blood seeped through her fingers and trickled down her face. An image of Jesus Christ bearing the crown of thorns momentarily came into her head. Movement out of the corner of her eye alerted her to the fact that the men from the priory gatehouse were now bounding up the hill towards them.

Pinned to the ground in the shape of the cross by the two burly men kneeling on his arms, whilst the third man bound his bloodied feet together with rope, Solomon managed to shout, "Run, Catherine, get away from here."

Without time to think, her instinct was to follow his advice and flee the scene. She ran towards her daughter, held her hand and said, "I love you, Mary, Genevieve," then blew her a kiss before heading towards the village store. She turned left in the direction of the well and then headed down Plains Road.

With her lungs burning, she was grateful for being momentarily stopped in her tracks when she met with the soon to be subterranean pipes of the waterworks. Two workmen were sitting under a tree having some food. They had removed their boots, allowing their darned socks to air. Oblivious to the commotion around the green, they were startled by her sudden appearance. Catherine jumped down onto the large sunken pipe in the middle of the dug-up road and carefully ran along its length.

The two workmen looked at each other, flabbergasted by the event and quickly decided to follow her. Like the workmen based at the road end near the Wheatsheaf Inn, they had been tasked with monitoring people coming into and out of the village. Any unusual behaviours or strangers to the village were always reported to Doctor Wainwright and any suspects detained. Catherine had been on their list of people to engage with.

Despite the burden of her clothes, her small nimble feet allowed her to navigate the dirty and slippery pipes with relative ease. She continued running, concluding that to stop would mean detention at the hands of the Order of the Priory, or even being re-admitted to the lunatic asylum.

Her throat and lungs felt on fire, but she could not stop running. The pipe was too narrow to stop and turn around to see how close the workmen were, but she could sense them following her, feeling the vibrations through the pipe and she could hear their voices, their laboured breathing. They were too close for her liking.

Reaching the end of the waterworks, she jumped from the pipes onto the rough road and continued through a tunnel of trees which formed a natural canopy. The air was suddenly dank and cloying with the smells of nature. She could barely breathe.

She could see a busier road at the end of the lane. Now on impacted ground, which felt stable underfoot, she quickly turned to see both men still tailing her. They were not the youngest or fittest of specimens and their work boots sounded cumbersome, so she continued to evade their advances.

As she approached the main road, she could see a small clearing on her right. A beautiful wooden shelter had been erected which housed a depiction of the crucifixion of Christ. There was insufficient time to contemplate the positioning of a crucifixion if they were wanting to keep the location of the true cross a secret.

On reaching the main thoroughfare, carriages and carts rattled past, but did not stop to help despite her pleas. Her flailing arms startled some of the horses and they reared with fear. People shouted obscenities in her direction. Close to collapsing, and with blood and perspiration blurring her vision, she did not have the breath to shout or ask for help, running scared whilst being pursued had drained every morsel of strength. Her heels were now burning with the pounding of the various terrains.

None of the travellers stopped to help her, but she was not surprised, looking at the state of her appearance. They probably considered her to be some sort of ragamuffin or loose woman with her dirty clothes and bleeding wounds.

Further down the road towards Carlisle was an interesting house, with a half-timbered front façade. Someone was in the garden, a small man, he was busy feeding the birds. As she got closer, she could see he was standing in a sunken garden. A decision had to be made quickly. She either continued running along the road whilst trying to hail someone down and ask for their help whilst still being pursued by the two workmen or she could take her chances and ask for help from this gentleman.

As if fate had answered her prayers, the man in the garden looked up and spotted Catherine. She could tell he was shocked by her sudden and bedraggled appearance, as he seemed to recoil. The man caught sight of the two workmen chasing her. He looked at Catherine again with her bloody face and then back at the pursuing men.

Catherine ran into his garden and asked for his support, "Help me, please!" She could barely speak and felt close to collapse.

The workmen stopped running and slowed to a leisurely pace. With a pained look, they started chatting, probably contemplating the situation. They stood still and watched proceedings. They looked at each other and chatted once more. They slowly retreated their steps and eventually turned and walked away without looking back.

Chapter Forty-Three

As the elderly gentleman hobbled across his garden and into his home, he beckoned Catherine into the kitchen. A delicious smell of warm bread wafted in the air. He took off his flat cap and offered Catherine the wooden chair by the stove to warm herself through. As he put the kettle on the stove, his wife hobbled into the kitchen, bearing weight through a roughly chiselled limb off a tree. They introduced themselves as Clarence and Sarah. Their greying hair was thin, and their clothes portrayed poverty, with patches on sleeves, frayed edges and layers of worn fabric to keep them warm.

The kettle boiled and Sarah made them all tea. The liquid was warm and comforting but did little to calm Catherine's nerves, her hands still shaking.

The couple respectfully asked Catherine what had happened, especially since there was blood dripping down her face. True to her word, Catherine did not divulge any information that would be considered a secret. The only explanation she gave was there had been some sort of fracas in the village. In the pandemonium that followed she had then fallen, hit her head, felt a little delirious, panicked then scarpered, fearful of the crowds. In essence her words were true.

Sarah opened a drawer and withdrew a pair of scissors. The sharp blades glistened in her bony hand.

Blood pounded through Catherine's body, preparing for a fight. She was outnumbered two-to-one, but the couple could barely walk, never mind run. She toyed with the possibility that all this fragility was a ruse, to give the impression they posed no threat. The old man had positioned her by the stove, which was the furthest place from the door, her only known escape route at this moment.

Holding onto the kitchen table for support, with the scissors in her right hand, Sarah made her way over to a clean but worn-thin bed sheet hanging from the ceiling to dry. With the large blades, she cut a square of fabric from the greyed cotton. She asked Clarence to pour some of the hot water from the kettle into a bowl. Placing the piece of cotton into the hot water, she left it to soak for a few minutes whilst they chatted before wringing out the cloth and passing it to her guest. "For your head, pet," said the old woman.

Catherine said thank you for the thoughtful gesture, her nerves starting to settle once again. She folded the square in half, and then folded it again to form a thicker pad and placed it over her tender wounds. The heat felt good, a different type of pain. The fabric now stained red.

Clarence asked how she was to get home which filled her with dread. With the current circumstances, she wondered if she could safely return to Rose Cottage. She thought about her parents and considered staying at their house, but her blood ran cold at the thought of her incarceration in the shuttered room. Another option was Petteril Bank House. Jeremy had said the house was hers, but she had no key. She could maybe break a window and climb in as she knew the house was now vacated, but the thought of her relying on Jeremy made her angry and defiant. She would not give him the satisfaction of her needing his help. A totally hopeless situation. She felt like crying.

Sarah must have noticed the subtle shaking of Catherine's hands and wrongly assumed she was cold for the lady started putting more kindling on the fire. Catherine was kindly offered a slice of bread and butter, but she refused, too nauseous to contemplate food.

Not wanting to outstay her welcome, Catherine thanked them for their kindness and stood from the chair, announcing her departure. She wondered if she could maybe make her way to Solomon's home, then she felt despair as to what had happened to her intended. The last time she saw him he was pinned to the ground by two strong men kneeling on his forearms, his ankles being bound by rope, stained with the blood seeping from his inflicted wound, a horizontal crucifixion. Solomon had told her to run.

To return to Solomon's house she would have to walk back along the water pipe and would be confronted by the two workmen. She appeared to have little real choice, maybe her only option was one of the workhouses for friendless girls until this situation had settled. Her bottom lip started to quiver at such a hopeless situation.

The elderly couple had obviously picked up on her indecision and suggested she could take as long as she needed to sort herself out when suddenly there was knocking on the door.

Limping, Clarence disappeared down the dark hallway. A sudden smell of tobacco wafted through the air. Catherine could hear deep, mumbled voices. Her heart once again went into defence mode.

Two well-dressed men strode into the kitchen. Sarah said, "Be kind to her, she didn't divulge the secret."

Without saying a word, the men grabbed Catherine by the arms and dragged her out of the house and into a waiting carriage.

Chapter Forty-Four

As on prior occasions, Catherine sat outside Doctor Wainwright's office at the Cumberland and Westmorland Lunatic Asylum, waiting to be called into his room. She had been interred in the asylum for over a week and kept in isolation to 'protect her from herself'. As she sat there, her heart was racing, her breathing staccato and shallow.

The door opened and a familiar voice beckoned her inside.

With unsteady legs, she made the short journey into the room and when requested to do so, sat in the familiar leather chair. Knowing Doctor Wainwright was the Grand Master of the Priory, she suddenly realised the significance of some of the items in his room. The boar's head on the plaque above the door had XX VV engraved underneath, the symbol of the Twentieth Legion of Valeria Victrix, a mighty force of the Roman Empire destined to protect the true cross.

Doctor Wainwright sat there in silence with a smirk on his face which made Catherine feel uncomfortable. Rather than stare him out, she continued to look around the room for further confirmation of his involvement with the priory.

Eventually he spoke, "Well, well, well. My dearest Catherine, why do you think you are here?"

On this occasion, she felt silence was preferable.

Doctor Wainwright filled the void in conversation, "You are here because …" he stopped mid-sentence. "Forget that. We both know why you are here. Let us not continue with the pretence. Do you want to know who else is here?"

Catherine gave an almost imperceptible shrug of her right shoulder along with a subtle lift of her left eyebrow.

"Solomon Smith."

Catherine could not hide her shock. Her mouth opened wide like a chick needing to be fed more food.

253

"Solomon's father Shadrach is here. Vincent and Vera Kavanagh are here. Samson Cohen is here." Catherine's shock turned to anger, her lips now taut. The doctor started laughing. "Do you see the link? Do you see what happens to people who interfere with our cause?"

"On what possible grounds are you holding them?"

"There are numerous witnesses to Solomon's madness. A rage so strong he was seen to wield an axe and threaten innocent members of the public. He is a risk to himself and others, oh, and to property too."

"And his father?"

"A very sad state of affairs. He has spiralled into a deep depression since the loss of his wife, so melancholy that he destroyed everything in his house that reminded him of her."

"Your lies are so cruel." Catherine turned her head away for she could not bear to lay her eyes upon him.

"Vincent and Vera, well they are both demented. Can't remember a thing and getting very confused. When they do speak, everyone knows they are deluded."

"Are they married or brother and sister?"

Doctor Wainwright paused. "I assumed they are married and now I feel such a fool. Are they possibly related?" He was met by silence. "Then another reason to hold them here for their own good. Incest is not tolerable. And before you ask, Samson is confused. A delirium, brought on by poison spreading through his veins from a cut on his leg."

Catherine was trying hard not to explode with anger.

Wainwright continued, "The Order of the Priory has existed for nearly two thousand years, created to protect the whereabouts of the cross on which Jesus Christ was crucified. The cross stood proudly on the column outside of St Constantine's since the church was built in 1356 and has survived extreme weathers. Nobody guessed that a cross so important to humanity would be displayed and left outside for all and sundry to see. Over the centuries, people have tried to burn it and have taken swords to its timbers, yet they have barely made their mark. Whilst others from the Order have made a pilgrimage to our very own Garden of Eden and been cured of their inflictions by a single touch of the cross.

"Sadly, it is only in recent times we have had to take drastic measures to entomb the cross once more. As chemicals, acids and tools are discovered and developed, we could not take the chance of allowing this sacred cross to perish by so called progress. People are losing their faith in God. They still attend church, they still marry, baptise their children, hold funerals for their loved ones and pray for things they want but evil exists amongst us. There seems little evidence of a God when there is so much suffering. People want to destroy, kill, cause chaos, seek revenge, desecrate religious artefacts, steal from holy sites. All in the name of progress. Satan truly is amongst us. Where there is good, sadly there is evil in equal measures."

Catherine remained silent, reluctant to say anything in case she jeopardised her delusion of sanity. She was reminded of what the old woman had said on the day she left the asylum, something like, 'Mark my words, you'll be back here soon enough, in Satan's house, the devil knows what you did, he likes you being here'. She shuddered, wondering if the old woman really did hear the voice of Satan. Maybe she was sane, and it was everyone else who was crazy. Doctor Wainwright was still talking; she had missed the start of what he was saying.

"...but the secrecy can destroy you. Rots away at your insides. There is no outlet, no escape, an internal prison, suppressing everything that is important to you.

"As a psychiatrist, secrets both intrigue and anger me. I want to know what is going on inside the minds of the mentally disturbed. I *need* to know what they are thinking, what makes them happy, what motivates them, what drives them mad. To me, ignorance is certainly not bliss.

"And now I have a dilemma. What do I do with you all? I know your secrets, but you now know mine and I am not comfortable. You and your associates have each played a part in revealing the location of the cross. Do I incarcerate you all here in the lunatic asylum for ever and a day? Do I trust you to keep the secret, yet forever worry that one day you will inadvertently reveal the truth? Vincent and Vera were part of the Order, but Vincent was losing his mind, he was too much of a risk. There are so many mentally ill people. As you know, the asylum is teeming with patients. We were supposed to house around two hundred insane people, but we are nearing seven hundred at the last count. The world has gone mad. We cannot cope with the volume of unstable people. Do you each meet an unfortunate death so we know that you will never divulge this long-kept secret?"

Fuming, Catherine wanted to explode. Everyone she cared about in that village was now in the asylum. Jailed for seeking out truth and made to appear insane to protect an ancient secret. As a Christian, how could Doctor Wainwright force this travesty on innocent and decent people? Surely Christians were taught to forgive and forget and trust in God, trust in each other, see the good and refrain from evil. Labelling people as insane, when they were clearly of sound mind, was not a Christian principle. But what could she do? Everyone knew she was a lunatic; no one would believe her word against a renowned and prominent psychiatrist such as Wainwright. There seemed little chance of escape other than to play his weird game.

"What about the Greek gentleman. Did you kill him?"

The doctor took a moment before replying. "Ah, a most unfortunate accident. It was suicide. He decided to jump rather than be incarcerated here."

Catherine could understand why.

"Tell me what you are thinking."

Her clenched fists wanted to punch him in the face, her fingers wanted to gouge out his eyes. Violent thoughts were building in her head such as strangulation, imagining her hands around his throat, squeezing until he ... He was taunting her, forcing her to attack him, confirming her status as a dangerous lunatic. With all her might she fought against all the mental and physical aspects of hate.

"Hmm ... a silent lunatic, catatonic, uncommunicative." His words were long and drawn out as he was writing in her file.

Pushed to her limits, she finally spoke, "Where is Jeremy? What does he have to say in all of this?"

"As you already know, Jeremy is not a well man. The syphilis is eating away at his insides. He has so many unfulfilled dreams, to travel, to build, to find a cure for his dreadful disease. He has so much wealth, yet very little time."

"Why doesn't Jeremy touch the cross? You mentioned before that people come to Edenvale to touch the holy cross and be cured of their diseases."

"Ah yes, a very good point." Doctor Wainwright squirmed in his chair. "Jeremy did touch the cross but all I can say he is not all that pure of heart. He rested his hands on the cross and a rash appeared on his palms. He recoiled as if petrified and in pain."

Catherine was unsure how to react. His confession had surprised her but at the same time not. In the priory gatehouse Jeremy had blatantly said he would rather be a Satanist, so why was he still a member of the Order, allowed to wine and dine with protectors of the cross, hearing their secrets?

Doctor Wainwright's eyes were the size of pinheads. "You have two choices, Catherine. The first is to stay here, incarcerated in the asylum where I can keep my eye on you. From here, I can ensure you get up to no mischief. I label you as insane, deranged, mental etcetera if you so much as utter anything about our secrets." Doctor Wainwright stared at Catherine with an evil glint in his eye, obviously wanting her to know he was utterly serious with his threats.

She dared to ask, "And the alternative?"

Enjoying the performance, Doctor Wainwright once again smiled as if he was the most genteel and pleasant person ever born. "You agree to marry Jeremy and together you will undertake psychological experiments on my behalf. I would like to discover the key to happiness. Beauty, wealth, health, food, servants, exquisite clothes, fine wine, why are we never happy? With each passing year we have so much more knowledge, engineering is surpassing itself, innovation and the industrial revolution, so why do we always strive for more?"

Intrigued but wanting to appear reticent, she casually asked, "And what will this experiment entail?"

Doctor Wainwright laughed, "Another excellent question." He swivelled in his captain's chair, stood up and took a couple of steps to the shelving unit behind him to retrieve a small globe which he spun teasingly on its axis. "You will go to the lengths of the world in order to find happiness."

Not convinced, and certainly not trusting anything he said, she enquired, "And if happiness eludes me?"

Doctor Wainwright made a diamond shape with his hands, tapping the tips of his fingers to his lips as he contemplated his answer, "Then you, and I, and everyone else in this godforsaken place will forever be miserable."

"And what about Jeremy, is he happy with this?"

"I want to be honest with you. Jeremy is the most honest person I know and that scares me a little."

Catherine had to agree with this statement. Jeremy was brutally honest. He did not understand tact and diplomacy or if he did, he chose to ignore them.

"The marriage is not for Jeremy to monitor you but vice versa. I want you to monitor him, in secret, and feed back to me."

She was not expecting that admission. "Are you asking me to spy on him?"

"No, not all, just keep an eye on him. His medical diagnosis of syphilis, well it is not fully understood as yet but it appears to fuddle the brain given time. He could be a liability, with his penchant for the truth, and with the syphilis rotting his brain, well, as you can imagine, it is not an ideal situation." Wainwright leaned forward and rested his forearms on the desk. "You have seen the villagers in Edenvale, you met Clarence and Sarah, we are old and getting older. We need new blood, but we are reluctant to share our secret. We need people we can trust, people we can rely on to lay down their life to protect the secret. Will you do this, Catherine? Keep an eye on Jeremy and protect the secret at all costs?"

Catherine considered her response. "If I do this, will you allow me to see Solomon? I need to tell him that I love him and to apologise for what I am about to do. And if I marry Jeremy, will you let Solomon and his father leave the asylum?"

For once Doctor Wainwright was silent.

Chapter Forty-Five

New Year's Eve and the congregation of St Constantine's Church had engaged in cheerful songs, supportive prayers and inspiring sermons. Except for one person, everyone was on a high, hoping for wonderful things from 1864. The time was now ten minutes to midnight, so they made their way outside to be met with a light dusting of snow.

Reverend Thornton expertly shepherded his flock, so they were all huddled together. A few people held candles and the moon occasionally made an appearance creating a silvery glow for which they were thankful.

"Since the 1500s, our church has been dedicated to the memory of St Constantine. I believe we are the only church in Great Britain to commemorate this saint. He was born in the year 272 and when his father died in 312, through his inheritance, Constantine became an Emperor of Rome. Our Lord Saviour Jesus Christ was said to have spoken to Emperor Constantine in a dream, informing him of the significance of the cross and the need to protect this sacred artefact from Satan and his demonic disciples. Constantine only trusted his mother and requested she locate the cross of Christ. For years, she traversed holy lands and read many scriptures in search of this elusive treasure. Legend has it that on the 14th of September in the year 313, Helena was mesmerised by the presence of fresh basil, growing in the shape of a cross in otherwise barren land. On turning the earth with her bare hands, she discovered three crosses of crucifixion buried in a shallow grave but well preserved by the dry heat from the warm sands.

"A gravely ill woman was brought to the site. She touched two of the crosses with no apparent change to her condition. On laying her bony hands on the third cross, she made a miraculous recovery and to this congregation the rest is history. The Church of the Holy Sepulchre was created to protect Golgotha, also known as Calvary.

"Our stained-glass windows will continue to honour St Constantine and his mother Helena for finding and protecting the most sacred and holy of crosses, but the time has come when treasure hunters seek glory, money and accolade for selfish means. As you know, our small and beautiful village on the banks of the River Eden, our own Garden of Eden, has been breached on many occasions. Our links with Constantine and Helena, our name Edenvale, the fact we are situated close to four tributaries, makes our secret harder to keep from a more global world. Therefore, as of the 1st of January 1864, our church will now be dedicated to the Holy Trinity."

The crowd gasped in complete surprise at what they had just heard. People started discussing the revelation, so Reverend Thornton quickly continued to keep his flock focused.

"We will continue to use the triquetra symbol to show the three coeternal hypostases of the Father, Son and Holy Ghost and ask for their protection and guidance. Also, with permission from higher authorities, we have declared that our village will from now on be called Wetheral."

Another gasp of disbelief, then heated discussions took place amongst the parishioners.

"Yes, I know, I know, I see and hear your discourse, but from tomorrow we live in the pretty village of Wetheral. Records from the priory show reference to a wetherhala, meaning a flat piece of land near a river where wethers were kept. Therefore, we are at least keeping with a reference to our history."

"Sorry to interrupt but what are wethers?" asked Mrs Humphries.

"Castrated male sheep," said Mr Dawson.

Mrs Humphries blushed from head to toe and suddenly felt extremely warm, despite the cold.

The vicar continued, "I know it's not a very exciting name, but it will prevent those treasure seekers finding our secret."

Separate conversations flowed.

As it was nearly approaching midnight, Reverend Thornton cleared his throat and continued, "I would quickly like to say a few other things. It has also been agreed that the River Lyne will be diverted further over time so they cannot locate us based on the Garden of Eden having four tributaries and the county borders are to be changed so we are no longer classed as being in Eden. Finally, as we have had to demolish the stone monument marking the cross, we are now in the process of erecting a new red sandstone cross. This will be a long column but with a small cross, four actual projections so more like an X as in XX VV. Currently, our Lord's cross is in the undercroft at Oak Bank, but we quickly need to find a new location."

"Richard, it's nearly twelve," said Doctor Wainwright.

Reverend Thornton looked at his pocket watch, "Yes, yes, then please let us all hold hands and countdown to midnight."

Doctor Wainwright took hold of Catherine's left hand and Jeremy Fisher took hold of her right hand. In synchronisation with the rest of the congregation, they counted down until, "Five ... four ... three ... two ... one ... Happy New Year!"

Everyone embraced and wished their loved ones, family, friends, acquaintances and fellow members of the Order of the Priory all the very best for the new year.

Outwardly, Catherine played her part to perfection but inside, she could not hide her sadness as to what the future would bring. Could she ever find the elusive emotion of happiness?

Solomon would remain forever in her heart. She had taken him for granted and only losing him had made her appreciate the wonderful love they had shared and how happy they could have been if she had only given their love a chance. All those years ago she had failed Sam, taking too long to realise her love and now she was failing Solomon. Wainwright had refused her request to visit him so he would never know how she truly felt about him and why she had made the decision to cruelly abandon him with everything they had been through. Tears welled in her eyes that she had ever doubted her love for him, and now they were separated by physical and mental walls of an asylum.

December 1976

Wing Commander Sherrard gathered the entire personnel of Spadeadam in the formal meeting room. Everyone had been warned of imminent change.

"Greetings fellow service men and women. I've gathered you all here today—"

Teddy the security guard interrupted, "Sounds like we are at a bloody funeral."

Restrained laughter was heard, and Wing Commander Sherrard could not help but smile. He patted down his outstretched hands to quieten the crowd.

"Apologies for the grave introduction."

Groans from the room.

"As we have had numerous discussions about the future of this facility, as of today, I can confirm we are to be officially known as RAF Spadeadam. Geographically, we are still the largest RAF base in the whole of the UK, with nearly ten thousand acres at our disposal. Even with an expanding civil population, Spadeadam remains the RAF's most remote location, with barely a soul living close by. This isolation gives us tremendous advantages.

"Over the years, the RAF has been involved with various government warfare projects, from the Blue Streak ballistic nuclear missile in the late 50s early 60s to the more recent satellite surveillance launch base.

"I can now say a decision has been made for the future direction of this facility. Our new role will be as an electronic warfare tactics range. We already have a secure and remote infrastructure. We already have a runway and control tower. With our geographical size and isolation, coupled with the marshland, peat bogs and rivers, we have natural protection so we can undertake surveillance and target practice from the ground and skies. We have the coast nearby and the challenging terrain of the Lake District mountains for our aircraft to navigate.

"We will be a training force for elite pilots from across various disciplines including the Navy, Army and NATO forces. They will come from far and wide under relative anonymity to receive this specialist training."

The room was unusually silent. "Any questions so far?" Sherrard took a sip of water.

"Nuclear warheads, space rockets, surveillance systems, gathering intelligence, reconnaissance techniques. Sounds like we could potentially be giving away all our secrets we've built up over the years to foreign regimes," said a voice from the back of the room.

Sherrard recognised the accent as John Stone's. He replied, "Ultimately, as our motto dictates, we are here to seek peace in order to prevent war, and if that means working in collaboration with allied countries then so be it.

"Hadrian's Wall passes alongside this very facility. For hundreds of years, the Roman Empire was unstoppable. They had wealth, treasures, forts, good food, built roads to network with other areas for trade and supplies, forged armour and weapons. They even had running water and bath houses. They were advanced beyond their years. But it all fell apart for several reasons.

"They became a monster, a massive dinosaur. Strong and powerful yet too slow to mobilise and spread too thinly over vast swathes of land. Terrifying but at the same time vulnerable because of its size. For such an advanced civilisation, the Romans were outnumbered and outclassed by barbarians, simple tribes, the Huns, the Vandals, the Saxons, as examples.

"The Romans became a challenge, too clever, too influential for their own good and this created uprisings. Their extravagant lifestyles became too costly, they were haemorrhaging money. Corruption at higher levels imploded the cause. They could not find any more slaves to do their dirty work. Remote, wealthy emperors living in luxurious palaces, protected from adversity, were no longer idolised or feared when their minions wallowed in poverty. There was bound to be a backlash eventually.

"There have been so many wars through the ages, that we need to learn from these events in order to prevent the same mistakes being made. We need to communicate, share our ideas, work with our friends, neighbours, allies and understand our enemies. Like the Roman Empire, the British Empire ruled by force, fought for land, occupied countries and dictated a way of life to too many people. Now is the time to lead by example, and hopefully people will see there is another way of doing things. A peaceful way, a nurturing way, working in collaboration with others. We are preparing for war but only as a deterrent to maintain peace when others see the knowledge we possess and the damage we can inflict.

"History is not there to be erased. History must be protected in order to learn. We need to protect our heritage, our culture and our beliefs at all costs.

Yes, we have secrets we would never divulge but there are others we should be willing to share. Otherwise, lessons will never be learned. Men, women, children and animals have sacrificed their lives for the freedoms we enjoy today. Please do not let them die in vain."

A female voice was heard from the right-hand side of the room, "I agree with a lot of what you say but I don't recognise our once great country anymore. When the Treaty of Rome was signed, I felt this was a good thing, former enemies becoming allies and signing a pact which would hopefully lead to peace. Even though I had some reservations, overall, I felt that the UK joining in was probably a good thing. But when I see what is happening day-to-day on our streets, the union strikes, vandalism, arsonists, protestors trashing cars and shops, the hatred and fighting amongst ourselves, it's heart-breaking. Our ancestors didn't die for this." There were mumbled agreements from the crowd. "Over the years, various governments have wasted so much time and money, millions of pounds on failed military projects whilst its citizens are living on the bread line. I really hope this isn't another expensive blunder."

A male voice interrupted, "I agree. It's like the bloody lunatics are running the asylum."

Present Day

"My name's Jessica and I'm the clinical psychologist. Dr Parton has asked me to come and have a chat with you regarding your admission to hospital." The thick, black frames of her glasses were stylish, and her blonde hair was as straight as silk. She wore no makeup other than a tinge of red lip gloss. "I've read over your file so have a general idea, but I'd like to get to know you first. Is that all right?"

Millie nodded her head, aware that her own hair was a frizzy mess. She had avoided looking in the mirror for many a week, too depressed to even care but her bony body was testament to her breakdown.

"Can you tell me a little bit about yourself, where you work, your husband, your family, that sort of thing."

It took Millie a few moments to muster the courage to speak. "I'm a nurse, so I should've known better. Ending up in here, well, I should have spotted the signs earlier. Although, I've never really worked in mental health before." A sigh calmed her nerves.

No one knows everything, Millie."

"I guess so." A pause. "My husband is Jack. He's a joiner by trade but prefers to call himself a carpenter. He says it sounds more artistic, more creative. As for my parents, they have been fantastic over the last few months. I don't think I could have coped without them."

"Did you have a happy childhood? Any brothers or sisters?"

"I'm an only child. I think my parents would have liked more children, but it just didn't happen for them. Other than that, yeah, it was happy times."

"Do you have children, Millie?"

"I would love to have children, that was why we were renovating the house, to have a home ready for them. Jack even turned one of the bedrooms into a nursery. Everyone said not to do it. That it would bring bad luck, tempt fate."

Jessica took a while to respond, as if she was contemplating reacting to the comment, but she didn't. "Tell me more about Jack. What made you fall in love with him?"

Millie wasn't sure what these questions had to do with her breakdown and her admission to hospital, but she didn't have the energy to argue. "Jack was an only child too, he seemed more mature than the other lads at that age. He had lovely eyes and a cheeky smile. But there was a sadness. I wanted to look after him."

"Why was that?"

"He was neglected as a child. I didn't know him then. We went to different primary schools, then we met at secondary. As we got to know each other in the later years, he told me his mam and dad neglected him as a child, which was why he lived with his nana. Up 'til then, he had to fend for himself. Often trying to sneak food. Feeling hungry all the time. I felt sorry for him. And now, it's as if he has tried to overcompensate, trying to give us everything he didn't have as a child."

"Is this relating to the house?" Jessica looked down at her notes. "Fernleigh?"

Even the mention of the name made her shake. The rate of her respiration increased, and she felt hot yet cold, as if her peripheral circulation was shutting down, with the heat diverting to her core.

When Millie didn't say anything, Jessica spoke softly, "In your own time."

With a tremble to her voice, she managed to say, "Fernleigh was an old Victorian villa. Jack bought it at auction. Got it really cheap as it was so run down and neglected, nobody else wanted it." She paused, her eyes staring into space. "I've never thought about this before but maybe this is why the house resonates with him so much. They had both been abandoned and unloved for many a year and were in a sorry state, waiting for someone to love them and bring them back to life. Oh, I feel sorry for him now. Jack spent months, and thousands of pounds, on the renovations. We nearly fell out about it on a number of occasions as he worked all the hours he could, trying to make it immaculate for us, which he did."

Jessica didn't say anything, she only nodded, and the silence was awkward, so Millie continued, "Anyway, he finished the house and true to his word, it was amazing, like some sort of posh show home, real state of the art. He kept the original character to the place but added modern touches."

"So, when did things change?"

Millie started breathing through pursed lips, trying to calm her breathing. "Once the house was finished, we started on the garden. It was a lovely sunny day and really warm. I remember it vividly." She paused again, aware that her throat was starting to thicken. "Jack had hired a little ride-on excavator thingy, one of those grabby things to dig out soil." She paused to slow her breathing. "He wanted to clear out the pond to make a lovely water feature."

Jessica noticed the glisten in Millie's eyes. "And I believe he found something."

For a while, all Millie could do was nod. "He found a body. The police pathologist, archaeologist, I'm not sure who was involved, confirmed it had partially been preserved, due to the conditions of the mud or peat in the pond. The body still had some hair and skin on the bones, even after nearly two hundred years." Tears started to fall. "I'm sorry."

Jessica offered her a box of tissues, "In case you need them."

After taking a couple of tissues she continued, "We were told the skeleton was a woman, maybe in her twenties, so similar to me, and that she had been murdered." Millie's nose was now running but sniffing wasn't sufficient. She took a couple more tissues from the box which was now within arm's reach.

"How did they know she was murdered? Maybe she had just fallen in by accident."

"The police report concluded it was impossible to say what had happened exactly but there was evidence of damaged tissue, with something sharp having pierced her bones, but nothing conclusive, too much time had passed. However, she was definitely murdered. She was …" Millie paused, covering her nose and mouth with her hand to hide the subtle quiver of her bottom lip. "She was … there was still some evidence that she had been wrapped in sheets and tied up … and her personal belongings …they had been thrown into the pond on top of her." Wiping her nose was no longer sufficient. Her voice had acquired a nasal tone, so she blew her nose to relieve the pressure. "Sorry about that."

"No need to apologise."

Millie cleared her throat which was now painfully dry. She took a sip of water.

"Just take your time, Millie. I appreciate this is hard for you to talk about."

She blew out a sigh. Her lips, eyes and nose felt uncomfortably swollen. "There were picture frames, but unfortunately the water had ruined the photos. There was jewellery. A brush and a comb. Bottles of perfume, that sort of thing."

"And were the police able to identify who this lady was?" asked Jessica.

"No, not really, but during the renovations, we found a newspaper clipping stating someone had been publicly hanged for murdering numerous people. We think this lady may have been one of his victims. Personally, I think the body in the pond was his wife, based on a photograph we found in the bedroom."

"And is this why you can't live in the house?"

"Well, yes and no. From the start, the house always felt spooky to me. Sad somehow and when we came across this newspaper from 1845, saying that someone called Samuel Thompson had been hanged, we decided to investigate the history of the house. Jack and I went to the building society with whom we have the mortgage and asked to read the title deeds. We were shocked by what we found." Millie took another sip of water. Her head felt like it was going to explode, her head pounding with pain. "The title deeds were held in an underground vault. All temperature controlled and that. We were escorted to a small office. Through the glass partitions, we could see rows upon rows of moveable metal filing cabinets which the lady jostled with until she located our deeds. She brought them through to us and placed them on the desk. I wasn't sure what to expect but the deeds were huge, just one big bit of paper, filling the entire desktop. The deeds were so old but beautifully written in that fancy calligraphy writing. There were conditions to the house such as the owner wasn't allowed to run a pub or a milliner's shop from the premises. The deeds were very specific, stating things like you could have a maximum of five chickens, three goats and two horses on the land. It really was interesting."

"So, who owned the house prior to you?"

"Samuel Thompson, the man who was publicly hanged for all the murders. There was no way I could live there, knowing what had happened."

"I can see why you would feel that way. Given time do you think you could come to terms with the house's history for it was a long time ago?"

"No, it wasn't just the finding the body and the history of events. I started seeing things, sensing things."

"Can you put into words what those things were?"

Millie's hands started to shake. She held them in her lap, trying to suppress the tremor. "Breezes, cold spots, the smell of lavender, creaking floorboards, footsteps, shadows moving, mists forming. She would even whisper in my ear which would cause me to shudder.

"Occasionally, I would have a horrible metallic taste in my mouth which I think was blood. My skin would crawl with goosebumps, creating a tingling sensation throughout my body, as if I was numb but at the same time hypersensitive, it was the weirdest sensation.

"I tried so hard to stay in the house, but I sensed her presence everywhere. Whenever she was there, I would get a blinding headache. She would roam the house at night. Jack would be annoyed about the electricity bills because I insisted all the lights remained on. However, this may sound strange, but I preferred the bedroom being in darkness and I know that doesn't make sense. I would hide under the duvet, too scared to look. I was worried if the light was on, I would see something. Like her standing there next to me, watching me sleep.

"Sometimes I get too hot in bed and put my foot or leg out of the bed to cool down, but I was scared she would touch me. I would often wake up drenched in sweat. I had to sleep with the door closed. I was too scared to open the bedroom door and make my way to the bathroom. The corridor was too long at night. There were stairs to the attic off that landing. Oh, and I kept hearing a baby crying. For months I barely slept. Too terrified."

"But you never actually saw anything? I mean, as in her ghost or anything tangible?"

"I know what you are getting at. You're saying I'm mad and that all of this is in my head but at times I see her vividly. She has long, wavy hair and she teases me with her gentle voice. I can't hear the words, but her voice is like a lullaby to me. I want to sleep, I need to sleep but as soon as I do she torments me. I dream of her and Jack, together, in bed, if you know what I mean." Sobbing, Millie took some time out to settle her breathing. "They are together … making love … she's always on top of him but she's looking at me and smiling."

"Is this affecting your relationship with Jack? Have you spoken with him about your dreams?"

She nodded a few times. "Kind of. He says I'm being silly, and he totally reassures me that he loves me and would never do anything like that but I'm so confused. It seems so real. I wonder if she is trying to tell me things."

"What things?"

"Maybe Jack is having an affair or is considering sleeping with another woman. That kind of thing. It's been a while since we've been … intimate."

"Which is understandable, you've had a lot to contend with."

"I know what I need to do. I know I'm being silly. I just want us to move on but I can't. Jack loves the house so much. Literally, his blood, sweat and tears went into renovating the house and it truly is perfect, in every way. Except one - her. Time and again I've asked him to sell it, so we can pocket the money, pay off our debts and make a fresh start but up until now he won't. He says I just need time, to have myself a few good sleeps and I'll be back to normal and we can move on. I've tried. I've lived there. But this woman haunts me. I can't even begin to describe her, she's so beautiful, wild and free, and she's always smiling, and I feel so sorry for her. She was murdered yet, oh I don't know, something about her gives me the creeps. Jack thinks it's all in my head. He has never seen or sensed anything, or so he says, because I reckon he had some bad vibes about the attic and bedroom. He thinks I just need time. So, for the last few weeks I've been staying at my mam and dad's house, but this ghost enjoys tormenting me and has followed me there."

268

"So, selling the house may not necessarily stop these visitations. Have you seen her since you've been in here?"

"Thank goodness, no. Not yet anyway."

"Well, that's something positive to think about. Being here, talking through your experiences, you have made the first step on your journey. Is there anything else you need to tell me, that you feel is relevant?"

"Actually, there is one more thing I'd like to say which I've not felt able to admit to anyone else. When I stayed at the house, I would regularly have sleep paralysis. I would be awake but couldn't move or speak. I would try to scream but I couldn't. Jack would often say I was mumbling in my sleep, but I was desperately trying to call out to him to help me.

"I looked on the internet and people have described an incubus and succubus, demons that terrorise you as you sleep. I'm always lying on my back and he's on me. Pinning me to the bed, panting over me, smelling me, forcing me to do things. And don't ask me how I know, but the woman hates him. She so totally detests him, and I sense her anger and fear. And I know from a picture we found in the bedroom that this man isn't her husband. This demon has a large scar down the left side of his neck and his eyes are evil.

"This is another reason why I'm so tired. I've been taking all sorts of stimulants, coffee, that sort of thing, trying to avoid sleep but then she torments my waking." Millie could not stem the flow of tears. She wasn't sure if this therapy session was helping or hindering but it finally felt good to be listened to without anyone telling her she was silly or imaging it or telling her what to do.

Jessica took a while to respond, "That must have taken a lot of courage to say. You've been brilliant in sharing your thoughts, your experiences and your concerns with me today, so thank you, I really appreciate that. For our next session, we'll work together on a plan on how we move forward from here. How does that sound?"

"I'll try anything. I just want my life back."

Exhausted, Millie slowly made her way back to her room. In one sense she was thankful for the privacy but in another sense, she dreaded being alone. Not a good start to the new year. At least her room didn't have mirrors. Probably assessed as too much of a risk for those deemed suicidal. Anyway, she had avoided mirrors for the last few weeks, dreading seeing the damned woman standing behind her, smiling.

The light was starting to fade even though it was only just after four in the afternoon. She walked over to the window with the intension of closing the curtains, but something caught her attention. She was residing in a relatively new section of the hospital but the view from her window was overlooking the old Cumberland and Westmorland Lunatic Asylum. Three workers in high visibility waistcoats and wearing protective helmets were exploring one of the empty buildings. She had recently read online that developers were looking to convert the old asylum buildings into residential accommodation. Her body shivered as goosebumps trickled down her arms. From what she had experienced whilst renovating an old, abandoned house with a gruesome past, the dead don't die, they linger.

Then she saw her, a fine mist swirling across the hospital grounds. Long, wavy hair loosely tied up, high-necked blouse, long skirt, laced leather boots, and that cursed smile. She disappeared through the closed door to Cumberland House. Appearing to be nothing more than a shadow or breeze, she followed the workers as they moved from room to room. On reaching the top floor, the woman looked out of the window and looked over at Millie, and waved.

Her blood ran cold, as if every last morsel of heat had drained from her body. Millie had to warn them. She repeatedly knocked on the window until her knuckles became too painful to continue. With her palms, she continued banging on the window and started shouting for more impact. She screamed, the pounding on the pane intensified until the nurses ran in to the room to assess the situation. Despite Millie's pleas, the nurses insisted there was no one there fitting the description of a grey Victorian lady.

Maybe she *was* mad, or maybe *they* were mad, maybe *everyone* had a little madness inside them.

Author's Notes

Creating a work of fiction is basically making things up as you go along. The characters are avatars, the scenes are animations, and the story is moulded from dreams, thoughts and moments of brilliance tinged with madness. Dear reader, it is up to you to unearth the truth and lies in *House of Asylum*, only please do not lose your mind in deciphering which is which.

Only joking, I'll give you a little synopsis of some of the main points.

Most of the buildings and structures in House of Asylum are real although not necessarily correct for the time period.

The Cumberland and Westmorland Lunatic Asylum opened its doors in 1862 as a result of the Lunacy and County Asylum Acts of 1845. Legislation was passed through parliament forcing counties to provide free health care for those deemed mentally ill. Many of the original buildings still stand today, but most have been converted into residential dwellings, including the asylum's church and mortuary.

The name of Edenvale is fictional but the village of Wetheral is real. There is reference to the name originating from the wethers who fed off the flatter farmland near the River Eden.

Oak Bank Hall, also known as the Killoran Hotel, started life as a grand residence and in the 1960s was associated with holding top secret meetings for those who worked at Spadeadam. The imposing dwelling has now been converted into residential apartments.

All that remains today of the 15th century priory is the gatehouse. Owned by English Heritage, the building is free to enter and explore. In case you are wondering, there really is a sign about seeking sanctuary / asylum.

Numerous saints are mentioned within the village: St Mary, St Cuthbert, St Martin and St Constantine. The church at the heart of the village was dedicated to the memory of St Constantine but is unlikely to be the Roman Emperor Constantine. There are historical references to a 6th century Constantine of royal descent, who is portrayed as a legendary leader along

271

the lines of King Arthur. Supposedly, this Constantine gave up the crown to become a hermit. There are references to a hermit who lived in the nearby cells close to the priory although this was a completely different time period. There are also references to a Constantine of Scottish descent. Whichever Constantine it was, the church later became known as the Holy Trinity.

The cells of St Constantine are carved into the rock face approximately 40 to 50 feet above the River Eden and are accessible through beautiful ancient woodland owned by the National Trust. The cells are open all year round.

Corby Castle, with its stunning waterfall, is visible from the west bank of the River Eden. A small chapel is hidden within the red sandstone. The castle was home to the Howard family. Henry Howard commissioned the white marble statue 'Faith' following the death of his wife, Maria and their baby during childbirth. The statue is housed within the Holy Trinity church.

Standing one hundred feet in the air above the River Eden is the impressive Wetheral Viaduct, also known as Corby Bridge. Built in the 1830s, to carry the Newcastle to Carlisle railway line, the arches were briefly the highest viaduct in the world.

At the intersection of the A69 to Wetheral stands the Wayside Crucifix. Constructed in the 1950s, this was commissioned by a Christian cell movement to represent the Passion of Christ. Their plan was to place a crucifix on every road into Carlisle, but this was the only one erected.

Wetheral village green is a triangular shape of grass, flat at one end but bizarrely shaped at the other end with almost sheer drops. The Wetheral Cross once stood at the centre of the green until this was moved to the raised mound (where the cross is supposedly buried in *House of Asylum*).

References to Roman Emperors, Kings of England and top-secret government experiments are all based in truth. Emperor Constantine and his mother Helena became saints after supposedly finding the true cross on which Christ was crucified. XX VV really is inscribed in the walls near the cells of St Constantine. The Twentieth Legion of Valeria Victrix served along Hadrian's Wall and the boar was their emblem. The Domesday Book failed to list Carlisle as an English city and Henry VIII did commission the fortification of Carlisle's castle and medieval walls. Spadeadam was at the heart of secret government experiments, including the Blue Streak nuclear missile.

So, although this story has elements of truth, it was concocted from a weird dream I had one night. In my dream I was ill, and my family and friends insisted I go and seek rest and recuperation in the village of Wetheral. I stayed in *Rose Cottage* although in my dream, the house was painted white. Little did I know that the village was an open lunatic asylum. I was allowed to wander the streets, but road works and train delays always stopped me from leaving the village. It was one of those dreams where I tried to escape but each path brought be back to the asylum. I will let you come to your own conclusions.

Acknowledgements

My sincere thanks go out to Roy Burns and Eric Dent for their valued input into the workings of Spadeadam. Having worked there, it was fascinating to hear their stories which helped in bringing a forgotten project back to life.

My thanks extend to my dear friend, Fiona Mills, for her unwavering support throughout this journey. We have physically and mentally walked thousands of miles together over the years and we have laughed and cried along the way.

Finally, I would like to say thank you to Stephen, Ethan and Orlissa. We have such a short time on this earth and family means everything to us. When searching for happiness, for us there's no place quite like home.

You are cordially invited to attend a weekend
of exquisite dining, fine spirits &
entertainment

To celebrate the wedding of

JF & CF

Date:
Sunday 9th December 1866 at 11 a.m.

Arrival:
Friday 7th December 1866 between 1 p.m. &
3 p.m. on the shoreline of Derwentwater,
Lake Road, Keswick

Venue:
Derwent Isle House, Vicar Island, Keswick

For attending this special celebration of love, you will receive a gift
of £1,000

Please note, you must stay for the entirety of the weekend and
participate in all events. Refusal or inability to cooperate will
render this invitation and gift null and void

R.S.V.P. To the above address by 27th November
1866

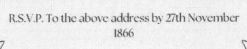